TAKING THE WATERS

"Hello?" I called. Nobody answered.

I saw Norah Platt's cane propped against the tub in her room, but the cot was empty. I peered in, wondering where Norah was. The tub was making the same gentle, water-in-motion sound as my own, and then I looked into it.

The first thing I saw was Norah's toes, bobbing up to the surface of the smelly tank. Then I saw that the toes were on her foot, which was normal enough, and the foot was at the end of her leg, but the leg was no longer attached to Norah. Both her legs floated in that tank, and so did her torso, and so did her head, but none of them were any longer joined to each other.

Norah Platt had been disassembled.

NARABEDLA LTD.

Frederik Pohl

A Del Rey Book

BALLANTINE BOOKS • NEW YORK

CHAPTER
1

When Woody Calderon told me about the offer he couldn't refuse, but was going to anyway, he blew my mind. He had done that often enough before. I expected a certain amount of weirdness from Woody. It came with the turf, because he was a musician, after all.

I hadn't expected this particular variety.

Woody was a cellist. I was an accountant—for, among other artists, him. Woody paid me a retainer plus my hourly charges to handle his money, except that he rarely had any, and to keep him out of trouble with the Internal Revenue Service, which I sometimes couldn't. I wasn't getting rich on Woody's account, because his career wasn't making him rich, either. It had started off, like, *wow,* with a wonderful first-year string of successes, when he won the Tchaikovsky prize, and debuted at Carnegie Hall, and had the critics comparing him to Casals and Rostropovich. But then he hadn't had a second year. At first he was a prodigious wunderkind—the kind that makes thirty-year-old cellists weep. Then, all of a sudden, the critics began to open their reviews with, "While not up to the brilliance of intonation and impeccable musicianship of his debut, Woody Calderon's new recital is nevertheless . . ." Nevertheless disappointing, is what they were saying, and Carnegie Hall lost his telephone number.

Nevertheless, and this time I am talking a happier kind of nevertheless, he really was the kind of cellist you could fairly compare with anybody you liked, even if he wasn't getting either the bookings or the reviews anymore. I kept him on as a client partly because I was certain that sooner or later he would make it again, and partly out of sympathy.

The sympathy was a personal thing. It happened that I, too, had had a brilliant first year. I was a baritone. I sang in all the glorious places: La Scala, Covent Garden, the Met—

1

I did them all. Oh, I only had little roles, to be sure—some-body's father or somebody's jailer—but it was only a matter of time until I'd be doing Papageno or Tonio. Everybody said so. At that time I even said so myself, to the girls I was having so wonderful a time dating. And we all might have been right, too, if it hadn't been for the damn wardrobe mis-tress's damn kid that gave me the damn mumps in Chicago. I didn't get sick enough to die, just sick enough to wish for it. When I was well enough to sing again I couldn't.

I do not wish to tell you what it felt like when the doctors began talking about how sometimes, even with the best of care, mumps had consequences—well, not the disease itself, so much, as the side effects of some of the treatments—well, in layman's terms, Mr. Stennis . . .

They weren't very good at layman's terms. They were better at medical terms like "Guillaume-Barré syndrome" and "tracheal stenosis" and "I hope you understand, Mr. Stennis, that there is no *possible* question here of anything like mal*practice*."

Well, there wasn't. I made sure of that. I checked it out. But the trachea and the larynx had got involved. The warm, strong baritone voice had been turned off.

And, unfortunately, not just the voice.

It was not a good time for me, those days right after I came off the critical list.

I did have a safety net. My mother, bless her prudent, departed soul, had laid down the law while I was still in college. If, against all her sound motherly advice, I were going to go in for something as madly chancy as a singing career, I had to take the precaution of studying something employable as well. So I'd taken a full load of accountancy courses, done well in them, had all the credentials I needed to put them to use.

So, instead of being a star, I began preparing the tax re-turns of stars . . . and of a lot of non-stars I didn't have the heart to turn away, like Woody Calderon.

Woody came in for his appointment with me an hour late, and eight hundred dollars short. I was working out with the weights beside my open window, and he nodded approv-ingly. "Keeping in shape, huh? Good, good. But listen, you're going to have to stall them for me again, Nolly," he said. "I haven't got the money."

Since the I.R.S. had been threatening to attach his assets

for the money, that didn't sound like good news to me. "I can't. They mean it this time. Next step is they file on you."

"Yeah," he said, nodding vaguely. Woody's name isn't Woody, it's Bruce. But he doesn't look like a Bruce. What he looks like more than anything else is Woody Allen—unsure, unfocused, and all. "I was kind of afraid you might say that. Well, gee. I dunno, Nolly. Maybe I should take the offer from Henry Davidson-Jones."

That was when I sat up straight. "You didn't tell me about any offer from Henry Davidson-Jones," I said.

"Well, it just came up."

I waited. Henry Davidson-Jones was a name that mattered. For one thing, he was about as big a benefactor of the arts as the world possessed. He was C.E.O. of a huge financial thing called Narabedla Ltd., but where he found time to run the business I could not guess. He was always doing six things at once, and they always turned out to be raising money for chamber-music groups and sponsoring ballet companies and generally doing all the things angels are supposed to do, except that as far as I knew he wasn't sleeping with any members of the corps de ballet.

Woody was looking tickled and apologetic, both. I waited him out. "Matter of fact," he said, "I just came from his office. I got a call from his secretary. I thought, I don't know, I thought maybe he was going to offer me a shot in some quartet or something." His voice was rising. Woody stands about five feet tall, tops, even with lifts in his shoes, and when he gets excited he chirps like a bird. "Only it wasn't that. He started out telling me how unfair the critics and the managers were, and how he really thought I deserved a break—well, I sure agreed with him about that. And, I mean, Nolly, he *knew,*" Woody piped earnestly. "He's heard me. Probably even bought his own tickets, because I sure never knew he was ever in the audience. He told me how fine I was at those impossible chords and, you know, like in those Paganini runs where you're lucky if you just get all the notes in, and he said my intonation was flawless—"

"It probably was," I said, because, as I've mentioned before, in my opinion Woody really was some kind of a marvel. Other than intellectually, I mean. "Could you get to the point?"

"He offered me a job!" Woody yelped.

"And you're thinking twice about whether to take it, for God's sake? With the I.R.S. breathing down your neck?"

He said apologetically, "Yeah, but it's kind of weird, Nolly. See, he started out by asking me all kinds of personal things—no, I'm a liar, he didn't ask anything at all. He was *telling* me all this stuff about myself. Like how Yvonne and I broke up last year and there hasn't really been anybody else since. Like how my family isn't really very close. All I have is a couple of cousins, really; and I've been chasing around so much trying to get a break that I've practically lost touch with all my friends—well, I don't mean *you*, Nolly; I mean—"

"I know what you mean, Woody! Get to it! This is beginning to get really bizarre."

He looked at me worriedly through his Woody Allen glasses. He couldn't help seeing that I was suddenly very tense. In fact, I could see my hand shaking, and so could he.

"Davidson-Jones said there was a little, well, like a syndicate, sort of, a bunch of people who had kind of a private concert circuit."

"And he offered you a contract to play for them."

"Right, Nolly! Long-term. Years, anyway. And they'd pay me a hundred and a half a year, plus traveling expenses, and because they were all foreigners the whole net would go into a Swiss bank, no taxes, and—"

I held up my hand. It had stopped shaking because I wasn't in any doubt any longer. I finished for him. "And he said the only drawback was that you'd be completely out of circulation while you traveled, and couldn't hope to keep in contact with the people you knew."

Woody gave me a long, worried stare. "You heard about this? He said they were Brazilian millionaires."

"I heard," I said. "A long time ago. Before I lost my voice. Henry Davidson-Jones made me the same offer, only then they were Arab oil sheiks."

We sat and stared at each other for a minute. Then Woody said, "You didn't take it? Why not?"

"I didn't get the chance. I had a date at the Chicago Lyric Opera two days later, and then I got the mumps."

We had another session of staring at each other. Then Woody said, "Listen, Nolly, that's interesting, but it doesn't help. What I want to know is, do you think I should do it?"

I couldn't answer right away, because there were too many answers floating around in my head. They didn't agree. The first answer that suggested itself to me was that it surely was a way to keep the Feds from attaching his cello. It was no Stradivarius, but it was a good $6,500 contemporary instrument that he would pay hell trying to replace if he lost it to the I.R.S. The second answer that came to mind was that he certainly hadn't had any better offers lately. The third, however, was positively *no*.

But I didn't have to say any of them, because Woody's head was moving in the same directions as my own. He straightened up, all five feet of him, and said sorrowfully, "It's true that that could square me with the Internal Revenue, and it's a long way the best offer I've had. But honest, Nolly, I don't like the sound of it."

All I could do was agree.

So we talked for a while about whether I could hope to keep the government from foreclosing on his fiddle for a while, and how he might be able to get some fill-in work with a New Jersey orchestra to eat on, and by and by he went away, looking dejected.

And three days later I got a letter containing a cashier's draft for a thousand dollars, issued on a Pittsburgh bank and mailed from Baltimore, with a note that said:

Pay the bastards off for me, Nolly, and credit the rest to what I owe you. I'll let you know how the tour goes after a while.

Of course, there was only one tour he could have been talking about. So he had my curiosity turned up high, but it all sounded fine enough.

What wasn't so fine was that the next day there was a little story in the *Times* arts section that said Woody Calderon had been in a light plane that crashed twenty miles off the South Carolina coast, no bodies or survivors found, everyone on board presumed dead.

CHAPTER
2

The first few days of June aren't the ulcer season for accountants—that's early April, just before filing date—but June comes close. Early June is when I have to lash the clients with the sixty-day deferments into getting it all together for June 15th. My clients being what they are—because it is quite true that concert musicians do not well comprehend the real world—means that I have enough on my plate at that time to keep my mind occupied.

I did think about Woody as time permitted. I even mourned him. Not so much as a friend, of course, because he'd been right in saying that we weren't very close. But he was, by God, a cellist I loved to listen to, and he was missed. He wasn't just missed by me, either. Even the critics who had done him in were now regretting his loss, though I didn't notice any of them apologizing for shafting him while he was still around.

After half a dozen twelve-hour days I had the last of the sluggards' W-2 forms and airline ticket stubs entered into the computer, and their checks to the state and the Feds and everybody else made out and clipped to their returns so that all they had to do was sign and mail.

Then I closed my door and got on my exercise bike. It's a good thing to do while I'm making phone calls, and, after I thought for a while, I dialed my oldest, and homeliest, friend, Wiktor Ordukowsky. "This is Nolly Stennis of the accounting firm of L. Knollwood Stennis and Associates, Mr. Ordukowsky," I said. "Isn't it about time you let me proposition you again so we can have a nice, tax-deductible lunch?" He was agreeable, and we settled on the Four Seasons.

Vic Ordukowsky is not only an old buddy from both high school and Columbia University, he also thinks he saved my life. Maybe in a way he did, after the mumps did me in, and anyway ever since then he has felt obliged to keep it saved. In school we saved each other's lives in class as a matter of routine. We had partnered each other in those desperate semesters on tax law and estate management. We made up weird and wonderful financial transactions to set each other, then helped reduce them to orderly columns of figures for the professors to check over. We coached each other for examinations, and took notes for each other when we cut classes—Vic more for me than I for him, because I also had those everyday sessions with my vocal coach to add to my burden. It worked, though. We both graduated up near the top of the class, and the job offers came in.

Of course, I turned them all down. I was going to be a *singer*.

What made me think of Vic Ordukowsky was that the job offer he had accepted had come from Narabedla Ltd.

When I got there Vic was at the bar, chatting with a Caribbean-tanned old man with "corporation lawyer" written all over him, and a woman I easily recognized to be one of the mayor's chief administrative assistants, and, although the Four Seasons is used to having plenty of high-powered people there, half the bar was rubbernecking at them. Mostly at Vic. He had on a dove-gray open-throated shirt and a dove-gray raw silk jacket over it; he smelled of good cigars and expensive barbers, and he was, as I have said, the homeliest man I know. (Of course, that was before Narabedla, so I hadn't yet found out what homeliness was like.) Vic's looks never stopped him. He looked like Mr. Potato-Head in high school, too, fat face and eyes a quarter-inch apart, but the girls never let him alone.

"Let's go inside," said Vic, terminating his conversation, and I followed. Accountancy Rule No. 1: Never drink at the bar before lunch; the expense account looks better when everything is on the meal check. They seated us immediately, although the big room was full, and they put us right next to the pool. Vic ordered one of those filthy European things that taste like burned bicycle tire steeped in cough syrup; I had a glass of white wine; and we did the necessary.

"I have asked you to lunch, Vic," I said, pro forma, "because I want to make a presentation on behalf of my accounting firm, L. Knollwood Stennis and Associates. We believe we could provide for Narabedla very satisfactory service for such accounting matters as are not handled internally."

Vic returned my serve neatly. "I'm really sorry, Nolly," he said, "but it's the policy of Narabedla Limited to perform all its accountancy functions with in-house staff. Since we're privately owned we are excused from a lot of filing—and so we have the option of keeping many of our financial affairs quite confidential. However," he added, getting carried away with the spirit of the game, "if at any future time these policies should change I will certainly see that your firm is considered."

He beamed at me. I beamed back at him. The letter of the law was satisfied; we had had a business discussion, and 80 percent of the cost of the luncheon had therefore become deductible as a business expense. "So how have you been?" he finished, as the drinks came.

I said, "Fine, fine, Vic. You're looking good yourself. Lost a little weight?"

"I wish," he said glumly. Vic had been chubby even in high school, but when he started earning big bucks he really let himself go. He had to be three hundred pounds. Where he found those good-looking suits that actually seemed to fit him I couldn't guess. He gave me a rueful grin. "Mary-Ellen's been putting on a little weight, too."

I said, "Oh." His wife had been a skinny little thing when they married; a few more pounds wouldn't have hurt her.

"She's up to two hundred," he said, sipping his Fernet-Branca almost as though he liked it, and added quickly, "She looks great, though. The only thing is, it gets kind of tricky to, uh, make contact. If you know what I mean." He gave me a look both comical and gloomy and began to tell me about his doctor's advice, which was no good because, basically, it came down to eating less—and, my God, hadn't he been trying to do that for years?—and his wife's best girlfriend's advice, which was to put planks under the mattress so Mary-Ellen wouldn't, you know, sink out of reach.

It was a great, friendly lunch. We had a bottle of wine with the artichokes and the stuffed veal, swapping personal stories and reminiscences and getting mellow. When I judged he was mellow enough I said, "I've got a little problem, Vic."

He mopped the last of his crusty bread in the last of his

cream sauce, looking at me. "That was true about company policy, Nolly."

"I know that, Vic."

He nodded and waved to the waiter for coffee. "It isn't money, is it? Because if it is, hell, Nolly, I know you're good for whatever you need."

"Not money. Just a problem. I have this client, or at least I did have him . . ." And I told him about Woody Calderon, and the offer he couldn't refuse, and the thousand-dollar cashier's check.

Vic refilled his coffee cup twice while I was talking. He drank it hot and black, swallowing it down as though he wanted to make sure he blotted up the last of the wine before he said anything he maybe shouldn't.

Then he sighed. "That's funny," he commented. "So what are you going to do? Pay off his I.R.S. tab?"

"I already did that. There's two hundred dollars left over."

"So that's your fee. Just keep it— No," he said, nodding as though the dentist had just told him the tooth would have to be recapped, "I know. It isn't the money that's worrying you. You want to know if I know anything about it, as far as Narabedla and Mr. Davidson-Jones are concerned."

I said, "You can see where I might be curious."

"I don't mind your curiosity, Nolly." He thought for a moment, beckoning for more coffee. "You understand, Narabedla's *huge*. I don't know everything that goes on in it. Maybe nobody does but Henry Davidson-Jones himself, and I'll bet even he can't keep track of the details. I have a specific job. I'm U.S. investments and subsidiaries, that's all. I audit the statements from the other offices and prepare a consolidated profit-and-loss for the board meetings—that takes my time and seven other people's, just for that. I don't have a thing to do with, for instance, any of the offshore holdings, except now and then when one of the U.S. executives makes a trip to Europe or somewhere for meetings and we get his expense records. And I certainly don't know anything about Davidson-Jones's personal philanthropies. He's never discussed his interest in the arts with me. He's never discussed *anything* with me. I've never met the man."

"It was just a thought," I said.

"I'm sorry I can't help you, Nolly," he said warmly, his

big face friendly enough and regretful enough. To make up for it, he said, "How about a brandy?"

So we had a brandy, and Vic told me why the Mets couldn't possibly repeat last year's season, while the Yankees were bound to improve, and when the check came he grabbed it. "Narabedla's got more money than you do," he said. And then, while we were waiting for his credit-card imprint, he said suddenly, "There is one funny thing."

I took a deep swallow of the cooling coffee, then I sat up straight, wishing I hadn't had the final brandy. Something was coming.

"It's not a secret," he said seriously—to himself more than to me, I thought. "There's no reason you shouldn't know about it."

He paused to add in the tip and scribble his name. I didn't even breathe. "It's just this woman," he said. "She came into the office a month or two ago. Irene Madigan. From Beaumont, Texas, I think, only she was staying at that women's hotel downtown—the Martha Washington, is it? God knows if she's still there. And she didn't belong in our department at all. She just came in off the street and somebody got rid of her by shooing her onto me."

He paused to put the pen back in his pocket, then remembered it was Restaurant Associates' pen and dropped it on the plate. He sighed. "This is just between us, Nolly?"

"Promise."

"The last thing I want to do is get the company into some embarrassing situation. Well, what it is, her cousin had some kind of deal with Mr. Davidson-Jones. And the cousin disappeared, too."

CHAPTER

3

There have been times when I missed my little old office with the kind of despairing passion a former grand duke might have held for the droshkies and white nights of old St. Petersburg. Whatever else it was, it was *sane* and, not counting such times as the 14th of April, never scary.

The firm of L. Knollwood Stennis and Associates comprised altogether six people, counting me and the receptionist. The other person who really mattered was Marlene Abramson. In ways I did not like to admit, she was more important to the firm than I was.

When Marlene was nineteen years old she married a brilliant young medical student. For the next seven years she spent her time bearing three of his kids, supporting them all while he finished school, keeping up her own studies on the side, and providing an impeccably kosher house.

Then, one night, the medical student, now a gynecologist, took her out to an expensive dinner in the kind of place where you can't make a scene and told her about the physiotherapist who was about to make him the kind of attentive, loving, *sharing* wife he had always dreamed of.

Marlene was a wonder. She didn't even tie up his assets for the next thousand years. She only told her lawyer to make sure the kids got all there was for them to get, and philosophically walked away from Central Park South to see what the world had to offer to a divorcée with kids. Whatever else it had had, it hadn't provided another man.

By the time I got Marlene, the last of the kids was starting college. Marlene was "over thirty"—had to be well past forty-five, I calculated—and her principal interests were dieting, fussing over the incompetent, and waiting for the grandchildren. L. Knollwood Stennis and Associates suited her perfectly; there were plenty of unworldly incompetents among our clientele. And she suited them better than I would have believed possible when I hired her.

Marlene was a creative and smart bookkeeper, who didn't like to admit that she was also a CPA. She could have walked out of my office any day and taken half the accounts with her. She didn't because she had no reason to. She had as much vacation time as I did, which was almost all the time there was when either of us could be spared, and on the first business day of every year she would tell me how big a raise she wanted. I would give it to her. We never argued about it. She knew what the cash flow was as well as I did. She wasn't greedy, and neither was I.

She was also my good friend, so she was the one I told about the missing cousin of this Irene Madigan. I had, of course, told her about Woody Calderon long since. She listened attentively. Then she whistled. It wasn't a very successful whistle, because this was one of the days when she was giving up smoking and her mouth was full of chewing gum, but it expressed astonishment and concern.

"So what about going to the police, Nolly?"

"Would you? What do you think?"

"I think like you think. No. You got nothing solid for them to go on and, Jesus, what's the use of it, they can't even find the three kids that ripped off my stereo and the silver dollars from Harrah's Club in Vegas."

"*D'accord,*" I said. Marlene had been practicing her French to get ready for a week in Paris, and I had been helping her. Us operatic types, or former operatic types, get to learn a little of everything.

"So where's this Irene Madigan now?"

"She's not in the Martha Washington, anyway. She checked out two weeks ago. They wouldn't give me an address."

"She might be in the Beaumont, Texas, phone book."

"She might," I agreed.

"So maybe you could call her," Marlene went on, thinking things through. "But if you did, what would you say to her?" I nodded, and Marlene nodded back, and then she stood up and bawled, "Sally! Bring us a little coffee, there's a darling."

I waited for her program to run. Coffee is Marlene's prescription for everything, especially for getting started in the mornings you can't get started in, and even more for solving problems that don't have any solution, like justifying a client's thousand-dollar charitable contribution that he doesn't have receipts for. Or this one.

After Sally popped in with the coffee, Marlene told me two long, irrelevant stories. I listened to them patiently, knowing that, like the hum of the cooling fan when the computer is going, they were the outward sign of the processing that was going on in her head. The first story was about the *schwartze* who cleaned her apartment, and how the city bus driver who was her lover was suspected of fooling around with a Board of Transportation payroll clerk. The second was about the *shicksa* who was her daughter-in-law, who not only was Milwaukee's biggest customer for the Pill but was thought to be considering a tubal ligation. I listened. I knew how Marlene's mind worked, so I wasn't surprised when she made the abrupt transition back to the subject. She was saying that it would serve the *shicksa* right if Marlene were to come to stay for a weekend and put aspirins in the Pill holder, and finished with, "Wait till she wants to be a grandmother herself, she'll sing a different song. So why don't you just go to him and ask?"

I hung on. "Ask who what?"

"Ask Mr. Henry Davidson-Jones if he can explain about Woody, of course. You know him already."

"I don't *know* him. I met him once or twice, a long time ago."

"He wouldn't remember you?"

I said reluctantly, "I guess I could remind him."

Marlene took a sip of her cooling coffee and made a face. "Sally!" she yelled over her shoulder. "The coffee's worse than ever, even, sweetheart!" And to me she said, "You've already thought of all this stuff, both ways, right? And what it is, you just don't want to do it."

"Not a whole lot. I don't know if it's a good idea to ask a millionaire embarrassing questions."

"And what's the reason you think it would be embarrassing? Have you got the idea Mr. Henry Davidson-Jones has some weird habit of murdering musicians?"

I looked at her squarely. "Do you?"

"Nah! Who needs to kill musicians? Dope, booze, cigarettes, women—they're all busy killing themselves. Anyway, Nolly," she went on, "I tell you what. I'll write you a note you can put in your pocket, 'Dear Mr. Henry Davidson-Jones, better not kill this man, because a friend knows exactly where he's going, and if he doesn't get back safe the friend goes to the cops.'"

I grinned at her. "Maybe I'll give it a try," I said.

"Thatta boy! Only Nolly, listen. If things start to look not so good, make sure they read the note. You don't know, Nolly. You're too trusting, you don't know the world, you've got no idea what kind of weird business you could be getting yourself into." And on that point she was righter than even Marlene herself could have guessed.

CHAPTER

4

It is not my nature to go skulking around like Sam Spade. I don't have a talent for it.

On the other hand, I was curious.

Curiosity wasn't the only thing. I really was concerned about Woody Calderon. I didn't like his being dead. He was sort of a friend as well as a client, and, besides, he was a hell of a fine cellist, no matter how many critics had decided not.

All this being true, I am ashamed to admit that I was actually enjoying myself. An accountant's job is not unrewarding, but nobody ever called it thrilling. If I couldn't be an opera star, it was at least an interesting change to be a private detective for a while. So I did twenty push-ups to clear my head, and when I was good and aerobic, I went the whole distance. I sat down and wrote a note to Henry Davidson-Jones:

Dear Mr. Davidson-Jones:

I don't know if you will remember me, but years ago you were good enough to offer me a tour as a singer.

Unfortunately, illness damaged my voice. However, since then my voice has come back. I am contemplating trying to return to singing, and I would be honored to audition for you.

Of course that wasn't really true. The kindest thing you could say about my singing voice was that just a little bit of it was still there, maybe. Enough so that singing in the shower, with the water splashing on my head and the tiles of the shower stall bouncing the sound back to me, sometimes didn't sound bad at all. It was the kind of voice that people at a party might think pretty wonderful when everybody was gathered around the piano, especially after a few drinks. It would never be a star's voice, but Henry Davidson-Jones might not realize that.

So a week later I was down in the World Trade Center, eighty-odd stories up, talking to a woman who looked like a photographer's model, seated at a gilt table with a bud vase and a telephone and nothing else. I showed her my letter from Mr. William Purvis, secretary to Mr. Henry Davidson-Jones, saying that Mr. Davidson-Jones was willing to receive me.

She took me right in.

Mr. Davidson-Jones's office was not a bit like my own. Mr. Davidson-Jones's office was something like a private sitting room off the lobby of a really first-class hotel and something like heaven. It was furnished in Rich. It had a clump of palm trees growing out of a tub in the middle of the room, and flowering vines—hibiscus, maybe?—climbing the far wall. I won't even talk about the furniture, which was mostly antique couches. I won't talk about the ceiling, or not exactly, because it didn't have one. What it had was a sky.

I don't mean it was a real sky, because even if the ceilings were glass you couldn't look out of the top of the World Trade Center without seeing a lot of upside-down Japanese tourists in Windows on the World. But what it was could fool you. There must have been some sort of planetarium projector somewhere, because Mr. Henry Davidson-Jones's ceiling gave every appearance of being studded with actual stars. I could even recognize some of the constellations. The easiest ones, anyway. About the easiest there is is Orion, with its three stars in a row for the belt, and there it was,

flanked on one side by Sirius and Procyon, on the other by
Aldebaran and the Pleiades. Behind a scattering of flowering
vines on one of the side walls was a ceiling-high tank of
tropical fish. It was illuminated from within, beautifully lighting a bunch of two-dimensional angelfish, and a lot of bright
red and green and orange tetras.

And all this on the eighty-somethingth floor of the North
Tower of the World Trade Center. He was not only a very
rich man, Mr. Henry Davidson-Jones, he was also one willing to spend money to indulge himself.

The other kind of man he was was a relaxed and self-
assured one.

He opened the door for me himself. He shook my hand
warmly, and he greeted me by name. Actually, by my nick-
name, which showed either a grand memory or an even better filing system. "Nolly, my boy, what wonderful news
about your voice! Come in, sit down, would you like a
drink?" You could feel the warmth and charm soaking into
your pores. He was projecting that cordial intimacy that
makes careers for actors and politicians, and con-men.

I let him lead me to a leather armchair that had a table
next to it containing both a whiskey decanter and a silver
coffeepot with a clean cup. I expected him to say, "Name
your poison." He didn't say anything more, so after I had
sat down and gazed around I offered, "You've redecorated
your office since the last time I was here."

He allowed himself a smile of pleasure. "Crazy, isn't it?
But I admit I love it. It was a present from the board for my
twenty-fifth year with the company."

It was not much of a challenge to my arithmetical powers
to figure out that that made him at least fifty. He didn't look
it. He didn't look any older than the last time I'd seen him,
a forty who could pass for thirty-five in a nightclub, and
maybe twenty-six on the squash court. He had one of those
expensive tans, and no thin spots anywhere in his hair. Although he was no taller than I, he had a lot more presence.

"Will you sing for me, please?" he asked, as though that
were the thing he had been waiting for to make his day. I
assured him I would. He spoke into a telephone on the
desk—well, I guess it was a desk. It looked like a drawing-
room table with four different vases of flowers, but there
turned out to be a phone somewhere among them.

Almost at once a door opened. A nice-looking elderly lady

came in and smiled at me. She lifted the lid of a kind of secretary-looking thing and revealed a keyboard. "Miss Harfst will accompany you. It's only electronic," Davidson-Jones apologized, "but it has a good tone, I think."

It did. It took me a moment to get used to the idea that even a millionaire can keep a recital accompanist on premises for whenever he may take a notion to hear somebody sing, but when I suggested to the woman that we try the "Champagne Aria" from *Don Giovanni*, she nodded and began to play immediately. She played through it once, beautifully, and the tone of the piano was all Davidson-Jones had promised.

The "Champagne Aria" is a delightful, fast-paced piece, not too hard if you watch yourself on the breathing. I sang it, really, fairly well. Davidson-Jones listened with full attention, but without comment.

"Would you like another?" I offered. "*Pagliacci*, perhaps?"

"No, you've done well," he said, giving the accompanist a smile that meant she could go. She did. "My congratulations, Nolly," said Davidson-Jones. "I never thought I'd hear you sing like that again. Are you ready for some coffee, then?"

I let him pour me a cup of Marlene's recipe for dealing with everything, and took the difficult plunge. "I don't suppose that offer is still open after all these years, Mr. Davidson-Jones, but what made me think of it was what happened to Woody Calderon."

He didn't spill a drop of the coffee. He didn't even look surprised. "Ah, Woody," he said sadly. "What a pity. What a terrible loss to music. Yes, Nolly, I had hoped to help his career on a bit, and I am deeply saddened that it can't be done now."

"He told me about your deal," I said. "It was funny that it was so much like the offer you made me all those years ago, I thought."

He nodded in agreement. "Rich people are all pretty much the same, aren't they? They do have their functions, but as a class they're simply inordinately secretive."

"Yes," I said, wondering whether to ask him if he thought he was like that. It didn't seem a good idea. Then I took the plunge on what also didn't seem like a good idea, but maybe an essential one. I took a deep breath. "And then there was the young woman from Texas who had a similar offer from you, I believe.''

He looked polite. "A young woman from Texas?"

"Her name was Madigan. I think her first name was Tricia."

"Tricia Madigan," he repeated to himself, listening to the sound of the name as he spoke it. He shook his head. "Excuse me a moment, Nolly." He picked up the phone again and spoke quietly into it. After a moment he put it down. "I'm sorry, Nolly, we don't have any record of any woman named Madigan. In fact, I'm not sure we've been able to do anything for any young woman artists at all for some time. I do remember a black girl with a wonderful contralto voice, but that must have been a year or more ago. Oh, and there was Louise Cerregon. A harpist. She was from Oklahoma—Tulsa, I think—but that was a good many years ago, I'm afraid. I believe she gave up concert performances to raise a family." He shrugged deprecatingly. "Often enough, artists have more interest in their personal lives than in their art. I'd be the last to blame them, Nolly, but it *is* a pity. I always have a personal sense of loss when someone turns down one of these tours, or, as in your case, is unable to take it. But believe me, I accept those decisions. I'm only an amateur impresario. When I can help, I do, but I'm not God—why, I said that to your friend Woody, now that I think of it, when he declined my offer."

Then he sat back and looked at me seriously. "So now, I think, it's time to tell you what you want to know. Whether or not the offer of a tour is still open for you."

I stumbled. "Well, I didn't really expect—"

He cut me off. "The particular group who was interested in signing you is no longer available, of course. But I think I should be candid with you. You've established yourself in a good career, isn't that true? Money can't be a problem; you're grossing better than half a million dollars a year, even though you overpay your staff. You could do more if you wanted to go after more billings. Apart from not having married, you're really pretty much settled down, wouldn't you say? So I can't believe you'd be willing to give all that up, just for a tour that wouldn't net you any more than you're getting now, and certainly could not by its very nature lead to the sort of reviews and future bookings that could build a career."

"Well . . ." I said, swallowing; he was very well informed on me.

"Also," he continued soberly, "although your voice has certainly improved to a considerable extent, I wonder if it would be up to the demands of an operatic career. You can't always pick and choose your roles, you know. You could do your voice great harm in just a few engagements. And there's not much demand for concert appearances for someone who is not a star . . . and could you, do you think, really make it back to the Met? I'd be afraid not, Nolly."

The old son of a bitch hadn't missed a thing.

I said sullenly, "Maybe not."

"Or maybe yes," he contradicted brightly, catching me thoroughly off guard. "Tell you what. Would you like to try a small part just to see how it feels to you? I'm helping to organize a gala for the Philadelphia Academy of Music. We're doing Beethoven's Ninth, and we will be needing soloists for the final movement, if you want to try out. No need to decide now; just give me a call if you like the idea, any time in the next month. And thank you, Nolly, thank you very much for coming in to see me!"

So in the express elevator, dropping breathtakingly back to the real world, I was morose, worried, and wondering.

Morose because, in no time at all, Davidson-Jones had recognized and told me truths about my voice that I already knew . . . but had hoped an outside observer might not.

Worried because he had lied to me about Woody Calderon. Calderon hadn't turned him down, I was sure of it. Woody might not have *accepted* (but if not, where did he get the thousand dollars?), but he surely would not have *refused*.

And wondering because something about Davidson-Jones's office was sticking uncomfortably in my mind. I couldn't quite swallow it down, and I couldn't quite diagnose what it was. Perhaps it was, I thought, something about his starry ceiling. Certainly that was a quaint and unusual thing for the chief executive officer of Narabedla Ltd. to have in his private office.

I went back to my own place discouraged and dubious.

It's funny that it didn't ever occur to me to spell "Narabedla" backwards.

CHAPTER

5

Well, time passed.

You know how it is. You let things slide. You come to a block of some kind. Then you don't forget the things, exactly—God knows I didn't forget either Woody or Henry Davidson-Jones—but you put them aside for the moment, because it's really hard to see how to take the next step, even if they're important. Other things come up. The old ones sort of slide into that stack of things that you damn well know you have to get around to, real soon now.

Only you don't.

I didn't get around to doing anything more about Woody's death because I ran out of ideas, and besides it was vacation time.

Once we get the sixty-day deferments out of the way on June 15th, then it's pretty light work until the sluggards with the four-month deferments come due in August. There aren't many of them, either, because if you need four months you probably need six, which is the most the I.R.S. will give you without much misery befalling, and so June and July are our best getaway times.

I got away.

Marlene and I each take a couple of weeks then, and my turn came first. I had airline tickets to Milan, with a return from London-Heathrow, and a Eurailpass to get me around betweentimes. That's the best way to do it, I've found. Europe isn't all that big, and you can get almost anywhere from almost anywhere else by rail overnight, and with the pass you don't have to make reservations. You get on the train. You go.

My "vacation" is also business, of course. I mean it really is. I've defended it successfully in two audits, one of them really bloodthirsty. I have an arrangement with most of my artists' representatives to split a commission now and then,

20

and so I turn up bookings for some of the artists as I travel.
I had dinner with some of the people at the Teatro Lirico in
Milan, went down to Rome for a day, then on to Naples to
the Teatro San Carlo, then back to Milan just in time to buy
a ticket to La Scala when I saw that it was *Trovatore* that
night. One of my sopranos was to sing in that production
later in the year. I don't often pay for an opera ticket, but
as I had made up my mind at the last minute I didn't bother
to get comped. In the intermission I wandered around the
sparsely filled theater, looking at the busts of Verdi and
Leoncavallo, with nothing more on my mind than whether
to head for Paris or Vienna the next morning.

The thing was, I was feeling pretty good. I promised myself that I would get up early enough the next morning to
run a mile or so before the Milanese were abroad to gape at
me. I didn't even feel the usual heartburn when the baritone
got a solo curtain call; I had made up my mind I was past
all that, as well as other things I once had enjoyed a whole
lot, and the renunciation was bittersweet but no longer
painful.

When I got back to my room in the Albergo Termini I
checked the time and called my office. It was nearly six in
New York, but Marlene was still there.

"How's business?" I started as usual; and as usual Marlene said:

"You shouldn't ask. Jack Pershing came in today with the
return and a check for the balance due."

"That was due on the fifteenth!"

"What a memory," she said admiringly. "Listen, Nolly,
I told you we shouldn't let somebody like him mail it himself.
Oh, and I forgot to say, the check's postdated two weeks."

I didn't say what I wanted to say. Marlene wouldn't
have minded, but sometimes the overseas operators listen
in. I just said, "So now we have to figure penalties and
interest—"

"It's already done, Nolly. Don't holler on Jack; he's got
wife troubles. How's Italy?"

"I sat in the royal box at La Scala tonight," I reported.
"Same place Mussolini used to sit, before they hung him
upside-down."

"Don't let it give you ideas. Nolly? Listen." Then a pause.
There's always that bit-of-a-second delay in transatlantic
telephone calls, while the voices go to the satellite and back;

it makes conversations sound a little strained. But Marlene was sounding a little strained on her own, too. "That Irene Madigan woman."

"Who?" I said. Then I remembered. "Oh."

"Yeah, that one. With the cousin. Well, she came into the office looking for you last night. She figures that this guy—you know who I mean? I don't want to say the name."

"I know who you mean."

"Well, she figures he knows something about her cousin."

"He swore to me he didn't."

"I know, I told her all you said. But she still thinks so, and she wants to do something about it."

I swallowed. What in the world could an unknown woman from some place in Texas do about Henry Davidson-Jones?

"Are you still there, Nolly?"

"Sure. What's she going to do?"

"Well, for openers she's following him around. She said he was on his way to Nice in his yacht. By now she's probably there, too. In the Holiday Inn. The one at the airport."

Then she stopped talking. The satellite bounced silence back and forth between us.

"You think I should talk to her," I said.

"Me? Nah, Nolly. I don't know what you ought to do. I'm just telling you. But, you know, you could be going that way anyhow, couldn't you? And, listen, Nolly, she's not a nut. She's a nice *goyische* kid, real worried about her cousin Tricia."

"Who is, I suppose, a soprano or something."

Marlene giggled. I hadn't expected that. "Soprano, huh? You want to know what Tricia is? She's the Texas state champion baton twirler."

There was, after all, no reason I shouldn't go to the Côte d'Azur. A lot of my clients performed there now and then. Especially dancers, although I didn't have many of those. The Coast isn't what it used to be, but, after all, where did the Ballet Russe de Monte Carlo come from?

So I checked out of the Termini just in time to catch the late-night train to Nice.

It didn't have a real sleeping car, nothing but *couchettes,* but miraculously I managed to get a first-class one. So the only other person in my compartment was an elderly Spanish woman on her way to Port Bou. She snored, even above the noise of the train, but I slept well until the porter shook me awake.

Irene Madigan wasn't in the hotel. But she had checked with the reservations clerk to find out I was coming, and left a message that said she would phone me at noon. That was fine. After the train ride I needed to get the juices flowing again. So I worked out for an hour, not pressing very hard, in the Holiday Inn's exercise room. I didn't mind loafing a bit. I ate a very decent breakfast out on the sun deck, watching a Concorde take off from the airport just beyond the road, splashed around in the tiny pool for a while, and was in my room when the phone rang.

"Mr. Stennis? I'm Irene Madigan. I really can't thank you enough for coming here."

Nice voice. Nice manners. I said, "That's all right. Where are you calling from?"

Half a laugh. "Actually I'm in Monaco right now. I'll be back at the hotel tonight—rather late, I'm afraid. I was thinking—I mean, well, I don't suppose you'd like to come over here?"

In for a penny, in for a pound. I wasn't really sure I liked to. But I did it. I arranged to meet her at four o'clock in front of the Grand Casino.

There was no problem about getting there. The Nice airport was a five-minute walk away from the hotel, and there was a direct bus. At half past three I was standing in front of the plaque the Société des Bains de Mer had put up to Sergei Diaghilev, wondering how I would recognize Irene Madigan when I saw her, when she came up behind me. "Please tell me you're Knollwood Stennis," she said, "because I don't want to be arrested for soliciting strange men in Monaco."

"They don't arrest you here for that. They might tax you," I said, shaking her hand. "I'm Nolly."

She looked at me with a kind of good-natured surprise. "I was afraid—I mean, I thought you might be more like, you know, an accountant instead of, well, I mean, with muscles and all."

I gave her a neutral smile. (Or should I say a "neuter" smile, meaning let's don't go so fast into any boy-girl thing.) I said, "Do you mind telling me what you're doing here?"

The pretty smile left her face; what was left was stubbornness. That went with her hair, which was red, but the face was still pretty. She said, "I'll go wherever he goes, and he's somewhere around here. See that big white yacht by the breakwater? That's his. Only he isn't on it, I think."

"You think?"

She unslung a pair of field glasses from around her neck and thrust them at me. "See for yourself."

Without much interest I followed orders. The yacht was certainly a beauty, easily a hundred-footer. A couple of small, Oriental-looking sailors were touching up the varnish on the railings, but no one else was in sight.

"How about your cousin?" I asked.

"I haven't seen Tricia, either. Don't you think I would have told you if I had? All I did see was—well, I don't know, but I think it was a little old man. He came on deck this morning. One of the crew came running over and made him go back below—he could have been another kidnap victim."

"He could have been Henry Davidson-Jones's father."

"I don't think so, Nolly. He was an awfully *ugly* little old man. But," she said, resigning herself to my dogged skepticism, "you're right, he could have been anybody at all. There's only one way to find out."

That had a sound I didn't like. I took time to think that over, looking at her. Irene Madigan was worth looking at. About my age, almost my height, wearing white slacks and a silk blouse. I observed that she had Côte d'Azur eyes that were almost the same color as the sea. "Why did you come here, Irene? Why didn't you just go to see Davidson-Jones in New York?"

"He won't see me in New York. Last time I tried I was thrown right out of the World Trade Center," she said grimly, and then lightened. "Listen, I owe you. Can I buy you a drink or something? Maybe lunch? I'd actually rather lunch, if it's all the same to you, because I've been hanging around watching that yacht all day and I haven't had anything to eat."

So we found a place on top of that garish American hotel they've cut into the rock in front of the Grand Casino, and she told me the story of her life.

Her missing cousin, Tricia, was from the poor side of the family. Still, they'd grown up close. Then Tricia went off to start her own life, the big ambition of which was to be a Dallas Cowgirl and make it with every player on the Rams.

Then she discovered baton-twirling. That looked like the first, best step to her goal. "Only," Irene said, "she got kind of mixed up with some guy. Then she got into the Hare Krishnas. Then we lost touch for a while." Meanwhile Irene herself had married young, moved to California, divorced almost as young, and spent five years trying to make it in the movies. I could see that she might come very close. She had; but never a really decent part. And the rich side of the family, I judged, wasn't all that rich, because she had supported herself with odd jobs in Hollywood. "Checker in a supermarket. Travel agent. I even drove a cab for a while," she said. "I had my little trust fund, but I didn't want to touch it until I had to. But now . . ."

She paused, with a forkful of shrimp halfway to her mouth, looking out at the sea. She finished uncertainly, "Now I feel as if I have to. Do you think I'm a nut?"

I reassured her. "You can't be a nut, because Marlene doesn't think you are."

So then I had to tell her all about Marlene, and my business, and why I was an accountant rather than a lead baritone at the Met, although I didn't tell her all of that. I couldn't tell her all of that. She was too pretty and too nice, and maybe a little bit too sad, and I didn't want to discuss mumps with her. So I jumped ahead to Woody Calderon.

And so we came to Henry Davidson-Jones.

She told me her story. Tricia had come out to Hollywood, too, hoping to convert baton-twirling into at least an occasional walk-on in a bikini. Never got off the ground. Went back to Beaumont to start over; but meanwhile the two cousins had picked up again, and when Irene decided she wasn't going to get discovered in Hollywood, being then thirty-one while the maximum discovery age was about twenty-two, she went back to Beaumont herself.

Tricia was all excited. She'd had this wonderful offer. She called Irene one evening to tell her about Mr. Henry Davidson-Jones and his promises of half a million tax-free dollars spread over a period of four years, and Irene had wished her well and got down to the serious business of washing her hair.

"And about five o'clock that morning," Irene told me, "the phone rang again. It was the Port Arthur police. They said Tricia had been in a car accident. She was dead."

I felt a chill grazing the center of my spine. "And the car

went into the water and they never recovered the body,'' I guessed.

"Oh, no, it wasn't that way. They had her body in the morgue, and I identified it.''

She looked like crying for a moment—I mean, not as though she were going to do it, but as though she'd done too much of it lately. "I was her closest living relative,'' she said. "So I told them they could use her organs for anybody who needed them. I called up Henry Davidson-Jones's office in New York to tell them about it. They didn't send anybody to the funeral, but they did send the biggest damned wreath of flowers you ever saw—I think. There wasn't any name on it, but the florist said it came from New York.''

She finished eating her shrimp. Then she said, "I wonder whose body it was I had cremated.''

CHAPTER
6

The sun was shining bright off the Mediterranean, a tour bus was off-loading summery men and women with cameras, at the table next to us four young German boys were arguing over whether Mutti would be angry if they all had another sweet. It was not an ambience for this kind of discussion.

I nearly choked on the last of my omelette. "But you said—you said you saw her in the morgue!''

"I thought I did. I saw a young woman who looked as much like Tricia as Tricia would, with her head all mashed and her nose pushed up under her left eye, and all the exposed flesh I could see all bruises and gashes. I did make an official identification for the police. She was driving Tricia's car and wearing Tricia's clothes and carrying Tricia's

pocketbook. That was six months ago, Nolly. I really did
think it was Tricia. Wouldn't you?''

I was almost as exasperated as upset. ''Come on, don't
ask rhetorical questions. You changed your mind, right?
Why?''

She said, ''I was putting away all her papers. And some
papers I saved *about* her. I couldn't even look at them for
months. But I saved everything, and then I decided to bundle
it all up and do something with it—maybe burn it; maybe
send the whole batch off to some other relative, if I could
think of one. And I found myself reading the actual police
record of the accident. They gave it to me for the insurance.''

''Was there a lot of insurance?''

''There wasn't any at all, but the police didn't know that.
They were just being nice. The truck broadsided her at a
quarter after five. They had the time exactly, confirmed by
witnesses. They didn't call me right away—it took a long
time to track me down; they had to check back through my
California addresses and everything, because Tricia still had
the old address in her pocketbook. But it was a quarter after
five when it happened, all right. And when Tricia called me
on the phone it was a little after six. I was watching the NBC
network news.''

I didn't say anything right away. I wanted to make sure
I was understanding what she was telling me. To help out,
I invoked Marlene's cure-all and ordered coffee from the
very English waitress. ''American coffee,'' I specified,
pointing to where it said that in the menu.

It wasn't really going to be American coffee, of course,
because all French people think that Americans really would
put chicory in their coffee if they only knew how, but I was
grateful for the distraction so I could think. Irene Madigan
left me alone to do it. When the coffee was served, and
poured, and tasted, and we had both made a face, I said
tentatively, ''I suppose you're absolutely sure about the
time.''

''I thought you'd ask me about that,'' she said. ''I would,
too, if I were you. But, yes, I'm sure. The reason I'm
sure . . .'' She hesitated, then shrugged. ''The reason I'm sure
is that I had just started my period. I was flowing heavily, and
I'd waited for the commercial to go to the bathroom, and
Tricia's call caught me on the way to change my Tampax.''

"So there's no doubt," I summed up. "She called you around six."

"Right."

"That was three-quarters of an hour after she was supposed to have been in the crash."

"Yes."

"So," I sighed, reluctantly, "it wasn't Tricia who was in the crash. You cremated somebody else."

"You've got it," Irene Madigan said, and began to cry.

Sitting at a restaurant table with a crying woman is not my favorite thing. I avoid it when I can—usually successfully; the last time I'd been in that position was when one of my old girlfriends asked me straight out why I didn't try to make love to her anymore, and I straight out told her what the mumps had done to me. Which was a mistake. Actually, I should have been the one crying. But the reason doesn't matter. People look at you. They make up their own scenarios to account for why she's crying. "He beats her." "She's pregnant and he won't marry her." Or maybe, in this particular setting, "He lost all their money in the casino and he doesn't even have the decency to kill himself." It makes no difference if you're innocent of all charges. It doesn't even matter if, actually, you've been more of a louse than anyone looking on could possibly guess, and once or twice in the old days I was close enough to that. Whatever. They look at you. And you know damn well that if the crying woman should say exactly the right thing, one of the men in the restaurant would come over and punch your face out.

This time I was certifiably as innocent as anyone could get. I looked back at the furtive glances and the hostile stares—girls in bikinis, men in shorts, an elderly couple, she in a sort of lavender miniskirt, he with an ice-cream suit and the worst toupee I've ever seen, fingering his cane dangerously as he glared at me. I tried to project innocence to them all, and wished I could think of a way to stop Irene Madigan crying.

Fortunately, she stopped herself.

"Sorry," she sniffled, reaching for a dry Kleenex. I patted her hand. She smiled damply back at me, and a lot of the voltage began to go out of the stares. "The thing is," she said, wiping her nose, "I'm so damn *helpless*. Who would believe me?"

"I would. I do."

"And who's going to believe you, Nolly?" She returned the hand-pat to show she didn't mean to hurt my feelings. "If you had anything convincing to say you would have been talking to the cops long ago, right?"

"Well, but the two of us together . . ."

She looked levelly at me, waiting for me to figure out the end of the sentence for myself. I did. I shrugged.

She said simply, "Forget that." She rummaged in her handbag again. I thought it was for another Kleenex, but what came out was a couple of sheets of Xerox paper, stapled together and folded several times. She pulled one set of pages off and handed them to me. "Take a look at this, Nolly. I practically had to sleep with a guy from the *Wall Street Journal* to get it."

I unfolded and glanced at the heading: "Estimated Balance Sheet for Narabedla Ltd. Unofficial."

It was unofficial, all right. It was the *Journal* staff's best guesses about some very well kept financial secrets. Vic had told me they didn't have to file very many reports. They certainly didn't volunteer any. Almost every line was marked "Estimated" or "Provisional" or "Projected from Earlier Data."

But what it added up to was—remarkable.

I knew the huge empire called Narabedla Ltd. was huge. I hadn't known about the shipbuilding firm in Taiwan, or the Japanese computer company. I had no idea Narabedla held such large interests in a hundred American firms. None of your standard blue chips. *Better* than the blue chips. The list included most of the biggest money-spinners in the high-tech industries. Gene-splitting. Computers. Industrial chemicals. Pharmaceuticals. Avionics. If a company was going somewhere fast in a growing market, Narabedla owned a piece of it. A *big* piece. This summary changed my idea of what "big" meant. By these figures, Ford, ITT, any of the companies of Big Oil—Narabedla was right up there with them, and could maybe have bought and sold some of them.

Irene asked, "Did you read the part about the lawyers?"

I had. I hadn't missed its significance. Not one but four of the hottest, winningest firms in the country were on retainer to Narabedla. Which meant to Henry Davidson-Jones. Which meant . . .

I sighed and put the paper in my pocket. "Legal-wise," I said, "they could kill us."

She set her chin. "All the same, the son of a bitch kidnapped my cousin."

I said reasonably, "We don't know that for sure. We certainly don't have a clue about any motive."

"Sex, Nolly!" She pointed to the yacht across the bay. "Sure, that sounds crazy. A man like Henry Davidson-Jones wouldn't have to kidnap good-looking women and lock them up in a harem. God, his big problem ought to be fighting them off! But if he *did* do that, what better place could there be to do it in than a yacht like that? You could hide half an army. Forty or fifty screaming harem girls would be nothing."

"Irene," I said soothingly, "that wouldn't account for cellists and baritones."

"So maybe he's gay, too. Or maybe he likes music when he makes love." She scowled at me. "I don't know *why*, I just know *that*, and if you've got a better theory, tell me what it is."

I didn't have a better theory, of course. I only had a whole lot of doubt and confusion. I said, "It's the craziest thing I ever heard of."

And that was true. But I hadn't then been to the second moon of the seventh planet of the star Aldebaran.

CHAPTER
7

Things did start to get really crazy about then. I got pretty crazy myself. I found myself doing things that I was very sure Marlene would have defined as *meshuggeneh,* and I wouldn't have had any right to disagree.

We took the elevator down to the lobby of the hotel, way

at the bottom of the casino's hill. I found a pay phone, collected a stack of those dumb little French telephone tokens, and began calling every luxe hotel in the area. To each one I said the same thing in my best Berlioz French—I mean the opera composer, not the guy who runs the language school: *"Bon jour. Je voudrais parler avec M. Henri Davidson-Jones."* Eight times I tried it, working my way through Monaco, Menton, and Beaulieu, and when I started on Nice I hit pay dirt. *"Moment, m'sieur, s'il vous plaît,"* said the operator at the Negresco, and a moment later I heard a male voice saying:

"This is Mr. Passerine, Mr. Davidson-Jones's secretary. Who is calling, please?"

I didn't have an answer for that question, unfortunately. I am very good at planning, up to a point. I had figured out a way to find out where Davidson-Jones was staying; it had worked; I just hadn't thought far enough ahead to have decided what to do when I found him.

So I improvised.

I said, "Mr. Passerine, please hold for Mr. Rmfmf in Chicago." And I put my hand over the mouthpiece for a moment.

Then I gently hung up.

"Why'd you hang up? He's there, isn't he?" Irene demanded.

"Right. He's there. Now you tell me what we do about it."

"We go and confront him!"

"You tried that in New York. He wouldn't see you."

"We'll sit in the lobby until he comes out."

"They'll throw us out, Irene. That's a classy hotel."

"They can't throw us off the sidewalk in front of it, can they?"

"I wouldn't bet." Then I said firmly, "Anyway, I want to think this over before I do something foolish."

And she said, "Oh, *shit.*"

She turned her back on me and walked away. I didn't follow. I didn't know what to say if I did. I just watched her as she walked into the lobby casino and began feeding coins into the one-franc slots.

I tried to think of what I ought to do next. No good ideas turned up, except that my feet were beginning to hurt; Monaco is an up-and-down place, and I'd jogged over from the bus stop. On cobblestones. I decided to sit down while I thought; so I walked over to the bar and got myself a Campari-soda, not because I had changed my mind about trendy European aperitifs, but because it seemed like the right thing for that place; and I sulked.

That's candor. "Sulked" isn't the word I would prefer to use. It just happened to be the right one.

I got into a debate with myself, for the lack of Irene Madigan to take the other side. I told myself that I owed her nothing—anyway, nothing but common courtesy, and I'd certainly given her more of that than she had given to me.

It occurred to me that she was really on the edge over what had happened to somebody she loved. I should have been more understanding, I thought.

I also thought that I probably seemed, well, excessively cautious to her. Not to say chicken. That was understandable. Actually I *was* more prudent than she, if only because the person I was principally concerned about was only a client, not a blood relative. Irene should have understood that, shouldn't she?

She hadn't, though.

That bothered me, in a part of my mind where I was pretty tender already. I guess you could call it the area of personality I thought of as "manliness." The old girlfriend who had wept at dinner at Il Gattopardo ran into me a year or two later. She didn't cry this time, she only looked me up and down and chatted for a while and then made up her mind: "Why do you have to be so macho, Nolly?" she asked. "Hang-gliding? Muscle-building? Why don't you just relax and quit trying to be Rambo?" We didn't part real friendly that time, either. She'd been through both Esalen and est by then and was, of course, absolutely sure of her diagnosis of me: Acting ballsy to cover up the fact that I wasn't.

So it meant something to me that Irene Madigan might be thinking of me as a coward. I wanted her to understand where I was coming from. But when I went looking for her among the slots to explain all that to her, she wasn't there.

"There's something funny, all right," I told the telephone, which told the satellite, which told Marlene back in New York, "but I don't know what I can do about it. I don't know where Irene went."

"No names!" Marlene scolded, half a second tardily.

"All right, but I don't know where she went."

"She just split on you?"

I said fairly, "Well, I sort of walked away on her, too. We had a little disagreement. But I thought I knew where she was."

Silence transported via satellite for a second; then, briskly, "So, tell me, Nolly, what are you going to do now?"

"I don't know," I said.

That produced more of that expensive silence. After about seventy-five cents' worth I said, "I think I might as well catch the sleeper to Madrid. I was hoping to see some of the Spanish opera people tomorrow or the next day."

"Oh." No inflection. Just an "oh."

"Maybe," I said, "when I get back to New York, I'll talk to the police, I think."

"All right, Nolly," said Marlene, and I couldn't tell whether the tone was disapproving or just attenuated by distance.

So I hung up.

Then I had a drink.

Then I had dinner; and all the time I was thinking about it, and right between the *avocat vinaigrette* and the baby lamb chops I got on the house phone to seek a truce.

No luck. Even bad luck; Irene Madigan had checked out. As far as I could see, that closed out the account.

It didn't *feel* closed out, though. And then I remembered the Narabedla Ltd. xeroxes Irene Madigan had given me. I fished them out of my pocket and glanced at them.

Then I began to read in earnest. It was a shame to give those perfect little lamb chops only a part of my attention, but it was really fascinating. The more I looked at Narabedla's holdings and operations the more awed I got.

Nor was it just the money-spinning power that was impressive. What Narabedla did with the money was curious, too. Quite a lot of it they gave away.

Political contributions—well, sure. Big companies keep the government as crooked as they can with gifts. Narabedla seemed to be paying off more than half the Congress—310 separate contributions to congressional campaign funds, all for the legal maximum of three thousand dollars each.

That was a million dollars right there.

I was a little startled to see that most of the names I

recognized were likely to be liberal Democrats instead of the what's-good-for-business-is-good-for-America types that usually got that kind of corporate dough. I was even more surprised to see what some of the other donations had gone for.

Narabedla was angeling a large number of scientific and educational institutions. A hundred and fifty thousand to one university, eighty-five thousand to another, nearly a quarter of a million to a foundation—all to finance research on AIDS. There were twenty-five or thirty grants for medical research on a dozen other ailments, ranging from salmonellosis to flu. Fifteen thousand to the World Esperanto Association. Forty thousand to an astronomical observatory, "to undertake an analytical catalogue of pulsars and related objects." Another twenty-five thousand to the same place that was marked, "Supplementary grant for the study of anomalous novae." Sixty-five thousand to one university and eighty thousand to another for grants "for basic study of particle physics and Einstein-Rosen interactions." A big one, nearly half a million, to CalTech: "Survey of earthquake precursors in the Palmdale Bulge."

It wasn't all science and politics. The list went on for three pages—a few thousand here, a lot more thousand there, to a long list of do-good organizations—peace groups, civil rights groups, groups of all kinds from the NAACP to the Unitarian-Universalist Church of America; and I'm not even beginning to talk about the music conservatories and chamber-music quartets and struggling opera companies.

He was quite a good and responsible citizen, Mr. Henry Davidson-Jones. The total made my eyes pop. His Narabedla donations had totaled more than eleven million dollars in the latest known year. There was certainly, I told myself, no reason to think that anybody like that would do anything as pathologically felonious as kidnap people.

With that in mind, after dinner I had them call a taxi to take me to Nice-Ville; and all the way to the station my thoughts were fully occupied with the task of changing my mind.

It wasn't hard to do. I got it done by the time we arrived at Nice-Ville; philanthropist or not, there were just too many questions about the man. So I checked my bags at the station and took a taxi back to the Promenade des Anglais along the beach, and the Hotel Negresco.

*   *   *

In the days when I was a budding opera star I got a number of chances to live high on the hog. I took as many of them as I could afford. I sang in Nice, once, and stayed at the Negresco. Once. I valued the experience greatly, especially when I saw the bill. Which, fortunately, was picked up by the people at the opera festival, because if I had had to pay for it myself I would have been working that week for nothing.

It was not likely they would remember me at the Negresco, although beyond doubt there was a card file somewhere in the hotel's guest files with my name on it and the fact that I liked my bacon very crisp. But I remembered them very well. I played no games. I headed for a house phone, got the never-sleeping Mr. Passerine, and said, "This is Knollwood Stennis. I want to see Mr. Davidson-Jones, please."

"Mr. Stennis," he said placidly, "it's nearly midnight. I certainly can't disturb Mr. Davidson-Jones at this time."

"Yes, you can," I said. Then I took a deep breath. "I want him to tell me what happened to Irene Madigan. Not to mention her cousin, Tricia, and Woody Calderon."

Smooth Mr. Passerine didn't turn a hair. "Whatever your reason is, Mr. Stennis," he said politely—reasonably politely—"there is no way I'm going to bother Mr. Davidson-Jones now. If it is important, you can telephone in the morning. After ten."

And he hung up on me.

And I had run out of programming.

The troublesome part of all that was that well-mannered Mr. Passerine had all reason on his side. No titan of finance wants to be bothered at midnight by somebody who wants to accuse him of implausible felonies, does he?

I looked at my watch.

I still had time to grab a cab from the stand outside and get back to the station in time for my train to Madrid—even if one stretched imagination as far as it could go and supposed it would be on time.

I might even have a few minutes to spare. Time enough, perhaps, for a few discreet private-eye-type questions here and there. It was at least worth trying, so I summoned up all my discretion.

It wasn't enough. I was not nearly discreet enough for the Negresco, which houses Arab oil zillionaires and German newspaper publishers, not to mention royalty. When I asked

the reception clerk if she had happened to notice a good-
looking, redheaded young woman with Côte d'Azur eyes
who might have been asking for Mr. Davidson-Jones, I didn't
see her move a muscle to call anyone. She simply said, actually with a quite friendly smile, "I am sorry, sir, but we
are not permitted to discuss our guests." And then, when I
looked behind me, there was the doorman in his monkey suit
with a large, polite porter standing attentively beside him.

I left with as good grace as I could manage.

There was a taxi with a Senegalese-looking driver at the
stand across the street. I waved him over.

Then I hesitated.

Even the best hotel may have somebody, somewhere, who
will take a tip. If I could just find out from some such person
which suite Davidson-Jones was in, I could pound on the
door until he let me in. Or until someone threw me out,
whichever came first, but how bad could that be?

So why not try it? What was the worst that could happen?
I might miss my train, of course, but that would be only an
annoyance, not a tragedy. No one was expecting me at any
particular time in Madrid. I would very possibly get thrown
out of the hotel. I might even get punched out, by either the
porter or the doorman in the organ-grinder hat. But the Negresco would probably prefer to avoid violence, and besides,
in a pinch I could ask them to look up that old card-file to
show that, once anyhow, I had been on their protected-
species list myself.

What the hell, I said to myself courageously.

So I pulled two hundred-franc notes and my business card
out of my wallet and handed them to the Senegalese, patiently standing by the open door of his cab. In my very best
French I said, "I must go inside the hotel for ten minutes.
If I am not back by then, go to the police."

It turned out I was in error, on at least two counts.

The man I thought was Senegalese said in unaccented Harlem: "Shit, man, you just don' *learn*." And what he hit me
with I never found out.

And that is how I came to travel to the second moon of
the seventh planet of the star Aldebaran.

When Irene Madigan said you could hide anything at all
on a yacht the size of Henry Davidson-Jones's she was ab-

solutely right. She just didn't go far enough. She hadn't imagined what the limits of "anything" might include.

CHAPTER
8

I guess I'd better try to say what the second moon of the seventh planet of the star Aldebaran was.

It was disorienting. In fact, it was very, very disorienting.

I woke up with a lump on my head (but it didn't hurt) and a funny feeling that I'd lost some weight. I had. I was (as I discovered later) in the outermost shell of the cylindrical, far-from-natural moonlet that had started out as the second moon of the seventh planet of the star Aldebaran, but even there the gravity, or the rotation of the thing that I felt as gravity, was only about 80 percent of what I had experienced all my previous life.

One would think—I damn sure would have thought—that somebody who'd been knocked out, lugged aboard a yacht, shoved into one end of a black box, and dragged out of the other a million zillion miles away—I mean, you'd think that anybody like that would be hopelessly befuddled, if not blown entirely away. It wasn't like that. It was disorienting, sure, but I knew right away what had happened. I mean, all but the details. It could have been Mars or the moon or the fourth dimension or the year 2275 A.D.—but I knew right away, no question at all, that what had happened was *weird*.

Of course, at that point I didn't see any of the really weird ones. What I saw was a redheaded hippy-looking middle-aged man whose name (I found out) was Sam Shipperton, standing over me while he read the note that had been tied around my neck. "Aw, shit," he moaned, "they're going crazy back there. What the hell am I supposed to do with *you?*"

He did, after a while, figure that out.

What Sam Shipperton decided to do with me was weird enough in itself. In my opera days I knew a Canadian voice coach named Daisy, who had worked for British intelligence back in World War II. She was twenty-two years old when she finished her training, not very worldly; on her first assignment they slipped her into Naples just ahead of the Salerno landings, and something went wrong with the arrangements. The safe house she was supposed to stay in wasn't safe anymore.

The chief of the *partigiani* who was her control had a real-life career as a stage magician. He improvised; and that night young Daisy found herself on the program at the Teatro Reale, doing a strip-tease before eight hundred howling members of the S.S. Panzer Division "Heimat." It was, she told me, very drafty.

It was not quite the same for me when I arrived on the second moon. I didn't have to take my clothes off for the audience Sam Shipperton put together for me. On the other hand, my audience was nothing as homelike and relaxing as Nazi soldiers. My audience wasn't even human. There weren't eight hundred of them, there were only six. But, oh Lord, I'd rather have faced the Wehrmacht. One member of my distinguished audience was shapeless and slimy, two were spidery, and the other three were even worse. (I mean just to look at. I'm not saying anything about the smell.)

The man named Shipperton didn't give me time to get set, or even to eat. These people, he said—he actually used the word "people"—were very busy, and you had to perform for them when you could, because you might not be able to get them together later on. So I performed. I chose a number at random, and for them I sang the "Catalogue Aria" from Mozart's *Don Giovanni*—Leporello's song about the Don's many conquests.

It wasn't my favorite aria, not to mention that it wasn't even in my proper range. It was just the one that I was most sure I could get through without rehearsal, because I had done it so often in the shower.

I didn't have a stage, just a sort of cleared space in a viny, greenhousy chamber, which was not at all drafty. It was closer to the temperature of a steam bath. The arrangements were as peculiar as the circumstances. There weren't any rows of seats. One member of the audience actually sat in a kind of a chair; two hung from tree branches. A little black shiny thing that more or less resembled an oversized bedbug scurried in and perched on the piano as I sang. I was on a sort of dais, or maybe a kind of slave block, rather than a stage. Heaven knows what the lighting system was. I didn't see any spotlights. The light seemed to come from the air around us, not from a projector, which had the effect that I could see the audience clearly—not in this case an advantage. And my accompanist was a woman named Norah Platt. She knew the Mozart score well. She'd played it in London when it was new. She looked no more than middle-aged, but she was, she told me, two hundred and fourteen years old.

CHAPTER
9

Once my "audition" was over, I got ordered around a lot. For hours. By everybody. It was "Wait here," and "Get in there," and "We'll be ready for you in a minute"—over and over, while I was hustled into things like elevators (only I never felt them move) and out of them into places that smelled funny and looked worse.

I didn't really make much sense out of what I was seeing. Two questions kept pushing themselves to the top of my mind. Neither of them had anything to do with the second moon of the seventh planet of the star Aldebaran. The first question was, would Marlene be ticked off at being left to deal with the post-filing problems of our clients? And the second was, what in the world had got into me to get myself into this fix?

I didn't have good answers for either of them, or, indeed, to any of the million lesser questions that kept bobbing up. I don't remember when I noticed that I felt curiously light. I don't know at what point it occurred to me that I wasn't going to get a chance to slip into a phone booth (because there weren't any phone booths) and call the cops (because there wasn't anything that looked like a cop, even a French one) and get rescued, because nobody seemed to care about the fact that I needed rescuing. Everybody appeared to have concerns of their own.

When I say "everybody," I am including some mighty strange bodies. There were other people around—people who sometimes looked at me curiously and sometimes said, "Hi." But sometimes they weren't people at all—didn't even look like people—looked more than anything else like the kind of things you see on Saturday morning television.

Of course, I wasn't in really good shape for any of this. I was still catching up from the little difficulty in front of the Hotel Negresco. My head hurt, and I was still dizzy. After you get coshed you're unconscious, all right, but being unconscious isn't at all the same as a good night's sleep. I was shaky with fatigue—well, I was shaky, anyway. Part of it was fatigue. Part of it was the dawning conviction that somehow or other L. Knollwood Stennis had got himself into worse trouble than any tax audit.

"Don't worry," said motherly Norah Platt. "It will all straighten itself out after a while."

She had said it before, guiding me around from weirdness to weirdness. She kept on saying it. She was a tiny little woman, with a white bush of hair and a pink, horsy face. She beamed up at me with bright blue eyes as she led me along a corridor, doing her best to be reassuring.

"Are you really two hundred and whatever it is years old?" I asked her.

She sighed and smiled forgivingly. "Oh, Nolly—may I call you Nolly?—you're so full of questions. Yes, I am, but it's better if you let Sam Shipperton tell you all that sort of thing. I'm sure he will, as soon as he's ready to see you. In there, please." And when I went "in there" it was a nearly bare room, with a door ajar. "Sit there," said Norah, "and wait till Sam calls you." She bustled over to peek in the door.

"He's here, Sam," she called. "Have you got his sandwiches?"

"On the table," said a man's voice. It sounded impatient, and then it lowered volume as it returned to a rumbling and chirping conversation on the far side of the door.

"Eat," said Norah, taking the lid off a covered dish to see what was under it. Sandwiches, wrapped in a white linen napkin. She approved. "Yes, these are fresh cut, and they look quite nice, don't they? You haven't eaten a thing, have you?"

I ignored the sandwiches. I said, "Who's Sam Shipperton?"

"But you've met him, dear! He's what you might describe as our booking agent. He's the one who arranged your audition. Poor dear man," she said sympathetically, "you're all confused, aren't you? And you haven't had any sleep, and I suppose you're quite confused by all this."

"You suppose exactly right!"

"Yes, well, it's always easier when you come as a volunteer. Still, once you make the adjustment you'll find it's quite nice here."

"Start with that! Where's 'here'?"

"Why," she said patiently, "I'm told that this is the second moon of the seventh planet of the star Aldebaran, but we just call it Narabedla. Won't you try your sandwiches? I asked for the chopped cheddar and watercress specially, but if there's something else you'd rather have—"

"What I'd rather have is answers!"

She pursed her lips. "Oh, indeed? Answers to what questions?"

"Well, to begin with, what are all these Loony-Tunes?"

"Loony-Tunes?"

"The funny-looking things! The *creatures*!"

"Ah, the *natives*," she said, nodding. "They are a bit offputting at first, aren't they? Well, to begin with, let's take the ones who were auditioning you. Meretekabinnda is the Mnimn—the little short one in front, you know?—he's really quite nice, and very interested in Earth music. Then there's Barak, who's a Ggressna, and I think there might have been an Aiurdi and a J'zeel. I'm afraid I didn't really pay much attention to them—it was a rather last-minute engagement, you know, and I simply didn't look. I suppose one of the Eyes of the Mother was there as well, but they're so small one doesn't always see them. Well, one wouldn't, would one? I mean, that's more or less what makes them so useful to everyone, isn't it?"

I snarled, "How would I know?"

"Yes, of course," she said soothingly. "Is that the sort of thing you wanted to know?"

"You left out the most important part! They aren't *human.*"

"Well, of course they aren't human, Nolly," she said crossly. "We don't perform for human audiences here, do we? It's all the Fifteen Peoples—at least, the few among them who care for such things. Binnda and the others are the impresarios. They decide whether or not a given company can perform for their clientele, do you see?"

"I don't!" I glared at her. "Are you trying to tell me that this whole thing is just a scheme of Henry Davidson-Jones to kidnap opera singers for a bunch of Martians?"

"Oh, no, Nolly! Not only opera singers. And certainly there aren't any Martians. And nobody gets kidnapped— well, your own case is quite unusual, isn't it? And Mr. Davidson-Jones does much, *much* more than arrange tours for artists. But," she sighed, "from your point of view at the present time, well, yes, I suppose you could say that. Nolly? I'm really terribly sorry, but I do have another engagement. So if there's nothing else you need just now—"

"I need to know what's going on!" I yelled, but Norah just smiled serenely.

"When you're as old as I am," she said, "you'll learn to take just one day at a time." I scowled at her. She didn't mind. She just said, "Sit down on that nice, comfy puff, love. Eat something; you need your strength. Sam will call you when he's ready."

And she left me there, in that room with not even a chair, just a sort of warm, vibrating hassock that did its best to put me to sleep.

How do I explain what it was like to find myself, without warning, on the second moon of the seventh planet of the star Aldebaran?

The answer is, I don't. Not so anyone can really understand, anyway. I was like a chimpanzee suddenly snatched out of his African jungle home and dropped in the middle of

Times Square. Nothing made sense. Everything was either scary or infuriating.

I should have been better off than the chimp, because I was better informed. After all, I was a pretty sophisticated, reasonably well-informed human being. I had traveled all over the world. I had heard all about the things people said about life on Mars (none there) and flying saucers (all unreal) and the far stars and the universe in general. I'd even watched Carl Sagan and Frank Drake and all those other somebody-must-be-out-there people on the Johnny Carson show, explaining how they were pretty sure that there probably were almost certainly some other intelligent races in the universe, most likely . . . but, unfortunately, not very *many* of them, they would add, because they'd been listening real hard on the big radio telescopes for a long time, and what they'd heard was zilch.

That was the big difference between me and the chimp. The poor chimp would have been astonished to find this new world possible. I, on the other hand, was triply bewildered, because I knew perfectly well it was *im*possible.

So I wasn't just angry, exhausted, and confused. I was in traumatic, if not indeed terminal, culture shock, and that was before I'd even met the Mother or seen the statue at Execution Square.

"I said you can come in now," snapped the voice of Sam Shipperton.

It woke me up. I'd drowsed off on that warm, vibrating hassock, with one of the sandwiches uneaten in my hand. Sam Shipperton was standing over me, and he wasn't alone.

The—ah—the *thing* with him was not at all human.

It was the same thing I had seen on top of the piano while I was singing, only now I could get a good look at it. What it mostly looked like was a big bedbug, the size of a dachshund. Maybe it looked a little more like one of those extinct things I used to get as rubbery plastic models out of the gum machines in Asbury Park. Those were called trilobites. This particular trilobite-looking thing was standing on the table and chirping up at Shipperton as he stood there.

It was chirping in English, but so shrill and so fast that I couldn't quite make out the words. "Yeah, yeah," Shipperton said absently, glowering down at me. "I'll take care of it."

There was a final admonitory burst of chirping from the bedbug. Then it hopped down from the table and scurried out the door.

"So *they* say," Shipperton said sourly after it. Then to me: "What a mess. You've turned up at a bad time, Stennis. But come on in, while I figure out what the hell to do with you."

I was still half asleep. I had no better ideas, so I followed, munching on the sandwich and staring around.

In my time I've been in any number of booking agents' offices. Never one like that. Like any agent, Shipperton had a big desk. It didn't resemble any regular desk. It wasn't mahogany or bleached oak or knotty pine or any of those other trendy things. It wasn't wood at all. I didn't know what it was. Most of the desk was ebony black, but the top of it was, I suspected, one huge computer screen. It was a mosaic of small, square images. As Shipperton absently reached out and tapped on one or another of them, they flickered and flowed, faster than my eye could follow. They meant something to Shipperton, though, because he was staring at them disconsolately.

The rest of the furnishings were standard enough—well, some of them were. Somewhat standard. That is, he had the kind of impressive-expensive furniture that you'd get in the office of a really big-time agent, or a small-timer willing to invest the money to look big. There was the traditional casting couch, huge, deep blue, and upholstered in what looked and felt like real leather. There were a chair and a hassock to match, and a coffee table with a vase of fresh-cut flowers between two tastefully displayed sheaves of magazines. The magazines were dentist's-office regulars—*National Geographic* and *People* and so on, with *Variety* and the *Hollywood Reporter* mixed in. All recent issues, too. The flowers were harder to be sure of. One kind was lilacs. Another might have been hibiscus, and another I didn't recognize at all, but collectively they smelled sweet. There was a deep, figured rug, maybe Persian. And there were no windows at all.

The reason there were no windows was that every inch of wall space was filled with small, square pictures, from about hip height to the ceiling.

I thought at first they were photographs. Silly me! They

were more of those computery kinds of things, because I
saw that as Shipperton played with his desk top some of them
blurred and changed. The one good thing was that they were
all of people. *Human* people. Most of the pictures were of
people I'd never seen, but then I recognized the sweet old
face of Norah Platt. It occurred to me to see if I could find
Woody Calderon among them, but Shipperton didn't give
me time.

He took his attention off the desk top and gave it to me.
"What a day," he said morosely. "The Polyphase Index is
still dropping, in spite of everything, and what I just had to
tell the Mother was that your audition was a bust."

I had already made up my mind to say what I wanted to
get off my chest regardless of anything this man might have
to say. I plunged right in. "Shipperton, I was brought here
by force and against my will. That's kidnapping, and that
makes you an accessory to a capital crime. And—" I
stopped in the middle of my planned speech, having taken
in what he had just said. I finished, "What do you mean,
my audition was a bust?"

He said sourly, "A bust. As in forget it. I thought for a
minute that I might talk some of them into letting you sing
for them, like any regular artist. But you stank. So that's
out; and now what am I going to do with you?"

I opened my mouth. Then I closed it again. I'd made my
protest; it was on record, for whatever that was worth—
certainly not much. I didn't really have anything more to
say.

Sighing, Shipperton got up and went to a little desk at the
side of the room; it opened and revealed a coffeepot with
cups. He filled two of them and shoved one at me before he
sat down again. "I wish they hadn't dumped you on me right
now," he complained. "Things are still real tense over that
colonization thing with the Bach'het, and everybody's pretty
tired of song recitals anyway. No," he warned, as I started
to open my mouth, "don't give me an argument right now.
Just keep it down while I think."

I didn't see any alternative to that, and besides I wanted
to finish my sandwich. So I did.

Whatever Shipperton was, he didn't look like a traditional
booking agent. He wasn't one of the female ones in a tailored
suit, and he wasn't one of the fat and fifty ones with a big
cigar. Shipperton looked to be about thirty-five. He was

wearing a plaid lumberjack's shirt with the sleeves rolled halfway up his forearms, showing a blue tattoo of a peace sign. He had a strong, long nose, and red sideburns to go with his red hair. The hair came down to his shoulders. He pulled restlessly at a strand of it as he said, "You can't tap-dance or anything, can you?"

I almost choked on the last of my sandwich. "No, I can't tap-dance! Let's get to the point. I was knocked out and kidnapped, and I want to go home right away."

"Forget that," he snapped. "That's just out. O-u-t, out. You know, I really hate it when I have to do orientation. They're suppose to take care of that on Earth." *On Earth* echoed awfully in my mind. So it was all true, then! "So just listen up. First, you can start out by forgetting about American kidnapping laws, Stennis. You're not in the United States now."

I stuck to my guns—unloaded though they might be. "Henry Davidson-Jones is. Sometimes, anyway. He'll have a lot to explain to the cops as soon as Mar—"

I swallowed the rest of Marlene's name . . . a little too late, maybe.

"You were going to mention a name?" he asked politely.

"Woody," I said promptly. "Woody Calderon. Where is he?" Shipperton looked puzzled, and I amplified: "He's a cellist. You snatched him maybe three, four months ago."

"Oh, that guy." Shipperton nodded and reached for his desk top. "Let's see if I can skry him for you." When he touched things on the desk top, it turned into a mosaic of panels, like the one on his walls. Each little square had an image—a piano, a woman's face straining in song, kettle-drums—there were dozens of them. Shipperton put his finger on the one that displayed a cello.

At once nearly all the wall pictures disappeared. The few that remained expanded and turned into human faces with cryptic numbers and figures around them.

Woody Calderon's sad, smiling, ineffectual face looked at me out of one of the pictures. As Shipperton did something else, the other pictures disappeared and next to Calderon appeared a drawing of an alien. It was a sort of sticklike, praying-mantis parody of a more or less human, or anyway biped and erect, figure.

"Woody Calderon, right," Shipperton said. "He's fine. He's on tour with the Ptrreek right now. He ought to be back here in—let's see—well, maybe a week. It might be more than that; depends on whether Barak wants him for anything. Friend of yours?''

"A very good friend," I said belligerently. "I was the one who reported him missing to the police." That was a stretch of the truth, but, I thought, worth putting in on the chance that it might worry Shipperton.

It didn't at all. The word "police" didn't even register. He just said, "Well, your friend Calderon's doing all right for himself here. He's made a good adjustment. He's done three tours already—all modern stuff that the other cellists never learned—and he's got a nice cash balance in his bank account to show for it. Now, let's talk about you."

"The only thing about me is I want to go home!"

"But we can't let you do that, Stennis," he said gently. "Get used to the idea, will you? You're on Narabedla for good. There's no sense in getting on my case about it. I don't have anything to say about it; I can't go home either."

He didn't sound as though that bothered him. "Well, who *can* do something about it?" I demanded.

"Nobody on Narabedla, that's for sure. Nobody human, anyway, and, believe me, I promise you none of the others care. But look," he said reasonably, "will you listen while I tell you the score? You're an extra. We didn't try to recruit you. We didn't want you. We're just stuck with you, and your tryout didn't impress those guys. As I see it, you've got no place here."

"That's fine with me! Send me home."

He just shook his head.

In the clear, cool glow of hindsight, I can see that Sam Shipperton wasn't at all a bad man. He didn't even look like a villain. What he looked like was any midwestern liquor-store dealer, settling down to a career after having his fling with the counterculture, bothered by some unexpected business worry on his weekend off. His clothes were California casual; he had beige Adidas on his feet, and when he got up to refill his coffee cup I could see the authentic leather label on the hip pocket of his Levi's. He put the cup down and sat on the edge of his desk, looking at me with wary cordiality. "What they suggested for a second choice," he said, "was that you be employed administratively. Administratively my ass! Sometimes they're real stupid back in the home office. I'm the only administration we've got here, not counting natives, and there isn't enough work to keep me busy, really. So—"

"Hold it a minute," I ordered. "You're going a little fast there. If that was the second choice, what was the first?"

"Ah, well," he said, sounding embarrassed, "we can forget that one. It really was not a good idea."

"What was it?"

He looked uncomfortable. "They suggested slow storage." I blinked at him and he explained. "They slow you down, you know. Just keep you on ice, so to speak—oh, not real ice! You wouldn't feel a thing, it's just that if we woke you up five or ten years later you'd only think a couple of hours had gone by."

"I don't like hearing that 'if' in there. What do you mean, 'if' you woke me up?"

He said defensively, "Well, that's kind of the point, isn't it? What would be the use of waking you up? What would be different in ten years? If we could find something for you to do then, we could find it now." He looked at me seriously. "But you should remember that slow storage is always an option, Stennis. So don't screw yourself up trying to do it to us, okay? Because you're the one that'll get screwed. Keep in mind that we're not running some white-slave gang. Narabedla Limited's a perfectly legitimate import and export business—legitimate by local standards, anyway, and it really doesn't matter what it is by any others, does it? The Fifteen Peoples get what they want. Narabedla Limited gets what it wants. And the artists get, really, not so tacky a deal at all. There's money to be made, and there's fun to be had. You'll see. Of course, most of the people who come through volunteer for it, you know. They know what they're getting into—well, they sort of do, anyway; maybe we weren't all up front with them about the geography, like. They've got talents that they can sell here for a better price than at home, they get well paid, there's no problem—anyway," he clarified, "after the first shock there isn't. Maybe right at first they're pretty pissed off. But when they see what a sweet deal they've got— What's the matter?" he asked irritably, as I cut him off in the middle of his sales pitch.

I reminded him, "You said I failed the audition."

"Oh, yeah." He thought for a minute, brushing his hair out of his eyes to look at a Patek-Philippe watch on his wrist. "Well," he said, coming down, "I'll have to see what I can do about that, won't I? All right. Get out of here and let me work. I'll talk to Binnda again. Maybe he'll have some ideas. Right now you probably ought to get some sleep. There's a vacant house you can use; I'll get a Kekkety guide to take you over, and— Now what? No more complaints about being kidnapped, you hear me?''

"Not about my being kidnapped. I just want to know what happened to the woman I was with. Is Irene Madigan here?''

"No, you were the only one to come through lately. She isn't here. And, Jesus, I hope it stays that way.''

CHAPTER

10

What Shipperton called a "Kekkety guide" turned out to be a silent, slim little person who looked more than anything else like one of the deckhands from Henry Davidson-Jones's yacht. He didn't speak. He just led me along some pleasant little streets with occasional pedestrians nodding to us as we passed. All very homelike, in an Andy Griffith kind of way, and all the time I was trying to get a handle on the terrible crazy confusion that had replaced my dull, pleasant, normal life.

I knew that I wasn't exactly unique.

I knew that in the history of the human race many, many millions of people have been snatched without warning out of their normal lives into some strange new captivity—college professors taken by terrorists in Beirut, farm girls abducted into the brothels of the big cities, Africans captured for the slave trade, Europeans shanghaied onto Moorish galleys. Well, sure. Such things happened. But they didn't happen to *me*. Although I'd worried about a lot of things in my life, I'd never worried about the right one, because it had never occurred to me that I might someday become a simple export commodity with nothing to say about it.

I still had plenty of worries. I worried about what had happened to Irene Madigan. I worried about what Marlene was going to do when I didn't show up. I worried about how my clients would survive without me.

I worried a lot, too, about myself. I didn't *want* to become a member of Narabedla Ltd.'s large clientele of touring artists dedicated to presenting Earthly performing arts to entertain the cognoscenti of the Fifteen (alien) Peoples and their twenty-two inhabited planets. All the same, I didn't like having failed the audition.

Before Shipperton sent me off with the Kekkety guide he let me run sketchily down the artists' list. It was formidable. Not counting Norah Platt, the ancient pianist, Woody Calderon, the cellist, and Irene Madigan's cousin, Tricia, the baton-twirling one, there were six sopranos, three mezzos, eleven tenors, four other baritones or bass-baritones, two basses, and a boyishly slight, pale-skinned castrato, all of whose pictures were on Shipperton's walls. That was just the singers. There were also violinists, pianists, harpists, percussionists, sitarists, harpsichordists, and a scrawny ebony-black man who played the djidjeraboo. There were jugglers, acrobats, gymnasts, unicyclists, half a dozen black guys who had once been a kind of generic imitation of the Harlem Globe Trotters, and a man who drew in chalk on sidewalks; a glassblower specializing in instant animals; two heavy-metal and one punk rock group (but their war paint, dreadlocks, and Mohawks were wasted on the audiences here); there was a lion-tamer with six lions and a man with a flea circus; and a man who imitated bird calls; and two mimes; and a small but otherwise first-rate ballet company; two break dancers, and a Jamaican who played steel drums.

Obviously Narabedla Ltd. had been doing a lot of business over a long, long time.

And those were just the artists who, being human, had originated on the planet Earth, Shipperton explained. He told me that his office didn't handle the nonhuman others. He said he was really glad of that.

The Kekkety guide got me nearly to where I was going before I came out of my fog long enough to look around.

"Hold on a second," I ordered, pausing. We were in a quiet kind of intersection in what almost might have been a small town back on Earth. There were four different streets leading away from the little square, which was a star-shaped plot with a couple of flowering fruit trees. What caught my eye was one of the ugliest statues I had ever seen. The statue was life-size. It was a man, a very human and terrified-looking man, and a monster. The piece looked a little like the Laocoön group, except that there was only one man in the coils of the monster, and the monster was a lot worse-looking than any terrestrial snake.

"A bronze general on a horse would've been a lot nicer," I told my little guide. He peered up at me curiously, but didn't respond.

I turned away from the hideous statue and gazed around at the intersecting streets. The first street on the right appeared to be a sort of Greenwich Village mews, with gaslights and wrought-iron gates. The next looked like a little English village that the local historical authorities wouldn't let anybody change, thatched-roof houses with diamond-shaped glass panes in the windows.

When I started toward the third the guide tugged encouragingly at my arm, and I followed him into it. The street looked like one of those Southern California hillside places with buildings pressed tight against each other, poised between brush fire and mud slide, except that these dwellings didn't have any carports. (Why would they? I hadn't seen any cars.) The fifth house on the right had a scarlet door with a lion's-head knocker, framed by two lemon trees in fruit. The other thing it had was a little swinging sign that said:

Malcolm's Place
14 Riverside Drive

There wasn't any river for it to be on the side of, I observed, and while I was staring at the door the guide turned and trotted away.

I was on my own. One of the little black bedbugs paused in scurrying along the street to gaze at me. It didn't linger. Evidently I wasn't very interesting. I reached out for the doorknob.

It disconcerted me to find that it was locked.

Shipperton hadn't said anything about a key. He certainly hadn't given me one. I looked under the doormat hopefully; no key there. There was no one in sight to ask for help, or even advice.

Apart from being really worn out, I think I was by then so numbed by the shocks and weirdnesses of the previous twenty-four hours that the reasoning and competent part of my brain had just thrown up its hands and gone to sleep. (The rest of me urgently wanted to follow its example.) I couldn't think of anything to do about the problem. I simply stood there for a minute or two, contemplating the door, until without warning it was opened by a tall, surfer-looking young woman who said, "If you want in, why don't you knock instead of just rattling the darn doorknob?"

She was naked. By "naked" I mean not a stitch.

The numbness that affected my brain was powerful stuff. I said politely, making no adjustment to the fact that she didn't have any clothes on at all, "I'm sorry. I thought this was supposed to be the house I was going to stay in, but I guess you live here."

"Hey, no, I'm just visiting," she said, giving me an appeasing smile. "You want to talk to Malcolm Porchester. It's his pad. He's getting his chalks together, but he'll be right out." She picked a kimono kind of garment off the back of a chair and wrapped herself in it, looking me over the whole time. Then she brushed past me, with lots of touching, giving me another smile on the way. She closed the door behind her, leaving me alone in what did not now appear to be my house at all.

Considered as a home which was apparently not to be my own, it was rather attractive. There was a Chinese silk rug on the floor. There were comfortable leather armchairs on one side, and a table and chair set on the other. The remains of a breakfast for two were on the table; they had had fruit, biscuits, and something that looked like it had been an omelette and made me realize I was very hungry. More than hungry. I deeply regretted the sandwiches I had left uneaten. My tongue was moving restlessly around the inside of my lips. I was just making up my mind to steal one of the leftover biscuits when a big, stoop-shouldered man came through the door from the other room. He was fortyish and stocky, and he wore a three-piece suit in gaudy crayon colors with tassels and brass buttons. "Oh, sorry, mate, didn't hear you come in," he said, voice soft but deep. "I was in the bog. Mind telling me who the hell you are?"

"I'm Nolly Stennis. Shipperton said this house was vacant—"

He gave me a deep scowl. "Damn the man! I've told him it's my own digs and no bloody Holiday Effing Inn. Why didn't he give you Jerry Harper's place? Still," he said, amiably enough, "that's not your fault, is it? In any case, I'm on my way to tour the B'kerkyis for two weeks, so you're welcome to sack in here while I'm gone. Malcolm Porchester's the name. Happy to know you. Make yourself at home. Just don't drink the liquor or borrow the books, if you don't mind—and if my Fortnum and Mason parcels come in, they're private property, not issue. Has Tricia left?"

I said diplomatically, "A young lady did let me in, yes. Then she went out."

"That's her. Tricia Madigan. Couldn't be bothered to say good-bye to me, could she? Well, give her a tickle for me when you run across her, and tell her I'll be back in a fortnight." And, picking up a heavy squarish case with a strap on it, he shouldered it and was gone.

Well, I thought. At least *something* was accomplished. If nothing else, I now knew for sure where Irene's cousin Tricia had gone.

CHAPTER
11

I slept on top of the bedclothes, fully dressed. There was only the one bed. It smelled of Tricia Madigan's perfume and of faint, private aromas, and I just did not choose to get in between those recently used sheets. I'd gobbled down the rest of the biscuits and fruit as soon as Malcolm Porchester was gone, and I might have slept longer if I hadn't heard rustlings in the other room.

While I was waking up, making up my mind to investigate the sounds, I heard my name called.

It was the voice of Norah Platt, my accompanist from the day—or was it the night?—before. When I peeked through the bedroom door I saw that she was standing primly in the front doorway, waiting to be invited inside, but there were two others present in the house who had not waited for an invitation. They appeared to be the same sort of small, brown men, Oriental-featured, that Shipperton had called "Kekketies." They had skinny, muscular legs sticking out of khaki shorts. They didn't bother to look at me. One of them was running a vacuum hose across the Persian carpet. The other was clattering dishes in the kitchen. The table had been cleared and the room picked up, and as soon as I was out of the bedroom both of the men ducked silently past me into it to begin stripping the bed.

"Good morning, Mr. Stennis," Norah Platt said politely. "I hope I'm not intruding. I thought you might like some help settling in."

"You never had a better thought," I told her.

Norah Platt was a tiny thing, no more than five feet tall. Her hands were in proportion. I wondered how she could span an octave on the keyboard, though she had seemed to have no trouble when she was accompanying me in my debut before the weirdies. That time she had worn a high-collared, long-sleeved evening gown. This morning she was wearing a decorously knee-length pleated skirt and a less decorous halter top. She filled it quite well.

Looking at her, it was hard to believe that this woman had been alive during the lifetime of George Washington. Apart from the fact that she was smoking a slim cigar, she looked like anyone's favorite staying-young grandma.

She acted like a grandmother, too. She began talking at once. She told me that she was aware I hadn't had much sleep and hated to wake me, but Mr. Shipperton had come up with an idea about what to do with me; no, she didn't know what it was, but he'd tell me all about it. As for "settling in," she knew what kind of assistance I needed before I knew it myself. I certainly wouldn't have to make my own bed, because the Kekkety folk would take care of all that.

"You know," she said, waving toward the little brown people, "the servants. They're called Kekketies. They come with the house. All mod cons, you know. No, they don't talk, but they'll understand when you give them orders. If you want something special, just tell them, or leave a note for them on the fridge." On the subject of clothes: "I'll help you choose a wardrobe this afternoon, if you like. There's no dress code here. A lot of the men just wear shorts. Or less." On the subject of food: "I'll make a basic list of supplies for you to give the Kekkety folk. Do you cook? So many men do, now. There are quantities of ready-cooked things available if you order them, and the Kekketies will do you a meal if you like. They're not bad on anything in the standard cookbooks. I think it's nicer to make my own. Of course," she added apologetically, "it's not like Home, is it? If there's something in particular you fancy—a particular brand, perhaps—you'll have to order it, and that can take weeks. Also, you've got to pay for it out of your earnings, and of course at present—well, I'm sure you'll have plenty of earnings once you get started. I mean, if you *do* get started. Can you eat kippers?"

I perceived that it was not an irrelevant question. The servant in the kitchen had not just been doing dishes. Food smells were coming from it, and one of the little men padded silently past us to deal with them. "I supposed you would want breakfast," Norah apologized, "so I took the liberty of instructing them to make you something. There wasn't all that much to choose from in Malcolm's larder. I hope it's what you can eat."

It was, actually, very little like anything I would have ordered for myself. There was a very large pitcher of what tasted exactly like fresh-squeezed orange juice—that was the good part—but there was an equally large thermos pitcher of what I hoped would be coffee but turned out to be strong, dark tea. There was a rack of thinly sliced toast (quite suitably, Englishly, cold) and something that, Norah said regretfully, "Isn't a real kipper, but it's not bad, actually. I eat the things myself when I can't get the authentic article from Home."

It was close enough to a real kipper to fool me. I've never liked the things enough to have much practice with them. I managed to get some of it down and filled up on cold toast and orange juice, while Norah consented to accept a cup of tea, talking away as I ate.

When I dawdled over the last of the cold toast she got up, wincing a little, and courteously took a seat on the couch before lighting up another cigar. She shifted position two or three times before she found one she liked on the couch. "It's the damp," she said, trying to settle herself comfortably. "Old bones, you know."

I had already noticed that the air was distinctly soggy. They kept the humidity that way, she explained, for the convenience of some of the "natives"—"Poor Barak, for instance, he does dry out so, and some of the others rather need to stay in water all the time. And there's more oxygen in the air here, they tell me, though I've long since got so accustomed to it I don't notice things like that. You do understand what Narabedla is like? I mean physically?"

I didn't. She tried to tell me. "It looks rather like a soup tin, one might say—or a series of tins, one within the other. We're in almost the outermost shell. There are two shells that are principally for artists like ourselves, when we're not on tour, and then there are five or six others for natives. Some of them do require such special conditions, poor dears."

"Oh, yes," I said. "The poor dears. But look, that sounds more like a spaceship than a moon."

"It does, doesn't it? They say it used to be a moon, though, and then somebody, I think it was the Aiurdi, but it might've been one of the others, rebuilt it. Oh, not for us! But then they didn't need it for whatever it was meant to be in the first place, and now they let us have it. Well, part of it. But I mustn't keep on jabbering away! You're to be in Mr. Shipperton's office in half an hour, so I won't make a real visit of it this time, but I'm at Fifteen, The Crescent, and I'd be delighted to offer you dinner tonight. Perhaps a few friends might join us? There are some very nice people here—although not usually," she added, with a disdainful little smile, "on this particular street. Nolly? If you'd rather not come to dinner . . ."

I realized I'd been staring into my teacup. Norah must have thought I was trying to think of a good way out of accepting her invitation. "Oh, sorry, Norah. I was just thinking about—about . . ."

"Of course," she said with sympathy. "One is always—

what shall I say?—*pensif,* a bit, just at first. But usually one isn't brought here if there's a wife and kiddies or anything of that sort?" The tone of her voice made it a question.

"There isn't anyone like that," I said, "but I do have friends, and I'm a little worried about them." I told her about Marlene and Irene Madigan, and my worry that Henry Davidson-Jones would do something unpleasant to them if they got curious about me.

"Oh," she said, nodding, "Irene Madigan. That would be the cousin of our Tricia. She's a silly young thing, but there's no real harm in her."

It took me a moment to realize she was talking about Tricia, not Irene. "Anyway," I said, "I don't want them kidnapped too. I've got to get back before they get into trouble."

Norah puffed cigar smoke at me sympathetically. "Yes, we all feel that way at first."

I said forcefully, "I'll go right on feeling that way! These people have no right to abduct human beings, or trick them into coming here. I don't care how pleasant this place is, it's a prison, and I'm going to get out."

"Nolly, dear, it's simply not possible to get back, you see. I know it's quite a wrench at first—"

"It's a *crime.*"

She said crossly, "Well, of course it is, if one takes that point of view." She stubbed her cigar out vigorously, then smiled. "I sometimes wonder," she said, all bright-eyed and accommodating again, "if there's something in the air in this house. Malcolm Porchester used to go on saying that sort of thing, too. And he wasn't the first. Of course, Malcolm's never tried to do anything *serious* about it—what is there that one could do, really?—but he did go on endlessly on the subject. Well, Nolly," she said practically, "mustn't keep Mr. Shipperton waiting. You know the way to his office? Second left past the Execution—and don't forget dinner tonight. Sevenish, if that's convenient for you."

Norah Platt hadn't left me a whole lot of time, but there was enough for a quick shower. I took it. I needed it. I was irritated by the fact that I didn't have time to get aerobic first—I hate to bathe and *then* work up a sweat—but there wasn't anything to keep me from taking another shower later on, if I found some way to work out.

The discontented (but not deprived) Malcolm Porchester hadn't left me much of a wardrobe that fit, but there were clean socks and underwear at least, and I helped myself. He had, after all, put only his whiskey, his books, and his Fortnum and Mason packages off-limits.

All this made me, I thought without guilt, probably a little late for my next go-round with Sam Shipperton, but why should I worry about inconveniencing a kidnapper? So I didn't rush to his office. I took time to smile at a couple of passersby (who smiled back affably enough, but kept on going on their own errands), and to look around this soup-can sort of a moon I was living on.

Having been clued in, I saw that Norah Platt's description of the moon called Narabedla might well be accurate. Looking back down the ill-named "Riverside Drive" I thought I could see that the road did, in fact, seem to curve up slightly at the end. It was hard to tell, because the street dead-ended at a cluster of trees. In fact, anywhere I looked I could see no farther than a few dozen yards, never more than fifty or so, before something blocked the view. There wasn't any sun in the sky, either. There wasn't even any sky. What had looked like blue sky with fleecy clouds was actually a ceiling no more than twenty feet over my head. As soon as I studied it closely I could see that it wasn't real. I didn't study the grisly sculpture Norah Platt had called "the Execution," because I didn't like looking at it, and besides I wasn't enjoying my sightseeing. I was too busy rehearsing what I wanted to say to Shipperton.

He didn't give me a chance. "You're late," he greeted me affably, "but that's cool; Barak won't be ready for us for a little while yet. Did you ever conduct?"

He caught me off balance. "Conduct what?"

"Conduct an opera, naturally. You certainly can't sing. Sorry, but you just don't have the voice anymore. Well, maybe the natives wouldn't know that, but we have a reputation to maintain, you know. But Jonesy sent along a lot of stuff about your career when you were in opera, and Barak's taken an interest in you. That's what we have to do now, go and talk to Barak. Then if he's still interested, and if Meretekabinnda and the Mother go along, you might fit in. Somehow. Not singing, naturally. What I thought of was conducting, maybe, but there's always the chance that Binnda'll want to do that himself. That would be out then, of course, but there must be something you could do. I hear they have prompters that don't sing at all, just keep the real singers going—"

"Hold it," I said. "What are you talking about? What do you mean, prompter?"

"Isn't that what you call them? I mean some little job you could do. You must know *something* about opera."

"Shipperton," I said, nettled, "I know a lot about opera, but you're going too fast for me. Back up. Who are these people you're talking about?"

"What people?"

"Well, this mother, to start with."

"Not 'this mother,' *the* Mother. The Tlotta-Mother, to be exact. And Barak and Meretekabinnda. They're the bookers, who else? And the tour managers, and the impresarios. Even Neereeieeree—"

"Who?"

He repeated it slowly, and more distinctly. It sounded like a five-syllable whinny. "Neereeieeree. He's one of the ones you sang for. He said he might be interested in an opera company. He's Aiurdi. I don't guess you know what that means, but they've got three whole planets, not counting colonies, so there'd be a whole tour right there if Neereeieeree said yes."

That diverted me from my purpose for a moment. "He liked my voice?"

"He thought your voice sucked," Shipperton said patiently, "but you don't have to *sing,* do you? There's never been a whole human opera company here, and Binnda's been talking about wanting one for a long time. Of course, it isn't up to him, but if Barak gets behind it, and the Mother doesn't object—hell. Let's take one thing at a time. Now, don't interrupt for a while, okay? Here's what we have to do—"

"Shipperton," I said, "it's no use telling me not to interrupt, because I'm not going to do anything until I get some answers. Are you telling me that Davidson-Jones makes his money out of what, in effect, is white slavery?"

Shipperton stared at me. "Boy, you're some kind of a weirdo, aren't you? Listen, Nolly, don't even *mention* that. Most of the Fifteen Peoples would throw up at the *thought* of having sex with a human being."

"I don't mean that kind of white slavery."

"I know what you mean. Jesus, pal, get off this kick. Narabedla doesn't do anything terrible. Nobody's a slave. Oh, sure, when they sign a contract they maybe think they're going to Buenos Aires or Saudi Arabia instead of here, but they sign up to do a job. And they do it. And they get the pay. What's wrong with that? Davy can't put an ad in *Variety* to say what he's doing, you know. He's not allowed to let people on the Earth know about the other civilizations."

"What do you mean, 'allowed'?"

"I mean by the terms of his trade franchise contract. Not just the artists; there's all the commodity stuff, and that's a lot bigger. The Fifteen Peoples are real strict about that contract. They don't want people on Earth to know about them. So he has to comply with the terms of the deal, same as you artists."

"I didn't make any deal!"

"Well, if you want to be technical, no, you didn't," he conceded. "On the other hand, if you'd come along in the regular way you probably wouldn't have had any contract to sign, because they probably wouldn't have accepted you. You just aren't good enough. You're just a wimp that got in the way, understand? You're stuck here."

"That's your opinion. It isn't mine. I'm not staying here, Shipperton, and when I get back I'm going to clean this whole stinking mess out," I said grimly.

"Oh, shit," said Shipperton, shaking his head. "I was wrong. You're not just a wimp. You're a wimp that wants to be a hero."

The reflexes of my mouth started opening it to respond to that, but then my forebrain took over.

I closed my mouth again. I didn't like what he said. But I had heard things like that before. The macho things I'd spent so much time doing, the hang-gliding, the muscle-building, the jogging, the marathon runs—for that matter, the recent half-witted attempt to break in on Henry Davidson-Jones in his hotel—I was acting out some kind of Clint Eastwood make-my-day fantasy. So Marlene had told me very kindly, and others less so, and what they were saying was that I was overcompensating for my unfortunate inability to prong the pretty ladies anymore.

So I didn't answer him. I just scowled. I didn't pursue the subject, and he didn't care about the scowl.

"That's better," he said again, and his face fell. "Oh, hell," he said. "Now what?"

I said, almost apologetically, "I just can't believe all this."

My tone must have struck him as plaintive, rather than belligerent, because he asked, quite tolerantly, "What can't you believe?"

"I can't believe that all these trillions of—well, people—all these incredibly advanced alien interstellar races spend all their time watching some human being play piano."

"Oh, grow up, Nolly! Most of them never heard of us. Most of the ones that have don't care. Look. Back home you had a nice little business handling taxes, right? But how many people ever heard of you? Well, it's the same thing here, proportionately. Narabedla's just another nice little business, and the word to remember is 'little.' There are three or four other undeveloped planets, like the Earth, that provide entertainers and commodities and things; we're *tiny*."

"All right," I said unwillingly, "but why entertainers?"

"Who else would be worth bringing in?"

"I don't know. Scientists?"

"*Human* scientists? Stennis," he said sorrowfully, "you just haven't grasped the picture, have you? We don't *have* any scientists, by their standards. Maybe in another hundred years—" He closed his mouth on the end of the sentence.

I pressed. "What were you saying?"

"Just that maybe in a hundred years," he said reluctantly, "could be a thousand, maybe we'll grow up enough so we can join. Maybe not, too. They've had some bad experiences. Anyway, I don't expect to live to see it, and the way you're going you won't even come close. Now, do you want to hear what's going to happen or not? There's always the alternative of slow-down if you'd rather."

"I'll listen," I said glumly.

"Thought you would. So, first, we have to talk to Barak. Who knows? It might work out, and it'd be better for you than trying to find some other way for you to pay your way here. We already have plenty of singers."

"And an orchestra?"

"Oh, yeah," he said, grinning. "You want to know about the orchestra. I keep forgetting you're new here. Come on, we'll take a go-box to Barak's place and we'll meet the orchestra there."

* * *

It turned out that a "go-box" was one of those things that looked on the inside like a little elevator, and on the outside like a comfort station in a public park. When the door closed behind us Shipperton said, "Barak," and turned to me. "The go-boxes go anywhere on Narabedla, but you have to have authorization to go to the alien parts. You don't have it. The thing's got a record of every human voice on Narabedla, so it'll know who you are. It just won't accept an unauthorized command from you. Barak's part of Narabedla's off-limits for you, except when you're escorted. Like with me now. You follow? You get in the go-box, you say where you want to go. You can go all over the human quarters on Narabedla, nobody will bother you, but that's all. You know what Narabedla is?"

"Somebody said it was the second moon of the seventh planet of the star Aldebaran."

"Yeah, but it's been remodeled a lot. It's your home base. There's four hundred human artists, all based here—didn't Norah Platt tell you all this?"

"Some of it."

"Well, the rest you'll pick up as you go along. We're here. Don't worry if some of the natives look, uh, funny. They won't hurt you. I mean, unless you do something to them first."

I didn't get a chance to see how funny the natives looked right away, because Barak's house was only a step from the go-box entrance and we didn't run into any natives. What I did find funny was how I felt. I'd been aware that my step had been springier than usual all morning, but now it was positively buoyant. I felt as though I'd lost fifty pounds in thirty seconds. When I said something to Shipperton he said, "You have. We're four levels up. A lot less gravity here. Come on, here's the place."

Barak's house wasn't a house like any of the ones I'd seen in the human quarter. None of the structures on this level looked even a little bit normal. The thing Barak lived in was a featureless, floor-to-ceiling prism of milky green glass. You couldn't see inside it, but a section of the angle split open when Shipperton stopped in front of it and pronounced Barak's name again.

There was a sound of piano music from inside. I hesitated.

Not long; Shipperton grabbed my arm to hustle me in—just in time, because the green-glass doors clicked shut about two inches behind my feet. It was a pity that they closed so fast. They cut us off from the outside air, and, oh my God, Barak's place *stank*. Years ago I dated a woman who kept five cats and lived in a one and a half room apartment. The aroma that came from Barak's room took me right back to the last time she'd failed to change the kitty litter.

That was the first thing that threatened to turn my stomach. The second was Barak himself. Barak was the source of both the music and the smell. He sat on a plump pillow in the middle of a sort of diamond-shaped room that was surrounded on all four walls by heavy, lustrous drapes. There were pillows scattered around a glassy tile floor, and a fountain was playing. The sound of the fountain was nice, and so was the piano that tinkled behind it, but they didn't help the stink. Barak himself was about the size of a collie, if you can imagine a collie shaped more or less like a starfish. Two of his arms were picking out a tune on a piano keyboard by his pillow—the music-lover at home, whiling away the moments as he waited for his guests to arrive—and four or five of his eyes swiveled toward us as we came in. Shipperton had seriously understated the case. Barak didn't look just funny. He looked really, truly, bizarrely *weird*. "Come-in-come-in," he said, in a voice that burped out the words like a series of farts, and lifted his body off the pillow on the other four of his legs so I could get a good look at him.

I think he did that on purpose. I think Barak was vain of the way he looked.

It takes all kinds to make up a universe. Maybe if I'd been Barak, or a female of Barak's species, I would have thought him pretty handsome, too. I wasn't. I didn't. I thought he looked awful. More than anything else he resembled a six-legged starfish who had been chrome-plated. All the "arms" (or "legs"—Barak didn't seem to make any distinction) ended in little clusters of pulpy digits; those were what he had been playing the showier parts of Chopin's "Fantasie-impromptu" with. The bottom part of the body wasn't shiny; it was hairy and not at all well kept—in fact, it was where most of the smell seemed to come from. It struck me that that was the bodily part that civilized people, or even beings, generally kept covered up. Barak didn't, and it didn't seem to bother him any more than the smell did.

"Sit-down," he belched invitingly. Shipperton picked a pillow for himself and pointed one out to me. There was something familiar about the way Barak spoke, and after a moment I figured out what it was. I'd had a voice coach who'd suffered from cancer of the larynx. As long as it was just bad he still managed to croak out scales and show me intonation. Then he had the whole larynx out. When I saw him after that he'd given up coaching. He had to. He'd had to learn to talk all over again, sort of burping out words in clusters. It was not a pleasing sound.

Neither was Barak's voice when he introduced himself. "Nolly-Stennis," he coughed, "my-name-is-Barak. You-once-were . . . Barak-too. Is-that-correct?"

I started to deny it, since I didn't have any idea what he was talking about, but Shipperton hissed, "Say yes. I think he's talking about some role in an opera."

Light dawned. "Oh, the *role,*" I said, trying to remember all the parts I'd ever sung. Then it clicked. "You mean, like, I sang the role of Barak once? The servant in the Busoni *Turandot*?"

He waved a couple of arms affirmatively. "You-were-Barak-yes?"

"Ah, I see what you mean. Yes, I guess I was." I reflected for a moment; it wasn't quite true. I decided to tell the truth, if only to show this weirdo that Narabedla's information agencies didn't always get the facts straight. "I did contract to sing the role, yes. I rehearsed it, and I was all ready to perform, but then I got sick." I hesitated a moment, then decided to try a joke—not one that I really thought very funny. "After that I would have been better cast as Truffaldino."

I could see from Shipperton's scowl that I had lost him. Barak protested, "No-no-voice-is-wrong." Then the starfish thought for a moment, while the six limbs stirred restlessly, then they folded themselves into what I took to be the equivalent of a nod. Barak laughed—I think—and said, "Ha-ha-ha-ha. Now-see-your-point. Understand. Lost-your-balls."

Even a dozen years after the fact, even when it was a silver-plated starfish that put it that way, I found myself flushing. It was bad enough to have to say such things to myself. Hearing them from somebody else was really nasty. But I only said, "That's approximately what I meant."

The starfish explained it to Shipperton. "Truffaldino . . .

chief-eunuch-in-opera. Understand!" The punctuated voice sounded almost enthusiastic. "Is-good-joke-you-make. Is-good-thing-to-hear. You-understand . . . Shipperton?" He didn't wait for Shipperton to answer. He burped on, "Is-interesting . . . human-societal . . . document-opera. You-Knollwood! Wish-to-know-all . . . strange-sexual . . . questions-raised. Turandot! Her-male-parent . . . order-sex-with-stranger. She-not-want. She-rather-die. Is-possible-so?"

Shipperton gave me a warning look. "As you can see, Barak is very interested in human social customs, as well as our music."

"I can see that," I said. The look in his eye told me I should take this dumb conversation seriously, so I thought for a moment before I added carefully, "Of course, operas are not exactly realistic depictions of life, Barak. But that particular element of the plot is, yes, based on things that have sometimes happened with human beings. Both men and women sometimes have been known to commit suicide for love, either because they were forced to, ah, have sex with somebody they didn't want to, or because they couldn't do it with somebody they did want."

"Fantastic!" burped the starfish.

Shipperton nodded approval. I hesitated for a moment, then offered, "But, look, Barak. That's not really a very good opera, you know. I mean, hardly anybody does it anymore; the only *Turandot* you ever hear in the major houses is Puccini's."

"Makes-no-difference!" Barak was silent for a moment, looking thoughtfully at me—that is, that's what I thought he was doing with most of those eyes, which were as featureless as a lobster's. Then he suddenly changed the subject. "Okay-you-sing-now."

I said, "I beg your pardon?"

"You-sing-now! What-role-you-know?"

"Sing *something*," Shipperton hissed uneasily.

I hissed back, "But you said I stank."

"*Do it.*"

There was no point in getting huffy, and the surroundings weren't right for starting an argument. So I said, "Well, I suppose I could—not any of the Barak arias, I'm afraid; I don't remember them at all—"

Barak's burps began to sound irritated. "Sing-some-damn-warhorse! Know-Pagliacci-prologo?"

"Well, sure, everybody knows that. I suppose I could manage that, if I had some kind of accompaniment—"

Barak waved an arm to shut me up. Without raising his voice he belched out an order: "Purry-you-come."

The drapes against the wall rippled, and through them a sort of sweet-potato-shaped creature came rolling and skipping into the room.

Purry was, maybe, even stranger looking than Barak, though that's a close call. Purry was about the same size as Barak, and it did (or he did) have short legs along the bottom of its (or his) body. He (or it) also had perforations all over the surface of its body, each cavity equipped with a set of muscles like lips or—well, like some other kind of orifice muscles worse than lips. Although it had warm puppy eyes, they were not attached to a head of any kind that I could detect, but that didn't keep it from speaking. "Here I am, Barak," it said in beautiful, golden tones that seemed to come from the holes in its skin. "Hello, Mr. Shipperton. Hello, Mr. Stennis. I'm Purry. I'll be your orchestra. Would you like me to play something?"

"Pagliacci-prologo," Barak commanded—and instantly out of that little creature began to come a volume of sound I would not have believed possible.

An orchestra? You bet Purry was an orchestra. Not just your skimpy thirty-piece opera bunch, either, but what sounded like the Chicago Symphony or the New York Philharmonic with all the seats in the pit filled, all ready for Mahler. It began:

"Dum dee-dum, dum . . . deedle-eedle-eedle-ee . . ."

It was the opening notes of the introduction to the Pagliacci prologue, as fine as I'd ever heard it played. I could make out every instrument, all from that one ocarina-shaped body that pulsed and swelled as it puffed air through all its holes.

Thank heaven, there are several bars of the introduction before the baritone has to come in. It gave me a chance to get my wits together, if not my voice. So when my cue came I was right there. There was a bad moment when I took a deep breath for the opening and almost strangled on that Parisian-pissoir stink that had hit me when I first entered the room, but I recovered and sang out:

Si puo! Si puo.
Signori! Signore!
Scusatemi, se solo mi presento . . .

And so on right to the end of the aria. It certainly wasn't the best performance of my life. But for somebody who didn't really have much of a voice left I belted it out pretty good, even hitting real close to that hard A-flat near the end that gives everybody trouble. I almost expected applause when I finished.

I didn't get any. Barak was silent for a moment. Then he said, "Purry-go-now. Shipperton-wait-outside."

Shipperton just got up and left. The little ocarina said politely, "Thank you, Barak. So long, Mr. Stennis; see you later. You were great!"

But I knew that wasn't true, and I hadn't heard from the impresario himself. I never waited for the next morning's reviews with more impatience than I waited to hear what that shiny starfish thought of my singing.

I never did hear that. After a silent moment, his arms writhing and his eyes wandering all over the room, all he pumped out was, "I-want-to-give-you . . . fatherly-advice."

That took me aback, because for a moment there I had almost forgotten about Marlene and Irene and Narabedla and the fact that the genius I was singing for was only a stinking starfish. I had almost felt like a real singer again.

Barak brought me down. I waited for the "fatherly advice" without joy. I'd never had much satisfaction out of it from my own father, and didn't expect any from a starfish.

I was right. He flailed three or four arms in my general direction. "Knollwood-Stennis!" he blatted. "You-live-by-rules-here!"

I said, "I beg your pardon? What rules are you talking about?"

"Rules-of-behavior! You-talk-go-home . . . okay-no-crime. But-you-hurt-somebody . . . you-get-hurt-back! You-kill-you-die! Not-counting-servants-of-course. Now-you-go!"

CHAPTER
12

When I was twelve years old some foreign traveler landed at Kennedy Airport from Pakistan or Bolivia or somewhere, and changed my life. The man got as far as the Immigrations desk. Then he keeled over in a faint. He turned out to have smallpox, and the whole city panicked.

My mother was the most panicky of all. Not for herself. For me. She was not about to let these diseased foreigners kill her kid with their nasty epidemics, so she not only got me vaccinated that very day, she packed me off the next week, sore arm and all, to a place called Camp Fire Place Lodge for the rest of the summer. Remember, I was twelve. I'd never been away from home before. It was already August. I didn't know a single boy in the camp, whereas all the boys there had already had a month and a half to get to know each other. So they weren't just other kids to me. They were a single monolithic mass called The Campers, and for the first teary forty-eight hours of my stay at Camp Fire Place Lodge I saw them as only interchangeable units of Camperishness.

Narabedla was not much different.

Forget about the aliens. Of course, they were a whole separate problem, and completely indecipherable at first, but that wasn't surprising. Unfortunately it wasn't just the aliens. Even the human people all blurred into each other. I could identify a few individuals. Norah Platt was my first accompanist. Sam Shipperton was the guy who ordered me around. Malcolm Porchester was Tricia Madigan's lover, and Tricia, of course, was Tricia. These four had traits I could hold on to and recognize; but all the rest were, basically, The Narabedlans. I did run into a few of them as I moved about. A few actually spoke to me in passing; but which who looked how and had said what was beyond my powers of retention.

It stood to reason, I told myself, that all these people were still people. Individuals. Some would be as content to stay here as Sam Shipperton. Others wouldn't.

Others might even be allies, and if I were ever going to get out of here, allies were what I would need.

I would have to start making friends.

So I kept my dinner date with Norah Platt eagerly.

It was indeed a home-cooked meal (more's the pity), and she had indeed invited a few people she thought it would be helpful for me to meet. Helpful to whom, she had not said.

15, The Crescent, was one of those thatched-roof jobbers, though once you got inside it turned out to be a whole lot like the house I'd borrowed from Malcolm Porchester. It even had one of those TV-looking things. When I walked in it was filled with appetizing smells.

When I made some conventional remark of appreciation, Norah said demurely that what she was cooking was nothing special, really. As a matter of fact it wasn't. Norah's culinary tastes had been formed in the late eighteenth century, when English cuisine consisted mainly of equal parts of barely warmed-through meat and of pepper.

As to her friends, there were two of them. Both were male, and although they weren't quite as old as she was, they were still plenty old enough to suit me. The older of the two was a tiny little Italian fellow, not much bigger than Norah herself. He had been born in 1822, which made him just about the right age to have been eligible to be Norah Platt's grandson. He wasn't, though. He wasn't related at all, except that they had all been picked up in one of the early Narabedlan experiments at importing human entertainers. His name was Bartolomeo Canduccio, a tenor from the pre-Verdi age of Italian opera.

The other was, or said he was, a Shakespearean actor. He was a mere youth of a hundred and fifty or so. His name was Ephard Joyce, and he was markedly deferential to Canduccio—because the tenor was his senior, I supposed—and equally deferential to me—because he was looking for a favor, I supposed, though what favor I might do for a 150-year-old Hamlet was a mystery.

I was astonished at their ages. I asked, "How come you're all so, ah, so, well—"

"Old," Ephard Joyce supplied, beaming. "We are, aren't we? You see, they take excellent care of us here—as you will discover, once you settle in."

It hardly seemed worthwhile to say again that I didn't intend to do any settling in. Anyway, Canduccio spoke up, matching Joyce's radiant smile. "It is precisely so," he agreed. "To be sure, at first it is discomfiting here, not true? One needs a little bit of assistance. Well, Mr. Stennis, I know this, and for that reason I have had prepared for you a little— a *regalo?*"

"He's brought you a gift, Mr. Stennis," Joyce said helpfully.

"Yes, a gift." Canduccio handed me something flat and square and wrapped in red paper—I supposed the stuff was paper, though it felt more like silk.

Norah urged, "Open it, my dear boy."

So I did. It was a book. A sort of a book. It was bound in maroon sort-of-leather, with lettering stamped in sort-of-gold. The printing on the cover read:

A Guide to Narabedla
and the
Fifteen Associated Peoples

The Property of
Mr. L. Knollwood Stennis, Esq.

"Do you like it?" Canduccio asked anxiously. "I had it made up especially for you, what is called 'hard copy' from the to-talk-and-to-see machine."

"He means the skry," Joyce explained, pointing to the thing that looked like a television set. "Haven't you been told what it is for? Ah, then let me explain. You can use the machine to secure information. And dear Signore Canduccio has made some of the useful information into a little book for you, do you see? It will be very helpful to you in getting settled in."

These people were hot on getting me settled in. It was getting on my nerves. Norah had brought in a tray of crystal glasses and a decanter, and while she was handing around an extremely sweet sherry I said politely, "Thank you very much," and turned the thick, heavy pages.

It was a picture book. The pictures were in full color and, believe me, they were grotesque.

The *Guide to Narabedla and the Fifteen Associated Peoples* was a kind of atlas of weirdos. The first page I turned to showed a thing like a stretched-out gorilla, twice as tall and half as thick, with bright pink feathers instead of fur. The next was a sort of combination of polar bear and hippopotamus, that lay in shallow water with its eyes half in and half out; oh, and it had a trunk like an elephant. The third—

"Why, that's Barak!" I said, and Norah leaned over my shoulder to see.

"Well, not Barak himself," she said encouragingly, "but, yes, that's what the Ggressna look like. They're very nice, apart from the fact that they do smell a bit doggy. Mr. Canduccio's book tells you all about them, do you see?"

I did see. For every one of these Fifteen Associated Peoples there was a sort of gazetteer text. It told me that Barak's Ggressna came from a planet called Ggres, and according to the book the Ggressna were one of the senior members of the Fifteen Associated Peoples. The piece didn't say just how senior "senior" was, but when I turned a page to a race called the Mnimns (ugly little things with snaky limbs and evil-looking mouths; I thought I'd seen one of them at my audition) I saw that the Mnimns had joined up, it said, on what the human calendar would have called the 11th of June, A.D. 1327.

A.D. 1327. More than six hundred years ago.

It's funny, but with all the wonders and startlements I had been exposed to, that historical date stuck largest in my mind. Six hundred years ago—when on Earth most seagoing ships still had oars, and land transportation was basically by ox-cart—these people had been flying around between the stars.

It was not easy for me to put my mind on dinner-table conversation. I tried. Everybody would like to be a good guest, and I wanted to go through the polite motions for Norah Platt. However, I also wanted, a lot more, to curl up with that book. My wants were in conflict—not to mention the wants of the other people in the room: Canduccio clearly wanted to be thanked profusely for his thoughtful *regalo,* and then to move on casually to whatever it was he wanted from me; Joyce wanted something, but I didn't yet know what. What Norah Platt wanted seemed to be mostly to show off her crystal goblets and damask dinner napkins, in their yellowed ivory rings.

"Will you light the candles, please, Knollwood?" she asked, beaming at me. Reluctantly I put the book down and we took our places at the table.

Ephard Joyce said grace.

I appreciated that. It gave me a chance to think about what it would be like if I could escape and get back to home base on Earth, and bring that book with me, and maybe bring along a few other things like the secret of the "go-box" and whatever other information the "skry" thing might have to offer. That sounded like a really good way to spend a slow evening on Narabedla, and I hardly heard Joyce finish his fairly long invitation to God to bless our dinners until Norah repeated a question to me. "I asked if you were a church-goer, Knollwood?"

I blinked at her. "Oh, not as a regular thing, anyway," I said.

She sighed. "I do miss those nice, long Sunday services," she said, handing around the platter of roast something. "There's nothing like that here, of course. Oh, Floyd Morcher has his own kind of services, but they're, what would one say, a bit *intense*. You haven't met Floyd? You probably will; he has quite a nice tenor voice, too, though not really up to dear Bartolomeo's. Still, every opera company must have at least two tenors, don't you think?"

I sawed gamely through my very tough slice of whatever it was, beginning to relax. Of course. What dear Bartolomeo wanted from me was a chance to sing in the opera company Shipperton was organizing. "I don't suppose I have much to say about that," I said.

"Oh, but I'm sure you do, Nolly! Barak's taken an interest in you, you know. A word from you could quite make the difference."

"He didn't act as though he liked me much," I pointed out, remembering my interview with him.

"Oh, well," she said philosophically, "he's Ggressna, after all. They don't generally like us much. Human beings, I mean. Or for that matter, much of anyone; they tend to be a bit standoffish. Not at all like, for instance, the Mnimn, who are quite affectionate.''

I changed the subject. I looked across at Ephard Joyce. ''Do you sing, too?'' I asked.

''Good God, no,'' he snorted, looking as though I'd asked him if he molested small children. Then he collected himself. He really loved opera, he explained, though of course the exigencies of one's own career kept one from really *seeing* very many of them. (''We do have many tapes and films, though,'' Norah put in.) Joyce's own training had been theatrical, but, really, they all amounted to the same thing, didn't they? If you knew how to hold an audience you could do it in any medium.

To my surprise, Joyce turned out to be American, though at least a century before my time. Even more surprising, he had played Polonius to the Hamlet of John Wilkes Booth. That's right. *That* John Wilkes Booth. He spoke of the association with pride and, even a hundred years later, with glowering resentment. ''*I* didn't shoot the President,'' he grumbled. ''The way the Washington newspapers carried on you would have thought I'd assassinated Lincoln myself. Actually I rather liked the man—would have voted for him, except that voting was really such a waste of time, wasn't it? And then Wilkes did that silly thing, and, *phffft*, that was the end of my career.''

''What did you do then?'' I asked, suddenly attentive in the presence of this man who had known the man who shot Abraham Lincoln.

''Oh,'' he twinkled, ''a gentleman called on me in my lodgings. He was quite mysterious about it, but what it came to was that he proposed a tour. The financial end sounded very attractive, you know. I thought it was going to be England or perhaps even Australia, but—'' He waved humorously at the room around him.

I put down my fork. ''You mean even *then* Davidson-Jones was recruiting people for this?''

''Even before then, Nolly dear,'' said Norah. ''Though it wasn't then Henry Davidson-Jones, of course. No, it was the man before him, Mr. Carruthers. Davy wasn't promoted until—when was it, Ephard?''

''Eighteen ninety or thereabouts, I think,'' said Joyce uncertainly. Then, nodding, ''Yes, it was eighteen ninety, all right. I remember, because I'd just celebrated my quarter-century here. Quite a party we had, eh, Norah? Half the colony joined in. Of course, we were much smaller then; Davidson-Jones has certainly expanded the trade."

I looked at him, marveling. "And you've been here ever since? Don't you ever want to go back to Earth?"

"Oh, we're quite happy here," he said, sounding disgruntled. "In any case, Nolly—may I call you Nolly?—what would I do back on Earth? I'm sure everyone's forgotten me . . ."

He left the sentence hanging, hoping I would deny it, but I couldn't. Instead, I pointed out, "They'd remember you real quick if you turned up now. A man who performed with John Wilkes Booth? Man, you'd be a sensation!"

"Do you think so?" he said, flattered. "Yes, I suppose that in a sense that might be true—though, of course, the thing's impossible."

"So you see," Norah began, but never finished, because just then I knocked over my wineglass. It splintered on the floor, spilling the sticky sherry all over her carpet. Over her shoulder she called, "Kekkety folk, come!" Then she turned to me, smiling gamely. "No, no, it's quite all right," she assured me. "The servants will have it made right in no time. No, really, don't say another word about it; accidents happen. Would you care for another slice of roast?"

Actually, nobody wanted anything more to eat. We drifted over to the other side of the room for coffee while three of the silent little servants, appearing out of her kitchen as if by magic, industriously mopped up the spill and cleared away the dishes.

It struck me strange that I hadn't seen them come in the door. The reason, it turned out, was that they hadn't. "They've got their own entrances," Joyce explained to me. "So you won't often see the Kekketies on the streets, for instance. And they'll never get sick, or steal your whiskey, or ask for more wages; as you see, we've solved the servant problem here!"

I was getting tired of being told what a paradise Narabedla was. I said, "Everything considered, though, I'd rather be in Philadelphia."

It was meant as a joke—that was supposed to be what W.C. Fields had ordered engraved on his tombstone—but I shouldn't have expected these old geezers to recognize it. They not only didn't, they took it seriously. "But really, Nolly," Norah said, "can you possibly mean that you'd like to go back to the Earth? Oh, certainly, you have friends there, but you'll be making any number of new ones here. And this modern Earth frightens me!"

And Joyce said severely, "I confess that I am not well acquainted with the present Union at first hand, but we do get American newspapers here from time to time, you know. Also we have many newcomers like yourself, Knollwood. To me, the Earth seems quite frightful. Such weapons of devastation! In my time we thought Shiloh and Antietam were so awful that no one would dare wage a war again, but now you have bombs that can destroy an entire city! I shudder to think of living under such conditions. I'll wager that if Mr. Davidson-Jones should withdraw his protection it would be only a matter of weeks until Armageddon."

I put my coffee cup down—very carefully. "What are you talking about? What protection?"

"Didn't you know?" caroled Norah Platt, limping over to the sideboard to fetch a brandy bottle. "Mr. Davidson-Jones does not simply recruit artists like ourselves. He has vast interests on Earth, and not simply in America. He uses his influence to keep you ferocious Americans and those barbaric Russians—though, I must say, Dmitri Arkashvili is quite nice, isn't he?—from destroying the planet with those terrible weapons of yours."

I already had my mouth open to ask for more information about Davidson-Jones the Peacekeeper, when Norah's last remark caught me and I wanted to point out that they certainly were not *my* weapons; the delay cost me my chance. Canduccio, nose buried in his brandy glass, lifted it to say ominously, "Anyway, is *wrong*. Cannot return to the Earth never, for because if one disobeys Mr. Davidson-Jones or those who represent him is very serious. Forget not Jerry 'Arper."

"Jerry Harper was something quite different!" Joyce protested. "He wasn't simply a malcontent, he actually—"

"Oh, please!" Norah begged. "Let's not talk about poor Jerry Harper. We're all friends here. We don't have to think about troublemakers like Jerry, or that foolish young black man, or, well, actually your Malcolm Porchester."

"*Personi cattivi,*" snarled Canduccio. "*Simila di* Ugo Malatesta."

He was looking at Norah Platt when he said it, but she just pursed her lips tolerantly. Joyce replied for her. "Oh, not at all, my dear Bartolomeo," Joyce argued. "Malatesta's an odd one, no doubt about it, but he's not a *revolutionary*."

"What's wrong with Malcolm Porchester?" I asked.

Norah said unhappily. "Oh, dear. I did want this to be a pleasant dinner. Do we have to talk about unpleasant subjects? Ephard, why don't you tell Nolly about your wonderful inspiration of playing mime roles in his opera company?"

So the hook was planted, and for the next little while I had to listen to Ephard Joyce's explanation of how the alien audiences just didn't seem to want an evening of Shakespearean soliloquies or human poetry-reading anymore, and did I think I might want my opera company—*my* company!—to do, perhaps, something adventurous?

"What kind of adventurous?" I asked.

It was Canduccio who replied. "We 'ave seen many of your new works on the to-talk-and-to-see machine, eh? Is very interesting, this one *The Medium*. Is by Giancarlo Menotti, who is of course Italian."

"I had hoped," Norah sighed, "that we could give it here sometime. It has only four singing parts."

"And no chorus," Canduccio added, and Joyce explained his own thinking on the subject. It seemed to him, he said, that it might be an interesting challenge for him to play the nonsinging role of the mute boy? When I told him that neither Shipperton nor Barak had shown much interest in twentieth-century music, it was Canduccio's turn to explain modestly how his tenor was particularly appropriate for Mozart or any of the early Italians, and he certainly hoped we might work together on something like *Idomeneo*—with, of course, a real tenor, not one of those wretched castrati like his much-loathed neighbor, Ugolino Malatesta.

I can't say I paid close attention. I had managed to open my book in my lap and between encouraging smiles at whoever was speaking to go on doing so, I was sneaking glances at the bizarre nightmare figures called the "Fifteen Associated Peoples."

Norah caught me at it. To get my attention she asked, "Cigar, Nolly?" offering them around out of a tiny silver humidor. I declined; so did Canduccio, not surprisingly—tenors don't like to rasp their vocal chords any more than they have to—but Ephard Joyce lighted up along with Norah. And, as she rose to bring over a little china ashtray, Joyce watched her walk.

"My dear Norah, you're limping again," he said accusingly.

"I'm sorry. One tires in the evening. The doctors do wonderful things here, but—" She gave a pretty shrug and changed the subject. "Nolly? Did I give you enough to eat? I'm afraid it wasn't Scottish lamb—it's something local—but actually it was quite nice, didn't you think?"

"It was lovely," I said, exaggerating only slightly—it would have been good enough if only cooked a bit more. "Are you sure you're all right?"

"Oh, quite all right." Then she added, with a deprecating shrug, "Dr. Boddadukti has promised to do me again as soon as he's, ah, free." The others nodded judiciously. "He'll have me right again in no time, once I make up my mind to it. But one puts it off as long as one can, doesn't one? I mean, one never knows what they might find. Meanwhile it's simply a nuisance."

"Is for all of us a difficult time," sighed Canduccio. "This affair with the Xseni and the Mnimn, who knows when it will be settled?"

"What affair?" I asked, perking up.

Norah explained, "Oh, it's been quite a turly-burly. The Xseni and the Mnimn have a claim to some planet, which they could solve easily enough, except that the Bach'het want it. Well, one feels sympathy for the Bach'het, after all—poor things, they don't have a planet of their own anymore—but there are only about a million of them, and the Mnimn are really *terribly* overcrowded. Meretekabinnda's a Mnimn, you know—the little one who was at your audition?—and he's had to go home to do something about the negotiations. I expect he'll be back soon, but it's created quite a stir, I assure you. It's sent the Polyphase Index into a real spin."

Sam Shipperton had used that term. "I don't know what that means," I said.

"Oh, heavens, I don't think I can explain the Polyphase Index to you," she said.

"It's something like the Stock Exchange," Joyce offered.

"It's more like the budget debate in the House of Lords, I think," Norah said doubtfully. "Ask Mr. Shipperton, next time you see him. It just means that the . . . well, money—it's not really money, but it comes to the same thing—is becoming harder for Narabedla to get."

"Is business of Fifteen Peoples, in actuality," Canduccio offered with a shrug.

"Like the peacekeepers and the Andromeda thing and all that," Ephard Joyce amplified.

I put the wineglass down in order to concentrate. "Peacekeepers? You mean they've got people on Earth to keep the peace?"

"No, no, Nolly," Norah said crossly, rubbing her hip. She winced slightly as she got up to refill Canduccio's glass. "What do they care what happens on Earth? The peacekeepers are, basically, the Tlottas—the Eyes of the Mother, mostly; surely you've seen them. They're the way the Fifteen Peoples have of keeping tabs on each other so they won't have a war—a very good thing, too, believe me."

"Like on-site inspection?" I hazarded. But Norah had never heard of on-site inspection.

"You see," she said, "the Fifteen Peoples have very strict rules about what they can do. Travel between planets, for instance. They, well, they don't really trust each other all that much, do you see? Narabedla here doesn't count. It's like what your people call a free-fire zone. But no one can go onto anyone else's planet without a, well, I guess you'd call it a visa. It has to spell out exactly who they are and what they're there for. Especially us; no contract, no tour. So you'll really have to sign with Sam Shipperton before you go anywhere, you know."

I was tired of saying that the only where I wanted to go was home. "And what's the Andromeda thing you mentioned?"

But Norah didn't know much about it, except that all the Fifteen Peoples were taking a great interest in it, and that was a good thing because it took their minds off territorial disagreements.

"Is a kind of spaceship, you understand?" Canduccio offered.

"Heaven knows, they have plenty of those," said Norah. She put the decanter down and stood holding the table for a moment, as though in pain.

"My dear Norah," Ephard Joyce said in alarm, "I think you mustn't put your operation off much longer."

"You do look a little pale, dear lady," piped Canduccio.

She smiled wanly at us. "It's nothing that a good night's sleep won't cure, I'm sure."

I know an exit cue when I hear one. "That sounds like a good idea for me, too," I said firmly, getting up. "Thank you very much for the dinner, Norah. And for the book, Signore Canduccio—and for the pleasure of your company, Mr. Joyce. It's been a pleasure to meet you. No, don't bother to come with me—I can find my way home!"

"Well, if you're sure," sighed Norah; and Canduccio said, "*Buona notte*"; and Ephard Joyce, escorting me to the door, patted my shoulder and said, "And don't forget about the mime parts, old man."

CHAPTER
13

It occurred to me on the way home that I had made a mistake at Norah's house; I should have followed up on their talk about Malcolm Porchester and the other dissidents. How was I going to make allies if I didn't find out who the prospective allies might be?

You can't do everything at once, I told myself. First find out what this place is like. Then figure out how to get out of it. So when I came to the corner with the ghastly statue, I detoured to stroll along some of the other streets. There was no one in sight, though there were lights in some of the little houses.

They seemed to keep a normal, Earthly day-and-night clock on Narabedla. The bright blue sky was gone. There were still clouds overhead, but almost invisible against a

faint twilight glow. There was plenty of light to walk by.
With my belly full of Norah's medium-bad home cooking
and medium-all-right brandy, I didn't hurry.

After all, I had no one to go home to. All I had was the
little maroon book under my arm. I was looking forward to
that, but it could wait while I sorted out the sensations and
concerns whirling around in my head.

Not counting the peculiar sky, the unusual feeling of light-
ness on my feet, and the occasional peculiar passerby (twice
one of those little bedbug things scuttled past me at high
speed), I might have been strolling somewhere on Earth.
Somewhere pleasantly warm, with flowers scenting the air
and trees and shrubbery everywhere.

The place was seductive. Everybody said so.

Still, if this was Heaven, then I was Lucifer, the angel
who couldn't get along in Heaven and wanted out. I wanted
out, too, in spite of the fact that the more I saw and heard
of this moonlet called Narabedla the more heavenly features
it seemed to have.

For one, there were, as I had been told, some hundred
other human artists to share Narabedla with. Nearly all of
them were obviously well traveled, cosmopolitan, sophisticated. If it turned out that, as everyone said, there was
simply no way for me to get back to the Earth and these
people had to be my only neighbors for the rest of my life,
at least they would be more interesting than the nurses and
U.N. employees I'd shared an apartment building with in
New York. Nearly all the Narabedla artists were young and
healthy. Or, anyway, like my recent dinner companions, so
remarkably well preserved that their calendar ages didn't
matter. Nobody on Narabedla coughed. Nobody had disfig-
uring facial scars or missing limbs. Nobody puffed and
wheezed and ran out of breath when he walked a few steps,
or had to pull a little oxygen tank along behind him to keep
his lungs going. And nobody looked any older than Norah
Platt, which is to say not much older than any normal Earth-
bound woman wondering whether or not she wanted to give
birth to one more child before menopause stopped her clock.

Of course, I wasn't an artist anymore. Shipperton had
made that clear.

Still, there were plenty of nonsinging jobs around an opera
company. I could direct. I could mime, if there were any
mime parts (and the hell with Ephard Joyce). I could con-

duct, if what's-his-face Meretekabinnda or some other creepy didn't rank me out of it. Worst come to worst, sure, I could sit in the box at the front of the stage and prompt.

Conscientiously trying to give Narabedla a fair shake, I tried to remember when I had ever in my life been in a nicer place than this one.

There had been one or two memorable ones. The Negresco, for one. Then, when I was an opera singer I stayed once in a hotel in California that didn't have rooms. It had bungalows. Each one had bedroom, sitting room, kitchen, and bath; there was a Jacuzzi for every bungalow and a swimming pool in every cluster. There was also maid service and twenty-four-hour room service; there were television, radio, and tapes; and, if you asked the bellboy in a way that didn't make him suspect you were the Man, there was your choice at any hour of any of the prettiest whores in Beverly Hills.

Even when I was a budding opera star that hotel was too rich for my blood. I kept the bungalow just one night—long enough to receive and suitably impress two newspaper interviewers. Then I retreated to the Quality Inn at the airport for the rest of my stay.

I had to admit that Narabedla was even better. And it didn't cost three hundred dollars a night, either.

Studied critically, there were flaws to be found in this Paradise. That imitation "sky" was not very convincing when you took a careful look. The ground I walked on did curve slightly—having been made aware of it, I could see the gentle slope upward that disappeared where trees and shrubs met roof. And yet those plants were pretty nice in themselves. For trees there were orange, apple, plum, fig, weeping willow, birch, and a dozen others, half of them in flower, half of the rest bearing fruit. For bushes and vines there were grape, blackberry, forsythia, lilac, boxwood, hibiscus—I didn't know the names of most of them. There were cleared spaces between buildings here and there, and some of them had fountains and rippling brooks, with little farm-garden plots where good things grew: tomatoes and pineapples and sweet onions you could pull out of the ground, rinse off, and nibble with pleasure. The air was a balmy seventy-eight degrees, even at "night," and there were occasional gentle breezes.

It was really a remarkably nice place to be.

I would have to be crazy to want to get out of it. But I did want that, all the same.

When I got to my house—or, more accurately, Malcolm Porchester's house—the TV-looking thing they called a "skry" was flashing.

It had a screen like a television set, all right. It was that screen that was blinking on and off, with a gentle lavender radiance.

Since Ephard Joyce had told me it was not only something to do with data bases but also something to do with communications, I could easily surmise that the flashing was some sort of attention signal. What I was supposed to do about it I had no idea. There was no dial with channel numbers, no on/off switch, nothing that looked at all helpful.

On the other hand, I didn't really care. If someone were trying to call me it could, I thought, only be Sam Shipperton. One of these days I would no doubt have to learn the thing, but not now. Whoever wanted me could damn well wait. It was what I wanted that was important, and what I wanted right now was—

Well, that got a little complicated. I wanted a lot of different things. I wanted to go home. I wanted to be in my own apartment, so I could duck across the street to the health club and get aerobic, and then swim fifty laps in the little pool. I wanted to talk to Irene Madigan and find out what had happened to her. I wanted to talk to Marlene and reassure her. I wanted—well, I wanted some things very badly, including the things the mumps had taken away from me a dozen years before; but as none of those wants were in my power to satisfy just now, what I *proposed* to do was settle down with a good book.

Namely the book Bartolomeo Canduccio had given me. So I checked Porchester's fridge. Yes, there was a six-pack of ale in it, and he'd only warned me off his liquor, not his brew. The ale was a Brit brand I didn't recognize, but when I popped the tab it tasted just fine.

I settled down with *A Guide to Narabedla and the Fifteen Associated Peoples* for a nice, late-night read. It was an attractive book. Although the texture of the pages was odd, the color printing was magnificent. (And Canduccio had said he'd taken it off the thing called a "skry." So it was a kind of duplicator, too. I wondered if Henry Davidson-Jones had had anything to do with the new full-color copiers Marlene had been after me to get for the office.)

A can and a half later I had discovered that the "Fifteen Associated Peoples" were all exceedingly nonhuman, not to say often disgusting-looking. There were really more than fifteen of them—there was an appendix for non-"Associated" races—but it was the big Fifteen who mattered. They were the major powers, each of them an alien race that had agreed to enter some sort of joint compact.

The only thing that I could see that they had in common was that they were all extraordinarily homely. There were the Ggressna, like Barak, whom I'd already met; there were the Mnimn, with three-cornered mouths, no noses, and rubbery limbs. There were creatures that looked like shrimps (only with transparent shells, so the innards showed through) and creatures that looked like pterodactyls. According to the specifications in the text, most of them were more or less human-size—well, within a couple of feet, anyway—but the only ones that looked anything like people were the ones called the J'zeeli. What they looked like were baboons with scales like pine needles instead of fur. They averaged about fourteen feet tall, with compound eyes and a sort of Mohawk of those needly scales across the top of their heads, and generally weighed (the text said) the equivalent of sixty Earthly pounds.

The text about the J'zeeli said they were originally from the planet of J'zeel (small hot planet around a small orange-colored star); there were 1,800,000,000 of them on J'zeel itself and another few billion on other planets they had colonized. (It didn't say what I found out later—that they smelled like a mixture of cinnamon and cat box, and the only Earthly entertainment they cared much about was hymns, marching songs, and musical-comedy numbers.)

According to the "Brief History of the Fifteen Associated Peoples" in the book, the whole shebang had got started something over 3,200 years ago, when a race called the Bach'het and a race called the Duntidons had been fighting a sort of slow, long-range war with conventional spaceships over interstellar distances. (Their two stars were only about a light-year apart, but they must have been really mad at each other to go to that trouble.) Then they were visited by the Ggressna, who had a sort of interstellar go-box that made things go a lot faster—well, the history ran twenty pages. I put it aside for later.

Besides the Fifteen there were a dozen or more other non-human beasties who were less important. (It didn't say why.) Some of them, like the Kekkety folk, weren't important at all; they were just around for the convenience of the others.

One of the unimportant species described was the human race.

When I came to that part I set the book down and worked on the ale for a while. I was *offended*. I mean, the human race had a lot of faults, sure, but it had done some pretty terrific things—skyscrapers, jet planes, atomic power plants, heart transplants—yes, and books and plays and the *Mona Lisa* and Beethoven's Ninth, for that matter. I didn't like seeing it brushed off by a bunch of things that looked like they'd come from the bottoms of cereal boxes. "Screw you and all your tentacles, wings, and creepy legs," I said out loud.

Which had an unexpected effect.

The skry thing stopped flashing. The screen lighted with a steady, gentle lavender, and a sweet, sexless voice said, "Welcome home, Mr. Stennis. Tricia Madigan called. She would like you to call her back."

It seemed my voice had turned the damn thing on. "Tricia Madigan?" I said out loud, and that did it, too.

"One moment," said the genderless voice. The screen paled. A moment later I heard Tricia's voice say "What is it?" and at the same time an image took form on the screen.

I was looking at Tricia Madigan again. She wasn't quite naked this time; she had a towel around her body and another around her hair, and she looked as though she'd been doing her nails.

"Oh, sorry," I said.

She grinned at me, unsurprised. "I didn't think you'd call back," she said. "Well, anyway. I thought after those old farts bored you to death you might like to have me give you the quick two-dollar tour of Narabedla?"

"Tour?" I said.

"Right," she said, nodding. "Just give me a minute to dry my hair and throw something on. Meet you at the square by the Execution in ten minutes, 'kay? See you there." And the screen went to no color at all.

*   *   *

She had said ten minutes, but actually I was there in five. Of course, Tricia Madigan wasn't.

I told myself that it was silly for me to leave my nice (borrowed) house in the middle of the night to meet this rather uninhibited woman, everything considered (and I mean everything). On the other hand, I told myself, it wasn't really all that late. And I did want to talk to her about her cousin. And it couldn't hurt to get a tour. And she really was a great-looking lady, with silvery-blond hair (well, it was, I was sure, whatever color Tricia Madigan wanted it to be) and the kind of body you'd expect on a Texas baton-twirler . . . and what was wrong with looking, even if I couldn't usefully touch?

So I strolled around the square, taking the environment in. A youngish couple passed, arm in arm, arguing with each other earnestly in low voices, barely responding to my nod as they went by. I looked around the square—not at the repellent monster-murdering-man centerpiece of it—just trying to make sense of what I saw. Each of the streets that radiated from the square was a different style and period of architecture. There were thatched-roof cottages, like Norah Platt's. There were high-rent-district ranch houses, like the one I had borrowed from Malcolm Porchester. There were townhouse condo rows, streets of brownstone fronts, white frame houses with the kind of porches you see in old Andy Hardy movies.

Somebody had put a lot of effort, not to mention money, into creating these residential streets on a moon of a planet many light-years from Earth. Just for the sake of having some entertainment? I could hardly believe it. What sort of wealth and power did these weird-looking aliens have, that they could squander it like that?

I looked up at the "sky" for help, but there was no help there. It was, I realized, a lot like the "sky" I'd seen in Henry Davidson-Jones's office in the World Trade Center—for the very good reason, no doubt, that it was designed by the same bizarre kind of people. It was almost comforting when, reluctantly, I turned at last to look at the agonized face of the man being crushed by the monster in the statue. At least the man was human. The monster definitely wasn't. Wasn't even a snake. As I looked closer I saw that it was more like a kind of wingless dragon; it had short, stubby limbs with claws like Velcro that gripped the hapless human figure, and fangs an inch long, poised only inches from the man's throat.

It suddenly looked almost familiar.

It took me a minute to remember where I'd seen it before: In the little maroon book Canduccio had given me. This murderous thing was, I was nearly sure, one of the Fifteen Associated Peoples.

I didn't like the implications of that. What was the statue meant to show? That we little Earth people were at the mercy of the weirdies? And if so, did they have to show it so graphically? The statue was a work of art. I did not think I had ever seen human despair, horror, and fear better portrayed in any piece of sculpture. Considered as a work of art, once I had psyched myself into doing that, it was breathtaking.

It was also scary, and I was not sorry when I heard the light tap of Tricia's footsteps.

She was wearing high-heeled shoes that made her just my height. She was also wearing very short pink shorts and a very tight pink top, and she looked just as good with her clothes on as off. She said, "Having fun? Come on, I want to show you something. If we go now we'll get there while we're darkside, so you can take a look before the sun gets around." She did not wait to see if I understood her. That was well enough, since I didn't. She just took my arm cozily into hers and led me toward that little go-box structure that looked like a comfort station.

As we were entering, she looked back at the statue and said, "Poor Jerry."

I stumbled. It wasn't that I tripped going into the cab; I stumbled over my own feet. I lurched against Tricia as she was starting to speak to the go-box control; she felt nice and warm, and she smelled even better, and she didn't pull away. But my mind was on something else. "Wait a minute," I said, making a connection. "Jerry? Is that, uh, that thing back there—is that Jerry Harper?"

She nodded sympathetically. To the cab she said politely, "Take us to the Lookout, please."

I swallowed. No wonder they called it Execution Square! And what kind of a place was I in, if they executed people by letting them get eaten by monsters, and then put up statues to commemorate it? "What—what did he do to deserve that?"

"Oh," said Tricia, thinking it over and biting her lip to

help the process along, "I guess you could say he really did deserve it. I mean, he killed four people."

"Killed! Four!"

She nodded sadly. "He went kind of crazy, you know? In a way, the whole thing was Jonesy's fault. He should've checked Jerry out a little more carefully. He wasn't married, all right, but, hey, what he didn't tell Jonesy was that he was having the heck of a hot secret affair with his ex-music teacher's wife, you know what I'm saying? And after he got out of slow time—"

"He was in slow time?"

"Well, but when he wound up here on Narabedla he wanted to get back to her. Blew his stack when he found out he couldn't. He wrecked a whole theater on Neereeie-eree's planet. Then they put him in slow time, I guess—I mean, all this was long before my time. So when he got out he found out ten years had passed, and she probably didn't even remember his name anymore, you know? So he started acting up again. Some of the guys tried to reason with him—well, they didn't just reason with him; one of them beat the hell out of poor Jerry because, hey, he made real trouble for the rest of us, you know? So Jerry just waited for his chance and set fire to their house while they were asleep. Really stank the place up for a week," she said fastidiously, "all that burned meat, until the air changers got it cleared up. It's okay now, though. Since then they've done something that fireproofed all the houses; and here we are on the Lookout. Watch your step getting out!"

And the door opened, and Tricia, smiling back at me, stepped out—

"Jesus Christ!" I yelled. "Watch it!" Because what she was stepping out onto was nothing.

I mean, *nothing*. Nothing at all. Under her feet I could see empty space. A sprinkling of stars and a few brighter things that might have been moons—and *nothing*. She looked exactly as though she had walked off the side of a space satellite and was getting ready to fall into infinite blackness.

Tricia turned. In the light from the go-box door I could see she was laughing at me. "Scary, huh? Come on"—stamping her foot—"there's a floor here, all right. Glass or something, I guess, but you won't fall through."

When I managed to force myself to follow her, one ten-

tative step with most of my weight still on the foot that was
in the go-box, then another . . . why, indeed she was right.
There was a floor. A *kind* of a floor. I couldn't see it. It
wasn't just glass; it was something reflectionless, a lot more
transparent than any glass. But it was hard and firm
underfoot.

When I looked down, it was like peering over the edge of
a diving platform poised over infinity, except that you
couldn't even see the diving platform. Behind us the go-box
door sighed closed, shutting off the interior light. The only
illumination left was starlight. A *lot* of starlight—I could
make out Tricia's features in it—because there were, I would
guess, about a million stars down there, ranging from next
to invisible to brighter than anything I had ever seen before.

"Let's see," said Tricia, glancing around with professional appraisal. "You know anything about astronomy?
Neither do I, but I've had this explained to me about a jillion
times. Those bright ones over there, they're called the
Hyades. You can see them from the Earth, they tell me.
Can't say I ever did, but then . . . Then there's that sick-
looking little red one up there, see where I'm pointing?
That's the companion star. Did you know Aldebaran was a
double? That makes two of us, but there it is. You can't see
that one from the Earth. It's too faint. Then we've got—
let's see . . . one, two—yeah, we've got three planets showing right now. Can't see our own planet itself; it must be
toward the star. I'm no expert on the planets, but that big
one is Elizabeth, I'm pretty sure, and the one next to it ought
to be Anne. The other one might be Maude. Or maybe Car-
oline. You know who named them? Norah Platt. She
couldn't pronounce the names the locals gave them, so she
named them after some of the queens of England. Wouldn't
you know? How do you like it?"

I just said, "Jesus."

I couldn't honestly say I "liked" it. It was too huge and
too awe-inspiring to "like." But it certainly reached right
down into the place where I kept my little soul and opened
it up to the drafty winds of the universe.

There were some cobwebby things that glinted starlight
now and then. "What are those?" I asked.

"They're solar-power collectors," she explained. "How
do they work? Aw, hey, Nolly, how would I know that?
They get like sunlight—only I guess you'd call it starlight;

it comes from Aldebaran—and they turn it into electricity, and that's what they run Narabedla on."

I squinted past them at something else that glinted, tiny and far away. "And that thing?"

"That's some other thing they've got. This place used to be for space probes, you know? I mean, this was where the people lived; that other thing is, like, another moon. It's where the probes launched from. That's what Conjur says, anyway."

I gazed around. "Which of the Fifteen Peoples comes from Aldebaran?"

"Oh, none of them. This was just a kind of neutral territory they used." She paused, looking me over appraisingly in the starlight. "Nolly? You know, you've got pretty good pecs for a singer."

"I'm really an accountant."

"Whatever. You know what? I guess I kind of like you."

I noticed that my hand was holding hers.

There are a lot worse things in this world (or whatever other world you may happen to find yourself on) than being told by a pretty girl in the starlight that she likes you. It brightens the air, it makes the senses tingle, it causes you to feel warm all over . . .

Unless.

Unless you've got your mind full of a million other things, including the particularly savage murder of a fellow human being (even if he was a killer himself) by a particularly gruesome monster, which event some bizarre creatures from another planet have erected a statue to commemorate.

And unless you're filled with anger and confusion over your recent kidnapping to a place that, a week earlier, you wouldn't have believed could possibly exist.

And unless you happened to have had, at the age of twenty-five, a particularly savage case of the mumps.

I let go of Tricia Madigan's hand.

I didn't really want to, because it felt good. It also felt strange, because I had got out of the habit of holding women's hands, or women's anythings. It even felt worrisome, in that sadly familiar way that any kind of normal man-woman come-on felt worrisome to me; the come-on was nice, but there wasn't any follow-up to come after the come-on. I changed the subject. I said, "Tricia, you know your cousin Irene's been going crazy, worrying about you."

There was a pause, then she looked at me. "Oh," she said. "I didn't know you knew Irene."

I said bitterly, "Do I ever know Irene." I told Tricia about Irene and her crusade, and about chasing all over Monte Carlo and Nice with her, and about Marlene, and about my attempts to beard Henry Davidson-Jones in his lairs at the World Trade Center and the Negresco.

She listened, watching my face carefully in the dim light. All she said was, "Gee, Nolly."

"Yeah. Gee. I'm afraid that she isn't going to quit looking for you. I'm afraid she's going to wind up here herself."

Tricia thought for a moment. "I hope not. I mean, for her sake. I just love Irene, I really do, Nolly, but I don't know if she could make the adjustment here. She's a real tight-ass about some things."

"About things like Henry Davidson-Jones's practices of kidnapping and murder, you mean?"

"Like murder? Oh, no, Nolly." The look she was giving me now was a lot like the look you give a little kid who refuses to go to sleep because he thinks there's a bear under his bed. "He never did murder, honest. Jonesy's not such a bad guy. If you mean Jerry Harper, hey, it wasn't Jonesy that sentenced him, you know. We did it ourselves, all legal and proper. Why, we had a real trial, with a jury and everything, because it was really bad of him to set fire to those poor guys. Ask your pal Ephard Joyce. Ephard was on the jury himself. Now . . . hold on," she commanded, looking down. "Here's what I wanted you to see. Look!"

I found myself squinting into a sudden bright orangey light that grew behind her. It was like morning sun streaming through a window, only about a hundred times brighter. I turned and, down below, past Tricia's pretty feet, there was a sudden corner of light that rolled into view and widened and became a sun, too bright to look at.

"That's it," Tricia crowed, shielding her eyes with her hand. "That's Aldebaran." And, "Darker, damn it!" she called, and the transparency under our feet obligingly grayed itself like photosensitive sunglass lenses, so I could look right at the thing. I could feel the warmth of it on my face.

Tricia grinned at me, pleased. "That's it," she said. "That's the whole show. Too bad we didn't get a chance to see the planet itself, but it must be coming up after the star now—and anyway," she added, prettily smothering a tiny yawn, "I'm not going to keep my little old head off the little old pillow forever, so do you want to go ahead with the rest of the tour or not?"

I looked down at the dimmed-out stellar disk below me. That thing is really the star Aldebaran, Nolly, I told myself. You're really here.

And then I said to myself, Go ahead, Nolly. Make the adjustment. And out loud I said, "Lead on, Tricia. Let's see it all."

In the little go-box, Tricia explained the transportation system to me. "There are lots of these things," she said, "and they go all over. Some of the places you can't go to, though. They'll take you anyplace in our sector, or where the foreign human artists live, like the Italians, the Russians, Chinatown, all that. I don't go there much, but there's nothing to stop you. And you can go to the shell, where we just were, so you can look at the stars whenever you like. Just say 'Lookout.' If you want to go to any of the funny-people levels—I mean, you know, the creepy-crawlies and all—you have to go with somebody who's authorized, like Sam Shipperton. And there's places you can't go at all, like the jump station, naturally. What's that? Oh, that's what you came here on, Nolly. It's what they call a matter transmitter, okay? But you can come here to this place anytime," she finished as the door opened. "I come here a lot. I usually take my showers here. You'll see. It's neat."

She was wrong about that.

It was not a bit neat. It was the opposite of neat. It was a green and jumbled jungle of vegetation of all kinds. It was illuminated with pinkish light from the ceiling panels; the light cast no shadows, but it was enormously flattering to Tricia.

Who certainly didn't need any flattery anyway. Who was looking all pink and pleased as she watched me staring around, half laughing as she saw my jaw drop. There was plenty to stare at. Stubby trees whose crowns spread against the roof panels, vines that swung from the trees, bushes, flowers, purple moss that had little scarlet blossoms in it, hedgelike shrubs that were full of pretty white and yellow berries. The place smelled jungly. It sounded that way, too. There were chirpings and whickerings and soft, sobby moans, and distant yowls that made me glad they were distant. "There's nothing here that can hurt us, Nolly," Tricia smiled. "Come along, I'll show you where I shower when I get tired of the one at home."

It wasn't really untamed jungle after all. There were paths in it. I followed Tricia's prettily waving hips down one of them, while she chattered over her shoulder. She named a dozen kinds of edible fruits and berries—half of them I'd never heard of, which was reasonable enough because the things with those names didn't grow on Earth. I didn't retain them, anyway. I was listening to a sound—a watery sound, like a forest creek running fast over rocks—that I hadn't heard at first because my attention was all on pretty Tricia. The sound got louder.

The path opened up into a glade. A few yards in front of us was a pond. At the far end of the pond, seeming to come out of the ceiling itself, was a waterfall.

That was the sound I heard, but it didn't sound exactly like any waterfall I'd ever encountered before. It sounded somehow gentler and slower, and the reason for that was that it *was* gentler and slower.

I understood that. Even at this level, I felt a little lighter than I'd been accustomed to back home on Earth, and so did the water. It fell in a leisurely, comfortable way, and splashed only gently when it hit the surface of the pond.

"Pretty?" Tricia asked, smilingly sure of the answer.

I obliged her. "It's *very* pretty. I have to admit that Narabedla's about the prettiest and nicest place I've ever been—anyway, in terms of amenities. I mean, there was this hotel in Beverly Hills . . ." And I told her about what had been my previous high-water mark for luxury, and added, "The only thing we don't seem to have here is the whores."

Tricia said demurely, "On the other hand, why would you need them?"

I found that we were holding hands again. I didn't remember how that had happened. More than that, she'd loosened a button or two in her blouse, and very visible was much of Tricia.

I backpedaled. Fast. I said, "I was just joking, Tricia." She listened attentively, absently stroking my arm. "I mean," I explained, "really, there's a *lot* missing here. Freedom, for instance."

She squeezed my elbow in affectionate disagreement. "Oh, no, Nolly, you're wrong about that. Believe me. You've never been so free. You can do anything you like here—well, hey, not *hurt* anybody—you wouldn't want to be like Jerry Harper, would you? You can't kill anybody, or rape anybody; you could get in a fight, maybe, if both you and the other guy wanted it, because that happens, you know? But not anything like *deliberate,* or *mean.* I mean, what would be the point? Whatever consenting adults, you know, want to do—"

"I'm talking about being *free.* Free to go home, damn it!"

She shook her head regretfully. "Aw, shit, Nolly," she sighed.

I started to amplify, but she got in ahead of me. "Forget about going home, Nolly," she advised. "Look on the bright side, for heaven's sake. What'd you have back home? Did you have anything half as good as you've got here? You're never going to get real sick, you know. You're going to live a heck of a long time—look at people like Ephard Joyce and that witch, Norah Platt. Course," she went on reasonably, "it isn't all free, exactly. You have to earn it. You have to do your thing for the cash customers if you want any special privileges or charge cards or anything, but, what the hey, that's what artists like to do anyway. Isn't that true? They like to perform. Why else would anybody be a performer? And you've got real good friends here, or anyway you will have as soon as you get over this tight-ass stuff." She gazed at me for a moment. "Tell you what," she said. "You ought to put all this stuff on hold till you can talk to Jonesy himself, next time he's here, just sit down with him and—"

"He comes *here*?"

"Well, of course he comes here, for gosh sake. What did you think? Every couple months, anyway. So now lighten up, will you?"

"But—"

"Butting's for bulls," she said kindly, opening the rest of the buttons on her blouse. "Come on. Let's have fun. I'm going to get under the shower."

So she did.

She threw the blouse in one direction and the skimpy shorts in another. I hadn't thought there would be anything under them but Tricia herself, and there wasn't. She dived into the pool, swam a dozen strokes, and came up under the waterfall.

"Come on, kidlet," she gasped, mouth full of water. "It's nice and warm, just what you need to chase the collywobbles away."

It would have taken a real trained-from-childhood eunuch, not a well-remembering one like me, to say no to Tricia Madigan. I took off my clothes—my own tired ones and the ones I'd borrowed from Malcolm Porchester's wardrobe—and I dived in after her. I was dimly aware that I was laying up a larger store of humiliation and regret for later, but I firmly turned off the voice inside my head that was trying to tell me so.

The pool and the waterfall were everything she'd promised.

The splash of water on my head was not only gentle, it was tepidly warm. It didn't beat down on me. It caressed me. Tricia was laughing as she splashed perfectly superfluous handfuls of water at me, and in a minute I was laughing, too . . . up to when we began touching each other. She took hold of me, smiling sweetly. Then she looked up into my eyes in surprise and uncertainty.

"My goodness, Nolly," she said, "you're not a priest or anything, are you?"

Unhappily, I said, "No, no, nothing like that."

"Or maybe you've got a secret pash back home that you're carrying a torch for, like Jerry Harper?"

I shook my head. Then I backed away a little, wiped the water out of my eyes, and said, "There's something I ought to tell you about. Do you know anything about the kinds of things that happen if you catch mumps when you're a grown-up man?"

And, oh, well, that was about the end of that.

Tricia was perfectly cheerful and friendly as we went back to our own level. But she went to her house and I went to mine, and it was a while before I saw Tricia Madigan again.

CHAPTER

14

I didn't have Tricia's company, but I wasn't without feminine companionship. I had Norah Platt. Right after breakfast the next morning she was waiting decorously behind the closed door of my bedroom while I, stripped naked, was exercising—sitting, standing, doing sit-ups and jump-ups, jogging in place, turning, bending—in front of my skry. From tiny projectors over the screen rays of bright blue light stretched out to fasten on shoulders, neck, knees, wrists, ankles, and elbows, marking the positions of all my joints and extremities as I moved. I wasn't doing it just for the exercise. I was being fitted for a new wardrobe; and when the machine politely thanked me and turned its lasers off and I was dressed again, Norah came out to help me pick out the kind of clothes I wanted.

The process left me with some doubts. "You sure this stuff is going to fit? When I go to a store they measure me instead of just taking my picture."

"My dear boy! The skry *has* measured you. And there aren't any stores. You do that sort of thing right here." She commanded the screen to display an assortment of slacks, shirts, underwear, shoes, socks—everything the well-dressed man-about-Narabedla might need. It didn't take me long to make my selections, mostly because I wasn't planning to stay long enough to wear them all.

But what I told Norah was that I didn't want to impose too much on her generosity. She seemed to appreciate that. "Of course, dear boy," she said, half apologetically. "The clothes do cost money, and you don't actually have any, do you? You really should work those details out with Sam—but for now, anyway, I'm glad to let you charge some things to my account. Heavens! I can't spend all I earn anyway, can I? And when you're singing lead roles . . ."

I stopped in the middle of pouring myself a cup of coffee. "But I won't be singing at all, Norah."

She looked startled. "I beg your pardon?"

"I thought you knew. I failed the audition. My voice is gone."

"Well," she said, biting her lip, "true, you weren't up to your best the other night, were you? But still—"

"Norah," I said, "that *was* my best. Shipperton says I can't sing. He says maybe they'll find something else for me to do, but singing, no."

"Oh," she said. "I see." I waited, while she thought for a moment. I couldn't tell what she was thinking about— maybe that I wasn't such a good credit risk, after all, and it might be a good idea to cancel the orders for some of the clothes. But after a minute she sighed and said, "Well, that's going to be a bit too bad for Ephard, I suppose. He was really hoping that you'd be able to fit him in somewhere in the troupe, but if there isn't going to be a troupe, or if you're only going to be . . ."

She trailed off there. I filled in for her. "Shipperton said maybe I could be a prompter."

"Oh, my," she said, shaking her head. "That sounds grim, doesn't it? You see, Nolly," she explained, "most of us are *artists*. There isn't really much for anybody who isn't, well, talented, to *do*."

"Not even sweeping the streets?"

"Of course not, Nolly! The Kekketies do that sort of thing, don't they? Of course, now and then one of the artists just doesn't seem to draw the audiences anymore, like poor Ephard, or he gets a bit too old—the dancers, for instance— but that doesn't happen very often, of course."

"Then what do they do?"

"Oh," she said vaguely, "different things."

"Like slow time?"

She jumped. "Oh, I *hope* not! No, there might be some sort of work . . ." She paused, lost in thought. Then she glanced at her watch, and stood up.

"But I can't think what," she said as she left.

I moved out of the way of the two silent little copper-skinned Kekkety creatures cleaning up the remains of the breakfast I had shared with Norah, trying to think what my next move should be.

What do you do when you're left to your own devices, in a house on the moon of a planet you never heard of before?

Sure, the most important thing is obvious. You try to figure out how to get home.

But how do you do that? I opened the front door of 14 Riverside Drive and gazed out. The street was empty, as usual. There was nothing to stop me from going out and reconnoitering the area; but what would I be looking for?

What I needed to begin with was information. *Know your enemy*. That was the right prescription for the situation, and there was no better place to acquire that knowledge than in the book Bartolomeo Canduccio had given me.

I went back to where I had been when Tricia Madigan interrupted my studies.

It was hard work. There was an awful lot to learn about our genial hosts of the Fifteen Peoples, the aliens for whose pleasure we were there in the first place. Canduccio's book was helpful only up to a point. It let me know that although there were fifteen fully participating species, only eight or nine of them had any interest at all in watching any human beings perform anything. I learned the names of a few more of them. (I don't say I learned to *pronounce* the names right away.) I learned that the creature named Neereeieeree (I had trouble remembering the name, but not the appearance), who had been one of my first auditors, was an Aiurdi, which is to say a creature like a round, radially symmetrical beetle, with spikes sticking up from its back, covered with a mosaic of scales that change color depending on its mood. I learned that the Quihigs were the Pekingese-sized ones that had heads like a hammerhead shark, hopped on two hind legs like a kangaroo, and had a long, forked tail that (the book told me) they swatted enemies with when provoked. I reminded myself to make it a point not to provoke any.

I say that I learned all that, but actually most of it just flushed through my mind and out of it again. Not much was retained. Anyway, in the back of the book there was a section about Narabedla itself, and that was more immediately useful.

I don't mean "useful" in that it gave me any practical ideas on what to do, only that it helped fill some of the gaping voids in my knowledge of what the hell was going on. For

instance, I learned that Narabedla's gravity was actually cen-
trifugal force derived from the fact that the whole *megilleh*
was spinning, but you couldn't tell the difference except
sometimes in the inner ear. It was only about 70-odd percent
of Earth normal, even down at the Lookout level. That was
so that the aliens who might want to visit Narabedla (as any
number of them apparently did, for reasons not necessarily
connected with the Earth import-and-export business) would
be able to get around; some of them weren't used to much
physical weight. In the upper levels, where most of the non-
humans stayed when visiting Narabedla, the apparent gravity ranged down almost to zero. The air pressure (I learned)
was about equal to, say, Mexico City's, the equivalent of
being a mile and a half up. The reason my lungs hardly knew
the difference was that the partial pressure of oxygen and
carbon dioxide had been increased. It was soggy, though. I
had noticed that the air was pretty damp, and that was because the water-vapor content was at least twice what I was
used to.

I closed the book and sat back, thinking. Or trying to.

I noticed that the house was very still. I got up and peered
into the bedroom—no one there; into the bath and kitchen—
and no one was in either of those. The Kekketies were gone.

It occurred to me that it was funny that I hadn't seen them
leave. The kitchen was neatly scrubbed and everything put
away. Did they have a back way out?

That didn't seem likely. There was, it was true, a narrow
door next to the refrigerator, but it looked more like a broom
closet than an exit to the outside world. I couldn't open it.
I supposed it might be where Malcolm Porchester kept his
really choice liquor.

"Funny," I said out loud.

And from the front door a sweetly musical voice replied,
"Mr. Stennis? I hope I'm not disturbing you. What's
funny?"

And when I turned and looked, there in the doorway was
something quite funny indeed; it was my ocarina-shaped
"orchestra" from the day before, the thing Barak had called
Purry.

Although Purry had opened the door, it—I'd better start
calling him "he"—*he* had been too polite to come right in.

I hesitated, too. It wasn't politeness. I just didn't know how you addressed a creature with no visible face, that stood knee-high on jointed legs that stuck out like a Dr. Seuss drawing of a caterpillar. "Well," I said at last. "Hello."

"Thank you," said the creature, taking it as an invitation. It slipped inside and shut the door behind it with one of the legs. "I guess you're wondering why I'm here," it said. I mean, *he* said. "Barak sent me. He thought you might want a little help settling in."

Settling in *again*! I temporized. "Well, Norah Platt's been very good about it," I said. "She's the one who—"

"Oh, I know Norah Platt," Purry informed me. "She has her own work, though, and I'm—well, I'm at your service. Plus it's really a privilege for me to spend time with you, Mr. Stennis. I've admired Earth music ever since I was first assigned to it."

"Thank you," I told the ocarina.

"So would you like me to show you around? Do you have any questions you'd like to ask? Can I help in any way?"

"If you're sure it's not too much trouble . . ."

"No trouble at all! Barak has instructed me to serve you."

"But isn't that an imposition on Barak?"

"Oh, no, Mr. Stennis! I assure you, it's quite all right. He has plenty of others to serve him, and in any case just now he is involved quite deeply with the Bach'het affair."

It was a good offer. "I'll take my book," I said.

"Oh, yes, of course," Purry said courteously. "You will find it very useful in preparing to visit some of the planets of the Fifteen Associated Peoples—that is, if you do."

"If? But I thought that was something I didn't have any choice about," I offered.

The little ocarina hesitated. "Not a choice, exactly, no," he said. "But let's hope that's what happens."

CHAPTER

15

I've explored a lot of interesting places with the help of native guides, one time or another, but usually the guides have been singers or musicians. Or at least human. A guide like Purry was a whole new thing for me.

He was as much a musician as any of them, as a matter of fact. Purry didn't need an instrument to play on. He *was* an instrument. All those tuned orifices on his body could produce the sounds of almost any instrument, even a human voice. (I admit he was a little fuzzy, like a Moog synthesizer, on the strings and percussion.) Moreover he seemed to know the scores of at least a hundred operas by heart—if he had a heart—not to mention any number of art songs, arias, spirituals, and instrumental pieces. He had a beautiful voice, too. That is, he had hundreds of beautiful voices whenever he chose to use them, but the one he normally spoke in was a sweet, high tenor that would have done well for Enrico Caruso.

When I got a chance I asked Purry why the Fifteen Peoples bothered with importing artists from Earth at all, when he was as good as any. "Oh, but that wouldn't be *real,* Mr. Stennis," he piped, shocked. "No, no. None of the Peoples would settle for an imitation—well, except perhaps the Ossps." Anyway, he went on, the sound frequencies weren't the whole of a performance, were they? Weren't they? Oh, certainly not, he declared, trotting along beside me on his stilty little legs. The sound was only a part. It was the totality, the gestalt, that mattered. Especially for some of the Fifteen Peoples, whose senses were not necessarily the same as those of humans—much more sensitive in some areas, he told me, and how could a mere reproducer like himself match not only the sounds, but the sight, the body temperature, the very smells of human performers? Not to mention that when he played an overture, say, he played it exactly as written, while us humans all put our own little spin of interpretation on it, and wasn't that really what art was all about?

Ocarina or not, I liked the guy.

The first thing he did was ask me what on Narabedla I wanted to see. I couldn't answer that. I didn't know what that was. I only hoped I'd recognize it when I came across it, so I told him to shoot the works; and he did.

We started out by walking the streets of the local human community. There were a couple dozen of them, all interlocking, none of them more than a couple of hundred yards long. It wasn't just houses. There was a library—"With a lot of your Earth newspapers and magazines, Mr. Stennis, although of course you can get them on your skry without going out of your house." There was a sort of restaurant/bar/soda-shop; we peered into it, and Purry introduced me to a couple of people sitting there, but they were a man and a woman, busy on a conversation of their own, and they didn't seem interested in talking to me. There were little parks and a pleasant (though oddly curved) pond. There were go-box stations at half a dozen of the intersections, so no one needed to walk very far except for the fun of it; and when Purry shepherded me into one of them I found myself again on the lowest level—the one they called Lookout.

Although I'd already been there, it looked different. There was something big in that immensity of empty sky beneath our feet that hadn't been there before, and Purry told me that it was that seventh planet that we were on the second moon of. It was a huge one. It looked a lot like pictures I'd seen of Jupiter, a great, bright, swirly, cloudy thing with no detectable surface. "And nobody lives there?" I asked, just checking.

Purry hesitated. "Well, Mr. Stennis," he said playfully, "that depends on what you mean by a body, doesn't it? None of the Fifteen Peoples do, certainly. They'd die; it's all poison gases and very high pressure. Still, there are living things there of some sort, I believe. Quite primitive ones. There are in most places. We could check it out on the skry if you like?"

I shook my head, watching the big thing follow its star down under the side of our moonlet. When they had both set I said, "There's an awful lot I need to check out on the skry. Maybe we should go back to my place."

"Oh? But really, Mr. Stennis, we can find a skry almost anywhere."

"We can't find food just anywhere," I pointed out. "I'm beginning to get hungry."

"Oh?" He sounded puzzled as he looked up at me. "But there are places where food can be bought. If you remember, I showed you one. The refreshment place. But I thought you said you didn't want anything."

"It wasn't so much I didn't *want* anything as that I couldn't *pay* for anything," I explained. "I don't have any money."

"I see," he said doubtfully. Then he made a sort of faint puffing sound out of several of his orifices, like the dying gasps of a pipe organ when the pump has been turned off. I took it to be a sigh. "No, I don't see," he confessed. "What is 'money'?"

By the time we got that threshed out I was getting really ravenous. "Money" as a medium of exchange for normal goods and services meant nothing to Purry. You did what you were supposed to do, you used what commodities you needed, and that was that. Nobody kept books. When I mentioned Norah Platt's fondness for imported kippers Purry saw the distinction at once. "Oh, yes, to be sure," he agreed. "For off-planet things, yes, of course, there is a medium of exchange. That is basically determined by the Polyphase Index in transactions among the Fifteen Associated Peoples—that is to say, by what you would call 'barter.' But for you Earth artists there are special arrangements, as set out in your contract for services."

"But I don't have a contract for services, Purry!"

"Yes," he conceded, "the situation is unusual in that way. It doesn't affect food, drink, and lodging, however. Shall we go to the refreshment place?"

But I wasn't ready for that. We wound up back at my place, where I discovered that the skry was flashing its gentle lavender attention signal again. Purry commanded, "Mr. Stennis's messages, please." There turned out to be three of them. A quick word from Sam Shipperton to say that Meretekabinnda was expected back in the morning, though why he was telling me that I wasn't sure. The skry's own sweet, sexless voice to tell me that the garments I had ordered were completed and already in my bedroom closet. And a message from Bartolomeo Canduccio to let me know that several of his recitals were in the skry's data-stores, and if I would like to hear how he sang I had but to order them up.

"There," I said, "is a man who doesn't know that I'm unemployed."

"I beg your pardon?" said Purry, looking uncertainly up at me.

"Never mind," I said. "Let's get to the food and drink. We can hear the man sing while we're eating."

So Purry did what was necessary to get the recordings going—actually, Canduccio wasn't half bad, if you like Mozart—and I drifted into the kitchen to see what was in the refrigerator.

"But don't you want something made for you?" asked Purry in surprise. He didn't wait for an answer. "Kekkety folk, dinner for Mr. Stennis," he ordered; and almost at once the little door that I'd thought was a broom closet opened and one of the silent little men came out. "And what would you like, Mr. Stennis?" asked Purry. "Something quick? There are premade meals in slow storage; I know that Mr. Shipperton always likes the what he calls macaroni and cheese casserole—"

"Fine," I said. "Get something for yourself, too."

"Oh, no," Purry said, sounding surprised. I didn't argue, because I wasn't really listening. I had been watching when the little Kekkety came out, and what he had come out of was something that looked like a closet. No doors. No windows. It was a go-box.

When Purry had given the order to the servant, who disappeared into the box to get it, I said, "Isn't that a go-box? Can't I use that one, instead of going to the one on the corner?"

"Oh, no, Mr. Stennis. Human beings can't operate the Kekkety things."

"Why not?"

"Well . . ." He hesitated. "They simply can't. The controls are not set for them, you see."

"But the Kekkety—" I did a slow double take. "Aren't they human?"

Purry shrilled in surprise, "Certainly not, Mr. Stennis! They're no more human than I am. They're *made*. They're what I believe you call 'robots.'"

I did a double take. "*You* are a robot?"

"Certainly, Mr. Stennis. An organic robot. I thought you knew."

"But you can talk!"

"Yes, Mr. Stennis. I'm din-Kekkety, you see. I have language capacities installed. The servant Kekkety simply have not been made with that capacity. Ah, your meal is arriving; would you care to wash up first?"

When I came out of the bathroom my dinner was all ready, and a table had been set in the larger room. Set for one.

Purry didn't seem to mind. He chattered on while I was eating. "As to this question of 'unemployment,' as you call it. I've queried the skry about it, to see what might happen if you do not actually sign a performance contract."

I sat down, sniffing the casserole appreciatively. "So what's the word?"

"I'm not sure, in your case, what would be done. There have been human beings who weren't artists; there still are, three or four of them. Mr. Shipperton, of course, and an associate of his who helps with bookings on other planets— he's away now. Also there used to be a human man who worked on the farms—I don't mean that he did the actual farming, of course. The ftan-Kekkety do that—oh, you've never seen ftan-Kekkety. Well, they don't have language capacity either, but they aren't made to look human. They're purpose-designed, you see, like me. But anyway, this human man was employed to help choose the varieties of things to plant, and he tested all the protein sources to see if they were to human tastes."

"I don't think I'd make a good farmhand," I grumbled, finishing off the macaroni casserole. There was a fresh fruit cup for dessert.

"Then there was another man who volunteered for one of the probes. I do hope you won't want to do that, Mr. Stennis."

"What probes?"

"The long-distance ones," he explained. "Not a *really*

long one. I don't mean anything like the Andromeda probe, just a two-thousand-light-year one."

I stared at the little thing. "And somebody volunteered for that? For God's sake, why?"

Purry said, "I believe he was hoping that by the time he got back the human race would have been allowed to join the Fifteen Associated Peoples, Mr. Stennis."

"Two thousand years! That's a lot of patience. And is it likely that that will happen?"

"Oh, Mr. Stennis," he said plaintively, "I know nothing of such things. Such matters are decided by the Associated Peoples, and they are quite careful. They've had some bad experiences, you know. In any case," he finished, "you seem to be through with your meal. Shall we continue the tour? Or would you like to meet some of your human colleagues? There should be a number in one of the refreshment places."

So we started a good old-fashioned pub crawl, me and my little pet ocarina.

No one asked for payment, just as Purry had promised. I started with a beer or two, and began to feel the effects fast. My jet lag, or I guess I should call it my go-box lag, was still hovering around, and by the time I had visited three "refreshment places" with Purry, and had a drink or two in each of them, it all began to blur on me.

I did get to meet a lot of my human colleagues, though. Purry introduced me to a dozen, and most of that dozen introduced me to others—even if I hadn't had the drinks, I couldn't possibly have retained them all. We stayed in the English-speaking area, but even there there were a couple of hundred people, and I met a large fraction of them. There was a middle-aged black woman who wanted to know how the Dodgers were doing, and a youngish, serious-faced man who wanted to know if I was right with God. There was a pair of xylophonists, male and female, who had just come back from a three-planet tour and were full of stories about the kinds of places that passed for hotels on the road. There was a trombone player who wanted to tell me all about the Andromeda probe, and probably did; but as I was talking to three other people at the same time I can't say I followed what he was saying very closely.

I did see a couple of familiar faces. Tricia Madigan looked in on one of the places as I was listening to a long spiel about how the Aiurdi really liked break dancing but the Ossps couldn't stand it; she was with a tall, skinny black man, and though she waved at me she didn't come in. And Ephard Joyce was sitting sullenly at the bar in one of the places. He turned and looked me full in the face. He must have heard that I'd failed my audition, because he cut me dead.

Purry got me home.

I don't think I could have made it by myself. He took me as far as the door, looked up at me anxiously, then excused himself.

I got my clothes off and myself into my neatly made bed, and closed my eyes. My head was full of strange people and strange things, but there were some familiar worries still bobbing about in my brain. Their names were Irene Madigan; and my good and faithful Marlene; and, a little bit, all of my other clients, any one of whom, lacking my good offices, might be even then strangling in the coils of a particularly savage I.R.S. audit.

There was one other thing I was thinking about as I fell asleep.

A dozen or more of the people I talked to in the bars were female, and I was quite aware that never once had any of those women come on to me.

I was pretty sure I knew the reason why. Sweet Tricia had not delayed in spreading the word that poor old Nolly Stennis had no balls at all.

CHAPTER
16

When I woke up the next morning I had some hard thinking to do. It wasn't, or at least it wasn't directly, about how I could get out of this place and back home.

What it basically was was curiosity. I wanted to *know* things, and as soon as Purry came through the door I said, "No grand tour today. What I'd like to do is just ask you some questions."

He reared back on his little legs, gazing up at me. "Of course, Mr. Stennis," he said, but sounding a little puzzled. "What kind of questions?"

I was ready. The little list was all in my head. "Well, to start out, the go-box. How does it work?"

"Certainly, Mr. Stennis," the little ocarina said agreeably. "To begin with, the local go-boxes will take you into any permitted area of Narabedla. You simply enter, announce your destination—"

"No, that's not what I mean. I mean, what *makes* it work? What is the scientific principle behind it?"

"Oh, I wouldn't know that, Mr. Stennis," he said in dismay. "My skills are merely linguistic and musical. I suppose we could find the kind of data you want on the skry—"

"Do it," I said. I watched with satisfaction while the little ocarina clambered up in front of the skry and began chirping out orders.

Hard thinking in the early morning had given me a plan, and it came in three parts. First, I wanted to go home. Second, in order to get home I had to find out where the weak parts were in Narabedla's security system. (Whatever that was. I hadn't seen any signs that anybody was worrying much about security.) Third, as long as I was going home, why not take something with me? Out of all this wonderful technology there had to be *something* that I could take back to Earth.

Not the go-box, however.

It took Purry half an hour of hard work to come up with anything I could understand, and then it wasn't any use. "The problem, Mr. Stennis," he said sadly, "is that the basic technological principles do not have any equivalent on your planet."

"You mean it's something we haven't discovered yet? Like electricity or the steam engine?"

"I suppose so," he said doubtfully. "The closest I can come is to that it relates to something that your scientists call 'Einstein-Rosen separability,' but what that is I don't know."

Neither did I, but I wrote down the name all the same; maybe the library would have something about it. "Spaceships, then," I ordered.

"Oh, the Peoples don't use spaceships! Off-planet transportation is just another sort of go-box."

"I thought you said something about probes?"

"Ah," said Purry, gratified. "Of course. The go-boxes can't work until there is a terminal for them, and the probes provide the terminals. Just a moment."

But that took a lot more than a moment, too. It wasn't that Purry was trying to keep anything from me. It wasn't that he was stupid, either—well, he was a musician, wasn't he? And I'd never met a musician anywhere who knew much about simple arithmetic (that was what they paid their accountant for), much less things like Einstein-Rosen separability. Purry didn't have any trouble finding out all the answers to all my questions through the skry. The trouble came later, because then he had to try to find English words for the answers, and a lot of the time the English words apparently did not exist.

As to spaceships—yes, certainly, there were two kinds of them for voyages on routes where go-boxes had not yet been installed. There was the kind they used for relatively short trips—from planet to planet, or to quite nearby stars—and they were "rockets." Well, not ordinary rockets; it took Purry a lot of sweat to find the term for the fuel they used, and it came out as "antimatter." Then there were the long-distance probes. One was just about to be launched to some very far-off place—ultimately Purry found a name for that place, "Galaxy M-31 in Andromeda." Those were light-sail ships. They required a special kind of light to propel them, though, and Purry hunted a long time before he came up with the word "pulsars." "They're a special *kind* of these pulsars, though," he said dismally, and he couldn't find any way of telling me what made them special.

The same with "slow time." The same with the "skry." The same with, for that matter, Purry himself, and the Kekkety folk, and all the other "robots."

After two hours of that sort of frustration I possessed a number of words, but nothing that I could see a way to build back on Earth. (I imagined myself going to NASA: "Okay, folks, here's how you explore Pluto. First you fuel your ship with antimatter—you don't have any antimatter? Well, get some! Then you put a go-box on the ship—what do you mean, you don't know how to make a go-box? Why, it's just a matter of Einstein-Rosen separability, after all!")

I wasn't really sorry when the skry lighted up to show Sam Shipperton looking out at me. He looked annoyed as he said, "Nolly, come on in. I need to talk to you."

Shipperton glowered at me over that flickering, flashing desk. "I'm expecting a call about you, Stennis," he said.

"What kind of a call?"

"It might be good news, but first we have to talk. You've got a problem."

"Sure I do. The problem is you kidnapped me."

He winced. "Will you shut up about that for a minute? That's not your big problem. Your big problem is this woman Marlene Abramson. She's going to find herself right down the tank if you don't do something fast."

I sat down on the chair next to his desk, suddenly alert. Was something happening back on Earth that might help me get out of this? I kept my face calm, and all I said was, "You don't even offer me coffee first?"

"Get yourself some goddamn coffee if you want it! But pay attention," he called to my back as I rose to do so. "You know what she's done? She's been to the FBI!"

I poured the coffee before I answered. "Well," I said judiciously, "yes, I suppose it's the FBI that a person would call in about a kidnapping."

"Don't make jokes!"

"That wasn't a joke, Shipperton," I said, sitting down. "I'm talking about real kidnapping, and maybe murder, too."

"Murder!" He gave me a stare of incredulous dislike. "Now what are you talking about?"

"Jerry Harper, for one. And then, when you took Tricia, you provided a corpse to substitute for her. You murdered some innocent woman just to cover it up."

"Oh, hell, Stennis, you've got some crazy ideas, you know that? Harper was convicted of murder himself—not by Narabedla Limited, or the Fifteen Peoples; it was a jury of the other artists right here. And that body that was substituted for Tricia came right out of the morgue. Some unclaimed hooker; it was lucky one was there, otherwise they'd have had to do it some other way. But murder's absolutely out of the question, believe me. Narabedla has never taken a human life. That's rule number one."

I sneered, "Are you trying to tell me that Davidson-Jones wouldn't be willing to kill somebody to protect his position? Say if he made some big goof and wanted to keep the weirdos from finding out about it?"

He looked puzzled, then shook his head. "Stennis," he said patiently, "the rule against murdering human beings doesn't come from the Fifteen Peoples. Most of them wouldn't care one way or the other. It's Jonesy's own rule, and he wouldn't break it. Now look," he said, beginning to build up steam again, "let's cut out all this crap. We've got to do something about this woman! She's blown the whistle on Henry Davidson-Jones, accused him of, Jesus, three counts of kidnapping, one of attempted murder, and—you're not going to believe this!—even a violation of the civil-rights statutes, because she says he abducted you and prevented you from getting back to New York in time to vote in some cockamamie primary election there. My God, Stennis! What kind of a woman is this? I never even *heard* of some of the things she's charged Jonesy with!"

I took a sip of my coffee and sat down again. I didn't even try to make my voice sound sincere when I said, "Gosh, that's really a shame."

He glared at me. "Damn straight it is! If she doesn't knock it off it'll be just too bad for her! Think this thing through, Nolly. First place, there's no way she can hang anything on Jonesy. How could she? He's got the money, he's got the lawyers, he's got real good friends in important places. All she can do is make a little trouble."

"I can see that," I agreed. "So then why are you all in an uproar about it?"

"Because," he gritted, "we don't *want* trouble. Davidson-Jones doesn't have to *have* trouble. He can take *steps*. Is that what you want him to do?"

I thought that over. I had a pretty good idea of what the steps might be, and Shipperton was right, I didn't want them taken. On the other hand, I didn't want to cave in too quickly. "I wouldn't mind having Marlene here for company," I said, not very honestly.

"What company? Is she a tap-dancer maybe? Or plays the kazoo? No, Nolly, if Mr. Davidson-Jones had to bring her here the only thing we'd be able to do with her is put her in slow time, and, honest, it'd be like having a stiff for company. Cripes," he went on, sounding injured, "maybe that's what I should've done with you in the first place. Here I am knocking myself out trying to find work for a busted-down baritone, with the critics getting tougher all the time, and what do I get for it? So what are you going to do?"

I didn't like what he was saying, but there was a certain amount of truth to it. I parried. "What do you want me to do?"

"Send her a postcard!"

That came out of left field. I blinked at him. "A what?"

"A postcard," he said. "This here is a postcard. I want you to write something on it so she'll know it's you. Tell her that everything's all right, you're just taking a little time off to think things over. And we'll send it to her."

I picked up the card he had tossed at me. It had a picture on the front of some beat-up row houses with some beat-up types lounging in front of them, and under the picture were the words: *Hi, mate, the best of Scottish luck from the Gorbals.*

I said, "What's a gorbal?"

"What do you care? It's a neighborhood in Glasgow. That's where you're supposed to be now. See," he explained, "we sort of laid a false trail after they, uh, picked you up in Nice. We got somebody to use your Eurailpass as far as Paris, then he bought a flight from De Gaulle to Heathrow, then a train to Glasgow, and stayed at a couple of hotels. He used your American Express card, so that's cool,

but we want Marlene to get somebody to check all this out,
otherwise what's the use? So write a nice little card for her.
Say, 'Dear Marlene, I just had to take a little time off. Don't
worry. I'll be in touch later.' Only put something in so she'll
believe it's actually from you."

"She never will!"

"Nolly," he said patiently, "*make* her believe it. Or do
you want her here in slow storage?"

"If you kidnap her, too, the FBI will really take an interest, Shipperton."

"Right, Nolly. That's our good reason for going to all this
trouble. *Your* good reason is to keep that from happening to
her. Write."

I argued for another few minutes, but in the long run I did
what he wanted me to do. I wrote.

I didn't see any way out of it. I said just what Shipperton
had told me, and added, "P.S., kiss Sally for me and tell her
I'll bring back some perfume from the duty-free."

Shipperton read it carefully. "Who's Sally?" he asked.

"She's our secretary. We always bring her something
back when we travel."

He gazed at me darkly. Then he shrugged and whistled.
One of the little bedbugs appeared. It took the card in its
little claws and, holding it high, raced out the door. As it
left, Shipperton relaxed.

"Now you're being sensible," he said approvingly. "Now
comes the good news. Well, kind of good news. Barak's back
from his meetings. Any minute now we'll be getting a call
from him, and if everything's all right we'll be off to see the
Tlotta-Mother."

As Shipperton appeared to relax, I began to tense up
again. I said, "I hate it when somebody says there's 'kind
of' good news."

"Aw," he said easily, "probably it'll be just fine. You
never know with the Mother, of course. But she's the one
with the most rank around here. She's a *Mother*. So you
have to get along with her—no, don't ask, I know what
you're going to say; wait till you see her and she'll tell you
what she wants you to know." He glanced at his watch.

"But—"

"No buts," he ordered. "Wait for the call." Then he

grinned. "If you want to talk about something else, we've got time. Did I ever tell you about how I got here?"

"You can if you want to," I said.

"Aw, Nolly, just mellow down, why don't you? I know how you feel. See, when I came here they didn't have a place for me, either." I stared at him and he nodded. "That's right. Just like you—well, almost. In 1972 I was in a rock group, trying to hit the big time in Houston, Texas. They picked us up, and when we got here they didn't want us at all!"

"Is that why you're doing this kind of stuff instead of playing your music?" I asked.

"Hell, they did give us a try. We bombed! It was a mistake to bring us, I guess. We tried out on four or five planets, but it just didn't work, you know?" He shrugged. "Jonesy said it was because our act was half technology, you know—electronic instruments, and makeup, and strobes and amplification. Hell, there wasn't anything we could show these guys about technology! So Chuck Plandome, he was our keyboard guy, he caught on playing accompaniment for an Irish tenor. Our own vocalist does Gilbert and Sullivan patter songs, and Frankie and I got administrative jobs. Frankie's on the road now. You'll see him, maybe, one of these days."

I got myself another cup of coffee, thinking. I decided to probe a little. "That must have been tricky, snatching four of you at once."

"They didn't really snatch us. It was more complicated than that. See, we were a new group, and, frankly, we had a few problems. I mean with the law. You could even say we were on the run—that was one reason why we all kept all that makeup on in public, and kept our private lives kind of secret, you know? So it wasn't any sweat for Jonesy, just a little mistake in judgment."

"I'm glad to hear you admit he can make mistakes."

"Oh, hell, man, everybody makes mistakes. Jonesy's been doing this for a hundred years, give or take. Maybe he's getting a little stale, overconfident—I don't know. Anyway, they took us on and then, when we got here, it was just like it is with you. The *reason* Jonesy made us the offer was that Frankie knew something. Frankie talked a lot, and one of the things he talked about was the Martians."

That stopped me. "*Martians?*"

"Not real Martians. That's just what they were called where Frankie used to work. Frankie probably shouldn't have talked about it, because I guess that's why Davidson-Jones came after us. I mean, well, back before we formed the group, Frankie used to work for a company in the Valley. In California, you know? They were one of those biotech outfits that did things like gene-splitting and stuff, making pharmaceuticals? That's why Frankie took a job there in the first place. He thought he might score something, but that wasn't the kind of drugs they made. Anyway. Even where Frankie worked, in the mail room, there was this joke about the 'Martians.' What it meant, every once in a while an outside director would come to the company with a suitcase full of papers. They'd have a secret meeting, and he'd turn the papers over. The people that worked there said it was all top-secret stuff. Like industrial espionage? You've heard of that? They said these were hush-hush reports they'd got—stole, I guess they meant—from places like Hungary and China and South Africa, where they were doing the same kind of work this company did. And they'd always be good ideas that the company would follow up on, and get patents, and make big bucks. They didn't want to say where they got them, so they'd say they were from the 'Martians.'" Shipperton grinned at me. "So guess who the Martians really were."

"Narabedla Limited?"

"Right on," he said.

"My God," I said. "Is that how Davidson-Jones gets so rich? Importing alien technology to Earth?"

"Just a little bit at a time, right," he nodded. "Nothing revolutionary. Never anything big. Just little bits of know-how to keep the Narabedla companies a step ahead of everybody else. They made big bundles out of it."

So much for my idea of bringing some wonderful new technology home with me! Well, there still might be something, I thought, and put that thought aside. As long as Shipperton was answering questions, I had a lot of them to ask. "So how long have you been doing this?"

"I told you. I've been here since 1972. Jonesy goes back to, I think, maybe somewhere before 1900."

"No, I mean the whole business of kidnapping artists."

"Oh, long before my time. Hundreds of years, anyway." He peered at me to see if what he was going to say would startle me. "You think that's long? Look, they've been doing the peacekeeper thing for eight hundred years now, and the Clouds of Magellan probes go back over two thousand.''

"Two *what*?"

"Two thousand years, right," he nodded, satisfied. "The Associated Peoples have been around a long, long time, Nolly. And you have to remember that Narabedla—I don't mean just you artists, I mean the whole schmear of importing things from Earth—isn't any more than a pimple on the ass of what they do. What do we bring in for them? Botanical specimens, art stuff—the Duntidons are crazy about Navajo blankets—a little bit of specialty foods and things. The Aiurdi drink tons of kvass. But that's just *Earth*. You look at the Polyphase Index, you'll see that the Earth sector is only about three percent of the total unincorporated-planets trade, and that's only about a tenth of the trade they do among themselves. Only it's not just trade; it's the big projects that they get together on, like the probes. The Andromeda one that they're just getting ready to launch? Well, they've been setting up for that since, let's see, since I guess just about the time the Normans invaded England. And those *cost*. They have to sort of rearrange a whole little star to propel it—no, don't ask me how; I don't know. And they've got forty or fifty of them on the way now. Some are just to other stars, but there's a bunch that are off to other, for God's sake, *galaxies*. Like Andromeda. That's the kind of thing their money goes into!''

"Have any of them arrived yet? I mean, to the other galaxies?"

"Oh, hell, no. The nearest one, I guess, is the one that's supposed to take a go-box to the Lesser Magellanic Cloud, and that's not due to arrive for something like forty thousand years yet."

I gulped. "They're patient people."

"They're nuts," Shipperton growled. He scowled at his watch again. "The thing is," he went on irritably, "these are all different races, fifteen of them. They don't all agree on anything . . . well, except the peacekeeping program, maybe, and they don't have much choice about that. That's why they got together in the first place. There were a couple of wars, a couple of stars got blown up—they figured they had to quit that, or they'd all be dead.''

"*Stars* got blown up?"

He nodded somberly.

"You mean they could blow up *our* star? The Sun?"

"In a hot minute," he said. "But don't worry. Why would they bother? We're no threat to them at all. And," he added earnestly, "we don't want to *get* to be a threat, do we? As long as the human race is just a bunch of charming primitives they won't bother us. Maybe sometime in the future, if we're lucky, they'll even let us join up—of course, you and I won't live to see it. But that's another good reason why Narabedla's a secret. The last thing anybody who wasn't crazy would want would be for some nut on Earth to get the idea of shipping an H-bomb or something through the go-box on Jonesy's yacht, for instance, as a terrorist threat. That's why you won't go back, Stennis. That's why *nobody* goes back. That's why—hold it."

The center of his wall screen was blinking that lavender flash again, and when it cleared Barak was peering out at us with three or four of his eyes. "The-mother-will . . . receive-you-now," he gasped.

"Coming right up," Shipperton said, but Barak raised a couple of his arms to halt us. He seemed to be looking directly at me, as near as I could tell with a multi-eyed starfish.

"Knollwood-Stennis! You-will-be . . . extremely-courteous-and-careful," he panted out. "Or-it-will-be-bad." He paused for a moment. Then he said, "I-hope-you-don't . . . taste-very-good," and vanished.

CHAPTER

17

What I didn't like about the situation was that Shipperton seemed pretty nervous. I could handle the fact that I had a lot to be nervous about myself. When my guide and tyrant was obviously biting his nails it made it a lot worse. "What's this all about?" I demanded when we were in the go-box. "Am I going to audition again?"

"Audition? Hell, no."

"Then what?" I persisted. "And what did the starfish mean about my tasting good?"

Shipperton just shook his head. "You'll see," he said as the door opened.

The place where we got out of the go-box was unlike any I'd seen before. It wasn't an open street. It was an anteroom, and it smelled of fish and rot and worse. Right in front of us there was a doorway hung with strings of glassy beads. It wasn't the only doorway off the little, stinky foyer. Another door was to our left, closed tight with a solid metal gate. A third was to our right, this one open. Through it I could see a largish room filled with stacks of what looked like fish tanks. Four or five of the little bedbugs were bustling around, but Shipperton didn't give me time to see what they were doing. He pushed me ahead of him through the beads. We had to step over a raised sill in the doorway, and then we were in a steamy room the size of a tennis court. It was hot, close to the temperature of a sauna bath; and it contained an Olympic-sized pool, oval-shaped.

That was where most of the smell had come from. The smell emanated, I supposed, from the Mother.

I had been thinking that, really, the worst thing about all these funny-lookers was the way they smelled. The Mother changed my mind because, although she smelled terrible, she looked worse. I stood there with my mouth hanging open until Shipperton punched me on the shoulder. His voice was strained. "Come on, Nolly, get your clothes off."

I blinked and looked at him. "Do what?"

"Get bare. Undress. Do it, man! You've got to get in the pool so the Mother can feel you!"

And when I looked at his tense, worried face I saw that he meant it.

All I was wearing was shorts, shirt, underwear, gym shoes, and knee-length hose. Given the right incentive, like somebody like Tricia Madigan waiting on a bed (and some hope of making it worth both our whiles), I could have been out of them in thirty seconds.

I took a lot longer than that. I was in no hurry to get into that pool, and besides I was busy looking around.

Shipperton and I were not alone in the room with the Mother. Barak was there, dancing irritably around on the tips of his six arms, and next to him was another weirdie, about belly-button tall and extremely ugly; I hadn't met that one before, but I recognized him as a Mnimn.

Those were the "visitors." There was more. The Mother evidently also kept "pets."

At least, the place she lived in was full of tiny creatures. A dozen or so of them were the familiar chocolate-brown bedbugs, skittering around the rim of the pool or diving into it, but there were at least a hundred other creatures visible. Some flew around like fat little hummingbirds, dive-bombing my head, tweeting to one another as they flew; they swooped away from the glass-curtained doorway, which I supposed was meant to keep them in. Some crept around the floor like little chameleons, and I thought the raised sill was what kept them from straying. The pool itself was full of fish-shaped things and octopus-shaped things and things with no fixed shape at all, swimming about sluggishly or earnestly, like the inhabitants of any suburbanite's tank of tropical marine life. And I haven't yet said a word about the Mother herself.

It was the Mother I kept my eyes on as I stepped out of my undershorts and hesitated at the brink of the pool. She was bloody *ugly*. What she looked like, more than anything else, was a sort of sea anemone with a body the size of a barrel and tentacles that stretched four or five yards around her. She was prettily colored in her main body parts—scarlet and blue and Day-Glo orange—and her tentacles were black and white and green. I supposed she had eyes. There was a ring of pale dots around the crown of her body, but they winked not; neither did they move.

One of the lizardy things came hesitantly to the rim of the pool for a drink of water, peering into it, and I saw what the Mother used the tentacles for. A quick flurry of water and the nearest tentacle had snapped around the little animal, drawing it, twisting and squealing, into a mouth that opened in the base of the body.

The mouth closed on it, and that was the last I saw of the little chameleon.

"Go, damn it, go!" Shipperton gritted. "Just be careful! Don't make any sudden moves—let her feel you—and *do it!*"

*   *   *

Actually, getting into the pool began to seem like a not entirely bad idea. I was not in the habit of appearing naked, even before aliens. I informed myself that they wouldn't have brought me all this way just to be eaten. Then I lowered myself to the rim of the pool and dropped into the tepid water.

The pool was almost shoulder deep, quite warm, and smelling really bad. After jogging along the East River in New York I sometimes used to walk down to the old docks, a few blocks from my apartment, where dead fish and condoms and watermelon rinds bobbed against the pilings; it smelled a lot like that. I bounced buoyantly on the balls of my feet, trying not to breathe, keeping an eye on the Mother's tentacles as they waved gently in my direction.

She made a sweet, soft moaning sound. Shipperton said urgently, "Get on with it, Stennis! Let her touch you—and, for God's sake, *relax*."

Relax! I did not think it was possible for me to relax in the pool with that huge, smelly thing, with smaller things bumping and nibbling at my body as I moved through the water; but I did my best.

One of the bedbugs hopped into the water and swam briskly behind me, butting me toward the Mother. Since I could see no alternative, I let it happen. I wasn't liking it a bit, especially as the longest of the tentacles stretched out to me. It was lined with pink cups, like the suckers on an octopus's legs, or the rosettes of leprosy. *"Careful!"* Shipperton cried.

The tentacle touched me.

The touch was gentle enough, but it didn't let go. The Mother pulled me insistently toward her. Other tentacles joined in the exploration of my body, moving caressingly over my legs and arms, into my crotch, over my shoulders into my ears, across my scalp, into my nostrils—I jerked away as one came toward my eye.

"Hold it!" Shipperton screamed. "Jesus, Nolly, that was a dumb thing to do! Don't *ever* make sudden moves when the Mother is touching you!"

The tentacles, which had twitched angrily as I jerked, relaxed again. More important, that huge and inescapable mouth, which had suddenly yawned a yard from my body, closed again.

I closed my eyes and let happen what would happen.

What happened was no fun at all. One of the shorter, slimmer tentacles found my mouth, gently pressed the lips apart and slithered delicately down my throat. It was a very good thing, I thought, resigning myself to fate, that I had often been complimented by dentists on my control of the gagging reflex. I simply stood there, even when another tentacle reached around my buttocks and entered me there.

Of all the terrible things that I had, one time or another, thought might sometime happen to me, being buggered by a sea anemone had never been one of them. It wasn't really painful. I've felt a lot worse from a proctoscope. It was just extraordinarily humiliating, and it went on for a long time.

Then I felt the slippery things sliding out of me. I opened my eyes. The tentacles relaxed. The Mother began cooing and moaning. Three or four of the little bedbug things began energetically pushing me away, and Shipperton, sounding relieved, said, "Okay, you can get out and get dressed now, Nolly. Wait outside. We'll tell you what the decision is in a minute."

And there I was, back in the anteroom, pulling my clothes on over my still wet body—nobody had offered anything like a towel—and waiting to hear my fate.

Although there was nothing between me and the Mother's sauna but the strings of glass beads, I couldn't see much. I could hear, all right, but I couldn't understand any of what I heard. Barak, the Mother, and the ropy-legged little Mnimn were making all the noises of their own languages, a nasty mixture of dove-coos and gravelly whines and belches, none of which meant anything to me. I did hear Shipperton, once in a while, speaking in English. He didn't say much, and what he did say seemed mostly to be yes-sir-no-sir-right-away-sir sorts of things.

A couple of the little bedbugs came racing through the curtain as I was peering through it, nearly tumbling me. They were carrying glassy baskets of what looked like yesterday's Italian meatballs, wet and crumbly looking. The bedbugs chittered at me impatiently to get out of the way. I did, looking after them as they entered the room of fish tanks. Carefully they lifted the meatballs out of the glassy baskets, one by one, and placed them tenderly in a tank. Other bedbugs were fishing around in another tank, and I could see that what they were scooping out with their little nets was a brood of very small, pale golden bedbugs.

They had to be their young. I began to see why the Mother was called the Mother. The meatball things were eggs; this room was undoubtedly a hatchery. To prove it, I saw the grown-up bedbugs gently herding the babies toward shallow pools on the lowest level, no doubt to eat and grow.

I didn't even notice that the debate behind me had ended until Shipperton tapped me on the shoulder. He looked both faintly annoyed and relieved. "Good news, Stennis," he told me. "You passed."

"Passed what?" I demanded.

He shook his head. "Binnda's going to take you home, and he'll tell you the whole thing. I haven't got time. Jesus! You wouldn't *believe* the things I've got to do now. Here he comes."

And he hurried away as the ugly little Mnimn pushed past the hanging beads. "Well done, my dear Knollwood Stennis," the Mnimn said. His English was excellent, his voice pretty nearly human—anyway, nearly that of some human with a really bad sore throat. "I'm Meretekabinnda. I'm a Mnimn. I'm going to be your impresario."

That was the first time I ever actually met Meretekabinnda. I'd seen him before. He'd been one of the five very peculiar members of my audience, that first night on Narabedla, when Norah Platt had accompanied me. I told him so.

"Yes, that's right," he said eagerly, pleased to be remembered. "You could've seen me at Nice, too, as well as other times. I've been on your The Earth quite often, you know! Now, Knollwood Stennis," he said, capturing my hand in one of his very strange ones and dragging me toward the go-box, "let's go to your house. We've got a lot to talk about—and, I wonder, do you happen to have anything of that good The Earth Scottish whiskey for a thirsty man?"

Well, a "man" Meretekabinnda certainly was not. Apart from being no more than three feet tall, he had no nose, his mouth was a hideous triangular affair, his arms ended in three-fingered pudgy fists, and his little short legs were bent like a dog's. He wasn't naked. In fact, it wasn't until I saw Meretekabinnda that I realized that Barak, and the Mother's little bedbugs, had been bare—it simply seemed right and proper that weird beasties should show off their weirdness,

and so when I took a good look at Binnda I was surprised
to observe that he was wearing a kind of diaper with metallic
spangles sewn onto it, and a kind of keys-of-the-city ribbon
and medallion around his—well, not his "neck." He didn't
have a neck, but there was enough of a shoulder to support
the ribbon where the neck would have been.

Man or not, he had some engagingly human traits. Most
of all he had enthusiasm. He also had warmth—"No, no,
call me Binnda, my dear Nolly," he chattered when I tried
his full name; "No need to be formal among fellow artists!"—and he had just about perfectly unaccented collo-
quial English, which was a big improvement over the
Mother's moans and Barak's gasps, not to mention the twittering of the little bedbug things that had been pushing me
around.

And he was a mine of information. He talked all the way
to my house. He filled me in on the Mother: "She's a sessile
female, you know. She didn't bring a fertile Tlotta male with
her, just the drones—drones? Oh, those little things you
called bedbugs; they go around and do things for her. Were
you frightened when she was examining you? Nothing to be
ashamed of!—though you're really a bit large for her to eat,
anyway. In one bite, I mean. But she's a really important
person, Nolly, and it's wonderful, for you, I mean, that she
liked you!" On Barak: "He's a Ggressna, poor fellow. Can't
sing at all. He loves human singing, though, and he's the one
that told the Mother about you. Not a bad guy, once you
get used to the funny way he looks." (I swallowed hard over
that one.) And, as we passed Execution Square on the way
to my house, in the row that looked like New York brownstone fronts: "That's a Duntidon there, eating your friend.
They're pretty civilized—now," he chuckled, "but they do
come in handy for executions. Oh, have I said something to
upset you? I'm sorry, Nolly; really, there's nothing to worry
about with the Duntidons these days, though in the old days
they had a hell of a nasty war with the poor Bach'het, before
they both signed up with the peacekeeping forces. But I'm
boring you with all this ancient history—and here's your
house, and do you happen to have any good single-malt
whiskey?"

I didn't. It didn't matter. Binnda emitted a high-pitched
screech, one of the Kekketies popped out of the kitchen,
Binnda issued orders in a language I hadn't heard before.

The servant understood it all right, though. He disappeared back into the kitchen and five minutes later emerged with a tray containing the whiskey, ice, and two glasses. By then Binnda had been hopping all over the house, issuing orders to the skry (which promptly began playing symphonic orchestral music of very Earthly provenance in muted tones), peering into my closets, bouncing on my bed. "I do love human furniture," Binnda sighed. "If one didn't have to keep up appearances I'd have some myself. Now. Let's talk about your career. We'll get along without a real orchestra to begin with; Purry's perfectly good, and the audiences won't know the difference on the Duntidon planet—oh, now, really, Nolly! I've told you! They're perfectly civilized now, most of the time!" And then he beamed. "Ah, here's the tipple! Your very good health, Nolly, and may destiny prosper our venture—and, say, do you happen to have anything to eat in the refrigerator?"

It took a while to get used to Binnda's appearance, and a while longer than that to get used to watching the way he ate and drank. His table manners were *foul*. I have heard of a man tossing a shot of whiskey down, but I never saw it done until I saw Meretekabinnda do it. He opened that large triangular mouth, revealing the bright grass-green tongue and the strangely colored inside. He tilted his whole body back, because he didn't have much of a neck. He threw the whiskey into it. His aim was pretty good. Only a little of it splashed on the furniture. He was less neat when he ate, because those powerful three-sided jaws ground up biscuits and cheese and potato chips so fast that crumbs flew in all directions. Especially because he never stopped talking as he ate.

His dream was going to be realized. There would be a real opera company; rehearsals would start tomorrow.

"Tomorrow?"

"Oh, yes!" he cried, delighted with himself. "Shipperton's finding artists right now—I do hope not all the good ones are off on tour! And we'll call the troupe the Bolshoi."

"But Sam Shipperton had another name picked out," I objected.

He stared at me out of the piggy little eyes. "What does Sam Shipperton have to say about it? No, it's the Bolshoi."

Even the Quihigs and the Ossps had heard of the Bolshoi, he explained, and they wouldn't know that we weren't the real thing. The orchestra would just be Purry, for the same reason. But we would have real human singers—"That's where you'll be so wonderful for us, Nolly, because you're just from The Earth and you'll be able to sing just the way they do in all the latest productions."

I spluttered some crumbs of my own on the carpet. *"What?"*

"What what, Nolly?"

"What the hell are you talking about? I'm supposed to be a prompter or something. I can't sing!"

"Oh, but we'll fix that up, Nolly," he protested. "Didn't Shipperton tell you? That's why the Mother was examining you, to see if you could be repaired."

"Repaired?"

"Oh, did I forget to tell you? Sorry. She said that your defects are repairable. I mean," he added hastily, "this 'mumps' thing that damaged you left physical injuries to those pipes of yours, but they can be fixed. A little sculpting of the larynx and the vocal cords, open up a few constricted air passages—nothing at all, really."

"You mean—" I began, having trouble getting the words out.

"Yes, yes, why not? Our 'doctors,' as you call them, do far more difficult things every day; ask Norah Platt. It won't be any trouble. One or two nights in the hospital, that's all, and you'll be singing as well as you ever did. Probably better. And while he's at it," he said, "he might as well fix up your balls, too."

Binnda stayed for a couple of hours after that. We talked about all kinds of things. I hardly heard them.

My mind wasn't really on what we were doing. It was on the promise that I might have both my voice and my balls back. Was it possible that, as Sam Shipperton had promised, I was really going to like this place after all?

Binnda helped that along quite a lot. He was a considerate, interesting, amusing person—once you got past the truly nasty way he looked. And he knew a great deal about opera.

He was sketching out a whole season for us. Did I think a simple *Pag* and *Cav* was enough for a bill? What did I think of Barak's idea of the Busoni *Turandot*? When I hesitated, trying to be diplomatic over that one, he bobbed his upper body—I think it was meant to be a nod of agreement. "Terrible idea," he said. "We'll forget that one. Not every opera from your The Earth is a masterpiece, after all. Of course," he added thoughtfully, "one hates to offend a Ggressna. They're really more or less the founding fathers of our association, as I am sure you know, but where would the Ggressna be without the Tlotta-Mothers? And the Mother happens to be a Mozart fancier."

I was having trouble following him. "*I Pagliacci* is by Leoncavallo, not Mozart," I pointed out.

"Yes," he twinkled, "but, you see, I happen to like *I Pagliacci*. And the Mother has entrusted me with all the details." Three programs would be plenty, he decreed. We could repeat them in different places on each planet, and certainly what we did on one planet would not be stale for another—and if we didn't have enough qualified human singers for all the roles we could use holographic simulations—though, personally, Binnda said disapprovingly, he didn't like to do that, except of course for crowd scenes and choruses.

And then, as the music from the screen came to the end of Richard Strauss's "Alpine Symphony" and started something else, Binnda raised his hand. "Listen!" he ordered.

It was symphonic music still, but it had a violin and it sounded vaguely Scottish, with that hop-skip rhythm. I am no expert on orchestral music, but I had heard it before. "Bruch?" I guessed.

"Yes, exactly. It is his Violin Concerto in A, Anne-Sophie Mutter as the soloist with the National Symphony Orchestra. A performance recording, not a studio. Mstislav Rostropovich is conducting," he said proudly. "But listen!" It was just at the beginning of Mutter's cadenza in the first movement, and somebody's raucous cough came through loud and clear. "That was me," Binnda said with a kind of gloomy delight. "Isn't it terrible? But I couldn't help it. The things you people put on yourselves! Perfumes, deodorants, I could hardly breathe! It got worse in the second movement and they threw me out."

I gaped at him. "You were *there*?"

"Why, Nolly," he said, superior, deprecatory, amused, "I have been to your The Earth often. Most of us would like to visit it, I mean those cultured ones like ourselves, but unfortunately their physiques are, well, unmistakable. For me it was not difficult. In some ways I look quite like a The Earth native, haven't you noticed? Wait, I'll show you how I did it.'' He barked a command at the screen. It did not stop playing the Bruch, but the screen obediently flickered and produced a picture.

The picture was Binnda. It was Binnda in disguise; he could have been a dwarf, or an exceptionally ugly six-year-old, wearing a shapeless trench coat and long blond hair. The nose was obviously false, of course. Maybe it wouldn't have been so obvious if I hadn't had the real thing right in front of me to compare. And the face looked different around the mouth; there were actual lips, not the triangular praying-mantis chompers that were Binnda's natural state. ''You wore a rubber mask,'' I said, comprehending. He nodded, gratified. It was a good mask. Probably it hadn't been studied very closely; people tend out of tact to avert their eyes from such obviously malformed faces.

''I have been in the audience in more than thirty performances of symphonic concerts, operas, and recitals on The Earth,'' Meretekabinnda said with pride.

I asked eagerly, ''Did you ever hear me sing?''

''Oh, yes! It was in your Stockholm, in Sweden, and you sang in the local language. *La Bohème*. You were terrible.''

I think it was around that time that I stopped thinking of Meretekabinnda as a revolting alien monster and began thinking of him as one of those more familiar monsters, a music critic.

To give Binnda his due, the Swedish critics had also said I was terrible. It hurt when I saw the reviews, but I probably was. The opera was *La Bohème,* and they'd sung it in Swedish, and I'd had to learn the part in four days because their previous baritone had come down with laryngitis. It was a pretty opera house; it smelled of over-roasted, over-boiled coffee from the bar at the intermissions (the Swedes don't go in for champagne in the pauses), but I would have liked it if the audiences had liked me. They hadn't.

I tried to remember if I had heard any particular ear-splitting cough from a member of the audience who happened to be a poorly disguised visiting creature from another planet.

Then it all came back to me. I wouldn't have heard Binnda however much he'd coughed. There had been too much competition. It was October. In Stockholm. Everybody in the audience had a cold. There's that scene where Mimi is hiding in a doorway, eavesdropping while Rodolfo is talking about how jealous he is. Then, according to the libretto, she coughs, and he discovers her. But not in Stockholm he didn't; the whole audience was hacking away, sounding like the seal pit at the zoo, and the Mimi had to strain her lungs to be heard over them.

Binnda was staring dreamily at his picture, waving one of those long arms in time with the Bruch slow movement. I said, unable to keep an edge out of my voice, "If you think I'm so lousy, why do you want me to sing for you?"

He looked at me thoughtfully, the three-cornered mouth working. "Oh, Nolly, I've hurt your feelings, haven't I? I'm sorry. I thought you knew you were having a bad night in Stockholm."

"Well, I suppose I did," I acknowledged.

"You won't ever have another," he promised. "Now, let's get on with our business!"

And we did. Meretekabinnda even acted out a couple of scenes with me from memory, and his memory was better than mine. Could we do *The Magic Flute*? he asked, and then at once wanted to hear me sing Papageno. "I'll sing the girl," he cried enthusiastically. "You ring your silly little bell, the three youths bring me in, you sing . . ."

And I did: "*Pa-Pa-Pa-Pa-Pa-Papagena . . .*"

And Binnda came in, vigorously croaking, "*Pa-Pa-Pa-Pa-Pa-Papageno . . .*"

"*Bist du mir nun ganz gegeben?*"

"*Nun bin ich dir ganz gegeben,*" he squawked back at me, and so on to the end of the silly, beautiful Mozart duet; he knew every word, though I was fumbling on most of the patter lines. "Yes," he said, waggling his neckless head in pleasure, "you'll do just fine, Nolly. And, once we get your plumbing back in order, maybe better than that!"

I never had a review I appreciated more.

I walked Binnda to the go-box entrance, the two of us chattering and sometimes singing a line or two at each other

as we went. One or two people looked out their windows
curiously as we passed. I didn't mind.

Rehearsals tomorrow! I was a singer again—or would be;
would be a real one, if Meretekabinnda's promise was good,
and I had never dreamed that would be possible again in my
life.

To say nothing of his other promise.

Strolling back toward the Execution intersection I let myself wonder about what sort of "operation" might be involved. The Mother's examination had been only gross, not
painful. Norah Platt had boasted of the fact that she was
kept in good repair, in spite of her incredible age. Sam Shipperton had sworn I would be well treated.

There was really nothing to worry about. Was there?

That is, I reflected, nothing for *me* to worry about. Not
counting what trouble Irene Madigan and Marlene Abramson
might be getting into . . . but, at worst, what would that be?
Henry Davidson-Jones might, in desperation, ship them to
Narabedla to shut them up; but was that so bad?

True, there was the loss of freedom. But I was beginning
to see that there were some pretty fine trade-offs for that.

Also true, I at least had the capacity to perform—that is,
to do the things the whole system was designed for. Marlene
didn't. Neither, as far as I knew, did Irene. They might not
fit in so well. They might easily, as Shipperton had threatened, have to go into this "slow storage"—but that wouldn't
really harm them; and some day, no doubt, they could be
brought out again to live quite happy lives.

Finally true, some of the aliens were not very likable.

I was looking at one that fit that description. It was the
monster that was eating the man in the statue in Execution
Square. Binnda had called it a Duntidon, and—yes! I remembered!—he'd even said that I might some day be performing on a planet inhabited by such things.

That did not sound attractive at all.

I stopped and looked at it more closely. In the dim light
from the nighttime ceiling panels it did not look any better
than by daylight. The mean-looking, slitted eyes. The talons
like knitting needles. The sharp teeth that were actually
pressing into the throat of the silently screaming man in its
clutches . . .

It took me a moment to realize that the last time I'd

looked, the teeth had still been an inch or so away from the man's throat.

I swallowed, hearing the two words reverberate in my brain. *Slow time*.

I did not want to believe what I had just thought of.

I made myself touch the "statue." I couldn't quite manage it. My fingers would not quite make contact with the terrible, contorted face of the man named Jerry Harper. There was something between. It wasn't a glass case. It felt tingly to my fingertips at the first touch. Then it felt quite painful, and I jerked my fingers away.

Slow time.

The statue was no statue.

The execution had not been commemorated. It was still going on.

In slow time, Jerry Harper was screaming, was in the talons of the Duntidon . . . was being murdered before my eyes . . . and had been, all the time I'd been on Narabedla.

And everyone who had passed that square in all those days had known it except me.

CHAPTER

18

But Nolly, dear," Norah Platt said patiently, "yes, of course it's too bad about Jerry Harper, but what can one do? He did kill those people."

"You don't have to make a public spectacle of his death."

"Really?" Norah pursed her lips. "Far be it from me to criticize others, but do you actually think it's a good idea to have executions in secret? I mean, what's the point? When I was a girl and my father took me to Tyburn for a hanging, please believe me, I resolved never *ever* to do anything that would put me on the gibbet. Yes, yes. I know you modern people have other customs, but have they really made any difference? To the amount of crime, I mean? No, I thought not; and Nolly, please, if we don't get started now we'll be late for our first rehearsal!''

She limped with dignity out of my door.

I followed. The thing was, I had forgotten for a moment how old Norah Platt was. As we passed the "statue" she paused to study critically the depth to which the Duntidon's fangs were penetrating Jerry Harper's doomed throat.

She didn't say anything, and neither did I.

I was in a somewhat peculiarly fractured state of mind. There was one of me boiling with outrage at the brutal murder of a fellow human being, raging at my captivity, calculating the chances of shooting my way out of this place (but where to find a weapon?), or taking a hostage (but how did you go about that, exactly?), or somehow, anyhow, breaking out of this slavery.

And then there was the other of me. The one whose ear tingled joyously at the word "rehearsal," and whose heart beat faster at the thought of being restored to all those powers I had kissed good-bye.

I don't really blame myself for hurrying after Norah Platt to the rehearsal hall. I guess there were times—oh, say, around the end of the year 1776—when even George Washington took his mind off the worrisome work of trying to free the American colonies from King George III, because he had a houseful of Christmas guests and a lot of mulled wine to drink up. Maybe even V. I. Lenin spent some of his Zurich days sitting at a sidewalk café with a seidel of brew, checking out the girls who strolled by. It stands to reason. You can't be a revolutionary all the time.

Especially when you've got a rehearsal to go to.

The rehearsal hall was the little theater where I had auditioned on arriving in Narabedla. Then I had been too confused to look at it very carefully. Now I saw that it was not actually a theater. A rehearsal hall is exactly what it was; there wasn't really enough room for an audience, just a couple of rows of seats (well, they weren't all *seats;* one part was a tank of water and another was a sort of artificial tree). There was a narrow stage, bare except for a piano on stage right. A plump young woman whom I had never seen before was plunking aimlessly at the piano keys.

The rubbery-legged Binnda was standing just at the steps to the stage. He left off talking to a pretty little man with long, curled hair to hurry toward me, long arms writhing in greeting. "My dear boy, my dear boy," he rasped, the three-cornered mouth working in what might have been a smile. "I hope you slept well? No? Ah, just the natural nervousness of the artist, of course, but you'll be fine! Shipperton has done wonders finding artists for our troupe. He must have been up all night! Let me introduce you to some of your colleagues. This is Ugolino Malatesta, our Idamante, and Eloise Gatt over there at the piano—say hello, Eloise!—will sing Ilia." I must have looked confused, because he took my arm—strange feeling, that rubbery, warm, snaky limb linked with my own—and walked me away. "Oh, didn't I tell you? Shipperton isn't the only one who was busy while the rest of you were all sleeping. I've chosen the operas. For our first production we're going to mount an *Idomeneo*!"

I gave him a suspicious look. "*Idomeneo*?"

"Yes, exactly. Won't that be wonderful? And the Mother is sure to approve, since she's such a Mozart fancier!"

How can you tell when an alien creature with no nose is trying to insult you? I couldn't. I kept a firm grip on my temper and only said, "You don't expect me to sing the castrato part, do you?"

"Of course not, Nolly!"

"In fact," I said, nodding, "there's no baritone part at all in *Idomeneo*, is there?"

Binnda gave me a wounded look. "But I thought you'd understand," he complained. "We'll do the *Idomeneo* first, so you won't have to sing until you're, ah, ready. Then we'll do two other productions, and of course there'll be parts for you. Big ones!" He peered up at me to see if I was angry, then was distracted as a couple of Kekketies came trotting in with armloads of paper. "Ah, here come the scores! Excuse me, Nolly, let me make sure they've got the right ones."

Shipperton's all-night labors had turned up eight or nine other human singers in the troupe. While Meretekabinnda was sorting the scores out, Norah introduced me all over again to the people he had already introduced, and to all the others present, too.

It was a good try, but it was Camp Fire Place Lodge all

over again. I was the new boy, and they were indistinguish-
able lumps of opera company. I did my best, rehearsing the
names. There was somebody named Floyd Morcher, a short,
dark, morose man in gray pants and gray turtleneck and gray
suede shoes. A tenor. There was a big man, no longer young;
he had a red mustache and fringes of red hair around a bald
pate. He also had a conspicuously red nose; he was a bass,
and he looked somehow familiar, but I missed the name because the second tenor was pulling at my arm. He was even
more familiar. He was Bartolomeo Canduccio, my acquaint-
ance from Norah's dinner party. "I hope you did like the
book," he said, wringing my hand to remind me that he had
done me a favor. There were three women, all sopranos,
ranging from young and Valley Girl looking to tall, dark, and
cadaverous. I told them all I was pleased to meet them,
though, really, I hadn't met them.

But I was pleased, all right.

The pleasure came welling up inside me. It took me by
surprise. Nothing had changed. I hadn't really recovered
from the shock of Harper's ongoing murder. I was still a
zillion miles from home. I still had all the problems I'd had
that morning . . . but I was in an opera company!

I found myself grinning at the other singers, smiling affectionately at Norah Platt, touched by the way Binnda
dashed around like the veriest human producer-director-
conductor-resident genius. Not counting the weird aliens
and the bizarre setting, it was so very like the first run-
through of any opera company on Earth. I strolled around
happily. Two of the women were engaged in an intense
conversation in a corner of the stage, in almost voiceless
whispers; when they glanced up at me I beamed at them.
I saw Bart Canduccio walk pointedly by the castrato, Malatesta, cutting him conspicuously cold; I observed it with
tolerant amusement. I was only too happy to oblige Norah
when she asked me to help her sort out the acts of the
piano reduction of the *Idomeneo* score. I was delighted
when four Kekketies appeared with trays of hot tea and
lemon juice for all us singers, and drank my own cup with
delight.

I was awash with good feeling. I was going to sing again!
I almost applauded when at last Binnda climbed up on a

chair, clapped his hands for attention, and cried, "Ladies! Gentlemen! Excuse me, I am the Prologue!"

It was an operatic in-joke—it was what the clown says at the beginning of *Pagliacci*—and Binnda got the little titter he was aiming for. Smiling (I *guessed* that three-cornered mouth was smiling), he began to speak. No, to orate. He said, waving his snaky arms, "This is an historic occasion. I feel humbled by the mantle that Fate has cast on me, the mantle of the immortal Diaghilev and Rudolf Bing. Never before in the history of the Fifteen Associated Peoples have we had the grace of a complete opera company to bring your wonderful The Earth human music to our many audiences in its original, all-human, faithfully produced form. You will perhaps have heard," he went on, his voice taking on a somber timbre, "that many of our friends among the Fifteen Peoples do not care for opera. You may even hear stories that powerful influences—I name no names—are opposed to the creation of this company. Perhaps there is a little truth to that. But it is not an obstacle. It is a *challenge*! On us in this rehearsal hall rests the divine duty to carry on the great traditions of Mozart, Wagner, and Verdi; of Chaliapin and Caruso and Madame Schumann-Heink; of La Scala and Covent Garden and the Met; above all, of the marvelous Bolshoi Opera of Moscow from which we take our name. You have all been personally chosen by me. I know you are as fine a company as has ever been mounted in any city of your human The Earth. If we fail, it will be my failing. But if we succeed— as I know we will succeed!—then that success will be triumphantly your own. And now, are there any questions?"

The man in gray raised his hand. "There's no brown sugar for the tea," he complained.

"A thousand apologies, Mr. Morcher," said Binnda. "That will be remedied at once. And now, if you will all take your scores, we will run through the opening of the first act of Mozart's immortal *Idomeneo*."

"What did he mean about obstacles and objections?" I asked Norah Platt.

"Oh," she said absently, rubbing her knuckles, "you know. There's always someone objecting, isn't there. Nolly? As long as you're not otherwise engaged at the moment, my fingers are giving me fits. Would you mind turning the pages for me while I play?"

* * *

All opera stories are pretty dumb, but *Idomeneo* is a little dumber than most.

From the point of view of any baritone it has one glaring fault—there's no baritone role in it—so I suppose it's possible that I could be a little prejudiced. I think not, though. The title role is the old king, Idomeneo, sung by the old tenor, Canduccio. Canduccio's pet hate, the pale, pretty little man named Malatesta, sang the role of the king's son, Idamante, and Eloise Gatt, one of the sopranos, was Idamante's girlfriend.

The story is, frankly, too silly to discuss. But on the other hand, the story doesn't really matter, because the music is, well, Mozart. Even sight-reading on a first run-through, it was—well—beautiful. Eloise Gatt had a really sweet soprano, with that mellow cantabile swinging-along sound that goes so well in Mozart, and Malatesta . . .

When Malatesta sang his first lines a shock went through me. I'd never heard a castrato sing before.

The part Malatesta was singing was written for a castrato in the first place. Of course, I'd never heard it sung that way. Due to the twentieth-century shortage of that particular type of performer, I couldn't have. The shortage hadn't begun in the twentieth century. Mozart himself had had to rescore the part for a tenor after the first production, because even in Mozart's time it was hard to find a singer who'd let his testicles be cut off to keep his golden boy's voice all through his life, and anyway after the first performance it was mostly given by amateur companies of the nobility. All of whom were determined to keep their gender equipment intact.

But Binnda wanted to give it as written, and fortunately he had Ugolino Malatesta on hand to do it.

It was pretty funny, when you stopped to think about it, to have Malatesta singing the part of anybody's son. Malatesta was the only human on Narabedla older than Norah Platt. He spoke six languages, English as good as my own—when he was willing to use it. He generally wasn't. He was smooth-skinned and spry and his voice was beautiful, and the single thing that gave away his age—not counting that chopping the testicles off young boys with beautiful voices had been out of style for a couple of centuries—was that he really didn't want to make the effort to speak in anything but his native Italian.

But his voice! It was a wonder. It wasn't just a soprano.

He could pull out of those old pipes a perfectly pure high C, fit for any pretty young coloratura, but the timbre was not like that of any woman who ever lived. It was unearthly. It was colder than a woman's voice, more majestic, more detached. It wasn't a boy's voice, either, because no boy soprano had ever had that much lung power. The top of his range was what I would have called a falsetto in any intact male singer—but there was nothing false about it in Malatesta—and there it had no sex at all. It had nothing to do with Mimi or Cio-Cio-San. It was simply a limpid, quicksilver miracle.

Malatesta knocked me out. If mumps had given me that voice, instead of simply wrecking my baritone, I might have learned to reconcile myself to the mumps . . . almost.

The other singers were all superb, too. The two sopranos, the gaunt, dark Electra and the plump, pretty little Ilia, could have sung in any hall on Earth. When we came to the Neptune, sung by the balding redheaded man, I suddenly realized where I'd seen him before. Eamon McGuire. Of course! It had been in Santa Fe, at the open-air opera. McGuire had sung the Commendatore in *Don Giovanni*. A long time ago, when I was still turning up at rehearsals in the hope of a last-minute fill-in, I'd gone backstage to ingratiate myself with him on the chance that, some day, I might sing the Don opposite him. Then he had dropped out of sight, and for twenty years or so he had from time to time been the subject of one of those whatever-became-of sessions. Drank himself to death, most people thought.

But now I knew what he had drunk himself to.

The second tenor part was the silent gray man who had complained about the lack of brown sugar, Floyd Morcher. I didn't have much trouble committing his name to memory because during the break he walked over to me and silently pressed a card into my hand. He turned away without waiting for me to read it. He didn't seem to welcome conversation.

The card said:

Jesus can help you even here.
I have services every Sabbath.

At the bottom he had signed his name. I stared after him, wondering exactly what kind of help he was offering. I hadn't forgotten there were flaws in this Paradise. I wondered what

Morcher thought of people who thought a good way to pun-
ish somebody was to have him eaten alive, in public, and
run the whole terrible event in slow-motion film so that it
would *last?*

From time to time we had an audience. They came and
went, human and alien. I saw Barak—well, I smelled him
before I saw him, but when I looked up there he was, burping
furiously at an alien that looked like a shrimp. I saw Tricia
Madigan briefly, with that huge, skinny black man I'd seen
her with in the bar. He was so tall that out of the corner of
my eye I'd taken him for one of the skinny, biped aliens with
the pine-needle Mohawks. But when I looked closer he was
human enough, and not that big—he was over seven feet,
but the aliens were sometimes double that. Tricia and he
watched for ten minutes or so, then Tricia blew me a friendly
kiss and they went out. Half a dozen aliens drifted in to
watch, and sometimes their chattering (or hissing or screeching) to each other caused Binnda to turn and wave his arm
at them reprovingly. One of them was one of those bedbug
things of the Mother's, the rest were only vaguely familiar—
especially one of the ones that hung from the tree.

After an hour Binnda declared a break. The singers went
off for tipple of their own—the soprano had said something
revolting about a teaspoonful of olive oil—and Norah Platt
offered me a cup of tea.

"Going well, isn't it?" she offered.

"I suppose so. Norah? I've been wondering about something. How come you're playing for us when we could have
Purry do a full orchestral accompaniment?"

All I had really meant by that was that I would have liked
having Purry present—he was about the closest thing I had
to a friend in that place. I had hurt her feelings. She said
with indignation, "Truly, Knollwood, would you actually
prefer that *thing* to a real, live artist? I know I've played a
few clinkers"—I restrained myself from agreeing—"and
I'm sorry for that. The old arthritis, I'm afraid. It's rather
awful today in the knuckles and the neck. And, of course,
the joints. But music isn't just *technique*. It's also *feeling,*
and how can one get that from a Purry?"

"Don't worry, my boy," said Binnda, coming up from
behind me. "We'll have the full orchestra for the dress re-

hearsal, this is just to get us together for a preliminary run-through. How did you like Malatesta? Simply superb voice! You don't hear that kind of thing at the Met or Covent Garden these days, do you? And now, let's get on to the second act."

And we did, and as Norah was cueing the Idamante for his first aria, I looked back at the dozen or so beings milling around in the seats, tanks, and perches. Most of them were weirdos, but a couple were human, and one of the humans was Woody Calderon.

When Binnda declared a lunch break I jumped down from the stage and grabbed Woody before he could get away.

He looked as cheerfully inept as ever as he pumped my hand. "Gee, Nolly, it's great to see you! And singing, they tell me! That's wonderful! Soon as you get over that little cold you've got, or whatever it is." He grinned apologetically at me. Then he said, "I heard you were here. Gosh. I hope it wasn't because of me or anything like that."

What I would have said to that I don't know, because what can you say to a Woody Calderon? Binnda came bustling up behind us and saved me the necessity. "Why, Woody," he called genially, "you're back from the Xseni planet, I see? I hear you were a great success! Join us for lunch? I've got a simple collation laid out in the courtyard."

"Oh, boy," Calderon said happily. "Come on, Nolly! You don't want to miss this!"

When we got outside I saw why. Meretekabinnda's idea of a simple collation was copied closely, I was sure, from the last opera gala he had sneaked into. It was an open-air luncheon, in an enclosed courtyard. The yard was planted like an English garden. White-linened tables were spread with canapés, fresh fruit, cut-glass bowls of reddish liquid with ice floating in it—"Nothing alcoholic, dear boy," Binnda rasped to me, "for we do have work this afternoon, don't we?"—and those slim, tiny Oriental-looking Kekkety servants hovering around to fill a fresh plate or whisk away a used one.

"Wow!" Woody Calderon grinned. "Smoked oysters!" They were, on top of Ritz crackers, held in place by Philadelphia brand cream cheese that had been tinted pink with paprika; there was also Beluga caviar, some other kind of crackers with more cream cheese, this time green and tasting of chives, with a little anchovy strip laid across each one, and cold shrimp that had not come out of a can, and five or six kinds of cheeses, Gouda and Edam and Brie and Port Salut and ripe, moldy Stilton. It wasn't exactly a lunch, but the rest of the cast gobbled it up, and so did Meretekabinnda.

When Woody had filled his plate I took him aside. There was a bench at the far end of the courtyard, under a flowering peach tree. I sat him down in it and said, "I've got an important question for you. Do you want to stay here?"

He choked on a macadamia nut. "Stay here? What do you mean, Nolly? We signed a contract!"

"*I* didn't! I was kidnapped."

"Gee, Nolly," he said remorsefully, "I heard something about that. I'm sorry. I honestly can't help thinking that it's kind of my fault, in a way. But, you know, this isn't so bad, is it? I mean, we've got work, we've got—"

I didn't want to hear the standard litany. "I want to go home!"

He stared at me through his Woody Allen glasses, honestly perplexed. "Why, Nolly?"

"We've been kidnapped, for Christ's sake! Isn't that reason enough?"

"Well, sure, there's that," he said reasonably, "but look at the good side. There's no I.R.S. here, you know. Nobody hassles me. It's not like back home, where nobody knew I was alive except the bill collectors and the critics that hated me."

I stopped for a minute, because an idea had just occurred to me. "Wait a minute," I said.

"Wait for what?" he asked defensively.

"The critics! I just thought of something. You really did get some lousy notices, didn't you? And suddenly I begin to suspect I know why."

"Well," he began, "you know how it is with critics."

I shook my head. "You know what I think? I think Henry Davidson-Jones got to some of those critics."

His jaw dropped. He forgot to swallow the latest smoked oyster.

"Figure it out for yourself, Woody." I was getting excited. "It makes sense. Davidson-Jones wants artists for Narabedla. Good ones—I mean, were you listening to those people today? They could've been stars back home! But stars have reputations, and if they've got reputations someone's going to miss them when they just disappear. Oh, sure, they cover it up—there was that fake plane crash for you. But if a lot of *famous* musicians all got wasted in a year, there'd be talk. He doesn't want talk."

Woody was looking at me with those unhappy, gentle sheep's eyes, trying to follow what I was saying. "He wouldn't do anything like that! Would he?"

"Wouldn't he? All he has to do is keep you from getting famous. That's easy; he gets to the people who make reputations. The critics."

"He *couldn't*."

"Of course he could," I said firmly, because the longer I talked the surer I became that I was right. "He could do it easily. He doesn't have to bribe them or anything, Woody, he's *Henry Davidson-Jones*. He says to one of them, 'Pity about poor Calderon, did you hear that sour note in the adagio?' and to another one, 'Well, young Calderon's playing a little better tonight, but you should have heard him last week in Phoenix. *Pathetic.*' And what critic is going to argue with the guy who underwrites the benefits and gives the prizes and pays for the scholarships?"

"Oh, my God," Woody moaned.

"So you don't owe him a thing," I finished.

"God," he repeated. I had him convinced then. I was sure of it.

But then I could feel him slipping away. He took another tiny sandwich and munched on it, thinking. "Well, maybe that's true," he said, "but it doesn't change anything, does it?"

"What do you mean, it doesn't change anything?"

"No, really," he insisted, beginning to get stubborn. "I've still got a good deal here. I don't have to do fry-chef work at McDonald's when I don't have an engagement, because Mr. Shipperton gets me all the engagements I can handle. And they pay in real money, you know. I've got a Swiss bank account, just like I was some big drug dealer! And—well, *listen,*" he said, beginning to glow, "you know what? There's a 1753 Guarnerius cello that's coming up for auction at Sotheby's pretty soon. I don't have enough nearly to pay for any of those big old instruments, of course, but I've got the catalogue; this one's been pretty well messed up and a lot restored, and it might go for under a hundred thousand,

and Mr. Shipperton says they'll advance me the price and I can pay back as I earn. I mean, a *Guarnerius,* Nolly! Mr. Shipperton says the folks here would like to see one anyway. Mr. Shipperton says if I want to put a bid in he'll have somebody cover the auction. Mr. Shipperton says—''

"Mr. Shipperton says 'Jump,'" I said bitterly, "and all you say is, 'How high?'"

He stopped chewing and looked at me. His eyes were hurt.

"You don't have to take that attitude, Nolly."

"There's nothing wrong with *my* attitude. What's the use of owning an expensive cello if nobody hears you play it?"

"I'll hear me! About a million Aiurdi and J'zeels and all those'll hear me."

"I'm talking about human audiences. Back in the U.S.A., where you belong."

"Well, see, Nolly," he said, "when I was back in the U.S.A. I didn't have any of those big audiences, did I? Now I do, and they're pretty nice people."

"Nice people don't get other people eaten up by monsters in a public place!"

"Oh, yeah," he said, nodding wisely, "you mean Jerry Harper. It's really too bad about Jerry. But, you know, he really was asking for it. You ought to remember, he started out by trying to sneak into a jump station."

"A what?"

"A jump station. A long-distance go-box. What you came here in," he explained. "The go-box thing they use to get you across space, you know? And then they put him in slow time and all and when he came out he just went ape. Blamed the people who caught him—well, they were human beings, too, and he kind of thought all us humans ought to stick together, so when they turned him in he got pretty cheesed off. But that didn't excuse burning them to death!"

I looked around. One of the Kekkety folk was coming toward us, his eyes on Woody's empty plate, but I waved him away. No one else was near.

"Woody," I said, "I want to know everything you know about these jump stations."

He looked worried. "What for?"

I said, "Because they're how you get home. I want to do that. Don't you think you owe me a little help? If it wasn't for you I wouldn't be here."

"Aw, Nolly," he said miserably, "you know I'd do anything in the world for you—"

"Not just for me. There's Marlene."

"What about Marlene?" And when I told him what Shipperton had threatened his eyes got round and worried behind the glasses. "Oh, I wouldn't want anything to happen to Marlene," he said unhappily. "But, gosh, what can I do?"

"Help me get back! Tell me how to get into a jump station."

"But there isn't any way! There are two or three of them on Narabedla, but they're all on levels you can't get to without Binnda or somebody to take you there, and anyway they're guarded all the time. Only the Tlotta drones can operate them, see? At least that's the way it is here; maybe on some of the out planets they're kind of sloppy. I mean, like a month or so ago when I came back here from the Tsigli planet they actually *asked* me where I wanted to go, if you can imagine."

I could imagine. My heart thumped.

I controlled my voice. "What would have happened if you'd just said you wanted to go to the Earth?"

"Oh, no, they weren't going to let me do *that,* Nolly," he said, shaking his head. "The drones wouldn't take me there without authorization from the Mother. Anyway, they'd have to know exactly what station you were going to. There's only one station on Earth, and that's on Mr. Davidson-Jones's yacht. You couldn't just tell them the *planet.* You'd have to tell them what you wanted was the *yacht,* do you see."

I kept my voice level. "And suppose you'd said that? That you wanted to go to Mr. Henry Davidson-Jones's yacht?"

He thought for a moment. "Why, I don't know. They'd ask their local Mother, of course, but she might not stop it. They're pretty sloppy on the Tsigli planet; it's a kind of a joke around here, you know."

I frowned. "But if it's as easy as that, why didn't Jerry Harper do it that way?"

"Oh, but that was what he was going to try next," said Woody. "Only he wanted to get even with those other guys first, you see? Which just shows you!"

"Shows me what, Woody?"

"How you really shouldn't do anything mean, don't you

see? Because if Jerry hadn't burned them up he'd probably be home by now."

When we started again, Meretekabinnda was talking to one of the Mother's bedbugs. He came up to the stage, still talking to it, but not in English; it scurried away as I approached. "Binnda," I said, "Woody says he had a great time on the Tsigli planet. Any chance we could go there with the troupe?"

"Why not, dear boy?" he said lavishly. "After we finish the tour I'm arranging now, of course; first we keep our commitments, then we look around for new ones, don't you agree? And there's one other thing. The Mother's drone says the doctor will be free by the day after tomorrow, so we can get your pipes fixed. You'll need a bit of time for it, but then we can put off your rehearsals for a few days—"

"Now, wait a minute! I don't know about this! I have to think it over!"

"Silly boy," said Norah Platt affectionately, coming up to us. "It's nothing to worry about; I do it all the time. And honestly, Nolly, Dr. Boddadukti is about the best barber I've ever seen. As soon as he's through with—what's the matter? Oh, did I say 'barber'? Of course, these days you call them just surgeons."

"Yeah," I said. I was not impressed by Norah's recommendation. The best barber-surgeon of her time, from the days when the same man did both surgery and hair-cutting, would have been about up to the level of a present-day supermarket meat-cutter.

Norah said, "Tell you what. I'm about due myself, Nolly. I'll go in with you, and we can both get fixed up at the same time. The day after tomorrow? Yes, why not? Just don't do any heavy drinking tomorrow night, there's a good boy, because Dr. Boddadukti might think that was the normal state of your blood chemistry and you'd come out of the operation roaring drunk!"

CHAPTER
19

Meretekabinnda's idea of beginning to stage an opera was pretty straightforward. He lined up the principal singers, gestured to Norah Platt to begin, and let them sing out straight through. It was pure oratorio style, with no attempt at moving them around. After lunch I went to the seats in the back of the house and leaned back, enjoying the music. Enjoying as much as I heard of it, anyway. The thought of this Dr. Boddadukti, whoever he was, performing surgery on my one and only body, kept getting between me and the opera.

"Catching some z's?" said a voice from behind me. It was Tricia Madigan.

I smelled her before I straightened up to look at her, a pretty, feminine scent of perfume and girl, mixed with a heavier, sweeter aroma of musk oil. She wasn't alone. The sweet musk scent came from the big black guy she was with. "You don't know Conjur, do you? This is Conjur Kowalski. You two guys ought to be friends, 'cause we're going to be seeing a lot of each other on the tour."

Perplexed, I shook his hand. It was a big one. He could have wrapped it completely around mine, and I was pretty sure that if he'd wanted to he could have squeezed mine into pulp. (Nolly, Nolly, I told myself, you have *got* to get back into shape.) He was good-looking, too—maple-walnut ice cream colored, with a Roman nose and an Afro hairdo. "Did you say you were going to be on the tour?"

Kowalski laughed, a deep voiced, friendly, we're-all-in-this-together kind of laugh. "That damn Binnda, he don't tell you nothing. We're like your double feature, you know what I'm saying?"

And Tricia explained, phrasing it as politely as she could, "Well, you know, Nolly, not all the funnies go ape for opera.

143

So Binnda thought he ought to put in some extra hooks to build the old box office up. That's us.''

I looked from one to the other. "You're going to sing?"

"Aw, no, Nolly. Conjur and I do a kind of act. We started—when was it, Conj? About a month ago? There was a kind of . . . Well, I guess you could call it . . . Well, the closest thing is the funnies had some sort of little convention, as you might say, on the B'kerkyi planet—wow, is that a weird place!—you know, a conference about something or other. Anyway, they're not that different from you and I, hon. They like to have a little fun along with their business, so Binnda brought us out there to play for them. We did our show and they loved it."

I looked from her to Conjur Kowalski. "What kind of show was that?"

She gave me a look of startled amusement. "Aw, you rascal, I don't mean anything *bad*. Like vaudeville, you know? I did my baton things. Conjur did mostly break-dancing. It's not his main thing, but the old Harlem Globe Trotters don't go over very well—"

"Those dudes are *not* Globe Trotters," rumbled Kowalski.

"No, 'course not. Only Jonesy must've thought they could do the same thing when he signed them on, only it doesn't work out here. And, hey, Conjur doesn't get along with them too well, do you, hon? When Conjur plays anything he likes to *win*."

I scowled at her. "Is that what you're going to do in the opera? Baton-twirling and break-dancing?"

"No, no, not *in* the opera! *After* the opera, maybe—like, it'll be a kind of a double feature. And anyway we're working up a new act."

"Which we best go practice some," said Conjur Kowalski, looking past me, "because here comes the Man." The Man, in this case, was Sam Shipperton, leading a dark, short, stocky man into the rehearsal hall.

"Sure, hon," Tricia said, getting up. "Anyway, Nolly," she said to me, "we just thought we'd look in on you folks to see how things were going. Come see us when you get a minute, okay?"

"You bet," I said, not really listening to her. Shipperton had brought his charge up to the stage, and Binnda had stopped the rehearsal to introduce him.

"Our other tenor," he said proudly. "Our good friend, Dmitri Arkashvili, who will sing the High Priest of Neptune. And just in time, my dear Dmitri, because we have almost reached your entrance cue."

"I've been digging them up for you as fast as I can," Sam Shipperton complained.

"Of course you have, of course you have. And doing a perfectly splendid job of it, too! Now, if we can resume from bar eighty—oh, dear, now what is it?"

One of the Mother's little bedbugs came skittering up to the piano, reared on its hind legs, and twittered at Binnda, whereupon he threw up his sinuous hands. "Take ten, everyone," he called and hurried over to the skry at the side of the stage. He began to chatter at it, and at once it lit up with the faces of half a dozen aliens, all different.

As I came up toward the stage to get a better look, Norah Platt addressed the bedbug. "What's going on?" she asked.

"I have only been told to inform Meretekabinnda he is needed," it said. Its voice was high and twittering, but what surprised me was that it spoke English at all. ("But of course they speak anything they like," Norah said tolerantly when I turned to her. "They're the *Mother*'s.")

The conversation over the skry seemed agitated. "Is it something about the rehearsal?" I asked Norah.

She was massaging her knuckles. "Oh, who can say?" she said fretfully. "I don't think it's anything to do with us, though—look, there's a J'zeel there, and they don't care about opera. I expect it's some Fifteen Peoples thing, Nolly. It'll sort itself out."

It didn't take long. Binnda snapped something angrily at the screen, the skry went blank, and he came back to us, muttering to himself. He stood in thoughtful silence for a moment, then climbed up on a chair. "Dear friends," he called, "I regret to have to tell you that my presence is required elsewhere, and so we must adjourn our rehearsal for today. I'm sorry. It's this Andromeda thing, you know; some last-minute details to be dealt with before the launch. But I'm sure it will all be straightened out by tomorrow." And then, as the company was stirring itself to leave, he came over to me, Ugolino Malatesta in tow.

"What a nuisance, my dear boy," he twinkled—it was amazing how close he could come to having very nearly human expressions on that wholly nonhuman face. "But I have a suggestion for you. It's been quite a long time since you sang in public, hasn't it? And one's skills need brightening after a long layoff? Well, dear Ugolino never seems to tire, and he's offered to coach you."

I blinked at him. "Coach me?"

"Oh, not that you need it, really—but it has been years, after all, and Ugolino is *so* good at technique. So if you won't take it amiss . . ."

What he said made perfect sense. I told him, "I won't take it amiss. I'll appreciate all the help I can get."

"Wonderful! And now"—he made a humorous grimace— "I'm off to see if I can get the Ossps and the J'zeel to agree on a launch time!"

Malatesta explained that his own home was pretty far away, and so we'd do better to have our first session in my own. In slow, careful, accented English, he said that, after all, the way to get started was to start, and no time was better than now. I had no objection at all.

As we passed through Execution Square I averted my eyes from the horrid scene. This time it wasn't deserted. There were six or eight people standing around, gazing at it curiously, like rubberneckers at a car crash. Malatesta muttered something I couldn't understand, but I didn't think it mattered. He was making the sign to ward off the evil eye, and I didn't think he was talking to me. Actually, I didn't comprehend very much at all of what he said to me for the first little while, because I made the mistake of letting him know I understood a little Italian, and that was all he needed. English vanished from his repertory. All future conversations were in Italian, and what I didn't grasp I had to get along without.

Once inside my house he got right to work. The language problem was small; there was no chitchat. He was a businesslike and hardworking teacher.

I was glad of his impersonal attitude. I would not have known how to take him if he had tried intimacy. When I looked at Malatesta, what I saw was myself. There was nothing effeminate about him; he didn't give off that aura of sexual interest that I sometimes got from gays. When we were working, which was almost all of that long, hard five-hour first session, he wasn't a person at all. He was a teaching machine. He stood me before my mirror and had me watch my mouth move, peer at the vibrations of my Adam's apple, pour out the vowels on the scale: *"Ah ah ah ah ah ah ah. Ee ee ee ee ee ee ee . . ."* endlessly up and down the full span of my register. And always instruction. "You must sing," Malatesta instructed, "off the *top* of your voice. It is the second most important rule of singing, that."

And all the other rules followed. Never shout. (Certainly not when I was singing, for that was a horrid, wolfish sound; but never at any other time, either, because that strained the vocal cords.) Keep the throat always warm. (If I were to visit the planet of the Quihigs, for example, I must always wear a natural wool scarf around my neck, *always,* because the Quihigs lived on a world of frequent chill drafts.) Get plenty of sleep. (A tired voice was a bad voice.) Always start the day's vocalizing in the middle register—it is time enough to reach for the upper and lower notes when the voice is warm, not before. Swallow at least four ounces of heavy cream, better still olive oil (but I must secure my own supplies of olive oil, he could not spare any of his) before each performance. Never press the voice when it is not right; it is better to cancel a performance than to give a bad one. Do not smoke! (Yes, he admitted, even that young fellow Caruso enjoyed an occasional cigar—one had heard his records, of course—but see what happened to Caruso, dead of throat cancer in his prime.) And, above all, to breathe one must always be sure to open up the *bottom* of one's throat, because that (at last) was Rule Number One.

And as I was singing my scales Malatesta was walking around me, studying my posture, watching my eyes to see if I was straining. He touched me all over with his papery hands, touched the breastbone, the cheekbones, the larynx, the lips—he even reached into my mouth and placed a feathery-light fingertip on my front teeth to feel if I was getting maximum reinforcement from the hard resonators in the skull. "It cannot all come from the throat, but," he instructed, "you must use your sounding boards to make the tone come out full and pure, have you understood?"

I had understood. I was even grateful. I was beginning to feel like a singer again.

I hardly remembered I was on Narabedla.

If there was anything wrong with Malatesta as a coach, it was only that some of his ideas seemed a few centuries out of date. I don't mean his sense of anatomy or his recipes for voice production. They were as good as any I had ever heard, in all my early years of teaching and practice. It was his ideas on performance that sounded peculiar. He insisted that I fill my lungs at every chance; that I take in all the air I could, so that I could release it in song with ease and comfort. That part was all right; but Malatesta was never satisfied unless he could actually hear me gasp from all the way across the room. I tried to object to that. Modern audiences, I told him, did not like to hear their singers suck air, no matter what it had been like in 1767. He laughed at me. "Modern!" he jeered. "But these audiences here, they are completely primitive! They are not in the least modern, those ones!"

How noisily the air entered my lungs, he insisted, did not matter at all. What was important was how it sounded when it came out—smooth, effortless, brilliant, with no change in quality from the bottom of my range to the tricky As and even Bs at the top.

Conversation wasn't difficult as long as he stuck to singing and talking about singing. That much Italian vocabulary had stayed with me. It was harder when we took a break and I got up the nerve to ask him about his, ah, condition.

He didn't take offense. He seemed to think it was perfectly normal to discuss his castration; only he would only do it in his native language. He was willing to speak fairly slowly, with good diction and using simple grammatical forms; even so, when he said, *"Ogn'anno, quattro mille ragazzi di dodici anni"*—he made a scissoring gesture with two fingers of his right hand—"tsit, tsit, *e dopo sono tutti castrati come me,"* I had to rehearse it for a moment before I understood he was telling me that four thousand boys got gelded every year. Then, when I must have flinched, he grinned. *"Hai paura, tu?"*

He was asking if the idea scared me. It did, though I didn't tell him why I had such a personal interest in it. I asked, *"Ma, perche?"*

He shrugged. *"La chiesa l'ha detto, hai capito?"* And when I frowned, he repeated, *"La chiesa."* And then, making a sign of the cross, *"Il Bibolo."*

"Ah," I said. "The *Bible*." It took a while, because my operatic Italian was not up to theological discussions, but it developed that what he was trying to tell me was that the purpose of this wholesale gelding was religious. It seemed there was an injunction in the Bible that forbade women singing in church, so the only adult sopranos they could have in their eighteenth-century choirs had to be manufactured. Boys were available, yes. But boys did not have the lung capacity, the muscles, the breath reserve of a grown-up. So they cut the ducts to the testicles to save the voices, and the choirmasters, piously deploring the horrid practice of child castration, never hesitated to employ the results.

Later on I tried to check up on what Malatesta had told me. It wasn't easy to find the right verse in the Bible. For that matter, it wasn't easy to find a Bible on Narabedla, until I thought to borrow one from Floyd Morcher; but I finally did locate it. I Corinthians 14–34. The key sentence was, "Let your women keep silence in the churches."

Four thousand a year . . . Narabedla suddenly did not seem so bad.

For five hours I tried to please him. Then I begged for rest. *"Ma, che cosa adesso?"* he demanded.

I said apologetically, "I'm tired. It's difficult, after all this time."

He stared at me in amazement. "You call this difficult? But if you could only know! As a child at the Conservatorio Sant'Onofrio I each morning must rise two hours before the sun to work. All day to work! To sing, study, work till eight o'clock in the night—it is in that way that one becomes a truly skilled singer!"

I said humbly, "But, maestro, I have not practiced in many years."

I thought he was pleased at the "maestro." He sniffed, but then he said, "Then, all right. Now! Let us have a simple drink together, and then I will leave you for this first lesson. *Camerriere!*" One of the Kekketies popped out of the kitchen, listened to Malatesta's quick order, in Italian so rapid-fire I could catch none of it, and returned in a moment with cups of hot, honey-sweet wine.

And all this time, five long hours of it, I had hardly remembered that I was on Narabedla, or that a few yards from my door a hideous monster was ponderously thrusting its fangs into the throat of a human being, or that I was to undergo surgery soon, or that Marlene Abramson and Irene Madigan, back on Earth, were endangered and worried.

I was *singing*.

Even Malatesta no longer seemed like a wretched victim of a barbarous mutilation. He was simply a colleague. He took as much pleasure as I did in the task of getting me ready to sing again. When he sank back, inhaling the steam from the cup, tasting it slowly and pleasurably, smiling at me out of those old, shrewd eyes—he was not only my maestro, he was very close to being my friend.

By the second glass he was boasting of his own exploits. He had studied with the great Farinelli; he had sung leads in Venice, Naples, and Vienna, in operas by Sarti, Galuppi, and Paisiello. (To him, Mozart was one of the new kids on the block. He hadn't been born until Malatesta's career was long over.) But when I tried to get him to tell me how he had come to Narabedla he suddenly became unable to understand me. To change the subject he went so far as to try a little English on me: "Is good, this wine, Knoll-a-wood, is that not true? And with the ladies is also very good, you understand?"

I nodded appreciatively to show that I understood, although in fact I didn't. "It is too bad," I said, as delicately as I could in the Italian that was only slowly coming back to me, "that such opportunities do not arise for you."

He gazed at me indignantly. His comprehension had cleared up as though by magic. "But for why should such opportunity not arise? Can I not make the love?"

I goggled at him.

"No, in truth!" he insisted. "One retains the essential instrument, is that not so? To become a father, all right, I agree, that cannot be, but to penetrate the charming parts of some fine woman, yes, certainly! One does so quite often, my dear Knoll-a-wood, with many beautiful ladies, not excluding the extremely charming Madam Norah."

Norah *Platt*? My eyes bulged. He gazed at me with a perplexed expression. Then he understood. Or remembered. "Ah, Knoll-a-wood," he cried. "But you are the one who— You suffered the malady which— Even though you possess the small jewels— But not to be able . . ." His voice trailed off and he gazed mournfully at me. "Ah, my poor little man," he whispered, and set down his empty glass, and patted me on the shoulder in the manner of somebody who is commiserating for a misfortune so terrible that it cannot be named aloud, and left.

And I was back in Narabedla, with all my worries, fears, and angers intact enough to make that night, too, one that was short on sleep.

CHAPTER
20

The next morning I woke early. I ran a mile round and round through the silent, empty streets, while the make-believe sky overhead paled and warmed and turned into morning sunlight.

Running is good for thinking. There isn't anybody to talk to. There isn't any phone to ring, or radio or TV (or skry) to interrupt. By the time I'd run my mile I had made a mental list of all the questions I wanted answered, and all the half-answers I needed explained. As soon as I'd showered and dressed I sat down with the book and the skry, trying to fill in the gaps in what I knew. It was time to get serious.

First, about the go-boxes, particularly the interstellar variety: could I use them?

Neither book nor skry answered that for me. It wasn't that the skry was unwilling to display any information I asked for; it was that the information about go-boxes was incomprehensible to me. The only solid fact I retained was that, yes, every interstellar box was operated by one of the "Eyes of the Mother"—the little bedbug things that were all over. What were the Eyes of the Mother? They were the unsexed "workers" that came from the eggs the real Mother had laid when she had not been recently visited by a male.

No help there; so what about the special transportation system the Kekketies used? I found no answer to that. I did find an awful lot about the Kekketies. The little brown "men" were called jur-Kekketies, and they apparently only existed on Narabedla itself and on Henry Davidson-Jones's yacht. Then there were the din-Kekketies, like Purry; they were smart robots that could do all sorts of specialized things (like make music, or translate languages) for the needs or pleasures of people (like me, or for that matter like any of the Fifteen Associated Peoples). There were also the ftan-Kekketies, which ran the farms and supervised some kinds of machinery; they came in a variety of shapes, because form followed function and the ones that, for instance, worked underwater looked more or less like octopuses.

There was also a special kind called the kai-Kekketies which apparently didn't do anything much but grow, whereupon they were "harvested" by the ftan-Kekkety "farmers." I didn't pursue that subject very far. I didn't want to know exactly what kind of roast I had eaten at Norah Platt's dinner party.

The Kekketies, it seemed, were indeed robots, but not the kind that you bought in a toy store. They were *organic* robots—more or less the kind Karel Čapek had meant when he coined the words, I supposed. And they were a fairly recent innovation in the lives of the Fifteen Associated Peoples. They had been pioneered by the Ossps, who had been admitted to membership as one of the Peoples only a couple of hundred years ago.

That was going nowhere useful. I got up, poured myself another cup of coffee, and started along a different line. What was this Bach'het trouble that had stirred the Fifteen Associated Peoples up?

According to Canduccio's book, the Bach'het were one of the four founding members of the Associated Peoples. The Duntidons (I knew who they were, all right) and the Bach'het (they looked more or less like eight-foot-long anteaters, and they communicated by flashing colors on their hindquarters, like fireflies) had come from planets of a pair of long-period double stars, and they had been fighting an interstellar war for a hundred years or more when Barak's people, the Ggressna, discovered them. The Ggressna had already begun exploring interstellar space with robot probes, and either the Bach'het or the Duntidons, the book didn't say which, had destroyed the probes, though not before information had been returned to the Ggressna.

A couple of hundred years later the Ggressna came back. By then they had discovered the go-box, so once their probes got to the Bach'het and Duntidon systems they had quick two-way transportation. Also they had made contact with the Tlotta—the Mothers and their workers and males—who were pretty smart, too.

Then (I skipped over some of the details) the Duntidons and the Bach'het acquired go-boxes of their own. The Bach'het launched an attack on the Duntidons; the Duntidons responded by blowing up the Bach'het star.

That ended the war. The only Bach'het to survive were the few remaining from the invasion forces. The Duntidons didn't come out of it too well, either, because a year or so later, when the shock wave radiation from the Bach'het nova reached their own planet, their unprotected biota got pretty well fried.

The Ggressna didn't care for people blowing up other people's stars. Their first impulse was to wipe out the Duntidons. The Mothers dissuaded them; and so they offered the Duntidons membership in a federation, on condition that they submit to antiwar control and inspection; and that was the beginning of the Associated Peoples. Then (skipping to the present) the few remaining Bach'het, now multiplied to a million or so and living in scattered colonies on other people's planets, wanted a homeland of their own, and so they had laid claim to a recently discovered planet.

That was the Bach'het affair. It had taken me half an hour to find it all out, and it was getting close to time for Norah Platt to come by to escort me to the day's rehearsals.

What had I learned?

Nothing very useful, as far as I could see. The big question was whether I could get home. The bedbugs were the key to that, I decided; and so I went back to the Tlottas.

By the time there was a scratching at my door I had learned a lot about the Tlottas. They were the peacekeepers of the Associated Peoples. The bedbugs, the "Eyes of the Mother," had the free run of everything, everywhere. They saw everything, and reported back to their Mothers; and the Mothers were insatiably curious.

I had a question for Norah when I opened the door, but it wasn't Norah who was gazing up at me cheerfully. It was my little ocarina friend, Purry. "Good morning, Mr. Stennis," he caroled. "I hope you had a pleasant night?"

"Marvelous," I said. "Where's Norah?"

"I'm sorry to say that Ms. Platt isn't feeling well today," he informed me, "so I've come to take you to the rehearsal."

"It's on, then?"

"Oh, yes, Mr. Stennis. Meretekabinnda finished his business with the committee on the Andromeda probe. He specially asked me to tell you that he's counting on you to be there this morning. He has a surprise for you."

"A surprise?"

"Actually," said Purry happily, "two surprises, but I think it's all right for me to tell you one of them. He's got the sets for *Idomeneo,* and he's really anxious to have your opinion of them."

So once again the opera singer took over from the dedicated dissident in my mind. I got to the rehearsal hall eager to find out what the "surprise" was, and then even that faded in my mind as I saw what was going on. I was *entranced* at what was happening there.

They were running through the whole of *Idomeneo,* as before. But it was not like any first run-through I had ever seen on Earth. In my experience, no one on Earth would have had a costume yet. In early run-throughs you're likely to get your Brünnhilde in a miniskirt and your Queen of the Night with curlers in her hair. The Commendatore doesn't come through a trapdoor out of hell. He ducks under the outstretched arm of a stagehand to deliver his doom-laden lines. And, of course, they do it all on a perfectly bare stage.

That's how it goes on Earth.

On Narabedla that (as with most other things) was very different. The principal singers all did have costumes; they were busy getting into them when I got there. Those remote-control clothes-producers had been busy all night, I supposed, and gaudy threads indeed they had produced. Mozart would have been delighted.

And then there were the sets.

The sets! But "sets" is the wrong word. On Narabedla they didn't use the conventional flats and backdrops. What they used were something very like holograms. You could see them. You couldn't touch them; there was nothing there to touch, nothing but light. When Binnda commanded, "Sets on!" they sprang up out of nowhere. I moved around the sets, staring at them. They were utterly solid-looking. And really three-dimensional; from out in the audience seats, or even from any corner of the stage itself, they looked incredibly and opulently *real*.

When the first *Idomeneo* scene appeared I gasped. Even the other singers looked startled, and Binnda was in heaven. "Do you like it?" he begged the cast, almost hopping with pleasure. "Here, look at the others!" And, as one by one they flashed into being, he catalogued them for us. "The throne room is from the La Scala production, the opening of the second act is copied from Bournemouth, and the last one is taken from the Leningrad Kirov Theater; I took the original pictures myself!"

There was a murmur of appreciation from the singers—almost unanimous. The exception was the Electra. She sniffed frostily. She was the dark, cadaverous-looking one, and her name (I got Purry to remind me) was Sue-Mary Petticardi. "*Idomeneo*," she said—she had just the trace of an accent, maybe French—"is set on the ancient Greek island of Crete, not in Egypt. I recognize that throne set. It does not at all belong to this opera. It comes from *Aida*."

Binnda pouted. "In our view," he explained, "the set is quite authentic. It faithfully represents your The Earth. Now! Places! First act! Purry, the overture, if you please!"

Norah Platt came limping in while they were still singing and sat down quietly next to me. I didn't ask her how she was; I could see by the strain on her face that her "old bones" were giving her fits. When they had finished the run-through Binnda disappeared for a moment to confer with somebody, and I walked around, congratulating the cast. I meant every word. They had been, well, sublime.

Then Binnda came back in. "We have time," he said, "for a quick run-through of our second opera. It will be *Pagliacci*. The Kekketies have the scores."

That's how I found out what the second surprise was. We were rehearsing *Pagliacci,* and I was to sing the Tonio.

"But I'm not ready, Binnda," I complained, half happy, half struck with sudden stage fright.

"No, of course," he agreed. "Don't worry about it. Simply do not sing too loud. And shall I tell you the other half of your surprise? Our third opera is to be again Mozart—

the Mother has requested that—and it will be *Don Giovanni,* with you singing the Don!" He grinned at me happily, the bright green tongue licking out of that horrid little mouth.

It was an ugly enough spectacle, but I could have kissed him. "Remember that you are not quite ready yet, dear boy," he cautioned. "So if you sing too loudly it will throw the other singers off."

"But you will be singing with the rest of them very soon," promised Norah Platt, putting a motherly hand on my shoulder, and Malatesta echoed, in Italian,

"Subito, subito cantare bellissimo, Knoll-a-wood!"

It was a heartening vote of confidence, but not unanimous. Floyd Morcher, who was singing the Canio, remained his usual isolated self, vocalizing at half voice off in one corner of the stage, and the Silvio was a man I had not met before named Rufus Connery. He didn't speak at all, only stood there with hostile patience, waiting for the rehearsal to begin. But I was pretty sure that I knew why that was. It was not necessarily that he thought I sang like a skunk. It was just that he was the other baritone in the troupe. I had sung the Silvio to somebody else's Tonio often enough to understand that Connery was not very likely to admire the voice of whoever was singing the larger role.

For I was the Tonio, all right. I got to open with the show-stopping Prologue; and, when we at last started, with Malatesta alternately nodding and frowning at me, signing when I should breathe and urging the top tones out of my mouth, I really did it pretty well.

I felt, almost, at home.

If there is a world composed more nearly completely of make-believe than the world of opera, I cannot imagine what it is. The stories of the operas are preposterous. The singers rarely look as though they could possibly feel and do what the roles require—the fifty-year-old Mimis and plump little Siegfrieds are chosen for voice, not plausibility. The swords are wood, the daggers are rubber, the sets are plywood and paint. (On Earth they are. On Narabedla, the sets were not even that much, being those mere immaterial shapes of light.) There is almost nothing in opera that is "real," and yet out of all this hocus-pocus and sham comes—well—*beauty*.

And anyway, although opera is a make-believe world, it is the world I had all my life wanted to live in. I actually *enjoyed* Rufus Connery's resentment. I was pleased to make an appointment to be fitted for my costumes. I let one of the Kekkety servants make me up for my role as Tonio. The greasepaint smelled good. I was home.

It almost made me forget about the cluster of spectators I had passed in Execution Square, all watching with critical interest something I turned my head away from.

Pagliacci is a short opera with a small principal cast—two baritones, two tenors, and a soprano. The Nedda was the pretty little Valley Girl, Maggie Murk; the second tenor, the Beppe, was Dmitri Arkashvili, the Russian who had sung the High Priest in the *Idomeneo* rehearsal; and, once again, they were all really good. Ruggiero Leoncavallo would have been pleased—if, also, totally freaked out by, for example, the likes of Binnda.

In the breaks I made it a point to chat with the Nedda and get on friendly terms—she has to hit me in the face with a whip, and I didn't want her to mean it—and tried to do the same with Morcher and Rufus Connery, just to keep the tension down among the cast. Connery was only professionally jealous; he would get over it by and by, I thought. Morcher simply did not choose to talk.

But his *Vesti la giubba* was as good as any I had ever heard, and that catch of the breath and controlled sob when he sings "Laugh, clown" was—well—beautiful. And it was, all in all, a happy time, right up to the moment when one of the Mother's little bedbugs skittered in to paw at Binnda for attention. When Binnda had listened to its message he clapped his snaky little hands and said:

"Ladies! Gentlemen! The Execution is finishing now! We will adjourn the rehearsals until tomorrow so that we can all go to watch the end of it!"

I don't know why I went there.

I didn't want to. I didn't know exactly what I was going to see, and didn't believe for a second that, whatever it was, I would enjoy seeing it; but everybody else was going. So I went along.

I found myself on the fringes of the Square. Maggie Murk and her tall, skinny friend, Sue-Mary Petticardi, were on one side of me, Floyd Morcher on the other. Together we were pressing forward to stare through the crowd.

It didn't at first look much different from the quick, re-

volted glimpse I'd had that morning. The monster's teeth
were buried deep in Jerry Harper's throat; the razor talons
were slicing through his breast, bones and all; Jerry Harper's
face—well, I didn't like to look at Jerry Harper's face. I
cannot enjoy the expression of agony.

The Square was densely packed with people—a good
many of them not precisely people, in the human sense.
Barak was there, elevated on the tips of his silvery starfish
arms, the eyes roving all over and the stench as bad as ever.
So were a couple of other aliens of the tall, black, praying-
mantis type, and a few of kinds I had not seen before. There
was a lot of conversation from the crowd, not all of it in
English, or even in any human language at all. Barak in particular was gasping away in that high-energy, breathy way
of his that sounded like a tire pump given voice, but he
wasn't speaking English. He lifted two of his arms com-
mandingly to wave a space through the crowd, and a group
of the little Kekkety folk came trotting through with various
items—some with folded-up cloth, one carrying a glittery
silver and crystal machine. They set the machine down next
to the "statue."

Barak choked out a sentence of command.

The servant at the machine did something to it. There was
a quick orange-colored emission from the machine—I suppose it was light, but it seemed almost to be a glowing gas
cloud—that sprang from the machine and spread to envelope
the statue.

And then the statue—came alive.

It was like a stop-motion still on a television program suddenly returned to normal action. The monster's great tail
flailed about. The pointed head with the dagger teeth shook
back and forth as it chopped at Jerry Harper's throat. Sounds
came out—a muffled roaring from the monster, a terrible
gurgling moan from Harper as he tried to struggle away.

Then Harper went limp. The Duntidon raised its head and
growled something that I knew was speech, though not in
any language I had ever understood. One of the Kekkety
folk silently handed it a towel, and it fastidiously began to
wipe Jerry Harper's blood off its face and talons.

Floyd Morcher said exultantly beside me, "An eye for an
eye, a tooth for a tooth, a life for a life!"

Maggie Murk said, "Oh, Sue-Mary, I think I'm going to
be sick!"

The servants unrolled a sort of body bag; two of them began to stuff what was left of Jerry Harper into it, while the others began to mop up the mess on the floor of the Square.

And Tricia Madigan reached forward to tug at my shoulder. "Had enough, Nolly? We're not doin' no good here, and there's going to be a bunch of people at Wanda's Place. How about if you and I and Conjur go off and crawl a couple of bars?"

Wanda's Place turned out to be the sort of refreshment place I had visited with Purry, but we didn't stay there. Conjur Kowalski took one look inside and shook his head. "Too crowded," he said. "We goin' home." He stalked ahead of us to the go-box, and where we wound up was at his personal pad.

Conjur didn't say much on the way. Neither did Tricia, because she was pouting over missing the excitement of the post-execution crowd at Wanda's Place. Neither did I, because I was trying to make sure that the queasy bustling sensation in my stomach was not going to lead to throwing up.

It is not every day that you see a helpless human being eaten up by a monster from outer space.

I concentrated my attention on Conjur Kowalski. He seemed to be as affected as I was by Jerry Harper's messy murder, but it took him a different way. Smoldering rather than sick. Conjur had a lot to smolder with. He was six long feet and ten skinny inches tall. His hands could wrap around a basketball the way I held an orange. He threw the door to his pad open and declared, "There be the booze, lady, and we wants us some *now*."

Tricia brightened. "Sit down, fellows," she said, and headed for the wet bar. She didn't ask what we wanted. She just started pouring, while Conjur stalked into the bathroom and slammed the door and I looked around.

Conjur's pad was no bigger than my own, but the plan was entirely different. He didn't have a big living room and a little bedroom. He didn't have any living room at all, except for a kind of little foyer with two chairs and a communications skry, but his bedroom took up a good deal more than 50 percent of the square footage of the apartment. The bed was round. It was also huge, big enough so that big Conjur could stretch out in it easily in any direction, with adequate room for another person (or four or five of them) besides. It was elevated on a platform a foot above the rest of the room, with the bar conveniently next to it at one point and what looked like about a ten-thousand-dollar stereo rig at another. And off in one corner, next to the bathroom door but not even screened, was a Jacuzzi big enough to hold parties in.

"Neat," I said morosely, taking the glass of J & B and ginger ale from Tricia.

"Aw, cheer up, hon," she said, depleting her own glass. She climbed up to sprawl on the huge bed, as though she had been there a time or two before, and looked at me in a friendly, chiding way. "You're not sitting down," she said. "You're all snaggle-toothed and mean, and you're gonna totally kill this party."

"Do you blame me?" I demanded.

"Who's blaming? But that thing with Jerry, hey, it happens, so why don't you just drink up and get mellow," she ordered. Then she raised her voice. "Damn you, Conjur," she called. "Are you ever coming out of there or what?"

The door opened and Conjur appeared. He had removed his shoes and they were in one hand; his pants had come off, too, and they were folded over the other forearm. What he still had on was a sort of Mexican-looking lightweight open-necked shirt and pale green jockey shorts. He hung the trousers up in a closet, neatly arranging the creases to match, and pulled on a pair of jogging shorts while he talked. They were partly green, too, pale green and white, and they were just about the right color to go with his café-au-lait skin. He had the longest legs I had ever seen on a human being, and they were solid muscle. "He right, woman," he growled at Tricia. "You don't be blamin' him for feelin' real low right now."

"Oh, knock off the damn jive talk," Tricia complained. She looked at me. "He was a speech major at CCNY, back home," she told me. "He just does that to put you on."

"I be doin' that way 'cause I be *feelin'* that way," Kowalski rumbled. Actually, in his normal voice he sounded like a speech major—a really good one, with natural talents. Conjur Kowalski had one fine, deep, round speaking voice. If the present incumbent ever gave them up, he could have done the Seven-Up commercials just as well. He glared at his drink and said, "Jerry Harper was a damn fool, okay, but they didn't have to do him like that."

"We're not going to talk about Jerry Harper," Tricia commanded. "How do you like Conjur's place, Nolly?"

"It's neat," I said again.

"Yeah," he said darkly, "but I tell you this, my man, I would trade it all for two rooms near One Twenty-fifth Street and maybe a contract with the Knicks."

"We're not going to talk about that, either," said Tricia. "We're just going to get relaxed and talk about having fun. You ever play any basketball, Nolly?"

"In college, but I was too short."

"Maybe you could throw some baskets with Conjur sometime. He still works out in the gym every day. In case he gets back, you know."

I was torn between two cues there—"in case he gets back" and "gym." "Gym" won out, and when I asked it turned out that, yes, Conjur had a gym. His own gym, he pointed out. He paid for it out of his earnings, and anybody else who wanted to use it had to pay for the privilege. Sometimes people did. It had a basketball court and a running track, not to mention all the Nautilus machines. I got right to the point. "I don't have any money," I said.

Conjur looked concealedly pleased, like a used-car salesman who sees an eighteen-year-old heading toward the Stingray with the bent frame. "You could get an advance on your contract," he said.

"I don't have a contract. They just snatched me."

"Shee-it," said Conjur thoughtfully, and Tricia said:

"But they can't do that. I mean, sure, they can snatch you if they want to, what can you do about it? But they can't make you go on tour. That's a real strict law. The funnies don't want each other kidnapping their people, so they have a rule that nobody travels to any of the planets without a voluntary work contract. You go talk to Sammy Shipperton; he knows he can't ship you off to the Ptrreek planet without papers. Make him give you a contract."

"Then you sure can use my facilities, Nolly," said Conjur graciously. "You shoot some baskets with me, I'll maybe give you something off."

"Fine," I said, but I'd been distracted again. "What's this about the Ptrreek planet?"

"Nobody told you about the Ptrreeks?" Conjur demanded.

"Nobody told me about *this* place," I said, disgruntled as I thought of it, "except Tricia started to give me a quick tour once, only—"

There was a moment's silence there, because I remembered how the quick tour had ended. So did Tricia. She said kindly, "You've seen a picture of it on the skry, haven't you?"

"Well, yes, but—"

"Show the man," Conjur ordered. "I'll fresh up these drinks."

And so Tricia Madigan took me over to the communications screen and summoned up a map of Narabedla. It very nearly took my mind off the sad fate of Jerry Harper, because it was pretty to look at—a sort of semitransparent illuminated, hologrammish model—and it answered a lot of questions. Narabedla, it turned out, wasn't really shaped like a soup can. More like a can of tuna fish, cylindrical but pretty squat. It wasn't very big, as moons go—no more than ten miles in diameter, maybe six miles through the axis of rotation. Even so, when I tried to do the arithmetic in my head, it came out a lot larger than it needed to be to house four hundred human beings on what was no more than a tenth of an acre for each little house.

"They built all this just so they could have a bunch of human beings performing for them?" I asked.

"Aw, no," rumbled Conjur Kowalski. "It *been* here, you know? They had some other use for it, like."

"Like what?"

"Oh, hell, Nolly, how would I know? It was just something they didn't need anymore. Maybe like a naval base for wars or something—they used to have them, you know, until they figured out nobody wasn't going to win any anyway. So when they started importing artists from the Earth they just cleared out a little corner of it, and here we are."

"I don't know much about their wars," I said, led away on another trail of thought and one that was far from attractive. If there was one thing I knew for certain about the people who had created Narabedla, it was that I didn't want their technology applied against the Earth in any way.

"You ain't *gonna* hear from me," said Conjur, "because I don't know nothin'. Ask old Floyd Morcher; he keeps digging into all that stuff, only what's the use? They don't do it no more anyway. Where's that liquor at, Trish?''

I made another mental note to myself, along with the one about seeing Sam Shipperton to talk contract, and studied the airy model that hung before my eyes.

It would be useful, I thought, to get around Narabedla. But Tricia explained that for that I didn't need a map. Most of the English-speaking human beings were within easy walking distance of my own house. The ones that weren't were only a go-box jump away, and from there it was never more than a five-minute walk to anywhere at all—anywhere we were allowed to go to in the first place, at least.

"But we can't go off Narabedla."

"Well, only on tours. When somebody's with us."

"But the aliens can go to Earth? Binnda said he'd been there."

Conjur shrugged. "Some of them do. The ones that can dress up to look human, anyway. You ask why? I dunno why. Well, they're all ape-shit to do it, only for all different reasons. There's the Ggressna, like Binnda, they just want to see what's coming down. There's the Mother, who would give her funny-looking little ass to go, only how can she? First she's sessile—that means she can't move much herself," the speech major explained to me, "and second can you imagine what would happen if she turned up on Times Square? There's the Ossps, and they got *bad* reasons. Happen they had their way they'd be there right *now,* you know what I'm saying?"

I was afraid I did. I felt a little chill on the back of my neck, thinking about what one of those high-tech alien races could do on Earth if it chose to. "And so it's against the law?"

"What kind of law are you talking about, man? There's no *law*. The Ggressna can't tell the Ossps what to do, no way. If an Ossp really wanted to go to the Earth nobody could stop him. Only he'd be in trouble, 'cause they've all signed the deal that says they won't interfere. See," he said, stretching—it was like a lion stretching—"the thing is, they can't let it be *known*. Otherwise it costs them. When Binnda goes to like Carnegie Hall he's living real dangerous. If anybody catches him and it makes the TV news, then he's in the deep shit. That's a violation of the Fifteen Peoples agreement, you see what I'm telling you? They come down on him *hard*. It'd *cost* him—not just him, but all the Ggressna. So he takes a chance. But if he don't get caught, why then there's no problem. He's got off on what he likes to do, and nobody's going to complain."

"And the Mother lets him go, because he comes back and tells her everything. She likes that," Tricia put in.

I remembered the question I had intended to ask Norah Platt. "But I thought the Mothers were the peacekeepers."

"Yeah? That's right, what about it?"

"But I thought that meant everybody trusted them, you know?"

"Man," said Conjur, looking pained, "nobody here trusts *nobody*. It's just like they can make you real sorry if you do something you shouldn't."

"And get caught at it," Tricia added, freshening up our drinks.

I tried a different tack. "How would they know?"

Conjur blinked. "Say what?"

"How would anybody here know if, for instance, Binnda got caught in Carnegie Hall?"

"Why, man, that would certainly make it onto the network news, don't you think? And of course all the radio and TV from Earth is monitored all the time. There's about a million funnies that keep tabs on everything that's broadcast from Earth. From all the other planets that they don't mess into, too."

"They're *spying* on us?" I cried.

"Who said spying? I mean, what in the world would they need to spy for? No, they're just interested. It's like they've got all these researchers, you know? Like people who study Earth customs, and, I don't know, people in the entertainment business, they pick up the shows and sell them, like. Like movies? Only of course they aren't movies. Anyway, there's no way it wouldn't get known all over if somebody on Earth came across a live Ggressna at the Met, or maybe a Duntidon walking down like State Street. It'd make all the papers, wouldn't it?" He hesitated. "And that's not all they're looking for, Nolly."

"Oh?"

He rocked his head back and forth for a moment. "No," he said, "there's worse than that. You know, some of these funnies are not so damn funny. Some of them's got real nasty attitudes about other species. If some of those birds got onto Earth there'd be *bad* times."

By then we were on the fourth or fifth drink, and I was actually beginning to like the combination of Scotch and ginger ale. We were all three sprawled out on the big, round bed, heads propped on elbows, about as relaxed as I had been since the moment I arrived on Narabedla.

Naturally something had to come along to spoil it.

What the spoiler turned out to be was a scratching on the door, and when Conjur let the visitor in it turned out to be one of the Mother's little bedbugs. It made straight for me. "Dr. Boddadukti is ready for you now," it piped, nudging me toward the door with its hard, warm little head. "Come! It is time to prepare for your repair."

CHAPTER
21

In one way, I didn't really mind the interruption. The party at Conjur Kowalski's pad had reached the point where I was pretty sure that fairly soon somebody was going to lay somebody, and I didn't see a role for me in that. So it was time to go.

In another way I was pretty uptight. Not scared. Tense. The feeling lasted all the while the bedbug led me through the go-box and along a sort of corridor. It wasn't a street. It even had a roof, and there were closed doors along the sides of it, though there were no furnishings. I didn't ask questions. It didn't speak again. Then I began to hear distant sounds of singing, and when the bedbug came to an open door it butted me inside.

The room inside was almost as bare as the corridors, apart from a bank of skry (I assumed they were skries) monitors that flickered with pretty colored lights on the wall. There, on a pure white, sterile-looking couch, were Purry and Norah Platt. They were not uptight at all. They were amusing themselves by singing "Greensleeves" together. At least Norah was singing, with a surprisingly decent contralto, while Purry was doing a real neat job of a piano and violin accompaniment.

I hadn't expected anything like that. It relaxed me considerably. I might even have joined in, except that all I knew was the first verse.

They stopped considerately to welcome me. "I'm glad to see you so bright, Knollwood," said Norah fondly, getting up and limping over to pat my cheek. She was using a cane, I saw, and the way she walked suggested that the joints were giving her real trouble again. "One's first operation is always a worry, don't you agree? But Dr. Boddadukti is a marvel. So much better than a human bar—a human surgeon. That is, simply in terms of natural equipment."

"He's not human?" I asked. It didn't seem important, but that fact had simply not registered with me before.

"Oh, Knollwood, of course he's not human. Why would they get a human being for something like this? The Duntidons are so much better. Dr. Boddadukti has done me for ages, and I'm so glad he's finished with his other work so he can get around to our little problems."

"Other work?" I started to say, but Purry broke in softly.

"Dr. Boddadukti is coming now," he said, and I looked up.

When I was at Camp Fire Place Lodge I had been lonely and unhappy, but never scared. That is to say, never scared until the time half a dozen of us were out a mile from shore with a counselor and the outboard on our boat quit. I wasn't scared then, even, until I saw that the counselor was. And I hadn't been scared here until I saw who Dr. Boddadukti was.

I could not believe it at first, but, yes, our surgeon, Dr. Boddadukti—the thing that was lumbering into the room, with a pair of the Mother's little bedbugs skittering beside him and one of the Kekkety servants close behind—the one who was about to perform any number of assorted perforations and incisions and heaven knew what else on me—

was someone, only I preferred to think of him as something, I had seen before, and not very long ago at that.

"How are you, Dr. Boddadukti," asked Norah politely, and I stood up to confront the creature I had watched only a couple of hours earlier. In Execution Square. With his needle-sharp fangs ripping the arteries out of poor Jerry Harper's throat. There were still traces of Jerry Harper's blood on the thing's razor-sharp claws.

It may be that Dr. Boddadukti responded to Norah's cheery greeting. I can't say. All my attention was taken up in staring at the monster.

It—well, I suppose I have to say "he"—wasted no time. He lumbered over to the far wall, gazed at the Christmasy colored lights of the monitors for a moment in silence. Then he said something. I suppose he *said* it, though what it sounded like was a combination of clicks and guttural growls. The Kekkety deferentially slipped in beside him and began pushing buttons.

Soundlessly, a part of the side wall opened up, displaying the entrances to two little cubicles. Between them were more of the screens and what looked like the control panel on a space shuttle. Boddadukti waved a claw at us sternly, and one of the Mother's bedbugs shrilled, "You are to remove your clothes, you two patients."

"Oh, sorry, Dr. Boddadukti," caroled Norah, sitting down to slip off her shoes. Purry translated into Boddadukti's clicks and rumbles for her, and Norah twinkled at me. "Come on, Nolly. This is no time to be modest. Off with the trousers, please!"

I glared at her. That involved my turning to face her, and as I opened my mouth to speak I felt a hard, hot hand—claw? paw?—on my shoulder, and smelled breath still redolent of human blood, and heard right next to my ear the voice of Dr. Boddadukti, rumbling, "Slajbachdajbaj," or something of the sort, which Purry translated as, "Dr. Boddadukti says that the human female patient Norah Platt has asked him how he is, but the true question, dear humans, is how are you?"

The Kekkety had pattered over and was busy unbuckling my belt. I pushed at him angrily. He didn't move. He was, I discovered, a lot heavier and a lot stronger than he looked.

I pushed him again, with more force this time, and made my stand. "Hold it," I yelled. "I am not going to get sliced up by some murdering monster with human blood still on his claws!"

"Nolly!" Norah cried in shock and outrage, stepping out of her bikini underwear—she had, I observed, a pretty nice figure for an elderly woman—*elderly*! "You mustn't speak that way about one of our most distinguished alien associates!"

"Shlazgajbazhmazh," roared Dr. Boddadukti—

And Purry out of one set of holes was translating what I said and what Norah said into the clicks and growls of the Duntidon language—and out of another set of holes was relaying to me Dr. Boddadukti's responses, which went in English: "Dear human friend, you must understand that I was merely carrying out the instructions of your own human court—"

And I was going on, "This thing is a dangerous *animal,* and anyway I was kidnapped here in the first place and I want *out*—"

And, all in all, that little room was filling with sound, none of it pleasing to me, and I would have left them all behind had I not discovered (limping over to the entrance with the little Oriental-looking Kekkety servant doggedly pulling my pants down around my ankles) that the door wouldn't open for me.

I hadn't seen anyone lock it, but the fact was that it was indeed locked. I was trapped there.

I turned to them as a Christian might have turned to the lions of the Colosseum. Purry was piping away in one language or another out of all of his holes at once, trying to keep up with me (still shouting) and with Norah (still remonstrating) and with Dr. Boddadukti (still clicking and growling).

We might have gone on in that way indefinitely if Dr. Boddadukti hadn't got tired of it. He didn't seem to lose patience with me. (How could you tell if he had? He didn't have a proper face.) His clicks and growls did not change in pitch or volume, nor did what he was saying (as relayed by Purry) become anything but the polite remarks of a cultured gentleman of the medical profession. Nothing he did could be construed as threatening, or even annoyed, though while he talked he did fastidiously lick away the little smears of Jerry's blood I had reminded him were on his claws.

He simply reached out, as though absentmindedly, and stroked the keypad of the consoles set in the wall.

From the wall there came a queer, shrill hum to add to all the other, already sufficient, noises in the room, and I began to feel rapidly and irresistibly at peace.

No, not exactly at peace. I had not forgotten that this being was a killer. I had not stopped being afraid. I simply didn't mind any of it. Ah-ha, I said wisely to myself, the son of a bitch is doping me. And out loud I said good-naturedly, "Sorry to take so long, Doc. I'll be out of these clothes in a minute."

And so I was.

The doctor didn't even look at me again. He was busy watching his monitors, perhaps, though he didn't seem greatly interested in what they displayed. From time to time he would suck at one of those razor-sharp talons, pulling it through his teeth (oh, of course, I said wisely to myself, sharpening them up for the operations). The act made a rasping, fingernails-on-blackboard sound every time he did it, but that didn't bother me either. Nothing did. Nothing seemed to be happening, except that every now and then I felt a kind of warmth, once quite hot around my throat and chest, once even hotter in the region of my scrotum, and a sort of generalized, all-over tingling, like standing next to a static electricity generator.

None of this hurt.

Nothing hurt, and I did not feel as though I would mind particularly if anything did.

When it stopped, nothing at all happened for a while, although I had a hazy notion, from watching Norah Platt give an occasional amused twitch or wriggle, that it was her turn to be examined by whatever kind of thing it was that had been examining me. I waited in good-humored patience, and in silence until Dr. Boddadukti said, "Scrajscrajbajgadda," and Purry translated it as, "He says there is no problem. Now both of you are to get cleaned up for surgery."

I bowed deferentially to Norah, and Norah inclined her head graciously to me and led the way. She went into the left-hand cubicle of the two that had appeared on the wall.

I went into the right. We were both still bare naked, of course. It no longer seemed particularly worth noticing.

Inside each cubicle was a thing like a cot, and a thing like a king-sized tub, full of greenish, faintly aromatic liquid, and a thing like a stall shower, but without any visible faucets. I thought of stepping into the tub, but the bedbug that had followed me nudged me into the stall.

It turned out indeed to be a shower, or at least something very like one at first. Needle-sharp sprays of something oily and sweet-smelling shot out at me from all directions as a door closed on me. I ducked involuntarily, but there was nowhere to duck to. I thought of trying to protect my eyes. Then I realized that whatever was coming at me had already found my eyes, but the sprays just there were gentle ones and my eyes didn't seem to mind it. The sprays didn't stab. They didn't sting; and they followed me wherever I moved.

Then the sprays changed. They became gentler and warmer, and they smelled different—a little like the roses of the Riviera, almost, I thought, wondering amiably if Irene Madigan were still there to smell them.

The sprays were quite soothing.

Why, I thought with amusement, I seem to be falling asleep right here.

I saw the door begin to open, the spray stop, the Kekkety reach in to catch me as I collapsed languidly to the floor; and go to sleep I did, then and there, without any further thought about it at all.

When I woke up I was thinking about Marlene and Irene Madigan.

Perhaps I had been dreaming about them, though I remembered no dream. I was lying naked on that little cot, turned on one side with my head pillowed on my arm, and my first waking thought was that Irene and Marlene must be worrying about me.

My second thought was that I seemed to have a slight sore throat, not to mention a dull ache in the vicinity of my belly and my balls, and my third was that—oh, wow! *Wonderful!*—the operation must be over!

I sat up and looked around.

I was alone in the cubicle with the cot, the bathtub, and the shower stall. The stall was empty. The tub was still filled with liquid, but it seemed thicker and soupier now, and it was gently swirling around in the tub, like a slow-motion Jacuzzi. It smelled different now, too, a sort of combination of ripe cheese and disinfectant.

"Hello?" I called.

Nobody answered.

The reason for that was that nobody was there. Not in my cubicle, and not out in the larger room with the pretty colored lights floating around the wall. My clothes weren't there, either. Naked and tentative I got up and peered around from my doorway, ready to duck back inside and demand pants if someone showed up.

No one did, and, actually, as I began to move around, the faint aches and worries seemed to ease themselves. I felt no worse than I would normally have felt after a night on a hard cot without a pillow.

I saw Norah Platt's cane propped against the tub in her room, but the cot was empty. I peered in, wondering where Norah was. The tub was making the same gentle water-in-motion sound as my own, and then I looked into it.

The first thing I saw was Norah's toes, bobbing up to the surface of the smelly tank. Then I saw that the toes were on her foot, which was normal enough, and the foot was at the end of her leg, but the leg was no longer attached to Norah. Both her legs floated in that tank, and so did her body, and so did her head, but none of them were any longer joined to each other.

Norah Platt had been disassembled.

By the time the outer door opened again and Sam Shipperton came in, fresh clothes for me over his arm, I was standing by the tub with Norah's cane raised in my hand. It was a good thing that it was Shipperton that came in first and not Dr. Boddadukti or one of the other weirdos. I would surely have done my best to smash in any nonhuman head that appeared.

Even so, it was a close thing. He ducked away from the cane in surprise, yelling, "What the hell are you doing, Stennis? Put that thing down!" And then, as I hesitated, "Come on, man! I got no time for this. Get your clothes on; Mr. Davidson-Jones wants to see you right away!"

CHAPTER

22

The trouble with you," Shipperton declared, steering me into the go-box, "is you don't fucking *appreciate* everything we're doing for you. Hurry up, get in!"

I got in, still seething. "And what are you doing for Norah Platt?" I sneered, though by then I had lost a lot of steam because I pretty well knew what he was going to say.

"Jump station," he said to the box. Then, as the door closed, he said what I had been expecting: "Dr. Boddadukti is fixing her up, that's what we're doing for her. Of *course* he takes her apart to fix her up, what do you think? How do you think *you* looked a couple of hours ago? Get out!"

I got out, as ordered, feeling a shiver of cold along my back. The pieces of my body fit together real well. They always had. I didn't like the idea that they had recently been disassembled and then stuck back together again. "I've got a sore throat," I complained, feeling my neck to see if the soreness was still there.

"Of course you do. That's because Mr. Davidson-Jones needs you, so I got you woke up a little early," Shipperton explained. "In here—move it, will you?"

"In here" was another go-box, bigger than the last. The door *shooshed* open. I started in, only half paying attention, because my fingers had felt something odd on my neck, but Shipperton grabbed my arm. "Hold it," he ordered. "Let them get out, will you?"

The new go-box wasn't empty. It was even bigger than I'd thought, almost the size of a one-car garage. It needed to be because it contained a couple of the little Mnimn, like Meretekabinnda (only Binnda wasn't one of them), and four of those big fourteen-foot praying-mantis-looking aliens, the Ptrreek, crouched over to keep their heads from going through the ceiling. They sputtered at me. The language was

172

their own, but I understood what they meant: it was, "Get out of the way." I felt my neck while the aliens shoved past and the two Kekkety servants muscled a couple of crates out of the box. One of the bedbuggy Eyes of the Mother followed them as far as the door. It paused there, gazing up at Shipperton. Shipperton said something I couldn't hear. The bedbug hesitated, sniffing at his ankle, then it trotted back inside. Shipperton pushed me in after it and the door *sqwuffed* shut behind us.

"Leave your dressings alone, will you, Nolly?" Shipperton ordered.

"It feels like there's something stuck on my neck," I complained.

"Well, sure there's something stuck on it," he said disgustedly. "Didn't you ever hear of bandages? I don't think you could pull them off, but don't try. You'll be sorry if you do. They'll just get absorbed by themselves in a couple of days if you leave them alone."

It wasn't easy to leave them alone. What I felt when I touched them was soft, slippery raised ribbons. They went in geometric patterns around my throat, all the way to the back of my neck, and they were warm to the touch, as though something unusual were going on under the ribbons. I swallowed, because I had a mental image of Dr. Boddadukti's razor-sharp claws slicing through my tender and undefended skin while I was unconscious. "Are you trying to tell me he isn't a murderer?" I demanded.

"Will you knock that off, for God's sake? Boddadukti is a volunteer. He doesn't have to fix us up, you know. He only does it because of his interest in exotic biologies."

"I know all about his interest in exotic biologies!"

"Just shut up," Shipperton ordered; and then, as the big door opened again, he snapped, "Out."

There was a Kekkety standing at the door. Shipperton nodded toward me and said, "He stays here. Stennis? Just wait a minute until I see if Jonesy's ready for you." He started to turn away, then stopped himself. He looked back at me. "One thing. Who's Wiktor"—that was the way he pronounced it, with a "W" "—who's Wiktor Ordukowsky?"

I straightened up with a jolt. "What? What about him?"

"Just that now you've got somebody else in the deep stuff,

Stennis," he growled. "Christ! I knew we just should've dumped you into slow time in the first place."

If there was one person I didn't want to add to the list of people who were likely candidates for trouble, it was Vic Ordukowsky. He was a homely fat man, but he had been just about the best friend I'd ever had.

When I had the mumps I thought I was going to die. When I was over the mumps, having left some important parts of my self-image in the hospital bed, I didn't think I was going to die anymore, I just thought that it no longer mattered. Singing and making love weren't just pleasures for me. They were, basically, the things my life was all about, and they were gone.

I knew I was supposed to construct some sort of new life for myself, but it didn't seem I had enough raw materials left to build it out of.

That was when Vic Ordukowsky saved my life. I ran into him by chance in Grand Central Station. We had a drink in Charley O's, and then a couple of pan roasts in the Oyster Bar, and when I was walking him to his three-hour-later-than-usual train he said, "Look, Nolly. You know what the trouble with good advice is? Good advice is what you've always known all along anyhow."

"So?" I said—not hostile, just getting ready to hear the same thing I'd heard a thousand times already.

"So this is the advice: Find something else to be good at. Then get good at it." And then, sort of offhandedly, "If you want to set up as an accountant, there's a woman named Marian Lambert—have you ever heard of her?"

"Sure. The contralto."

"She's a friend of my wife. Mary-Ellen says she's looking for somebody new to do her taxes. I'd go after it myself, but I'm not supposed to take on outside work. Anyway, what do I know about opera singers?"

So Vic had given me my first client. He also steered my second, third, and about half a dozen more to me over the next year or two, and if that hadn't saved my life I don't know what had.

I should never, never, I told myself, have involved Vic Ordukowsky in the Narabedla situation. Sure, I hadn't meant to do him any harm. I had had no reason to think it would mean any serious trouble for him. But he wasn't just vulnerable, he *worked* for Henry Davidson-Jones. That meant that the biggest part of his life was lived in the center of Narabedla's web. It would be no trouble at all to make him disappear.

And I was responsible.

When Shipperton came to get me I had made up my mind what to do about it. I was in full possession of my faculties. I nodded briskly to Davidson-Jones as I entered his office. He was sitting at his desk, a desk very like the one he had in the World Trade Center, though the office he was in now was a lot smaller. It had the same kind of never-mind-the-cost furnishings, but the ceiling was no higher than the one in the corridor, and it lacked that wonderful starry sky. It was just a ceiling. The walls were hung with drapes, and Davidson-Jones himself looked a lot more tired than the last time I had seen him.

I didn't waste time. I said, "I'll be glad to write Vic Ordukowsky any letter you want me to."

Davidson-Jones looked at me curiously. "You're not going to argue about it?"

"No. Give me a pen and some paper."

"Why," he said, nodding, "I'm glad to see you cooperative, Nolly. It won't have to be a letter. A card is good enough, and I have one here."

He tossed it to me; it wasn't from Scotland this time, it was from Copenhagen, and the picture was of the Little Mermaid in the harbor. "I guess I do a lot of traveling around," I said. "What do you want me to say?"

"Be creative," he told me. I picked up the pen and wrote quickly:

Dear Vic:
    Having wonderful time with the girl of my dreams. If you see your boss thank him for me, because without him I never would have met her.

He read it over carefully, and put it in his desk drawer. "Thank you," he said.

"Is that all?" I said, getting up. "Because I might as well be getting back—"

He sighed and rubbed his forehead. "Nolly," he said,

"I'm afraid it's not all. I want you to listen to something. You might as well sit down."

I did, stiffly; and he turned the switch on a tape recorder on his desk, and a voice began to come out.

It was Marlene's voice.

"My name," it said crossly, "is Marlene Abramson, I live at 308 West 75th Street in New York City, my age is none of your business, and now can I tell you what I came here to say?"

"What the *hell*!" I snapped, but Davidson-Jones waved me to silence.

"Listen," he ordered.

An unidentified man was saying, "Go right ahead, Mrs. Abramson. Tell it in your own words, what you said on the phone."

Marlene: "Well, Nolly began—what? Oh, all right. My associate, Mr. L. Knollwood Stennis, do you want his address, too? Anyway, Nolly began acting funny, I guess some time in April, it was. We have this client, Woody Calderon, and he came in and—oh, God, now what?"

Male voice: "Just to save time, we have all that preliminary material in your file already, Mrs. Abramson. Would you just tell us what occurred when you came here to Miami last Thursday?"

Marlene: "Wednesday. I got here Wednesday, not Thursday. I registered at the Fontainebleau." She pronounced it the way she always had, "Fountain-Blue." "They comp me there, because I used to do their tax records, but I have to pay my own bar bills and phone. Anyway, I called you people at the office here, but I couldn't get you off your duffs. FBI! Lordy, lordy, what do you people do with your time? A taxpayer comes and wants to report a kidnapping, and—"

Male voice: "Yes, Mrs. Abramson, you've said that."

Marlene: "I'm going to say it a lot more, you hear what I'm telling you? I pay taxes! I told you Davidson-Jones's yacht was right here, and you wouldn't do a thing. So I checked it out myself."

Male voice: "Mrs. Abramson, did you ever stop to think that if these allegations have substance you could be in a lot of serious trouble?"

Marlene: "Jesus, did I not! But Nolly's a nice kid, you know? Even if he's got a *goyische kopf*. Anyway"—she laughed a little; it was a pretty small, sad laugh—"I figured if I told you where I was going, and then if I got snatched, too, you wouldn't be able to sweep it under the rug anymore."

Male voice: "I see." Pause. "Then, after your failure to meet with Interpol, you decided to investigate yourself here in Miami."

"That's right. My God, Miami in the summer! But that other guy in the FBI in New York, Matson? Watson? Whatever his name was. He let it out that the yacht was here. So first thing Thursday morning, after I couldn't get you people to move, I rented a car from Avis and I went off to watch the yacht. Nothing was happening. All I ever saw was some of those Chinese people he has working there up on the deck sometimes, and I got hungry, and besides I had to go to the bathroom. So there was an I-Hop down the road—what? It's International House of Pancakes, haven't you ever seen one? And I ate, and when I came back to the yacht there was this silver-gray Bentley just pulling away, and I could see Davidson-Jones in it. So I followed it."

Male voice: "To the Shady Cypress Memorial Lawn, I think you said."

Marlene, "Right, the cemetery. And I pulled in after them, and I saw Davidson-Jones get out. He put flowers on a grave. Then he got back in the car and I ran back to my own."

Male voice: "And that was when you lost him?"

Marlene: "I didn't *lose* him, I just had a little trouble. Well, I hit a gravestone when I was turning around. And then this rent-a-cop comes out and gives me an argument, and by that time Davidson-Jones is long gone."

Male voice: "So you went back and looked at the grave the suspect placed flowers on."

Marlene: "Right. And it said, 'Henry Davidson-Jones, 1931–1933, beloved son.' So this other guy is a fake, and what are you going to do about it?"

The fake Henry Davidson-Jones sighed, reached out, and clicked off the recorder. "It's really surprising," he said, in a tone of wonder, "how much trouble your Mrs. Abramson can make."

I had to clear my throat before I could speak. It might have been just the effects of Dr. Boddadukti's fooling around with my vocal cords. Or it might have been the way I felt after hearing Marlene's flat, lovingly worried voice coming out of that machine.

"How did you get that?" I demanded.

He looked surprised. "I didn't have to get it. A man named William Matteson of the New York office of the FBI brought it to me. He came to my office and played it and asked me to explain." He grimaced. "Fortunately," he said, "I already had contingency plans for any question about my actual identity. But it's getting tiresome, Nolly. Mrs. Abramson's been busy. It's not just Ordukowsky and the FBI, she's been making a career out of talking to people. She has to be stopped."

"Lots of luck," I snapped. It was empty bluff, of course. He knew it as well as I did, and went on as though I hadn't even spoken.

"So what you have to do," he said, putting his hand on a telephone on his desk, "is call her and tell her that everything is really all right."

"Not a chance," I said positively.

Davidson-Jones sighed. He passed a hand before his face. Then he took the cassette out of the machine and replaced it with another. "Sorry," he said, with his hand on the button. "I put that wrong. I should have explained to you that we don't *need* your help. It would just be more convenient. For instance, at this moment Mrs. Abramson is back in your office in New York. There are some men nearby who can meet her when she leaves and dispose of her."

"You bastard!" I flared.

He said mildly, "I don't want to do that. Among other reasons, it would cause a lot of talk. However, I think the talk would die down once it became clear Mrs. Abramson was out of her mind. Listen to this."

He pressed the lever, and out of the new cassette came Marlene's voice again, but this time it was saying, "Hello, FBI? Listen, I didn't tell you the whole story last time. This Henry Davidson-Jones, I want you to know who he really is. He's Adolf Hitler. He's been hiding out with the saucer people, and he's going to kill the president and take over the White House."

The voice stopped. Davidson-Jones pressed the stop button and said, "That one's a phone call to the FBI. There's more. A call to the mayor of New York, to *The New York Times,* a whole bunch of them to your clients."

"Marlene never said anything like that!" I cried.

"No, she didn't," Davidson-Jones agreed. "But it's her voice all right, isn't it? Of course, it's not really hers. It's your friend Purry simulating her voice, but, actually, Purry is extremely good at that."

"No one will believe it's Marlene!"

"I think they will, Nolly, because the next thing they could find, if that's the way you want it, is Mrs. Abramson, dead of an overdose of LSD. Then they'd check her medicine cabinet, and they'd be sure to find six sugar cubes left in a box of twenty-four, and all of them laced with acid."

"You'd *murder* her?"

"I'd do what I had to do to save the project, Nolly," he agreed, "but murdering's something I haven't had to do yet. Do you really want to push us that far, Nolly? You can clear the whole thing up."

"But how—" I began. And then stopped, appalled, because I was beginning to sound as though I would cooperate.

"All you have to do," said Davidson-Jones gently, "is pick up this phone. Call her. Tell her to call off her dogs. Tell her you're all right, but you've got something going and you'll be out of touch for a while."

I snapped angrily, "Can't Purry do my voice too?"

He said patiently, "We want to make sure she *believes* you, Nolly. You're the only one who can do that. Convince her. Make sure the next thing she does is call the FBI and tell them it was all a mistake; or do I tell the people in New York to pick her up?"

"But there's still that tombstone."

"Oh, yes," he sighed. "There are a lot of loose ends to straighten out. We'll take care of that part. You do yours." He looked at me searchingly for a moment, then picked up the phone and dialed a number. I recognized it: it was my office in New York, complete with area code.

What wonderful technology they had, I thought bitterly as it began to ring.

"You're on," said Davidson-Jones, handing the phone to me.

"Stennis Associates," our receptionist said in my ear.

I closed my eyes. I took a deep breath. "Hello, Sally. This is the boss calling—yes, I'm all right, just real busy. Let me talk to Marlene, please."

When it was over I sat for a minute, trying not to shake. I didn't pride myself on what I'd done. Marlene had actually been crying on the phone.

I lied to her, copiously and imaginatively, just as Henry Davidson-Jones wished. I told her a long line of hogwash about how I'd been feeling as though I had a nervous breakdown coming on. I just needed to get away for a while, I said. My crazy ideas about Henry Davidson-Jones were just part of being overstrained and mixed up, I said. Everything would positively be *all right,* I said, and I promised I'd keep in touch every now and then. And I filled it all in with chitchat about whether Henry Stanley's New Jersey state forms had been filed, and how Terry Morgenstern's CDs needed to be rolled over—the kind of day-to-day stuff that only I would know about, so she would be sure this person on the phone was no impostor.

Toward the end of the conversation she stopped crying and began to get mad. That didn't make it any better, and I was glad when it was over.

Of course, I *had* to do that. For *her* sake.

But I couldn't make myself believe that. Not at that moment, not at all that day, and not for a good many of the days that followed.

Shipperton escorted me back to his office. We didn't speak. When we got there he poured me a drink and I took it.

"So now," he said tentatively, "can we figure there aren't going to be any more threats and arguments out of you?"

I didn't answer that. I didn't have to. When I had picked up that telephone to talk to Marlene Abramson I knew what

I was doing. I was making a major decision, and the decision was to stay on Narabedla.

"Would he really have killed her?" I asked.

He shrugged uneasily. "I don't think so. He never has. But it would have been bad for her, one way or another." He peered at me. "Are you all right?"

"What makes you ask that?"

"I don't know. You look—you look kind of funny."

"How should I look?" But I knew the answer to that. My conscience made it clear to me. It told me I should look like a man who had just got done ratting out on Marlene and on Irene Madigan . . . on all of my friends, on my clients, on my country—and most of all on my planet and the whole human race that inhabited it.

He poured me another drink. "You know what that tombstone was?" he said, making conversation. "It was his son. Right, he was married once; only his wife and his kid got drowned on a boat. They never found the wife's body."

"So he just took his son's identity?"

"Later on he did. Well, he kind of has to, now and then, doesn't he? I mean, he stays too young to have only one identity. The way you will, here."

"Are you giving me another sales talk?"

"Well, we really do need to get you to sign a contract, you know."

"All right."

He stared at me. "Really? Well, hell, Nolly! That's fine. Just a minute, I've got blanks here in my desk, and you can sign—"

He broke off in the middle of the sentence, peering at my face. "What's the matter now?" he demanded.

I finished my drink and put the glass down. My mind was made up. I said gently, "Sam, have you ever negotiated a contract with a CPA before? No? I thought not. Well, I hope you've still got your coffeepot. It's likely to be a long night."

CHAPTER

24

Narabedla was beginning to look better to me.

All it took, really, was a change of attitude on my part. I stopped thinking of Narabedla as a place where I wished I wasn't and accepted it as the place where I was. I'd done that before. It had been the same at Camp Fire Place Lodge. After those first few miserable, homesick days I found out that I was, after all, a camper, too. In my second week I won a Shark Feather for swimming clear across the bay unaided; I placed second in marksmanship in the competition with the .22 rifles; before the end of the season I was fourth man on the relay team and in the front row of the sing-alongs around the evening campfire, and when Labor Day arrived I didn't want to go home.

Calling Marlene had been the irrevocable step. Signing the contract had only confirmed it. I was a Narabedlan now.

On my morning run the next day I detoured by way of the little street called Rodeo Drive to inspect one of the perquisites therefrom. Rodeo Drive looked like any suburban condo development, stucco-walled townhouses with lawns and flowering trees around them under the pleasant (if make-believe) morning sky. I had no trouble finding the house that would be mine. It had daffodils in beds under the windows and marigolds in tubs by the patio in back. Shipperton hadn't yet given me a key, but, peering through the window, careful not to step on the flowers, I saw that there was furniture in it.

That wasn't a real problem. Shipperton had promised I could choose my own, and the contract I had finally beaten out with him provided for advances on earnings enough to buy anything that needed buying. It would be pleasant to pick out my own, I reflected as I jogged back to Riverside Drive, but I wondered what they would do with the old stuff.

Store it somewhere? Throw it away? What did they do on Narabedla with the things people discarded? For that matter, what did they do with the people when no Dr. Boddadukti could fix them up anymore?

I added those things to the long list of questions I hadn't yet had answered. I would get all the answers sooner or later, I promised myself. After all, I had plenty of time. I was going to be on Narabedla for quite a while.

Maybe, like Norah and some of the others, for hundreds of years.

Showered, breakfasted, and dressed, I headed for the rehearsal hall.

None of the opera singers was there yet, but Tricia and Conjur Kowalski were dancing on the stage, while Binnda happily beat time from the conductor's box. The surprise was that the music they were dancing to was World War II-era swing, and the person playing it was Norah Platt, wonderfully reconstituted out of the assemblage of cold cuts I'd seen floating in Dr. Boddadukti's tub. She seemed none the worse for it. She glanced up as I came in, winked cheerfully, and went on hammering out a jivey "Twelfth Street Rag." Ephard Joyce was sourly hanging over the piano, and he, too, favored me with a cursory nod. I didn't want to interrupt. I sat down and watched the jitterbuggers.

They were worth watching. Both Conjur and Tricia were in costume, Conjur in a zoot suit with the jacket cut down to his knees and a gold watch chain flying around his ankles, Tricia in a jitterbug skirt with tiny, tight white panties that showed every time Conjur flung her over his shoulders or between his peg-topped legs. I could see that she was sweating. I could almost smell her, the sweet, healthy smell of a pretty young woman expending a lot of calories and enjoying it. Norah, spry and smiling after her operation, was grooving right along with them on the piano, sounding almost like the old Glenn Miller and Tommy Dorsey days.

And the interesting part was that while I was sitting there, watching them take the A-train and swing along in the mood, I felt something. It was right in the crotch of my sleek new pants, where I hadn't felt much stirring for a long time. It was not really anything big, just a tingle, but it tingled in a way that suggested at least a hope that one of these days I

might very well be back in the kind of action I had thought
as lost as singing in the opera.

I didn't even hear Binnda call for a break. I came to, out
of my rosy glow, to find Binnda looking at me curiously.
"Dear boy, are you all right?"

I sat up. "Oh, I'm fine," I said, looking around. Tricia
and Conjur were mopping sweat off their faces and arms at
the side of the stage, and Binnda was standing over me. "I
thought you'd be rehearsing the troupe."

"Oh, we've given the troupe the day off, my dear boy.
More or less on your account, you know; Dr. Boddadukti
wasn't sure how your throat would feel just at first."

I said, with sincere pleasure, "It feels fine."

"Really?" He thought for a moment. "Perhaps I should
ask Ugolino to spend some time with you this afternoon—
just to make sure, you see? And then if he says it's all
right . . ."

"He will," I said positively. "I'll be ready to rehearse
again tomorrow."

"No, no, my dear Nolly! We won't be rehearsing *tomorrow*!" he cried, sounding shocked. "Didn't you know? Tomorrow they're going to launch the Andromeda probe and
we'll all be glued to our skries!"

"Really? Nobody told me. I didn't know it was such a big
deal."

"My dear boy! It is going to what your The Earth people
call M-31, the Great Nebula in Andromeda! Ever so far
away. We've never done anything this big before!" He
clucked at me reprovingly. Then he said, "But you'll see it
all tomorrow. Meanwhile, go off and amuse yourself a bit,
while I see if dear Ugolino can see you today."

That was easy enough to do. I strolled over to Norah,
preening myself. "Stennis," Joyce growled, acknowledging
my presence. I shook his hand, and kissed Norah's as I told
her how happy I was to see her, well, *alive* again.

"But of course, Nolly, dear," she said in a reproving tone.
"I told you it would be all right, didn't I? And I understand
you've signed quite a nice contract."

"Well," I said, "it's just a matter of bargaining, you know.
It's like an income-tax audit. You push the agent just as far
as you can. You stop right before the point where it would
be easier for him to go to court than settle; that's what I did
with Shipperton. And I've got a new house, too."

"What's an income tax?" asked Joyce, but Norah was frowning.

"As far as I know," she said thoughtfully, "there's only one house vacant just now. On Rodeo Drive, is it?"

"That's the one. And listen," I said, struck by an idea, "I think I'll have a housewarming party as soon as I get it fixed up. Will you come? Both of you, I mean?" I added, because, after all, the man was standing right there.

Joyce picked up his cue eagerly. "Yes, of course. Be delighted." He glanced around, and, lowering his voice, added, "I've been wanting to talk to you about something. Do you remember the thing you said the other night—about how I could do really well if I went back now? Did you mean it?"

I blinked at him. "Oh, that," I said, remembering. "Yes, I suppose so. I mean, well, definitely you would. If you showed up in New York you'd make the headlines, you know? Someone who actually knew John Wilkes Booth? Not to mention someone who's been here on Narabedla! Believe me, you'd have TV news people all around you. And, of course, if you decided you wanted to play Hamlet or anything like that, you'd have to fight the producers off, because there'd be a guaranteed box office from people who'd want to see what you looked like."

Joyce pursed his lips. "I see," he said.

Tricia and Conjur had drifted over to listen. "You stirring some more revolution?" Conjur asked—jokingly, I assumed.

"Oh, no. I admit you were all right, that's all. It's impossible to go back."

"Of course," Joyce echoed. But at least he'd forgotten to be surly about the fact that I wasn't helping him get a mime part in the opera troupe.

As he drifted away I patted Tricia's shoulder welcomingly. "You two are looking pretty fine on the dance floor," I said, and then got down to business. "Conjur? Did you say you had a gym?"

"Yeah?" he said suspiciously.

"Well, I'd like to work out in it, if that's all right with you."

"Twenty bucks an hour. 'Less you want to work out with me, then it's free."

"Work out? You mean shooting baskets?"

"Yeah, well, what I'd rather is a couple easy rounds," he

grinned, putting his fists up. "We could use the big gloves, nobody gets hurt. Just to get the old blood flowing, you know what I'm saying?"

I looked him over, ten inches taller than I was and twenty pounds heavier. And all muscles. "I think I'll pay the twenty dollars," I said.

Tricia was looking me over thoughtfully. "So it's true," she said. "You did finally sign a contract."

"And he's got a new house," Norah put in.

"And you're all invited to my housewarming," I said.

Tricia, frowning, said, "But there's really only one house vacant now, isn't there?"

And Norah said, "That's what I was trying to tell you, Nolly. It must be the one that used to be Jerry Harper's."

It was Harper's house, all right. Sam Shipperton confirmed it when I stopped by to pick up the keys.

When I opened the door and let myself in it had a bare and empty smell. There was furniture there—table and chairs, couch and coffee table; big king-sizer in the bedroom, knotty-pine chests—but there wasn't anything *but* furniture. No clothes in the closets, no food in the refrigerator, no pictures on the walls. The only thing that showed anybody had ever lived there was a stain on the kitchen carpeting, where somebody had spilled something, and a Kekkety was busily scrubbing away at that.

I don't believe in haunted houses. It was good I didn't, I thought, because otherwise I might have thought taking over the home of an executed man could have been bad luck.

I didn't spend any time worrying about it. I sent the Kekkety over to the house I had borrowed from Malcolm Porchester for my clothes. While he was gone I scribbled out a shopping list, food and drink for the larder, and by the time Ugolino Malatesta showed up to check my voice I had a pot of coffee on the stove. "But no!" Malatesta cried when he saw what I was drinking. "Coffee is acid! For your voice it is tea you should drink, quite hot and sweet, or best of all a little wine!"

"They're acid, too, aren't they?" I grinned.

But I humored him. I'd already stocked up on a Chianti that he sniffed and pronounced acceptable, and after a glass apiece we set to work.

He started me slow, with mid-range vocalizing, and it was half an hour before he would let me stretch to the limits of my range. Much less actually *sing* anything.

But then he did. And when he heard, he beamed.

I wasn't surprised. I didn't need Malatesta to tell me that my voice was back, all of it. I by-God *knew* that it was all there. Vocalizing in front of a mirror, with Malatesta gently touching cheek and throat and jawbone, grinning as he did, I could *feel* the rightness. I didn't look as though I were straining, because I wasn't. *"Cantare, allora,"* he said finally, contented, and sing I did. Audition songs. Snatches of arias. The kind of thing I did in the shower, when no one was there to hear. Everything I remembered I tried that afternoon for Malatesta, while he nodded and grinned at me. Snatches of "Glory Road" in the style of Lawrence Tibbett. Lieder I'd learned from records by Dietrich Fischer-Diskau. A few bars of Wagner, something from *Boris Godunov,* some of the Tonio from *I Pagliacci.*

And they all came out just the way I wanted them to. *"Bella, bella,"* Malatesta cried, with the fond delight of a coach whose student has surpassed him. *"Voi avete una voce bellissima, Knoll-a-wood!"*

And so I had. With the help of Binnda and Barak and the Mother, not to mention the good monster-doctor Bodda-dukti, I had the voice I had always dreamed of, and it was all *mine.*

I don't think that ever in my life I have been happier than I was that afternoon, on the second moon of the seventh planet of the star Aldebaran.

CHAPTER

25

When a mild-mannered accountant is suddenly transformed into an opera star—never mind whether it's on Narabedla or in New York—it keeps him *busy*. Every hour was full. When I wasn't picking out the furniture for my new house, I was vocalizing with Ugolino Malatesta. When I had time from either, I needed that time just to learn my way around my new home. With Purry and the skry I learned to tell the difference between a Hrunwian and one of the Tseni, and how to order records from Earth for my new stereo, and what to say to the Kekketies when I wanted my morning eggs over easy instead of scrambled.

I cannot tell a lie about it. I was having a ball. Best of all was the time I spent with Binnda, going over the plans for our new opera company's first tour. He had promoted me to something like assistant managing director, and together we went over the casts. *Idomeneo* was easy; we had Malatesta to sing the Idamante, and Canduccio, Morcher, and the Russian, Dmitri Arkashvili, for the three tenors. Eloise Gatt for Ilia, Sue-Mary Petticardi for the Electra, and Eamon McGuire as Neptune's voice.

The cast for *I Pagliacci* was no problem, either, because we already had everybody necessary right on hand:

Canio: Floyd Morcher.
Tonio: Me.
Nedda: The pretty little Valley Girl soprano, Maggie Murk.
Beppe: Dmitri Arkashvili.
Silvio: The other baritone, Rufus Connery.

It was the *Don Giovanni* that was the headache. There

was only one tenor part, so our tenors could alternate in the role and rest their voices, but we needed all three of our sopranos and both our baritones. The hard part was that we had to have a second bass. Eamon McGuire was fine for the Commendatore, but who was going to sing the very important role of my servant, Leporello?

Binnda, Malatesta, and I borrowed Sam Shipperton's office with the wall-sized skry to check out the available talent. There simply wasn't any. One of Shipperton's group, Dick Vidalia, had a bass voice, all right, but it was a hoarse, heavy-metal kind of rasp that made Malatesta shudder. "Better," he declared, "that we transpose the register and I sing this myself!"

"But, my dear Ugolino! That is not how Mozart wrote the opera," Binnda declared, his bright green tongue flapping in dismay.

"Could Purry fill in?" I offered.

That was even worse. Binnda drew himself up to his full height, reaching almost to Malatesta's chest. He stated firmly, "We will use only *human* artists or we will use none at all. Excepting choruses, I mean," he added.

"What about choruses?"

He twisted his nonexistent shoulders—I took it as a shrug. "We have just so many native human singers," he said, sounding a little defensive. "So we must make some compromises. Of course, the chorus parts are not very demanding. I thought for a moment of drafting all the surplus humans here to fill in as what your The Earth people call 'spear-carriers,' eh? But they do not have voices, after all, so why not simply use animation?"

"You mean holograms?"

"As your The Earth expression has it, yes. They will be quite satisfactory. Simply you will have to be careful not to walk through any of them on stage. Of course, that means that everyone will have to double for the choruses. Then we'll record your voices and use the optical simulations in performance—and, oh, my dear friend," he cried, beginning to glow, "wait till you see the finale of *Don!* We'll have the devils screeching at him as he descends into hell, and do you know what I'm going to use for devils? Ossps!"

I tried to remember which were the Ossps—the ones that looked like a cross between a lizard and a bat, I decided. True enough, they looked nastier than any devils I had ever seen on stage, but there was a question in my mind. "Won't that hurt the feelings of any Ossps in our audience?" I asked.

He stared at me incredulously. "Ossps? In one of our audiences? Ho-ho-ho, my dear boy! That is extremely funny! No, no, we are not likely to have any Ossps attending our performances—nor, indeed, would we have anyone else in the audience if they did."

We didn't find our missing bass that day, because Meretekabinnda had to hurry off to take part in the Andromeda probe launch. There was so *much* to do, he declared feverishly—and happily. He wanted to go over the theaters we would play in with me. He wanted to run through *I Pagliacci* again, and maybe make a start on the *Don*. He wanted me to make sure Sam Shipperton double-checked for any bass singers we might have missed.

But more than any of those, he wanted to be on hand for the ceremonies of the probe launch, and so he tootled off and left us to our own devices.

What Malatesta wanted was another coaching session, but I had a better idea. "Let's wait a while, please," I urged. "I'm getting pretty far out of shape, and I'd like to try out Conjur Kowalski's gym."

He acknowledged that a young singer needed his physical strength, and so I made a call on the skry and Conjur agreed to meet me there.

When I say it was a gym, I mean a *gym*. It was a combination of the gymnasium of a well-to-do suburban high school and the New York Athletic Club. He had the complete Nautilus machines, as promised. He had a double-barreled sauna, steam on one end, dry heat on the other. He had Indian clubs and weights and rings and those horsey things gymnasts vault over, and the horizontal bars to go with them; he had basketballs and softballs and bats and gloves; he had assorted sizes of shorts and jockstraps and shoes for every sport; and the whole thing, not counting the room itself, had to have set somebody back twenty or thirty thousand bucks.

The "somebody" was Conjur Kowalski himself. He'd imported every item, paid for out of his earnings on the Narabedla circuit. "So what else would I spend the money on?" he puffed, doing leg-curl sit-ups on the slantboard. "Anyway, I get some of it back from rentals. You ready to shell out the twenty bucks an hour?"

"My pleasure," I said, as off-handedly as any opera star who had just signed a really good contract.

"Shee-it, man!" he said in disgust. "I was hoping you'd want to work it out. I need a little competition, you know? Only not shooting baskets, what I want is some *competitive* sports. Some *body-contact* sports, you know what I'm saying?" He got up from the board and began ratta-tatting the punching bag with his bare fists.

"Another time, maybe," I said, not meaning it. "Can I start on the Nautilus machines?"

But an hour on the machines, and skipping rope, and working out on the bars made my body feel almost as good as my throat did. What the hell, I said, and agreed to put the gloves on with him—big, soft gloves, and face protectors, too; but he gave me three hard rounds. He had the reach on me and the weight and the height, and hitting him in the body with the marshmallow gloves hardly even made him grunt. I had to admit that he won all three rounds, but the third one was at least close.

When we packed it in and soaked in his little steam room for a while, Conjur was actually friendly. "You got to quit cocking your shoulder for your right, Nolly," he said, looking like an Arab ghost in the huge white towels draped around him. "I can always see it coming, and then you're off balance for a counterpunch. You want to try again tomorrow?"

"No," I said.

He laughed. "Then it's still twenty bucks. For the first hour, I mean." He got up and stood under the cold shower in the corner, howling as the water hit him. When he came back he was looking thoughtful. "Listen, Nolly," he said, "I got an idea. After we get a good sweat going here, how about if we jump down to the outside level and swim a few laps in the pool?"

"Too bad you don't have a pool of your own," I said.

"I thought of it," he said. "Ain't worth the price. Anyway, the one with the waterfall's nicer. Tricia's probably there right now." He gave me a friendly poke. "How come you don't go after that? It's Class-A stuff, my man."

"You ought to know," I said. I didn't intend to have an edge on my voice, but it was there and he heard it.

"Don't be gettin' tight-ass, Nolly," he ordered. "She do

what she want to do, that lady. I got no claim." He looked at me, struck by a thought. "You did get your tools all sharpened like they said, didn't you?" I shrugged and didn't speak. "Well, see," he said, floundering as though he were trying to be tactful, "what I want to say is you don't have to worry whose lady she is. She ain't mine, for a fact. Trish, she's a sweet chick, but she's, you know, she's *white*. I got no hate against no whites. But there ain't any nice colored ladies here, you know what I'm saying? It be gettin' time for me to get *serious*."

"Are you talking about getting married?" I asked, honestly surprised.

"And why would I not?" he demanded aggressively. "Cain't do it here. Cain't find no good black woman to hook up with, and if I could cain't have no kids—nobody does, you know? They put something in our food or something."

Conjur had started me on a whole new train of thought. "Are you saying you'd like to go back?" I asked slowly, trying to untangle what he was driving at.

"Effing well right I'd like to go back! Only I can't."

"No," I agreed, "nobody can."

"Aw, shit, man," he said, "that's not what I mean. I mean even if I could, I couldn't."

"What are you talking about?"

"I'm talking," he said patiently, "about how even if Sam offered me a ticket home I'd have to tell him no, thanks."

"That's crazy! Why is that?"

"I'm a deserter from the U.S. of A. Army," he said. "That's why I wouldn't go along with Jerry Harper when he tried to get out. It wouldn't work for me. See," he said, settling the towels around his shoulders, "right before I came up here, the Army had me in this asshole boot camp in Arkansas. You ever been in Arkansas? You ever been a *black man* in Arkansas? Then you wouldn't know, but there was this redneck drill sergeant, a permanent-party staff, and he was on my back every minute. So I popped him one. Then I took off for Chicago. Hitched the whole way, sweating bullets that the MPs would pick me up, looking for my draft card, which I didn't have anymore, you know? And while I was hiding out I heard about this cat who was looking to hire basketball players, no questions asked. I didn't ask any, either. So here I am."

I said, as tactfully as I could, "But really, Conjur, did you have to go that far? You could've reported him if it was really a race thing. I mean, even the Army has its civil-rights people—''

"Nolly," he said patiently, "you don't dig what I'm saying. You're talking now. I'm talking *then*. How long do you think I've been here?"

I blinked at him. "I don't know," I admitted.

"When I deserted was August 1940," he said.

That took me by surprise. I simply hadn't thought of the possibility—no, the damn *certainty*—that it was not only Norah and her friends who had been here for a longish time. "That's almost fifty years ago," I said wonderingly.

"You good at arithmetic," he complimented.

"No, but what I mean is, that's a really long time. How would they ever connect you with some guy that deserted even before World War Two?"

"Maybe they wouldn't," he said. "Maybe I could buy some papers someplace—only where would I do that? From a friend in the business? The people that hid me out would be able to handle that easy enough, but where do you suppose they've got to? The guy that run off from the Army in 1940 isn't going to have any friends around now, is he?" He opened his mouth as though he were going to say something else, then shook himself. "Hell," he said, "time's a-wastin'. Let's get down to the pool and get in those laps. You sweating yet? Okay, my man Knollwood, let's go do it!"

The pool was there, just as before, and so was Tricia. She was lounging on the side of the little pond, brushing her hair, and once again she was naked. She looked up with a friendly smile. "Hey, you guys. Listen, I was just going to start getting dressed so I could watch that, you know, probe launch thing."

"Plenty of time for that," Conjur growled. "We got some swimming to do."

We peeled down and jumped in, and it was just what I needed. I did a dozen fast laps to take my mind off Tricia's bare body. It didn't work. My own body was beginning to have a mind of its own again.

Or half a mind, anyway. What I saw when I pulled myself out of the pool and looked down was a lot more than I'd been used to seeing for twenty years, but it was also a lot less than enough for any practical use.

"Hold it," Conjur ordered from behind me. "Don't be gettin' out yet."

"Why not?" I asked reasonably.

"Count of you and me's going to get under the waterfall for a minute," he said, turning toward it.

"We are?" I asked. But he was already halfway there, so we were. I gave a perplexed glance at Tricia, who just shrugged her pretty shoulders in a way that made me decide I'd better stay in the water a while longer anyway.

I followed, and under the gentle, slow, tepid fall Conjur stood up and said softly, near my ear, "We talk here, nobody be hearin' us. I *hope*."

I had been about to ask him why we were doing this, but then I didn't have to. I closed my mouth with a snap. I squinted out from under the waterfall, at the flowering plants around the pool, at the little rabbity things that were watching us out of the corners of their eyes as they munched the tops off the grasses at the water's edge.

It had not occurred to me that the Narabedlans, who could do just about anything they set their minds to do, might from time to time want to hear what we Earth people talked about when we thought we were alone.

Conjur was reading my mind. "I don't *think* they be listening in on us here," he said, glancing around. "This old waterfall makes a lot of noise, and anyway there's not many people come here much. But I wouldn't take bets on the gym or any other place, because you might not like what would happen. You certainly will not like hanging out there in the square with old Doc Boddadukti coming at you for six or seven weeks."

I jumped. "Why would he be doing that to me?"

"Because of all that stuff you been saying about wanting to trash the man and cut out of here."

"Oh," I said, shaking my head, "but I've given up on that idea. There's no way, is there?"

"Suppose there was," he said.

I thought that over. Conjur certainly looked serious. In fact, he looked angry as he waited for me to answer.

From the edge of the pool Tricia called, "You guys! Hey, if we want to see the launch we better get up to a skry!"

I would have started out, but Conjur put a hand on my shoulder to detain me. "What about it?" he demanded.

I took my time. "If there *was* a way," I said, "I'd probably really like to know about it. But then I'd have to think it over. And now," I said firmly, "let's go see this launch thing."

The rehearsal hall was set up for us, with most of the opera people there and a giant skry screen filling the stage. There were Kekketies hovering around in case of need, and I ordered drinks for the three of us from one of them.

Purry was standing beside the skry, shifting from one foot to another with pleasure. "In just a moment," he called happily, "the transmission will begin, and I will explain what is going on for you."

We found seats, and the screen lighted up just as the Kekkety brought our drinks. It didn't look like much—mostly black, with some geometric patterns.

"What we are seeing now," Purry informed us, "is a reconstruction of the preliminary orbiting of the probe. We are not in real time yet. The probe has been going around the neutron star for, let me see, something like four billion revolutions now, at half a millisecond per revolution—that's something like four of your years, and for all that time the control teams have been stabilizing its orbit in preparation for the launch." In the screen there was a long ellipse traced in light, with a bright little point that was the star just inside one end of the ellipse. As we watched the ellipse shrank and rounded.

It was interesting, but I had something else on my mind. "Conjur?" I whispered, touching his elbow. He turned to look at me without expression. "It isn't that I don't care about the Earth."

"Check," he said, turning back to the screen.

Purry's voice was saying, "Now the orbit is perfectly circular, as you see. The control ship is getting ready to create the magnetic storm on the surface of the star."

I said to the back of Conjur's head, "Really, it's like any other immigration, isn't it? You should understand that. When your folks, I mean way back, were shanghaied into slavery from Africa, they didn't have any choice about it. I bet they all wanted to go back home at first. But, really, aren't you better off now?''

"Oh, *yeah*," Conjur whispered bitterly.

"I mean, every American came from somewhere, right? But once you've made the change, then you can't spend your time thinking about what it's like back home?''

He moved restlessly. "Watch the damn show," he ordered.

I did. Actually, it began to get interesting.

"This is the probe," Purry said, as a spidery, filmy thing took form in a corner of the skry screen. It looked like a spiderweb. "It's fifteen, ah, miles across," Purry went on. "Even bigger than the neutron star, but it's all made out of very thin filament. The whole probe only weighs about two hundred pounds." The image blinked out, replaced by a surly-looking dim red ball. "And that's a closer look at the neutron star. You can't see any features because it's spinning so rapidly. Although it's only seven miles across, it weighs as much as your sun at Earth.''

"Wow," I said. Conjur turned and gave me a curious look, but didn't say anything.

"Now," said Purry, beginning to sound excited, "we're almost at the critical moment! The control ship has set up its magnetic fields. Any time now they'll energize them, and a part of the containment of the neutron star will be breached. A great jet of energy will pour out, revolving with the star. Like a giant lighthouse, but millions of millions of times more powerful, and revolving two thousand times a second!''

I snapped my fingers at a Kekkety. "Time for another drink," I decreed. I was beginning to get into the swing of it. It was hard to imagine that a star could be that small and yet as massive as the sun and spinning that fast. It was like watching Carl Sagan explain the universe. I hadn't understood that, either, but it surely had been pretty to hear him talk.

"There it goes!" Purry shouted.

On the screen a burst of bright flame leaped out of the star and instantly became a disk of light. "They've got a match! The flare is locked in to the probe!" cried Purry. "Look, you can see the probe drifting outward!" And by squinting, yes, I thought I could. There was a cheer from the people around us, all of them peering as hard as I was at the faint, shadowy rim that hung in that disk of light.

"It's a success," Purry announced joyfully. "Now the control ship has to keep the magnetic fields locked onto the ship—as it's pushed away its orbit gets bigger and takes more time. It will be accelerating for a thousand years; then it will drift at eighty percent of the speed of light for more than two million more . . ."

He went on, but by then no one was listening to him anymore. The Kekketies were busy filling fresh drink orders. The babble of conversation grew. Isolated words and phrases sounded over the rest—"Jesus!" and "That's high-tech, all right" and "Holy *shit*."

I turned to Conjur. "Seriously," I said, "do you think people like you and me could go up against *that*?"

He stood up, gazing down at me. But all he said was, "Thanks for the drinks, Stennis. Come on, Tricia, let's get out of here."

CHAPTER

26

When the last of the rubbery transparent stuff over my scars had been absorbed, I had to submit to the Mother's questing tentacles again.

The second time in that smelly, shallow pool wasn't quite as bad as the first. It was bad enough. The trouble with the Mother was that her appetites were not in circuit with her mind. She really had no control over her feeding reflexes— or of her excretory reflexes, or of her egg-laying, which went on forever. When something edible came within range of her questing tentacles she ate it. You couldn't blame her, any more than you could blame someone with digestive problems for breaking wind in church.

Knowing all that, and knowing that sometimes she made mistakes in identification, I approached her very cautiously. The little chocolate-brown bedbug that had brought me chittered warnings to me from the edge of the pool, but I didn't need them to be careful.

It was an English-speaking bedbug, and quite conversational. As I was being probed it translated the Mother's coos and moans for me. "The Mother," it informed me as, naked, I waded toward her restless tentacles, "is quite pleased that two of the operas are by Wolfgang Amadeus Mozart, whose work she enjoys."

I stopped, as far from that brightly colored barrel of a body as I dared. The tentacles reached out for me. "So do I love Mozart. Very much," I said, wincing as the tentacle tip reached for my mouth.

"She has enjoyed watching your rehearsals on the skry," the bedbug went on, raising itself on a couple of its legs to peer down at me. "Be most careful now!" I couldn't answer, with the tentacle slithering down my throat, while the pale eyes of the Mother regarded me opaquely. The bedbug went on, "She hopes that the difficulty with casting the Leporello role is solved quickly. She does not wish *Don Giovanni* to be canceled." He paused to listen, while the Mother cooed gently and the tentacles slid out of me again. "You may come out," it finished. "The Mother says you are quite recovered, and asks why your Earth human Conjur Kowalski cannot sing Leporello."

I was halfway out of the pool by then. "Well," I said, "he does have a nice voice, but he hasn't had any operatic training, you see. Also Leporello and I have to disguise ourselves as each other, so he has to look at least a little bit like me. Conjur just doesn't."

The bedbug moaned at the Mother, who moaned back. "Then what are you going to do about it?"

"Binnda's working on it," I told them. "He's had a couple of ideas." I hesitated, because I hadn't liked the sound of some of them, but the bedbug was insistent.

"State for the Mother what the ideas were," it commanded.

"If I can. Of course, he could transpose the role for a different voice, but that wouldn't be authentic. Then he said

something about, ah, recruiting a bass from Earth." The
word I wanted to use was "kidnapping," but I didn't think
it was tactful. "That would take too long, he said. Or he
thought he could have Dr. Boddadukti alter the voice of a
tenor—there are a couple of them that are available, but that
might take a while, too. The last thing he said was—I'm not
sure I know what he meant—we could buy a bass from the
Ossps."

The bedbug chirped at me in dismay, and when it translated what I had said the Mother's tentacles flailed the pool
into froth. I jumped back to avoid being splashed, pleased
I wasn't in the pool anymore. The bedbug said severely,
"The Mother reminds you that that sort of trade with the
Ossps is interdicted! She will speak to Meretekabinnda about
it herself. Under *no* circumstances is he to make use of any
services from the Ossps! Now come, I will escort you back
to your quarters."

"Oh, my dear boy," said Meretekabinnda reproachfully
when I saw him in the rehearsal hall, "how could you *possibly* have said that to the Mother? I wasn't *serious* about
buying a bass from the Ossps."

"I didn't know that," I said. "I only told her what you'd
said to me."

"But I was only thinking out loud! Anyway," he said,
cheerful again, "I'm happy to tell you that the problem is
solved. Señor Manuel de Negras will join us this afternoon,
and he will sing Leporello."

I asked suspiciously, "Have you, ah, recruited him from
Earth?"

"No, no. He has been—how shall I explain it? He has
been unavailable. In reserve, so to speak. It's a complicated
political matter, my boy, but now, with the probe going so
well and everyone in a sort of era of good feeling I've been
able to secure his services. Here, look." He spoke to the
wall skry, and it obediently displayed the face of a man in
flamenco costume gazing belligerently out at us. "Señor de
Negras was originally recruited as a folk singer and dancer,
it is true. However, he has the trained voice; he studied in
Barcelona and at the Paris Opéra."

I studied the flat, peasant face. "He doesn't look much
like me," I objected.

"Oh, more than you think, dear boy," Binnda twinkled. "At any rate, he's about the same height and build, and that's all that matters for the disguise scene, isn't it? Believe me," he added earnestly, "he is quite satisfactory."

"Then why didn't you get him right away?"

"Because," Binnda said patiently, "there were political problems, didn't I just say so? Now! Before the rest of the cast arrives I would like to show you some of the theaters where we may be playing—as you will see, there are some technical difficulties we will have to face."

So he wiped the Spanish bass off the skry and began to display theaters, as the other singers trickled in. The first one he showed me looked, actually, a little like the old Radio City Music Hall in New York. It was a great, open, bright auditorium with a vast stage. The chief point of difference from the Music Hall was that the entire ground-floor seating area had no real seats in it, being a shallow lake of water. "This will be built on the Tlotta planet," Binnda announced. "The water, of course, is for the Mothers. Do you like it? I designed it myself, but, unfortunately, it is not finished yet. Neither is this one." He showed a quite handsome, quite traditional opera auditorium, all finished in white with gold trim. It looked more like the Kirov in Leningrad than anything else.

"It's a real opera house," I marveled.

"Oh, yes, exactly! Or it will be. This one is on my own planet, and I had hoped to open there—but," he added sadly, "because of the political questions we won't have it finished for some time."

"What political questions?" I asked.

"Nothing that is not now mere history," he said cheerfully, "I hope. Now, look at this! Hopeless, don't you agree?"

The skry was showing an open-air amphitheater, like the Baths of Caracalla bred to the Hollywood Bowl. "Can you imagine the acoustics?" he demanded with distaste. "They will destroy the sound, and this one is even worse."

The next one was almost Greek, a Spartan, empty open stage with tiers of bare seats rising around it. Binnda gazed at it in despair. "Do you see the problem? This is a Ggressna theater! Barak's people, you know? On his planet, where it *rains* all the time. Can you imagine trying to sing in the open, with raindrops falling into your mouth every time you open it?'' He shook his shoulders morosely and sighed. ''If only we could have something like Bayreuth. That wonderful hall! Nothing straight in it, no boxes to swallow the sound—''

''And no seats fit to sit in,'' put in Eamon McGuire, coming up to us with Floyd Morcher in trail.

Binnda blinked at him. Most of the company was gathered around us now. He seemed embarrassed. ''But,'' he said reproachfully, ''comfort does not matter. None of your theaters have seats that are right for me, you know. It is *music* that matters. And we had better get to it! Gather around me, everyone, while I show you what we are going to do for our *Don Giovanni!*''

What we were going to do for our production of *Don Giovanni* was—I'll put it as conservatively as I can—*wonderful*.

I've always felt that it was just about impossible for anyone to put on a perfect *Don Giovanni* on Earth. The technical problems are terrible. Both Mozart and his librettist, Lorenzo Da Ponte, were very casual about where they set their scenes. Act One of the opera alone calls for five different sets—a courtyard, a square, a country place, a garden, and the interior of a palace, and they switch around faster than any human stagehands can move them. In a place like the Met, with all its built-in elevators and turntables, it's possible—barely possible—to reset the scenes without totally destroying the pace of the performance, but most houses don't even try. They tend to ignore Da Ponte's directions and have Giovanni meet Donna Elvira in the same place where he stabbed the Commendatore, because the directions are too hard to follow. Da Ponte didn't care. In Mozart's time the audiences didn't, either. They were quite content to have the curtain rung down while the singers did their arias, with probably half a dozen encores. That gave the eighteenth century stagehands time to sweat the new set into position behind the curtain. It is a matter of record that the singers often complained bitterly about grunts and bangs and crashes that came from the other side of the curtain to punctuate their high notes, but they didn't complain much. They liked having the stage all to themselves, so they could milk all the bows the customers were willing to tolerate.

On Narabedla almost the whole set was one of their hologrammish things. Problems of moving furniture simply didn't arise.

A few props and settings had to be "practical," because we had to use them—the stone horse for the Commendatore to sit on when he's a statue, and the garden gate that Donna Anna locks in the first act, for instance, because Leporello has to bang against it. Everything else was only light.

Then there was the music. Da Ponte's libretto calls for three separate orchestras, which hardly any Earthly impresario can afford. Binnda could. He had three separate Purries tootling away, one in the pit and one on each side of the stage, but you couldn't see the Purries. All you could see was the unreal, hologrammed musicians.

Even a Purry is limited in what instruments he can duplicate, so Binnda allowed a little technology there, too. Some of the sounds were fiddled electronically so that we got the right timbre for violins, clarinets, kettledrums— whatever. It worked. Even the sound effects. The thunderclap in Act One was loud enough, and real enough, to jolt me. And it came, Binnda pointed out proudly, with a genuine Van de Graaf–spark lightning bolt that seared right across the stage.

When Binnda had finished demonstrating the sets for our third opera there was a patter of applause. Gratified, he bowed, waving those snaky arms deprecatingly. "I am so delighted that you approve," he said modestly. "I had only hoped to provide staging that would be equal to your talents." He stretched himself upright, peering past us into the rear of the hall. "Ah," he said, the green tongue licking out of the ugly little mouth with pleasure, "our remaining artist has arrived! Ladies and gentlemen, may I present our second bass, Señor Manuel de Negras!"

Manuel de Negras was younger than I thought from his picture. He didn't seem to be much more than twenty, tall for a Spaniard, very dark, with a solid, strong face that, every once in a while, broke out in a smile of pleasure as he looked around at the rest of us. When we shook hands he apologized to me, in Spanish, for having no English, and in English I apologized to him for my lack of Spanish. But both of us had a little French and Italian, naturally. When Binnda insisted on beginning at once to run through the first act of the opera, de Negras reading his lines from a script, we were able to say what we had to say to each other.

The man did have a good, rich, humorous bass voice, just right for Leporello. I was pleased when, halfway through the second scene, I was offstage long enough to go down into the audience seats and watch him deal with my discarded sweetheart, Donna Elvira.

Tricia had come by to see what was going on, and I sat next to her. "Do you know this guy?" I whispered to her. "Everybody else seems to."

"Never saw him before," she said. "Listen, is he saying what I think he's saying?"

He had reached "*Madamina: il catologo e questo*," where he tells Elvira about all the women I've had—a hundred and forty in Italy, two hundred and thirty-one in Germany, and so on. "I guess so," I told her. "He's adding up all my ladies for her."

She looked at me with interest. "So you play a real super-stud, right?"

"It's the story of Don Juan, after all," I told her. "And Leporello there is my servant, and his greatest wish is that he could run up the same score for himself."

"For Manuel de Negras, too, I bet," Tricia offered, looking up at him. "After where he's been, I mean."

"I thought you said you didn't know him."

"Well, I don't. Before my time. But I know where he's *been* the last ten years or so, didn't you? They put him away for trying to hijack a trip home, like Jerry Harper. Binnda just got him out of slow time."

With our last singer in place, we began rehearsing in earnest. Ten hours a day, every day; and it would have been longer hours than ten if Binnda himself hadn't been happily dashing off every now and then to congratulate the Ptrreeks, or with other Mnimn to be congratulated by the Hrunwians or the Quihigs, on how well each had done their respective parts in launching the Andromeda probe. "Purely ceremonial events," he confided to me as he came back from one more exchange of compliments, "but, oh, how good it is to have everyone friendly with each other again! Not counting the Ossps, of course. Now let's get busy on Act Two!"

That was the best part of all. When my voice was better it was not only better, it was *fine*. Binnda was delighted. Malatesta was proud. Norah Platt, once again bounding about like a twenty-year-old, was smug. ("I *told* you Dr. Boddadukti would make it all well, dear!") Floyd Morcher actually admitted he liked the way I did the Prologue, and even the other baritone stopped looking hostile and only looked glum.

If I was good as Tonio, I was even better as Don Giovanni. I looked the part—boots, cloak, plumed hat, sword at my side; it's a swashbuckling role, and I played it like Errol Flynn. I sang the part—forgive the immodesty—I sang it as well as any Don I'd ever heard. After the first fully staged run-through Binnda would have kissed me if I'd let him. "My dear boy," he cried, peering up at me and resting one of those scaly, three-fingered hands on my chest—he couldn't quite reach my shoulder—"you are *ideal*!"

I didn't dispute him. I thought he was right.

The only, very small fly in the ointment was in the acting. I was having trouble trying to find the right interpretation of Don Giovanni as a person. There are a thousand questions

about the Don that aren't answered in Da Ponte's libretto.
They start at the very beginning—has he really made it with
Donna Anna, or did she fight him off? What is his relation-
ship with his servant, Leporello?—is there friendship between them, or does the Don simply use him as a veritable
Kekkety? When he invites the statue of the dead Commendatore to dinner is he bluffing, or really fearless? What
I wished for was a good, theatrical, human director to help
my acting interpretation of the role. I didn't have one. When
I asked the closest thing I had to that, my coach, Malatesta,
he simply sighed and said in English, "Knoll-a-wood, merely
sing-a the lines." When I asked Binnda he shrugged his
upper torso and told me that I could choose any interpretation I liked, because none of the audiences would ever have
seen any other. When I said that I really *had* to know what
motivated the Don, Binnda thought for a moment, checked
the skry to see if he had any ceremonial mutual congratulations to go to, and then agreed to come over to my place
that evening for some of my good The Earth whiskey.

It was a welcome break for me, too. With two major roles
to get up, plus a full day of rehearsals every day, plus vocalizing with Ugolino Malatesta and, when I could find the
time, an hour or so working out in Conjur's gym, there
wasn't much left of my days.

There wasn't nearly *enough* left, because there was so
much more that I wanted to do. There was my house to
refurnish, my neighbors to meet, the rest of the opera troupe
to get to know. Not counting all the questions about Narabedla itself, and about the Fifteen Associated Peoples and
their multitudinous relationships and activities that I still
hadn't answered. I did from time to time remember to think
of Marlene and Irene Madigan and my abandoned clients
back on Earth. I remembered them with affection. I sincerely
hoped that they were all well and happy, but I can't say I
did any of those things very often. There was simply too
much in the here and now.

The probe launch to the Andromeda galaxy that we had
watched on the skry had been bloody awesome. As technology it was so vastly beyond anything human that I could
hardly take it in. Just to start with, these people harnessed
stars to their purposes! They set them working the way I

might turn the ignition key in a car. More than that, it was the incredible scope of the project that made my eyes widen and my breath come short, for they were starting something that would not come to an end for *three million years*.

And the Andromeda launch was only the newest and far-thest-ranging of their probes; they had already sent off robot exploring sailships to fifteen other external galaxies and star clusters, including a dozen major galaxies I had never heard of. (Purry told me human beings had never seen them, be-cause they lay on the far side of the core of our own galaxy.) A thousand other probes were on their way to the unexplored corners of our own galaxy, to the core, to the far edges of the galactic rim, to the spherical halo of stars outside the galactic disk. Many, of course, had long since arrived at their destinations. Some had found wonders (binary pairs, with one dense little star sucking the blood from its larger, more tenuous sister; black holes; nova shells). Some had found more practical treasures; they had identified sixteen planets with life, suitable for colonization or (like Earth) for sup-plying trade goods (like us). Another dozen planets were not life-friendly—yet—but they were seeding them with dust or chemicals or organic matter so that someday, maybe in a thousand years at best, they too could be colonized. There were eight other stars which had not yet developed planets; each had a sort of Saturn-ring disk of uncoalesced particles around it. Perhaps each of them, in a million years or so, might have started developing a solar system if left alone. They weren't left alone. One or another of the Fifteen Peo-ples, usually several of them in partnership, were busily shuffling those particles around to make a screen around the parent stars, to trap all their escaping energy to make power for their other enterprises. In a dozen places they were busy coagulating clouds of interstellar gases. Why? To make sun-shades. To stop the radiation from supernovae that might otherwise threaten inhabited places on the far sides of the clouds. In the empty space between the stars they had con-structed a thousand immense space telescopes—mirrors a thousand miles across, radio antennae forty times as big—to study the stars and systems they had not yet reached with a go-box.

And that was only the astronomical part. I could under-stand that—some of it. I could even understand, a little, some of the biological things they did, like making the Kekketies, and Purry, and a hundred other creations that did the work none of the Fifteen Peoples cared to do. I don't mean that I could understand *how* they did it, but *what* they did was simple enough to comprehend. But—mathematics! Molecular biology! Nuclear particle physics! Even Purry couldn't explain any of that to me. He couldn't even find the words in English that might translate some of the ideas, whether I then could understand the ideas or not, because such words did not yet exist on Earth. There was no need for them. The things the words referred to had not yet been discovered.

When Meretekabinnda showed up I tried some of the questions on him. He seemed tickled by the fact that I was interested in such things. "You're really quite peculiar, Nolly," he said affectionately. "Most of our guest artists from your The Earth don't care much for scientific things."

"They're performers," I explained. "Singers don't get worried about anything farther away than their press notices and the state of their vocal cords."

"Oh, yes, I suppose that's it. I know that on your The Earth you do have all sorts of chemists and astrologers and shamans. No doubt they would be more curious about such things. Well! How can I help you? The genetic things? That's mostly the Ossps, you know; we Mnimn don't deal much in such things."

"Well, that's what I wanted to ask you. The Fifteen Associated Peoples. How do you decide who's going to do what? How do you share out the business?"

"Ah," he said, bobbing his upper body. "I see. Well, you know what the Polyphase Index is?"

"Something like the Stock Exchange?" I hazarded.

"In a way, perhaps," he said doubtfully. "Here, let me borrow your skry. This is what it looks like."

The graph he displayed on the skry was in three dimensions and a whole spectrum of colors, and it changed and flowed before my eyes. It measured, he explained, the available and committed resources of each alien race for each shared project.

Binnda pointed out the tiny peaks that were devoted to the Narabedla project. It was almost too small to show. Even within it, we actors, singers, and baton twirlers were lumped together in a single little spike called "Cultural Activities," and we were the tiniest item in the group. "As you see," he said, "only eight of the Associated Peoples are committed to Narabedla. Pity, but some are simply cultural morons. But now when we come to the probes, and particularly the Andromeda project . . ." The peaks were a mountain range now, immense spikes of lilac and blue and green. "That's a *major* area of cooperation, you see! Oh, my dear boy, I can't tell you how much we have needed a success like that! And it's shared by every single one of the Fifteen Associated Peoples—except, of course, the Ossps."

"Right," I said. "And what do the Ossps do?"

"Genetics," he said shortly.

"Yes, I understand that, but why are they so—I don't know—disliked?"

"Because they are very dislikable, my boy," he said, refilling his glass. "It was probably a mistake to admit them to membership. Now, really, weren't we supposed to be discussing your interpretation of the role of Don Giovanni?"

"Sure," I said, refreshing my own drink, "but right now I want to hear more about the Ossps."

He said firmly, "You won't. I don't want to discuss them. If it was up to me I'd put the whole planet in slow time."

"But I'd just like to know—"

"*No*, Nolly," he said, and closed the three-cornered mouth with a snap.

I took a long pull at my drink, resentfully. We were both silent for a moment. Truth to tell, I'd lost interest in how to interpret the Don's motivations and needs; the good The Earth whiskey had loosened Binnda's bright green tongue, and it seemed like the best chance I would ever have to ask some questions.

I tried another tack. "All right, then what about slow time?"

"What about it?"

"Well, our new bass, Manuel de Negras. What was he in slow time for?"

"Ask him."

I said reasonably, "But that's hard, Binnda. He doesn't speak any English."

"Purry will translate for you. He's had Spanish installed for de Negras." Then he relented. "But, ah, my dear boy, why do you concern yourself with unpleasantness? Manuel de Negras did a foolish thing; he attempted to return to your The Earth. As others have done. With the same result: he was placed in slow time. It did him no harm. It simply removed him from circulation for a while. After all, slow time is not a bad thing; we all wind up there sooner or later, don't we?''

"We *do?*"

"We either do that or we die, don't you know? We Mnimn are not quite as well off as you people, you know. With good care and repair, your The Earth people can last for over three hundred of your The Earth years. Our theoretical limit is maybe two hundred and a bit. Then there's cellular degeneration, and then''—he shrugged wryly—"it's the slow-time vaults.''

"And what happens in the slow-time vaults?''

"You just sit there," he said wryly. "And you hope that sometime in the next thousand years or so—say, a week in slow time—people will figure out how to fix the cells. But even the Ossps don't hold out much hope for that.''

I stared at him. "So nobody ever really *dies?*"

"Oh, of course they do. It just takes a long, long time.''

I shook my head. "You must have a hell of a population problem.''

He bobbed his upper torso affirmatively. "That's why we're so busy looking for new living space. A planet like your The Earth would be a home for billions of, say, Bach'hets. And don't think there aren't a lot of people who'd like to use it for that.''

He tossed off the last of his whiskey, and slipped off the couch to the floor. "It's getting late," he said. "Now. I have been working on preparations for our tour. Never fear, you will be making your debut in a very few days! But you must have your rest to protect that golden voice.''

"All right," I said, getting up reluctantly to escort him to the door.

As he was leaving, he paused. "And when will you have that housewarming party you've been promising us?'' he asked jovially.

"Well, pretty soon," I said, gazing around my new home. All the furniture was in; I was as ready as I was likely to be.

"Please don't put it off too long. And make sure, please, to have plenty of your good The Earth whiskey, and a lot to eat. I've taken the liberty of mentioning it to a number of my colleagues—Ptrreek and Hrunwians, mostly. You don't mind?'' I shook my head. "It's really important for us to get together socially, you know. There are—well, frictions now and then. But the Andromeda probe has made things a lot friendlier, and I'm anxious for some of the others to get a really good impression of your The Earth. Even if they can't visit it themselves, as I have. You see, I really love the place! I only wish it could be opened up soon—"

He stopped, looking embarrassed. Alerted, I asked, "What do you mean, opened up?"

He said unwillingly, "Well, sooner or later it's bound to happen, isn't it? Some of the Peoples think it should be open now—oh, not as a *member,* of course, but for visiting. But I think the protected status will remain for a long time yet."

I shook my head. "I don't understand," I said. "Who are you protecting?"

And he said simply, "You."

CHAPTER
28

As all of my girlfriends had told me in the old days, a party should be planned for. I didn't have time for that, but I went ahead and had it anyway.

There wasn't any problem about whom to invite. I skried invitations to everyone I knew and crossed my fingers. The Kekketies provided everything I demanded of them, but I couldn't help worrying about whether I'd have enough room, or alternatively whether anyone would come, or whether I'd provided enough food and drink.

I needn't have worried. Everybody showed up, and most of them brought contributions of their own.

Tricia showed up early with Malcolm Porchester, back from his sand-painting chores. Both were bearing gifts. "I cooked for your party," Tricia said happily, setting down little trays with foil on top. She unwrapped a plate of what looked like pale fudge. "This is coconut burfy, and these sweet pastries have honey and pistachio nuts in them. And the quiche just needs to be heated."

What Porchester had brought was a white enamel tray and a couple of small sacks of powder. "To decorate your party," he grinned, and wouldn't explain. He set himself up in a corner of the bedroom, and I left him to it, because other guests were arriving.

Norah showed up with Ephard Joyce on one arm and my castrato coach, Ugolino Malatesta, spry and smiling, on the other. Ugolino had a huge, round-bellied bottle of Lacrimae Cristi, and Joyce was carrying Norah's contribution to the party, little silver-paper boxes of candied almonds and pecans. "I wanted to get something nicer," she apologized, "but you know how hard it is to get special orders filled now that the yacht's off in the colonies somewhere. Oh, you didn't know? Well, Mr. Davidson-Jones thought it best to keep it away from the major ports for a while. Because of the questions that were being asked, you know. No, no, don't feel bad, Nolly. I'm sure all those little problems you caused will blow over."

I kissed her cheek apologetically and turned to the next arrivals. I had almost forgotten there was anything to blow over.

Everybody came, starting with the whole opera troupe. Even Canduccio sulked in, looking daggers at Ugolino as he waltzed with Norah to the music Purry was pouring out, show tunes and gentle rock. Sam Shipperton was there, bringing a pretty little Chinese girl I'd never met. Conjur Kowalski followed them in—a little cool, a little reserved (as he'd been ever since the night of the Andromeda launch), but he brought a bottle of Jack Daniel's, crunched my shoulder good-naturedly enough with his immense right hand, and promptly began dancing with the pretty little harpist from across the street. Most of my neighbors had showed up, too. That was just as well for them. There were plenty of people, there was plenty to eat and plenty to drink, but one of my concerns turned out justified. The house just wasn't big enough for the party. We spilled out into the street, and so all of my neighbors were at the party whether they wanted to be or not.

And that was just the human beings. At Meretekabinnda's

advice I had invited all the aliens I knew, and a few I didn't think I did. Most of them showed up, too. Binnda brought two bottles of Glenlivet Scotch and another Mnimn named (I think) Fl'tstitsni. Fl'tstitsni was female. At least, I assumed so, watching them dance with all their limber limbs entwined around each other. The Tlotta-Mother didn't come herself, of course—she couldn't—but three of her bedbug drones were there, skittering around under everybody's feet and taking chittering part in the conversations, one of them in English. Even Barak came, bringing Dr. Boddadukti with him. I was not real easy in the Duntidon's presence, though he seemed affable enough. Barak himself was a little sulky because the Mother had backed Binnda up in declining to do the Busoni *Turandot,* but he seemed to enjoy the music and the dancing, burping out compliments to the couples on the floor. He only stayed a minute, though—complained he couldn't stand the smell of the Earth food and beverages.

That was a good thing. It wasn't until he and Boddadukti left and the air had cleared out a little that the rest of us could enjoy them.

Enjoy them we did. Well, most of us did, most of them. I made the mistake of trying Tricia's vegetable quiche, and she caught me at it. "Oh, isn't it any good?" she asked anxiously. "I was afraid I'd spoiled it. I couldn't get any hing to put into it so I used onions, even though they're not acceptable to Lord Krishna."

"It's fine," I lied, chewing without swallowing. "I don't miss the hing at all."

"But we always used hing in the commune, and, hey, nobody's eating the eggplant salad either," she said disconsolately, but then I felt a huge hand on my shoulder and turned to see Conjur grinning at me.

"You eatin' that stuff?" he demanded. "You got guts, Nolly. Listen, Binnda's looking for you. He's outside. Says he's got some people he wants to introduce to you."

The reason they were outside was that one of the "people" was one of those big things that look like a praying mantis, a Ptrreek, and another was one of the skinny baboons with the pine-needle Mohawks. Both were fourteen feet tall. They almost touched the imitation sky of the ceiling, but they weren't any uglier than the third "person" Binnda had invited. That was a Hrunwian, and he looked, more than anything else, like a five-foot, Cellophane-skinned shrimp.

I swallowed the miserable quiche as Binnda introduced us, beginning with the Ptrreek. "This is Mr. Tsooshirrisip, who is in charge of all exotic entertainers for the Ptrreek. He particularly admires works about your human The Earth superstitions."

I didn't try to shake hands. I couldn't have reached his, anyway.

The shrimplike Hrunwian, whose name I didn't catch at all, whistled something that Binnda translated as, "He hopes to see you soon. And here is Neereeieeree"—Binnda didn't so much speak the name as whinny it—"who is of course an Aiurdi. They have never had any of your The Earth entertainers on his planet, but one can always hope they will change their minds, can't one?"

"One can," I said. This time I did shake hands, although it was more like clutching a whiskbroom. Apparently it was the right thing to do, because Binnda beamed at me.

"Since not all of our guests can come into your rather small house," he said merrily, patting my shoulder, "suppose you and I bring them something from the bar, eh? Come along, then!" And on the way he whispered, "They're very important people, my dear boy! We're so lucky they decided to come—it can mean great things for our tour. And, oh, it's a fine party!"

I thought he was right about that. It was a good party, and I was being a good host. After I'd seen that our weirdo guests in the street had plenty of good The Earth liquor and even some of Tricia's not so good The Earth macrobiotic food, I circulated. I told pretty little Maggie Murk that she looked lovely in her off-the-shoulder, 1920s, flapper-skirted dress (which was very true), and the other soprano, Sue-Mary Petticardi, said, "Thank you," for her as she drew her away. I told Ephard Joyce I was glad to see him there (which was a lie), and he said to me, "You know, I've been giving a lot of thought to what you said. About me being a star back home, that is." I pointed out to Bart Canduccio where I kept the *regalo* he had given me, right next to the skry, and he informed me that I was a good enough fellow but that (looking poisonously at Ugolino Malatesta) some of my friends didn't deserve me. I told the Ptrreek, Tsooshirrisip (out in the street, of course), that I was delighted to see all our races mingling in social harmony—by then I was fairly well liquored—and he whistled something that my Purry translated as, "If you come to our planet I hope you're not as repulsive as the last bunch."

But Binnda pulled me away apologetically. "Don't mind anything he says," he whispered. "You'll win them over, I know you will. Have another drink." And he refilled my glass from the bottle he carried wound into one arm.

Apparently Binnda had not noticed that my glass was already half full. I had never drunk half-and-half Scotch and Jack Daniel's before. It didn't matter. The party was going well, and I was beginning to float.

I was also beginning to feel very conscious of the sights and smells of the pretty women who were gracing my home. I caught sight of Maggie Murk dancing with the Russian tenor, Dmitri Arkashvili, and it suggested something to me. Maggie was singing Zerlina to my Don Giovanni, and there had been something definitely warm-blooded in the way she responded to me in the flirtation scene in rehearsals. As soon as indefatigable Purry began the next selection I cut in.

Maggie felt as good in my arms as she looked and smelled. I whispered in her ear, "You know, this party won't last forever. I wonder if you'd like to stay a bit when it's over."

She snuggled closer. "But the Kekketies will clean everything up for you," she said demurely.

"Oh, well, I wasn't thinking so much of doing housework," I told her, tracing her rib cage with my fingertips. "Maybe not even stay here at all, you know? We could go down to that place with the pool and the waterfall, just the two of us, where it's nice and quiet—"

I felt a vigorous tap on my shoulder. I turned in annoyance to see which mannerless male was trying to cut in, but it wasn't a male at all. It was tall, dark, somber Sue-Mary Petticardi, glaring at me. "Malcolm Porchester's looking for you," she told me. "Maggie! Don't you think it's about time we thought of going home?"

I gazed after them, Maggie meekly following as the taller, older woman tugged her along. It was a downer, all right. Then I turned to see Malcolm Porchester at the door of my bedroom, beaming as he beckoned to me. "Come and look," he said proudly. Tricia came over to me, giggling an odd little giggle. She took me by the arm and led me into the bedroom.

There on my dresser Porchester had made a sort of sand painting, a picture of me (it did look a little like me) dressed in my Don Giovanni finery, making a sweeping bow. Porchester hadn't used sand. The stuff had produced almost a monochrome—white, yellow, brownish powders. I noticed that there were a dozen little plastic spoons arranged around the edges of the picture, but I didn't understand their meaning at first.

"Thanks a lot, Malcolm," I said. "It's beautiful, only how am I going to keep it from getting ruined?"

"It's not meant to *keep*," said Malcolm, sounding offended.

Tricia was already handing me one of the little spoons. "You get the first hit," she said. "I was the one that supplied the three different kinds of coke, but the artwork was Malcolm's idea. Go ahead, Nolly, take a toot. It's really all very mild stuff."

Comprehension struck. "Ah," I said, temporizing. "It's, uh, very nice of you."

I didn't entirely mean it. I'd never done cocaine, not even at parties. Back in the old days on Earth I had always been uneasy when someone brought out the little silver snuffbox or the plastic pouch, and I was twice as uneasy here. What were the drug laws on Narabedla? No one had told me. Was this going to mean something like slow time? Or even worse?

From the doorway I heard Binnda's voice. "What is this I smell? Can it really be some of your good The Earth coke? May I?"

So it wasn't against the local laws, after all.

Actually I didn't need cocaine, or the joints that my next-door neighbor, the figure-skater, was passing around. The drinks and the party had me high enough already. Everybody seemed to be having a good time. Even Norah Platt, in spite of her advanced years, was cutting the rugs with the best of them, and when she collapsed on the briefly vacated edge of the couch I knelt beside her. "Having fun? You look like a teenager out there!"

"Oh, I feel that way, Nolly dear! It's a wonderful party. And of course I'm completely recovered. Dr. Boddadukti is so *very* good, and doesn't even leave a scar—I do wish we'd had barber-surgeons like him when I was a girl! So gentle!"

Well, I'd had all those drinks. "But Norah," I said reasonably, "he drinks human blood."

"You never saw him do that!"

"I saw him lick it off his claws, and he didn't spit it out."

"Well," said Norah vaguely, "what difference does it make, really? The Duntidons don't eat *intelligent* beings anymore, so I suppose in a way it's a treat for him—oh, thank you, Ugo dear." She was talking to the castrato, who had brought over a pair of drinks for them.

I didn't even look at him. "What do you mean, any*more?*"

She looked exasperated. "Oh, Nolly, what difference does it make what they used to do in the old days when they had wars? One does hear these stories about the Duntidons, but they're all in the past, aren't they?" Malatesta somehow managed to squeeze into a space on the couch beside her, listening politely.

"In any case," he told me in Italian, slow enough for Norah to follow, "we do not need to see Duntidons very often, do we?"

"I think not," Norah said. "As I understand it, we'll be visiting the Hrunwians and the Ptrreek."

"Have you been to those places?"

"Nolly, dear," she said, "I've been to *all* the places. All the ones that let people in, anyway. Remember how long I've been here! These are quite nice ones. Well, true, the Ptrreek do smell a bit odd, and the Hrunwians are a bit rough and ready, you know. But there's a zoo on the Ptrreek planet; if we have time I'd love to see it again with you. We could pack a lunch, just the two of us."

"Careful, careful," Malatesta warned good-naturedly. "This good young man will think you have an amatory interest in him."

"Why should she not?" demanded Bart Canduccio, drunk and nasty. I hadn't seen him approach, but there he was, wavering as he stood over us. "She has already shown that she can take interest even in a eunuch!"

I could have told him that, true or not, that was not a good thing to say.

Malatesta's good humor dried up like spit on a skillet. He pushed himself away from Norah and bravely stood up to Canduccio. He snarled something unpleasant—all I could make out was the word "*ubriaco,*" meaning drunk—and Canduccio responded in kind. Operatic Italian was not enough to follow that exchange. All I could be sure of was that it was dirty, unpleasant, and loud. Loud enough so that the people around were turning toward us, and even Purry's music faltered as he peered over at us.

Norah stood up angrily. "Ugo! Bart! The two of you, stop this at once or I'll never speak to either of you again—oh, you *beast*," she hissed at Canduccio as he flung some more Italian at her and flounced out of the room.

Malatesta shrugged, triumphant. Norah turned to me. "I do apologize, Nolly," she said penitently. "Bart simply can't drink distilled liquor, it makes him crazy. And he's just the tiniest bit jealous, you know, because he stopped in last night and found Ugo and me watching a film together."

"A cassetta," Malatesta corroborated in English, grinning. "Your, how is it called, *Deep-a T'roat*."

Norah scowled at him. "But do go on with the party, please," she called to the room at large. "Tricia! Come dance with Nolly. Purry, start the music again, please?"

In spite of what Malatesta had said (not to mention what I'd seen with my own eyes when we were getting ready for our little operations), I had trouble thinking of Norah Platt as a functioning sexual person. The knowledge of her age kept getting in the way, and when Tricia whispered in my ear, "Was she, Nolly? Coming on to you, I mean?" I was shocked.

"She's two hundred years old!" I said.

"But, hey, that's not answering my question," she said, pressing against my chest. "And I saw the way you were hitting on Maggie Murk. You're wasting your time there, you know. Sue-Mary keeps her all to herself."

"Oh, hell," I said, startled. It was true that the two of them lived together, and spent a lot of time whispering to each other. But I just hadn't thought.

Tricia said dreamily, "You know, you do have pretty neat pecs. For a singer, I mean."

Dozen-year-old memories were coming back to me. I could feel interest developing inside me. "Tricia," I whispered, "I like yours, too."

And what might have come of it I don't know, but Binnda spoiled it. He ended the party.

"Dear members of the Greater Bolshoi Opera Company

and honored friends," he called, sounding very pleased with himself. "May I have your attention?"

He had climbed up onto the table next to the skry, steadying himself against it with one limber arm. "It is a tragedy to end such a joyous occasion, but all good things must come to an end. And I have an announcement to make."

That took care of the party. People turned toward him, even coming in from outside to hear. Already the Kekketies, taking their cue from him, were beginning silently to move about, collecting empty glasses and debris. Through the door to my bedroom I could see the Mother's drones carefully sweeping up the last few grains of cocaine—I supposed to take home to Mama.

When he had everyone's full attention, Binnda said, "This is more than a housewarming party for our dear Nolly Stennis. It is the beginning of a wonderful new episode in the dissemination of the operatic culture of your The Earth among the Fifteen Associated Peoples. My announcement is this: I have just reached agreement with our good friends from Hrunw and Ptrreek. Our tour begins at once! Tomorrow we leave for the Ptrreek planet, and our first public performance of this greatest of all opera seasons!"

CHAPTER
29

Kekketies took our bags away at the rehearsal hall, and Meretekabinnda made a little speech.

He introduced the honored guests, starting with Barak, slumping restlessly around the stage on his wobbly arms, going on to the Ptrreek, Tsooshirrisip. None of that was necessary. Nor were any of Binnda's compliments on how well

we were going to perform, and how splendid it was of the
Ptrreek to invite us, and how certain he was that, with our
debut following so closely on the wonderful accomplishment
of the launching of the Andromeda probe, the Fifteen Associated Peoples were headed for a new era of peace and
goodwill and constructive cooperation for the whole galaxy.

It got interesting when he warned us to behave. "The trad-
ing regulations of the Fifteen Associated Peoples are very
strict, and the Eyes of the Tlotta-Mother"—he waved at a
couple of the little bedbugs, crouched at the end of the
stage—"who are traveling with us will report any infrac-
tions. That means any breach of the regulations at all, my
dear friends. You must not, any of you, engage in any commercial transactions of any kind with any nonhuman person
for the duration of your stay on any planet. Is that understood by all of us?"

Pause. Then he raised his snaky arms and declaimed,
"Now let us move on to the go-box! Our tour is beginning!"

It was one of the big go-boxes, but even so it couldn't hold
the dozen of us humans and our baggage, never mind the
aliens. It took two loads to get us all in. "Ladies first," cried
Binnda cheerfully, shepherding Tricia and Norah Platt and
the sopranos into the first load, along with a couple of the
funnies—apparently claiming honorary status as females for
the purpose, though heaven alone knew what gender they
really were.

The door *whuffed* shut. I rested a hand on it, waiting for
it to come back for the rest of us.

It occurred to me that it was very like the door I'd entered
to visit Henry Davidson-Jones in his office.

I thought hard about that for a while, so that I hardly
noticed when it opened again and we got in and it closed on
us once more. It wasn't easy to concentrate. We were all
pressed together. Floyd Morcher was standing quietly, eyes
closed, moving his lips in silent prayer. Canduccio was os-
tentatiously pushing his way as far from Malatesta as possible; and there was a residual cockroachy smell in the place.
It couldn't have been from the bedbug, as it climbed into its
niche high in the wall and gazed down at us. It had to be left
over from our host, the Ptrreek Tsooshirrisip.

Then the door opened again.

Warm, wet air came into the go-box and smote us. Blue light came down from a dark-blue sky. Half a dozen other Ptrreeks were waiting for us, at the side of vehicles—I guessed they were vehicles, though what they looked like was giant-sized bathtubs mounted on tiny, thick wheels.

It was a wholly fascinating, absorbing, incredible spectacle—good God, actually setting foot on an *alien planet*!

I didn't do it justice. I was still pondering, and slowly, slowly, something had at last penetrated my poor Earthhuman brain.

I turned and looked back at the space-traveling go-box we had just come out of, exactly like the one that had taken me to Davidson-Jones's office for the phone call to Marlene. And it was only then that I realized what planet I had been on when I made that telephone call.

CHAPTER
30

The Ptrreek planet had a deep blue sky, almost a slate blue, with a tiny, bright blue sun in the middle of it, hammering heat down at me. And we were in a real city. It even had a skyline, and if you half closed your eyes you could almost think it looked a little bit like the canyons of Wall Street, or downtown Chicago. To make it seem a *lot* familiar, though, you had to close your eyes entirely, and even then, it didn't *sound* like anything on Earth. There weren't any taxicab horns, gears shifting, trucks backfiring. There were plenty of traffic noises that came from the wheeled bathtub things whizzing by, but the noisiest things around were the tall buildings themselves. They *creaked*. The Ptrreek skyscrapers weren't masonry, glass, and steel. I suppose they were something like wood.

They came in clumps, like bamboo clusters, eight or ten dark, skinny, needle-shaped towers bound together by closed passageways. The things that held them must have been loosely joined, because the clusters moved in the wind, and screeched as they moved. And all around us there were Ptrreeks, twice as tall as I was, wearing filmy, feathery cloaks in bright-spectrum colors and gazing at us curiously out of their faceted insect eyes.

As soon as I stepped out of the box I saw all this and the sudden pang of missed opportunities back on Henry Davidson-Jones's yacht receded in my mind. I was gaping around like any hayseed on his first trip to the Big Apple. It took a sharp nudge from Tricia to bring me out of it. "Watch it," she warned, and I did a little waltz step out of the way just in time to avoid being trampled by Tsooshirrisip, the big Ptrreek who had been on Narabedla with us. He loped past us to meet another Ptrreek getting out of one of the bathtub cars, the two of them chirping and barking and flapping their cloaks in what looked like joy. Then Tsooshirrisip turned and gazed at us. He beckoned to Purry, lingering modestly out of the way, and then chirped something at our company as they emerged.

Purry translated for us. "Mr. Tsooshirrisip welcomes you to the world of the Ptrreek," he piped, and added, "He also says he hopes you enjoy the clean stink of Ptrreek air after all those foul odors you have been living among; and now you are all, please, to get in the cars which have been provided for you."

I hesitated. "What about our bags?"

"Coming, coming, dear boy," Binnda called cheerfully from behind me; and indeed a procession of Kekketies was coming toward us clutching suitcases and cosmetic bags. I recognized my own. "You go in the first car with our hosts, Nolly," Binnda ordered. "I'll make sure no one gets left behind. And quickly, please! Mr. Tsooshirrisip is a very important person on this planet, and we mustn't keep him waiting!"

The cars were the bathtub-shaped things on wheels, and they were right funny-looking. For one thing, the wheels of the car I was directed to weren't much bigger than basketballs, and shaped the same way. For another, the things were built to the huge Ptrreek scale. Tsooshirrisip and his buddy simply strolled over to the car and stepped inside. (There wasn't any door.) Purry handled the situation by flinging himself at the side of it and scrambled up and in like an inchworm. That left it up to me.

The Kekkety with my bag heaved it aboard and waited politely for me to enter, but I could not quite see how to do that. At maximum stretch I could reach the side of the car with my fingertips. After all those workouts in Conjur's gym, I could have chinned myself out and struggled in; what stopped me was that I simply did not believe I was supposed to do that. After all, I was a visiting opera star! Cars were supposed to be user-friendly. Shouldn't there be some invisible seam that would open up and let me enter decorously? Steps that ought to extrude magically so that I could climb aboard?

There was nothing like that.

Then I felt someone encircling my legs from behind. It was my Kekkety porter, whose strength was a surprise. He got me halfway up and then one of the Ptrreek, laughing (at least, bark-chirping in what I took to be amusement), reached around with those spidery arms and lifted me the rest of the way.

That was as much crowding as they were willing to accept, though. When the Kekkety started to chin himself in after me, Mr. Tsooshirrisip pushed him off and drove away. Rapidly. The bathtub's acceleration was amazing. When it took off I went flying. I smashed into Purry, squashing a sort of organ chord of grunts out of his many apertures, and bashed my head against the rear seat of the vehicle. Which was, of course, right about at the level of my eyes.

Mr. Tsooshirrisip took his eyes off the other cars long enough to turn around and laugh. Then his partner pointed to his own head (both of them had pulled a sort of hood out of their cloaks and covered their heads with it), and then at mine and the sun. He said something which Purry translated. "He's warning you against sunburn, Mr. Stennis," Purry said. "Their blue sun is a strong source of—what is the word?—oh, yes, ultraviolet. You should protect your skin against it."

"What with?" I asked.

They had an answer to that. After Purry had debated with them a bit the smaller Ptrreek leaned back and flung a corner of his cloak over me. The texture was marvelously silky. The odor was something else again. That cockroachy aroma had seeped into the cloak, and being under it was a lot like being under a sheepdog's winter blanket, along with the dog.

The other thing was that with the Ptrreek's cloak over me I could see nothing of the city. All in all, it was fortunate that our "hotel" was only a short ride away.

After I had "checked in" and taken the "elevator" up to my "room" in the "hotel"—but none of those words meant quite the same thing as they would have on Earth—there was a scratch at the door and Tricia came in to see me. "Hey, Nolly," she said. "How d'you like this place so far?"

"It moves around a lot," I complained. From the street I'd been able to see the tall towers swaying, but from inside it was a lot more nerve-wracking as they rocked like the tops of coconut palms in a breeze. "Outside of that it's all right, I guess. If you like sleeping in a hammock."

She reached over and set the thing swaying. "Don't knock it. They've put them in specially for us. I mean, hey, we'd have a little trouble getting in and out of a Ptrreek bed, you know? Did you catch all the fuss when we came in?"

"What fuss?"

"The Ptrreek couldn't get our count to come out right. There's fourteen of us from Earth in the company, aren't there? Only the Ptrreek claimed they counted fifteen."

I added up on my fingers: three sopranos, three tenors, two baritones counting myself, the two basses, plus Ugolino, Conjur, and Tricia. Oh, and Norah Platt, who had come along to help in rehearsals. "Fourteen is what I make it. It's a bad mix, though—nine men for only five women."

She dimpled. "That's the kind of odds I like. Anyway, it's going to be tough for Binnda if they don't get it straightened out. They don't want any stowaways sneaking onto their planet. The other thing," she said, turning to go, "is that Binnda says they'll be bringing us something to eat pretty soon. Room service, can you believe it? But I bet it's just because they don't want us eating with them. Then Binnda says we should rest for an hour before we go to the theater."

"How much rest can you get in a hammock?"

She laughed. "You'd be surprised what you can do in a hammock, Nolly," she told me as she left.

She was right about the room service. Ten or fifteen minutes later, after I'd tried to make some use of the facilities in what I supposed was the bathroom—strenuous, but ultimately successful—a silent Kekkety brought in a tray for me. It looked exactly like the kind of thing they slop the passengers with on airlines. He set it on the floor and left silently, leaving me to decide how to dine.

There wasn't much choice. The floor was about the only thing I could reach. I pulled some cushions off an eight-foot-tall thing that was more or less like a couch and sat down.

The rocking motion was better sitting down, but not much. The meal was edible enough, in a TV-dinner kind of way, but the slow, sinuous waving of the room made me wonder if I really should have eaten it.

Tricia had said I had an hour to rest before we had to go anywhere.

I didn't really need to rest. All I really needed was to get out of that swaying room for a while. So I took my courage in my hands and found my way to the elevator (not a go-box, a real elevator, even if its height was five times its diameter and I had to stretch on tiptoes to reach the control dial), and five minutes later was walking out onto the street of the Ptrreek planet.

Two suns were in the sky.

I hadn't really been prepared for two suns. I'd forgotten about the warning of potential sunburn, too, but the tiny, hot, blue one was sinking toward the horizon and it was a large, red, dim one that was rising on the other side of the sky. If I stayed in the blue-sun shadow as much as I could, I reckoned, I would be all right . . . and anyway, what was a little sunburn compared to the exploration of a whole new alien planet?

It was *unearthly*. It was exactly the kind of adventure I had dreamed about when I was ten years old, watching *Forbidden Planet* and *The Thing* on late-night television, when my parents had left me with an indulgent sitter. I, Lawrence Knollwood Stennis, was actually walking around on the surface of a planet of another star, many light-years from home! Even Narabedla had been nothing like this.

A couple of Ptrreek, talking to each other next to one of the cars, had interrupted their conversation to peer at me. It was time to move on; I gave them a friendly wave and turned away, walking fast.

It was sultry hot, and the effort made me pant; it even made me choke a little from time to time. Something in the air, maybe? Mold spores or pollen or whatever? I kept on walking rapidly anyway. Binnda would not have taken us to a place where there was any real danger—I was pretty sure—but I didn't exactly know how the Ptrreek felt about having a short, hairy alien creature wandering around their town, even if he was a star in a visiting opera company.

Twenty minutes later, I still didn't know how they felt about it. Definitely, they hadn't mobbed me for autographs. They hadn't exactly ignored me, either. A couple of them had seemed to be taking my picture. A few others, now and then, had paused in their way from wherever they had been to wherever they were going to lean down and chirrup at me in their wholly incomprehensible language. They didn't sound hostile. They didn't seem to care that I couldn't understand them, either. They just chirruped for a moment, straightened up, and went on their way.

Of course (I told myself) the Ptrreek were full members of the Fifteen Associated Peoples. Funnies of any variety would hardly be startling to them. They'd no doubt seen them all. They were seeing aliens even then, because among the hordes of Ptrreek I passed there were a couple of Mnimn, like Meretekabinnda (though neither one was Binnda himself, and they paid no attention to me), a Barak-like Ggressna waving its silvery arms at a couple of the Eyes-of-the-Mother bedbugs, a Duntidon lallumping along at a great rate, and four or five others even odder. None of them seemed to notice that I was in any way unusual. Ptrreek was a busy and cosmopolitan place.

I liked it.

I was really euphoric, I think. Even the mantislike Ptrreek, with their gay, flowing cloaks and their inquisitive, thrusting horsey heads, seemed like possible customers rather than potential foes. And in any case, I was no longer up in that tower, whose motion made me think of an unfortunate January cruise I'd once taken in the Caribbean, when there was a gale-force storm and there hardly ever were any takers for the ship's six lavish meals a day.

That turned out to be an unwelcome train of thought.

For "cruise" made me think of "yacht," and "yacht" made me think of missed opportunities.

I stood still on the side of that Ptrreek street, in the shadow of one of those clusters of reedy buildings, thinking. I really could have done it, I thought. If I had realized I was on Earth I could have done *something*. Some derring-do, swashbuckling thing in the style of Conan, Rambo, James Bond—for that matter, in the style of the Don Giovanni I played with such bravura on the opera stage. Sneak-punch Shipperton? Hold a knife to the throat of Henry Davidson-Jones? (I supposed there might have been a knife, or at least a letter-opener, somewhere around his desk.) Take hostages, find a gun, and shoot my way out?

It wasn't impossible.

It all sounded like TV heroics as I thought about it, but it was at least an outside chance that somehow I could have overpowered Davidson-Jones and made him do something—if I'd known where I was. At least I could have tried.

But then I would not be here, with audiences waiting to applaud me and pretty Tricia showing every sign of wanting to show appreciation of her own.

Back in my still-swaying room, Binnda poked his head in to announce that we were leaving for the theater in ten minutes. "All right," I complained, "but this place makes me seasick."

"Oh, really, Nolly?" He considered for a moment, peering up at me. "I suppose we could get you some sort of shots if you like."

I vetoed that quickly. "I'd rather be seasick. It's just that I'm a little worried about my performance."

"As you wish, Nolly. The theater's at ground level, anyway, so that won't be a problem." Then he got serious. "Nolly? Have you seen anything of Ephard Joyce?"

I blinked at him. "Was he supposed to be with us?"

"Not at all! No, we have no place for him in the company. But there's some confusion about how many people made the trip here, and according to the Ptrreek somebody who looked like Joyce came in earlier, with the theater props."

"He really wanted to do some mime with us," I remembered.

"Then perhaps he'll come to the theater," Binnda said gloomily. He shook himself and sighed. "Well, I mustn't upset our star, must I? Tell me, is everything satisfactory? Have you admired your view?"

"Oh, is there a view?" I asked acidly. There were picture windows, all right, but the lowest sill was a good four feet over my head.

"You simply need to stand on something to look out," he explained. "Really, it's an honor to be given a suite so high up in the building!" He came closer, peering at me. "Do you know what I think? I think you're a little edgy, dear boy. A case of opening-night jitters, wouldn't you say?"

I considered that possibility, and then discovered another one concealed inside it. "What opening night? I thought we were just going to rehearse today."

He looked shocked. "Rehearse again? But we've already been rehearsing! For *weeks!* No, no, this is going to be our very first actual performance. Our gala debut, my boy! You cannot believe how excited the Ptrreek are to have us here. They're all agog to hear our *Pagliacci*—and you're going to sing the Tonio for them tonight!"

CHAPTER
31

The "theater" wasn't exactly on the ground, it was under it, and it wasn't exactly the kind of theater I had expected. We came into it from above, so I could see the whole layout at once. The stage was the first thing that caught my eye. It wasn't the standard opera-house arrangement, and it wasn't exactly theater-in-the-round, either; the stage was thrust out into the audience, like a strip-teaser's runway, and as the theater was filling there was a sort of hologrammic newsreel going on. Binnda chuckled and nudged me, pointing at it. What it showed was the familiar diagram of the Andromeda probe launch, the pulsar's beam of energy pushing the bright ring of the spidery spacecraft farther and farther away. That dissolved to show a couple of Ptrreek arguing earnestly about something, and then that too dissolved and I was looking at pictures of Malatesta in the robes of the King of Crete, and of Sue-Mary Petticardi singing Electra, and abruptly of me—me as Don Giovanni— waving my sword and bobbing my plumed hat as I invited the statue of the dead Commendatore to dinner. I couldn't help it. I laughed out loud. I hadn't expected an opera performance to start with snatches of coming attractions.

But then I took another look at that stage and stopped laughing. Those early arrivals moving into slant-board seats weren't human beings. They were Ptrreek. Twice human size and more; which meant that my perspective had to shift a gear. The place was *huge*. Bigger than any opera house I had ever sung in by far; and in a little while I would be all by myself out there, singing the Prologue, with all those thousands of alien eyes on me.

Binnda's remark had not after all been laughable. Stage fright was a distinct possibility.

It had been thirteen years since I'd sung before an audience. Worse than that, I was the one who would start the show. Tonio's prologue sets the scene for everything that follows. If he fails, everybody fails; and this time that "he" was me.

I had plenty of time to think about that in my dressing room while one Kekkety made me up and another helped me into my costume. I hardly noticed what they were doing. I wasn't even aware, really, of how odd my dressing room was, more like a closet than a room, though with a twenty-foot ceiling. I was concentrating on vocalizing while they did me, listening critically to my lost and regained voice.

It sounded pretty good, but would it hold up through the entire opera?

They say that having the jitters before a performance is a good sign. I hoped it was true.

Ready or not, I opened the door of my dressing room and made my way through the unfamiliar, high-ceilinged passages to the wings. Because of the construction of the stage there wasn't much room there, but most of the cast was there already, strolling around by themselves as they silently mouthed their lines or watching the first half of our double bill on stage.

I had heard the music as I was approaching. *I Pagliacci* is a short opera, and so we had Tricia and Conjur warming them up for us to the strains of 1940s dance-band tunes. In spite of the cramped space, it wasn't as cluttered as the backstage of a regular opera house—well, it *wasn't* a real opera house. There wasn't any tangle of weighted cables to fly the flats up into the rafters. There weren't any flats; the scenery was all optical, except for the parts we actually had to stand on or lean against or use.

So I could see well enough. The music was coming from Purry, pumping his heart away out of sight of the audience in a funny mixture of heavy-metal rock with a big-band sound. Conjur Kowalski was on stage doing a solo number to it, spinning around on the back of his neck like a kid dancing for quarters in front of the Fifth Avenue library. He was alone on the stage, but I could see Tricia in the far wing, waiting to come on. I leaned forward to peer out at the audience. It was a big, big hall, and it had filled up. It was loaded with Ptrreek as far as I could see—rows and clusters of them, hunched in their places, with their fluffy cloaks in every color of the rainbow. In the distance they looked like the colored sprinkles on a birthday cake, but what they smelled like was the same old cockroach.

Somebody tugged at my leg. I looked down at one of the Mother's bedbugs. "Mr. Stennis?" it piped softly. "Have you seen Mr. Ephard Joyce today?"

I shook my head, and it scurried away toward the practical furniture that would go on in the first act of *Don Giovanni,* as Conjur finished his solo. There was a sort of clicking, rustling sound from the audience as he took a bow—I supposed it was applause—and Purry switched to John Philip Sousa. Out of the wing came Tricia, stepping high in her Texas Cowgirl suit to the strains of "El Capitán." She did a fast three minutes of baton twirling, got her applause, and left.

Then the stage dissolved in polychrome light, like a kaleidoscopic rainbow fog; I couldn't see a thing, but when it cleared there was a whole 1940s big band at the back of the stage.

It almost looked real, for a minute. It did look real; the

only way I knew it was not was that I knew we hadn't brought along twenty-five musicians and a boy and a girl singer. (I was partly wrong about that.) The musicians had to be more of those neat Narabedlan holograms. They were good ones, too, because someone who knew the period had had to choreograph the way the trumpeters stood up, rocking back and forth with their mutes in their hands, the vibraphonist tap-tapping up and down the bars, the drummer tossing his sticks in the air between riffs. Of course the music was all Purry again, tootling out a medley that began with "Take the A-Train" and segued into a slow introduction to "Stardust." The boy singer stood up to do that number; then a fast "String of Pearls" and then it was the girl singer's turn.

That was a surprise, because she turned out to be real. The girl singer was Maggie Murk, from our own company. She hadn't said a word to me about her solo, which was a sultry, bluesy rendition of "Temptation."

When the set was over I applauded along with everyone else. Next to me Ugolino Malatesta was patting his thin, dry hands together as enthusiastically as anyone. "*Brava, brava!*" he called as Maggie came offstage. (On the other side the "boy singer" also got up and left, but when he reached the wings he merely disappeared, like any other hologram.)

"That was great," I told Malatesta.

"And you will be even more great," he informed me. "A wonderful day! If only that cretin Joyce had not got himself into trouble."

"Did they find him, then?"

"No. That," he sighed, "is the trouble. If they found him they would rapidly put a stop to his foolishness, but as it is he is no one knows where, doing no one knows what. But look, now they dance again!"

And the synthetic band started up as Purry launched into "Tuxedo Junction" and segued into "In the Mood" and four or five other grandfather's-day hits as Tricia and Conjur came jitterbugging out onto the stage.

They'd changed costumes. Tricia was wearing a bright red miniskirt with tiny, sequined red panties that flashed every time she moved. Conjur had his zoot suit on again, with the lapels that would have made two ordinary suits. They were works of art, both of them.

I was born too late for the big-band era, and all I knew about zoot suits and jitterbugging is what I've seen on the late-night movies. But I have to say they set my feet to tapping and my body to twitching.

And, as a matter of fact, a little bit to itching, too. Every time Tricia flung herself around I felt that long-lost little hint of a tingle in my groin. I didn't know quite how to feel about it—part *Welcome home* and part *Jesus, is it real?*, and all of it was pretty good. It took my mind right off being nervous, right up to the time when the (purely optical) rainbow curtain came down, and Conjur and Tricia took their last bows, and Binnda came flapping toward us from the dressing rooms, crying, "Places! Ladies and gentlemen, places, please! The curtain is going up!"

That took care of the possible stage fright, because Binnda broke me up. The whole cast broke out in giggles. He didn't just come in, he made an entrance. He had got himself up in an opera-impresario suit that would have done credit to Rudolf Bing on the first night of a Met season, with full white tie and tails, and what looked like ten-carat rubies in his shirt studs, and at least an inch of starched, snow-white cuffs that showed at his wrists. Well, at where his wrists would have been, if he'd had any. We all broke out in applause.

"Thank you, thank you," he beamed, delighted. "But please, it is time to begin the opera. Get ready, my dear Nolly!" And he hurried off to take his place on the conductor's stand.

It surprised me that there were no intermissions. I suppose the Ptrreeks had better bladder control than human beings. Certainly the stagehands didn't need the time of an intermission to reset the stage, because most of that was accomplished by a quick flick of a switch somewhere.

For whatever reason, intermission there was none. Three minutes later Binnda was in place and Purry started the overture. The "curtain" went up (or, it would be better to say, evaporated). And there I was, sticking my head out through the dissipating rainbow cloud to address a horde of thousands of weird-looking alien monsters.

We were a smash.

I was a smash. We took ten curtain calls. I got one all to myself, and the last one with the Canio, Floyd Morcher, and then Binnda came trotting up from the improvised conductor's box, all spiffy in his version of white tie and tails, and dumped two huge bouquets of red roses (well, they weren't exactly roses, but I knew what he meant) at our feet. "Splendid, dear boy!" he whispered, wringing my hand. "They love you! You too, my dear Floyd," he added.

But I was the one whose hand he held in his own scaly claw as together we turned to bow a lingering farewell to the audience, all the Ptrreek towering over their seats as they rubbed their spiny limbs together in the buzzy kind of sound that was (yes, really was) their version of applause, and the rainbow mist began to gather for the final curtain.

CHAPTER
3 2

Of course, there was a cast party after the performance. Binnda wouldn't have omitted anything as traditional as that.

Tricia picked me up to go there together. She was wearing a sheath dress with the skirt slit almost hip-high along one side, and high heels that made her exactly my height. She had done her hair in a sort of bun on one side of her head, and all in all she looked pretty spectacular. When I told her so she thanked me as though no one, ever, had said anything like that to her before.

I thought it was going to be a real good party.

The place for the party was in another tower of our cluster. To get there we had to walk through one of the aerial bridges that linked the clumps, a transparent tube, twenty feet or more in diameter, limber enough to flex a little as the towers swayed. It was like walking through a plastic soda straw. It twisted and swayed disconcertingly, and the only good thing about it was that we could at last see the view Binnda had told me about. The Ptrreek city was ring-shaped, like a Jell-O mold, with a clear space in the middle. The blue sun had set long since, but it wasn't dark. The bigger, dimmer, deep scarlet sun was still in the sky, and, if anything, it was hotter than the blue one had been. But when we got to the room where the party was being held it was *cold*. Evidently it had been chilled as a compromise so that six or eight different kinds of aliens could be comfortable in it. There were a couple of dozen Ptrreek towering over everyone else, with their bright-colored cloaks wrapped around them. I saw Binnda talking to Barak, loudly and with a lot of waving of arms and tentacles, as they headed toward a cluster of other aliens in a corner.

The humidity was high, too. It felt like a Christmas party in the Coney Island Aquarium, with the doors left open. I was glad I had worn a jacket. I wondered how Tricia was doing in her slit skirt, but she didn't seem to mind. "Now what are they doing?" she demanded, looking over to the corner of the room where eight or ten Ptrreek and as many other aliens were gathered around something. It wasn't easy to see past the huge Ptrreek, but as they moved I caught a glimpse of a large skry, showing that same old Andromeda probe. It seemed to be still on course, and the aliens were doing a lot of congratulatory screeching, chirping, barking, and yowling at each other.

Tricia sighed. "What we need is a drink, Nolly," she said, and waved an arm. One of the little Kekketies came trotting across the dance floor, where Norah Platt and Malatesta were moving slowly to Purry's music. As the Kekkety took our order Eamon McGuire approached me, his hand stuck out to shake.

"You were fine, Stennis," he rumbled. "Are you getting drinks? Yes, I'll have something too—a double vodka, if they've got it."

They had it. They had all sorts of Earth liquor, and Earth food, too. As the Kekkety came back with our drinks Floyd Morcher materialized beside us. "You don't really want that drink, Eamon," he said.

The bass looked rebellious. Before he could answer, Tricia tugged at my sleeve. "Let's get something to eat," she said, pulling me away. She whispered, "Morcher's assigned himself to keep Eamon off the sauce, but, hey, I'd just as soon stay out of it. Anyway, there's Conjur by the buffet."

Actually two buffets had been laid out along one wall, one of them at Ptrreek height and invisible to me, the other spread out on what I suppose the Ptrreek thought of as benches, but were actually at about eye level for us tiny humans. Conjur grinned at us. "Can you see what they've got?" he asked. "There's sliced ham, and there's caviar, and there's maybe potato salad—pretty close, anyway—and I think that stuff in the back is knishes, but I don't know if they're any good or not. I think the ham's real. I don't guarantee anything else."

"What's the pink stuff in the bowl?"

"You try it and tell me. Anyway," he added, "congratulations. You knocked 'em dead. How much you making on this?"

I blinked at him. My incarnation as opera star had so far submerged the accountant persona that I'd almost forgotten that I had a financial stake in our success. "You know about my contract?"

He nodded. "Three and a half percent of the gross. Everybody knows that one now, Nolly. You be gettin' *rich*. You got old Samuel duckin' and hidin' when one of us comes near him, 'cause everybody else wants a new contract now, too. So I guess we forget all that other stuff? You know? What we were talking about, down by the waterfall? Now that you signin' on for permanent party here, I mean?"

Tricia swallowed a mouthful of caviar to say, "Please, Conjur, don't start that business again."

"I ain't starting nothing," he protested. "I'm just makin' a comment on the passing scene, you know?"

"I haven't forgotten," I told him stiffly. "It's just that nothing has changed, has it?" And I didn't wait for an answer; I took Tricia by the arm and led her out onto the dance floor.

But what I said wasn't really true. I had forgotten. And at that moment, still glowing from my applause, with Tricia Madigan light and warm in my arms, I didn't want to be reminded of anything about the planet Earth.

The party was slow to pick up momentum, largely because all the aliens were knotted around the Andromeda skry. But at last Binnda remembered the reason for the party and came over to the buffet with Barak. He was happily waving his arms about as he greeted me.

"What a night!" he cried, the green tongue flickering joyously in and out of the hideous little triangular mouth. "I can hardly believe that everything is going so well! The probe is locked in again—oh, it was worrying us there for a moment, because it looked as though we were losing synchronization—and, of course, Nolly, you are the star of the evening!" He raised himself as high as he could to look over the buffet. He spotted the pink stuff and took a plate. "Did you *hear* the applause you got? You were a real sensation, my boy!"

I saw an opportunity and pressed it, "About that. How many people were at the performance tonight, do you know?"

"Oh, nearly eight thousand, I think," he said, ladling pink slop onto his dish.

"And what was the take?"

He paused and looked up at me. "The take?"

"The box-office receipts. The money that I'm supposed to get three and a half percent of," I explained.

The three-cornered mouth worked irritably. "My dear Nolly! I know nothing of such things! Sam Shipperton will explain it all when we return, I'm sure. And, really, my boy, how can you trouble me with this at this time? This is one of the happiest days in my life, what with your performance and the way the Andromeda probe is going—"

"Yeah," I said, sticking to the point. "But Shipperton isn't here to ask anything. Can't you tell me roughly what the box office was in U.S. dollars?"

"Absolutely not!" Then he relented. "If you're really curious, you could ask Floyd Morcher; he's always been interested in such things."

"Morcher?" I asked, startled.

"Yes, of course Morcher. It's that 'church' of his. He what he calls 'tithes' to that religious thing on your The Earth, and he is always checking the Polyphase Index to see how much they're getting."

He upended the dish and poured slop into his mouth to put an end to that subject. I peered around but didn't see Morcher. Then Barak, disdaining the food, reached out with a silvery tentacle to remind me he was present. "Good-performance," he belched in my face, "even-if-not . . . Busoni *Turandot*."

I took the tip of the tentacle he offered me; I suppose it was meant as a handshake. "Maybe we'll do that one later," I said, hoping not. I appreciated the congratulations, but his breath was as bad as his public-toilet-in-a-bus-terminal body odor.

"Especially-liked . . . dark-and-light-skinned-persons . . . calisthenics," he added. "They-do-more-now?"

Well, you don't expect a silvery starfish to have good taste. But all the same! Imagine preferring jitterbugging to *Pagliacci*! "I'll suggest it to them," I promised, in order to get away. "I see Conjur over there, talking to Ugolino."

When I got there I found that actually it was Ugolino who was doing the talking. He was telling our new bass, de Negras, and a couple of Ptrreek about the good old days when he was primo soprano for the court of the Cardinal d'Especcio in Mantua. Purry was busily translating his Italian into Spanish for de Negras's benefit and English for Conjur's and chirps and squeaks for the aliens. To do it he had to use one set of holes for each language, giving an entire new meaning to "simultaneous translation." It was an extraordinary performance.

I hated to interrupt it, but I felt obliged to relay Barak's request. Conjur shook his head. "Maybe later," he grunted. "Ugo's keeping Mr. Tsooshirrisip here happy right now, and, you know, it's kind of interesting. So why'd you leave, Ugo?"

"Ah, there was this *woman*," Malatesta piped ruefully when that was translated. "I had with her a small affair of the heart, which her protector, the cardinal, took amiss. It was necessary to depart, for health. One did not want a dagger in the ribs, have you understood? And in Milan there was a lawsuit concerning some jewels, and one did not wish to go to Rome—not Rome! There in Rome the singers were kept locked up for the whole season, so they would not catch a cold or perhaps there too be a target for an assassin, for Rome was not a cultured place at the time! So here I am." He peered over my shoulder at Norah, just coming back into the room. "Any word of our friend?" he asked.

She said sadly, "They think Ephard has left this planet, but that's all I know."

"How can he be such an idiot! Ah, you would think at

their ages they would have learned something, he and Can-duccio! I wish them no harm, but really . . .'' He put his arm around her, which made her look pleased. ''It is simply their jealousy, of course,'' he chuckled, in the manner of any rooster who has beaten out the other roosters to the hen.

The big Ptrreek issued an order, and Purry translated. ''But this is all very interesting to Mr. Tsooshirrisip,'' he said. ''He asks that others of you tell something about your life on your own planet before you were allowed to enter the civilized worlds.''

I looked around the room. Sue-Mary and Maggie were harmonizing in ''Down by the Old Mill Stream'' near the neglected skry, some of the other singers were drifting to-ward us, and Tricia Madigan was nowhere in sight. At the powder room, I supposed, and wished her luck. (I'd already tried the Ptrreek idea of sanitary facilities.)

The Kekketies were bringing us fresh drinks, and I decided to stay for the stories. I already knew some of them, but the party was getting to the relaxed state when just talking was pleasant, and besides it was interesting. Every one of us had a different history, every one of us came from a different time in the recent history of the Earth, and every one of the fourteen of us had had a different reason for being there. I was the only one who had no reason of my own at all, but Floyd Morcher came close. He had signed up on the promise of finding many, many people whose souls had not been saved; he accepted Davidson-Jones's offer in order to mis-sion to these poor heathen, and the exact nature of the ''peo-ple'' he found was only the first disappointment he had encountered on Narabedla. Eamon McGuire had been on Skid Row until Davidson-Jones's people promised him a new life and a cure for his drinking problem. Maggie Murk had been a singing teacher until, along about 1975, she got into trouble when a fourteen-year-old girl in her class blew the whistle on her for improper sexual advances. Narabedla was an unexpected way out, and she regretted nothing about coming here, because on Narabedla she had found Sue-Mary Petticardi. Who was, she said, a little over ninety years old now. Sue-Mary had been a French singer, converted to an Army whore for the Germans when they occupied every-thing north of the Marne in World War I. She wound up with syphilis and a shaved head. Narabedla had cured the syphilis and given her a career. She didn't miss her family, because they would no longer have anything to do with her after the Armistice. The Kaiser's infantrymen had left her with a great distaste for males, and when Narabedla produced Maggie for her, her life became complete. Norah Platt had been sick, too, though with tuberculosis, and when old Dr. Lafourrière came to the hospital—

I stopped her there. "Who was Dr. Lafourrière? I thought Narabedla was American?"

"Oh, heavens, Nolly, *nobody* was American then! Nobody important, at least. No, this was long before Henry Davidson-Jones and all those; Dr. Lafourrière was a French gentleman, quite old, even then. He's still here, you know. In slow time, of course, but I understand he hasn't quite died yet."

Mr. Tsooshirrisip, following the conversation through Purry's rapid-fire translation, put in a comment. "Mr. Tsooshirrisip points out that you humans from the planet Earth should be very grateful for being allowed to enter slow time when death is near."

Conjur Kowalski snorted. "Oh, we be *grateful,* all right. You just ask Mr. de Negras here, he tell you how *grateful* he is."

Purry squeaked in alarm as he translated that. Tsooshirrisip's reply was frosty. "Señor de Negras violated our hospitality," he declared. "He was placed in slow time because he was a danger to you all, and justly so. After all, why should he be allowed to travel to Earth when I am not?"

That put a damper on the little circle. Conjur didn't answer him. He just clamped a fist on my forearm and dragged me over to the bar. Barak intercepted us on the way with another testy request for more jitterbugging, and Conjur grinned and shuffled his feet and said, "'Deed we will, Mr. Barak, sir, soon's Miss Tricia gets back." Then, a safe distance away, he screwed up his face in pain. "Damn," he said. "You got to say it don't smell good around that one. You know what does it?"

I said doubtfully, "A lot of these aliens smell funny. Body chemistry, maybe?"

"Not Barak. He's un*civilized.* What we're smellin' is his

piss, Nolly. He does it all the time, 'cause he can't sweat. So he does like a dog when he hangs out his tongue; only Barak don't *have* a tongue, so he gets his cooling from evaporation in that ugly patch of fur by his dipstick, you know? He just leaks into it and lets it evaporate to cool off.''

''But it isn't hot in here.''

''Be grateful for small mercies, because that's why he don't smell as bad as usual.'' He picked up a glass and handed one to me. ''You get a chance to talk to our señor yet?''

''Not much. I don't speak Spanish, you see.''

''Get your Purry to help you,'' he advised. ''Manuel's just out of slow time for doing what you were talking about doing, and you might want to hear what he says. Or was all that talk about getting home just talk?''

Actually, he was beginning to annoy me. I thought it over. It was all complicated in my mind, but I said, explaining it to myself as much as to him, ''I'd *like* to go home. Sooner or later, I mean. But I wouldn't want to die for it, or kill anybody else—not even somebody like Boddadukti.''

''Would you want it enough to take a chance?'' he persisted.

''How big a chance?''

He shrugged, keeping his eyes on me.

''Come on,'' I said, angry now. ''Don't crap me. Have you got some way to do it or not?''

''I don't know,'' he admitted. Then he looked around to see who might be listening and lowered his voice. ''There's ways,'' he told me.

''What kind of ways?''

''Depends. There's lots of these aliens would like to go to Earth, if they could, only right now they're all too happy about their damn probe to get out of line. Only some of them ain't as happy as others, you know?''

''I *don't* know. Spit it out, Conjur.''

He said, ''After we split this place we're going to the Hrunw planet. There's a dude there who might be willing to do something about it, if you want.''

I stared at him. ''Are you putting me on?''

''I'm not. *He* might be. I never met the gentleman so far, but we could go pay him a little call if you want to.''

I hesitated. ''I'd have to think about it,'' I said cautiously.

''Why, sure you would, my man,'' he said, grinning.

"Wouldn't want you to stick your neck out without figuring everything out first. Now I better find Trish and do some dancin' for old Barak . . . but listen, Nolly. You get a chance, you do some talking with de Negras, you hear? I think you be interested."

Barak finally got his wish. A band appeared and struck up "Rock Around the Clock" and switched to "Shaboom" in the authentic Crew Cuts style—of course, it was all Purry, piping away behind the hologrammed musicians—and Tricia and Conjur did their thing. I had another drink while I watched them, turning over what Conjur had said in my mind. It was very unlikely, I told myself, that Conjur had a lead on any plan that would work—after all, nobody had ever got back from Narabedla before, had they?

Then, when they came off, the band kept going. Conjur's annoying persistence drifted to the back of my mind as I watched the gruesome spectacle of half a dozen Ptrreeks lumbering around the middle of the room as they tried to do what some of the opera troupe were doing. They seemed to be having fun.

I tried it myself, with Norah Platt, and then with Maggie Murk—well, not the real jitterbugging, the sort of prom-chaperone's attempt to be one of the kids. I took time out for a little more champagne.

Then I switched to the bourbon (real bourbon) and ginger ale (the bottles had actual Schweppes labels on them) and, by gosh, it wasn't such a bad party after all.

I even went around the floor a couple of times with Tricia, though it was obvious I wasn't up to Conjur Kowalski's standards. Besides, it was what she was doing for a living. When I suggested we sit the next one out she gave me a hug. "The other thing we could do," she said, "is, hey, we could split. You want to take me home, Nolly?"

Well, there was only one answer to that. I hesitated just for a second, remembering something. "I did want to talk to Floyd Morcher," I said.

"Oh, he's been gone for hours—took after Eamon, trying to keep him sober. We don't need to do that, though. Bring the bottle, why don't you?"

Actually, we each took one. I didn't want to try those midair passages again with all that liquor sloshing around in me, so we took the "elevator" down to the "lobby" and strolled across the now dark space (both suns were out of the sky) to our own tower. Even at that hour there were Ptrreek about, some of them gathered about another skry with the Andromeda probe still looping around its star, others going about whatever business might engage a Ptrreek. They looked at us the way vacationing senior citizens on Earth look at conventioneers in any Hilton or Hyatt, only these particular respectable "hotel" guests were fourteen feet tall. We waved amiably at them and continued on our way.

At Tricia's door she said, "Coming in for a minute?"

There was only one answer to that, too. We popped the cork of the first bottle—both of them were champagne—and drifted over to her window. Tricia had shoved a sort of coffee-table-sized thing against the wall. We climbed up on it and looked out. There were about a million stars in the dark sky. Tricia leaned against me. I put my arm around her, and one thing led to another.

Why, I thought in pleased surprise, it certainly looks like the operation was a complete success.

Indeed it was. Although I'd never made love in a hammock before, it worked out just fine. And I didn't think about the missing Ephard Joyce or about the probe to the Andromeda nebula or about what to say to Conjur Kowalski if he brought up the subject of going home again or, in fact, about much of anything else outside that hot, swaying, alien room for all the rest of that long night.

CHAPTER

33

The next day was, I guess, about the happiest of my life. And Tricia seemed to second the motion.

Reason told me that going to bed with me probably was not really the most earthshaking event ever in Tricia Madigan's experience. I knew of at least two of her quite recent lovers. She had not been sexually deprived. But reason just didn't enter into it. For me it was—oh—it was the first glorious day of a wonderful spring, after a winter that had lasted for a dozen long years. And the funniest thing was that I felt, well, *guilty*. Not about the morality of it, or anything like that. About Tricia's cousin Irene.

It was really stupid for me to feel as though I'd been unfaithful to Irene Madigan. There had certainly not been anything between Irene and me. But I did.

And, you know, I kind of enjoyed that feeling. It had been quite some time since I had had any opportunity to feel anything like that.

Everything in sight was going my way. I had my voice back. I had thrilled an audience. I once again had the use of the masculinity I'd been born with, and I had pretty Tricia Madigan to use it with. Who can blame me? I didn't have much concern with willful old men getting themselves lost, like Ephard Joyce. I wasn't worrying about people trying to lure me into some harebrained scheme for escaping back to Earth, like Conjur. I wasn't worrying about any possible future problems at all. I was simply exultant, and Tricia was fond enough (or just nice enough) to meet my mood, which lasted all through that day.

It was a good long day for us, too. The troupe was doing *Idomeneo*. It was the best of all possible operas for my purposes, which for that day were not entirely musical. It was

too long to need Tricia's opening number, and too lacking
in baritone parts to require me.

So we stayed in our room. We had our meals on trays.
Actually, it was a close thing whether we went to the performance that night or not, because I was much more interested in our own performances in the hammock.

But even miraculously repaired glands can do just so much
in one day, and when it came near time for the opera we
were there.

When I saw the first troops of tall, cloaked Ptrreek riding
the moving stairways down to their seats I made an effort
to count them. Of course, that was impossible, but it seemed
clear that the house (I didn't mind discovering) was not likely
to be quite as packed for *Idomeneo* (without me) as it had
been for *I Pagliacci* (with me) the night before. Even so,
there were thousands of Ptrreek coming in.

Which raised a question in my mind. Just how much dough
had I hauled in the night before? I knew I was earning plenty,
but I didn't exactly know what I was earning plenty of. They
all paid for their seats, I was sure of that. But what did it
come to in United States dollars? I couldn't just go to the
nearest currency exchange to find out. There weren't any
currency exchanges. So I asked Tricia, and she said shortly,
"How would I know? I get paid by the week."

"Oh, sorry," I said. Meaning, oh, so you're a little jealous, but I'll try not to rub it in. Then I remembered what
Binnda had told me. "Floyd Morcher's supposed to know
that sort of thing. Shall we go backstage and look for him?"

She shook her head. "Morcher's not real crazy about me,
you know. You go ahead; I'll see you inside."

She put up her face to be kissed, and I guessed I was
forgiven. When I got to the tall, skinny door to Morcher's
dressing room it sounded as though he were talking to someone inside, and when I knocked on his door he took a long
time to answer. He didn't open the door all the way. He just
slid it wide enough to peer out at me. "What?" he asked,
not invitingly.

"I'm sorry to bother you," I said, trying to look past him
to see who he was talking to. There didn't seem to be anybody there. Over his head, I could see the upper parts of his
room just fine; it was built to Ptrreek height, of course. I

couldn't see anything else. I explained that everybody said he knew all about Ptrreek finances, and, well, I was sort of curious about how much I'd earned.

He looked at me from under the cap of his costume. "Ask me later, Stennis. I don't have time now." And he slid the door firmly closed in my face.

It was almost funny. It was also almost deliberately insulting. I stood there for a moment, undecided between laughing and getting mad. I finally chose curiosity. I pressed my ear to the slippery, cool door, wondering if that presumed invisible other person would say something to reveal who it was.

That didn't happen. What I heard was two muted bumps together—*bumbump,* on the floor—and then Morcher's voice, low-pitched and passionate. It was a monologue that kept up for a long time.

It took me a while to realize that what I had heard was Floyd Morcher dropping to his knees and raising his voice in prayer.

I hurried back to the seat Tricia had saved for me. And then a few minutes later, when the "curtain" evaporated on the first act of *Idomeneo,* Morcher was singing lustily and beautifully. "So if he was praying to be in good voice," I whispered to Tricia, "his prayer was answered."

She was craning her neck to see what was going on on the stage, and all she said was, "Sssh."

Well, she was right, and I was rebuked. I settled myself to enjoy hearing the performance.

Hearing was about all I could do. The Ptrreek idea of an auditorium seat was a sort of slantboard, which was fine for a fourteen-foot-tall Ptrreek. It wasn't any good for Tricia or me. The Ptrreek had considerately (for them) set aside a short row of high chairs to one side of the thrust stage for us humans, but if the high chairs had been high enough to do us any good, viewing-wise, they would have been too high to climb, sitting-in-wise. They helped only minutely. We could see nothing but the tops of the performers' heads.

It was also very hot in the auditorium. The air-conditioning that had been overpowering at the cast party simply didn't exist in the theater. It was filled with their cockroachy smell, not to mention a considerable contribution from Barak, who was toe-dancing on the tips of all six of his limbs on the chair next to me.

None of that mattered, really. Mozart made up for it all, and the performance was up to the standards of the music. Malatesta's high, unearthly voice was absolutely superb, and so were the sopranos—so was everybody.

When it was over I clapped in delight. There were plenty of curtain calls to clap to, though, curiously, the audience didn't seem *quite* as enthusiastic over *Idomeneo* as they had been when I wowed them in *I Pagliacci*.

This did nothing to dispel my own pleasure. I clapped louder than ever and even ventured a "Bravo!" though Tricia turned and gave me a thoughtful look.

That evening I was in the sanitary facility attached to my room, trying to bathe, when I heard Tricia come in. Bathing wasn't easy. The Ptrreek didn't seem to take showers, or tub baths either. I was doing my best to sponge myself, standing on a stool to reach a thing like a hot-and-cold bubble fountain eight feet off the floor. "They caught him," she announced from the door. "Caught who?" I asked, reaching for a towel—at least there were towels, though it had taken a special order to the Kekketies to get them.

"They caught Ephard Joyce sneaking into a go-box," she told me. "They took him back to Narabedla. I don't know what will happen to him, but I guess we'll hear all about it at the party."

"At the party," I repeated, digging out my ears.

"Of course at the party," she said. "So, hey, come on and get dressed."

I finished drying myself. "I could do that," I agreed, for the sake of argument. "If that was what we really wanted to do, I could. The other thing we could do is just stay here and have our own party."

She grinned at me, and she gave me a kiss, but all she said, quite firmly, was, "Get your clothes on."

So we repeated the trek across the wobbling passage between the towers, and there were the rest of the company and the assorted aliens, just as before.

There was one difference. When we came in the Ptrreek greeted us with a round of their clickety-sticks equivalent for applause.

Even though my new career was only a day old, the reflexes of the performer were strong within me. If anybody claps, you bow. So I bowed, and when I looked around to take Tricia's hand to share the applause, she was standing facing me and she was clapping too. "But really," I whispered to her when we were inside the room, "I think they were applauding both of us, not just me."

"No, you don't," she said grimly. "Anyway, they weren't. No, you made a big hit, Nolly. You'd better circulate. I'm going to find a drink."

So I circulated among my colleagues.

Apparently I wasn't the only one who had noticed that the applause for the *Idomeneo* had been just a little sparse. Nobody was exactly cool toward me, but of my human colleagues it was only Malatesta (who was convinced it was his coaching that had made me a star) and Norah Platt (who wasn't in competition with me anyway) who sounded really adulatory. Even Binnda, busy explaining to Floyd Morcher and Eamon McGuire and a couple of Ptrreek that the The Earth impresario he most admired was Walter Felsenstein of the Komische Oper in East Berlin, greeted me only as "Nolly" instead of "my dear boy."

Norah was either really worried about Ephard Joyce or really angry at him. "Such a foolish little man," she said irritably. "But one doesn't want anything to happen to him, does one?" And Sue-Mary Petticardi let go of Maggie Murk's hand long enough to lean forward and confront Norah eye to eye.

"Foolishness is one thing," Sue-Mary told her. "Reckless actions are another. They will put the man into slow time, yes, but how long do you think they'll put up with this sort of provocation? He endangers us all!"

"Oh, no, really," Norah protested.

"Yes, *really*. Don't forget Jerry Harper! Now that one life has been taken, how safe are any of us?"

I intervened tolerantly. "You're worrying much too much, Sue-Mary," I told her. "These are civilized people, even if they do look a bit strange."

"Civilized people! You forget, I had four years of civilized people in the War, and they at least were human. These creatures are not *civilized*. They would kill each other in a minute if they could, and they certainly do not have any love for us!"

It was an interesting discussion, but I saw Morcher drifting away from Binnda's monologue, and I was reminded of what

I wanted from him. I intercepted him. "Can I have a word
with you?" I asked him. "Over by the buffet, maybe?"

He considered the request soberly, as though I had asked
to borrow money. At first I thought he was going to say no.
But apparently the attractions of the buffet turned the trick.
He was there before me, spearing rye bread and slices of
ham. As he put together a sandwich, he asked, "What do
you want?"

"I was hoping you could explain the money situation to
me," I said.

He grunted. Then he put his sandwich down, closed his
eyes, and whispered to himself for a moment in prayer.
When he opened them he took a bite of the sandwich and
chewed experimentally for a moment before saying, "It's
complicated. I can tell you a little bit, maybe."

I moved back a little to avoid the shower of rye-bread
crumbs. "That would be fine, Floyd."

He scooped some of that more or less potato salad onto
a plate to go with his sandwich and said, still chewing, "Do
you know anything about the Polyphase Index?"

"Well, I have a sort of a general—no."

He rolled his eyes. "All right, then I'll just start from the
beginning. The Ptrreek and all the rest of the Fifteen Peoples
don't use money."

"But the audience paid something for their tickets?"

"Yeah, in a way they did. It's complicated. It's all barter.
The way it goes, when the Ptrreek trade with other planets,
their big export is some kind of plant products they use in
their so-called medicine. I know what they trade for. They
trade about three pounds of the plant stuff for about an ounce
of a metal that is what you call radioactive. I don't know
the name of it. The way the Ptrreek pay for tickets is each
one of them commits to supply one-fourteenth of an ounce
of the plants they export. That's what you get three and a
half percent of."

"Wonderful," I said.

He didn't respond to that; he just piled another forkful
into his mouth and went on through it. "So now you want
to know what that's worth, and I can't tell you. I never heard
of that metal. Maybe we don't have it back home. The best
I can say is that sometimes they trade it for gold, and when
they do they get about forty times as much gold by weight.
Are you following all this so far?"

"Sure," I said. It was almost true; I was setting up the accountancy program in my head, but Morcher didn't wait for me to do the arithmetic.

"So, figuring gold at thirty-five," he said, "and with about eight thousand tickets sold, your share at three and a half percent ought to be a little over five hundred dollars."

"Five hundred dollars," I repeated slowly.

"For each performance," he added, rolling up a slice of bread and dipping it into what might have been guacamole.

I thought about that. Five hundred dollars a performance wasn't exactly minimum wage, but it was nowhere near a *star*'s income. Even the Met, notoriously stingy about its top singers, paid a good many times that, and they didn't have eight thousand people in the audience, either. I began to wonder if my bargaining with Sam Shipperton had been as big a victory as I'd thought.

"But it doesn't make any difference, does it?" said Morcher in gloomy triumph. "Because what do you have to spend it on?"

And he scooped the last of his food into his mouth and hurried off to see where Eamon McGuire had gone.

CHAPTER
34

When we got back to Tricia's room that night I paid full attention to Tricia Madigan for the first three-quarters of an hour or so, but later on, while she was rubbing skin cream or something on her face, I got out the paper and pencil.

Morcher had sounded as though he knew what he was talking about, but what accountant would believe a client's arithmetic? So I started over. Eight thousand "people" in the audience meant eight thousand tickets sold; I didn't think the Ptrreek did comps or press passes or twofers. At the equivalent of one-fourteenth ounce for each ticket, that meant about thirty-five pounds of the vegetable stuff pledged, of which three and a half percent was mine. Call it twenty ounces for me. A pound and a quarter, which was equal to, say, half an ounce of the mystery metal, or twenty ounces of gold. Which was worth, at—what was gold now? somewhere over $400 an ounce?—about, my *God,* eight or nine thousand dollars.

Eight *thousand* dollars.

But that was more than fifteen times what Floyd Morcher had estimated. True, he was a tenor, not a CPA, and he could easily have put a decimal point in the wrong place.

Accountants had been known to do that, too; so I went over it again, and refined it a little more, and still came out with the same figure. I couldn't be absolutely sure of it, because somewhere there should have been a conversion from troy to avoirdupois ounces that I wasn't sure how to make. But eight thousand dollars a performance was still pretty close, pretty close.

I scowled at the figures, and then I had an idea. "Tricia?" I called. "What do you know about Floyd Morcher?"

She didn't look around. "What's to know? He's a godder. He's trying to save Eamon McGuire's soul, or anyway keep him from getting drunk all the time. He doesn't like me because I'm a scarlet woman, and he absolutely *hates* our nice lez couple, Sue-Mary and Maggie."

"No, I don't mean that kind of stuff. I mean, do you know how long he's been on Narabedla?"

"Oh, gosh, hon," she said, wiping off the surplus goo and coming over to me. "I don't have a clue. He was here for ages before I got here."

"But how many ages?" I persisted. "Maybe fifty or sixty years?"

"Could be something like that, I think. I remember him saying something about Herbert Hoover once. Why do you want to know?"

"Because he was talking about gold at thirty-five. Gold hasn't been thirty-five dollars an ounce since the U.S. government called it all in, way back in Franklin D. Roosevelt times."

"Yeah? So?"

"So I guess Floyd's older than I thought," I said. "So I'm richer than I thought." I reached out to pull her into my lap, grinning down at her. "You want to know how rich? If I sing three times a week, that's all, I take in about a million and a quarter dollars a year."

"That's really neat, hon," she said, kissing me in congratulation. And then she said the same thing Morcher had said: "But what are you going to spend it on?"

The next morning, breakfast was set up for the human opera troupe in a small building just a step away from the "hotel." It took us a little while to find it. Everybody else had been steered to it the morning before, but that was the morning Tricia and I had elected breakfast in bed.

By the time we arrived, everybody else was eating. It all smelled good. The place had been furnished with three or four human-sized tables, obviously whipped up on short notice for us, and there was a buffet table presided over by four Kekketies acting as short-order cooks.

After we got our food I led Tricia to a small table for ourselves. "Actually," I said, tasting what I had ordered, "they don't make a bad omelette, Trish." They were definitely real Earth eggs, cooked in real Earth butter, undoubtedly imported specially for us celebrated artists.

She didn't answer. She was stretched halfway around in her chair to talk to Norah Platt, who was disconsolately toying with a soupy soft-boiled egg behind us. She was sitting by herself and looking as though she'd been crying. When Tricia turned back she was shaking her head. She told me, "They did it to him, hon. Ephard's in slow time."

"Pity," I said, reaching for the toast. It was still quite warm. "I wonder what the weather's like. Did you remember that I'm singing Don Giovanni tonight?"

"No, but listen," she said. She sounded serious. "Do you know what Norah says? She says you put the idea in his head, talking about what a hit he'd be on Broadway after a century or so."

I did vaguely recall some such conversation. "I never thought he'd take it seriously, though," I explained.

"I believe that. Look, Norah's pretty upset. I think I'll sit with her for a while."

"You're a sweet kid," I told her, and meant it. I was

surprised that Norah was taking it so hard. I knew that Malatesta and Bart Canduccio were competitors for her favors,
but I hadn't known that Ephard Joyce was in the running.

I left Tricia with Norah Platt. Outside of the hut I saw
Conjur, wearing a big floppy hat and squinting morosely up
at the bright blue morning sun. I told him about Norah and
expressed my surprise that she was so upset about Ephard
Joyce.

"Well, Knollwood," Conjur rumbled, "they all been here
a *long* time. Ain't no man that's going to last a hundred years,
is there? I think they kind of take turns, you know? Only
it'll be a goodly time before Ephard gets another turn at the
lady, where they put him now."

"It won't seem long to him." I smiled. I'd already figured
out that less than half an hour in slow time equaled a year
outside.

"It will seem *real* long," Conjur growled. "Knollwood,
why do you talk about things you don't know anything
about? Did you talk to Manuel de Negras yet?"

"Not much," I confessed. "I've been pretty busy. Tonight I'm going to sing Don Giovanni, you know."

He sighed. "Talk to the man. Get your Purry to translate.
You'd really be interested, I promise you that." He passed
a hand over his face and added, "You know what it's like
in slow time? You never forget where you are. When you're
in the place you know damn well how long it's being outside.
You know it'll be ten or twenty years before you get out,
and nobody's hardly going to remember you."

"That would be an annoyance," I admitted, "but it
doesn't sound terrible."

"What's terrible," he said patiently, "is wondering
whether they're ever going to let you out at all."

"But they always do, don't they?" I said, to reassure him.

He sighed. "Knollwood," he said, "you better get out of
this sun. It's frying your pitiful little brains."

Six hours later, in plumed hat and boots and sword and
cape, I was dragging my weeping Donna Anna, Sue-Mary
Petticardi, out of the purely illusory castle door on the stage
before an even fuller house of delighted Ptrreeks.

I had that *made*. I had never been in better voice. The
Spanish bass was a grand Leporello. Old Eamon McGuire
was a perfect proud Commendatore, and died magnificently
when I stabbed him. The girls were wonderful, fiery Donna

Elvira, icy Donna Anna, sultry Zerlina; but I rather thought, and got the impression that all of them thought, I was the most wonderful of all. I *was* Don Giovanni—courage of a lion in combat, guile of a serpent in seduction. It was the starring part in the finest opera ever written, and I was playing it to the hilt.

The audience agreed.

At the end I was dragged to a furiously flaming Hell by a chorus of demons. That was one of Binnda's brightest ideas; the hologrammed demons were actually programmed to resemble the ugly and unpopular race called the Ossps, half lizard, half bat, all hideous. The crowd roared. They kept on roaring all through the sextet that ends the opera, and when I came out for my first bow those fourteen-foot insects stood up for me.

The day had started well. There'd been a little letdown here and there, mostly professional jealousy, I thought, but it had definitely been a good day; and now it was ending with the kind of triumph I had hardly even dreamed of. When Binnda trotted out with the night's roses, in his beautifully comic opera suit, I decided my life was just about complete . . . and, of course, that's when it happened.

The misty "curtain" had just begun to gather around us when, without warning, it vanished.

The applause stopped as though chopped off. Binnda made a sound of surprise. So did I, while members of the audience, halfway to the aisles, paused to look back.

A harsh bright light snapped on to surround us. It seemed to be a hologram pattern, but I couldn't make out what it was; we were actually inside it.

A strident Ptrreek voice began a bass chittering from nowhere, addressing the audience. Twitters and rumbles of consternation came from all over the hall. I looked wonderingly at Binnda, whose three-cornered mouth hung open in horror.

"Oh, my dear boy," he moaned, wringing his three-fingered hands. "What a terrible thing to happen just now!"

I guessed. "Has Ephard Joyce done something serious?"

"Joyce? No, of course not, it has nothing to do with your The Earth. It's far, far worse than that. It's the Andromeda probe, my dear Nolly. It's lost synch, and it's headed for destruction!"

CHAPTER

35

I don't know if the theater ever did empty that night. When we left there were still a thousand or more Ptrreek roaming the aisles and chittering to each other, as the big skry rehearsed the disaster over and over, and when we got to our hotel lobby there was more of the same.

The lobby, of course, was not really any more like a hotel lobby than the "hotel" was like a human hotel. It didn't have couches, registration desks, or bellhops. It was a largish open space with six or eight cloudy spheres spotted around it, hanging in air. They were the Ptrreek equivalent of skries, and people (or at least Ptrreek) used them the way passengers waiting at an airport would use the coin-operated TV sets, or visitors to a Ramada Inn would use the house phones. They weren't being used for telephoning just now. The place was full of tall, cloaked Ptrreek, waving their powdery arms and chittering among themselves as they gathered around the globes.

I took Tricia's elbow and drew her to one of them to see what was going on. It wasn't easy to hear the voice coming from the skry—the Ptrreek muttering almost drowned it out—but that didn't matter, because none of us could have understood it anyway. It wasn't much easier to see the skry itself, either. The fourteen-foot Ptrreek weren't transparent, and even when we caught glimpses past them we were handicapped by our size. The skry was at Ptrreek level. We midget humans had as much trouble seeing as a three-year-old trying to watch his big brother's video game.

Wherever we looked, each skry showed the same scene. You didn't have to understand Ptrreek to know that what we were seeing was on-the-spot news coverage of the Andromeda probe disaster.

"Thank heaven," I murmured to Tricia, "that it isn't *our* problem."

Norah Platt, standing next to her, overheard. "Oh, Nolly," she said sadly, "don't you think it is? Anytime the Fifteen Peoples get into an argument their minor joint projects are going to suffer. And of course we're about as minor as any project could be."

"Oh, it can't be that bad," I said comfortingly. "They loved us. Didn't you hear the ovation they gave us?"

"Let me put it a different way," Tricia said. "Do you hear these Ptrreek?"

She had a point there. There were hundreds of Ptrreek in the lobby, and although the things they were saying to each other were incomprehensible, they were clearly furious.

I shrugged and complained, "I wish I knew exactly what was going on."

"Just look," Tricia ordered.

Actually, it was clear enough. I already knew that the probe had lost its synchronicity with the flare from the pulsar. What the skry showed was the detail, slowed down and enhanced. We could see the searchlight-beacon of energy from the star fall slowly behind the orbiting spiderweb. The huge, flimsy light-sail probe wasn't meant for such rough treatment. It tipped and crumpled in upon itself, and each time they saw that happening every Ptrreek in the audience simultaneously emitted a sort of high-pitched, chirping groan.

"Well, hell," I said, "I see that they're upset, of course, but I bet they get over it. Space launches have gone sour on Earth, too."

"Not like this," Norah said direly, and went on to explain. What made this one particularly nasty was that the Andromeda probe was a high-level cooperative effort, involving almost all of the Fifteen Peoples in one way or another. The Ggressna had supplied the filmy probe itself. The J'zeel had done the instrumentation, with some contributions by, of all people, the Duntidon. The Ptrreek were the ones who had supplied the apparatus that controlled the magnetic field of the neutron star; they were the ones everyone blamed first, because that gave them operational control of the launch. But that just made them madder, because not all of the instrumentation was Ptrreek. The Ptrreek blamed the J'zeel, the J'zeel complained that the B'kerkyi data on the star's natural magnetic fields was faulty, the Duntidons assailed the Ggressna for making the probe so weak, and they all blamed Meretekabinnda's Mnimn, who had had general supervision of everything. Everybody was mad at everybody else.

"Look at Binnda," Tricia said, nudging me.

I hadn't seen him come in. It wasn't easy to see him now, because he—and a Purry—were encircled by a score of the Ptrreek, leaning down to chirp furiously at him. Reinforcements of Ptrreek were lunging toward him to join in, like the kind of argument you used to see around the speakers' stands in Union Square.

"Poor guy," Tricia whispered. "Maybe we ought to help him out."

I wasn't sure he needed it. He had blown a fuse. He stood there, bellowing up at the huge, expressionless insect faces towering ten feet above his head. What he was saying I couldn't tell, because it wasn't in English. It wasn't in the Ptrreek language, either, because the Purry was kept busy translating back and forth, from clicks and whistles into grunts and roars.

Whether he needed help or not, he was getting it. Norah had already started determinedly toward the scene, and Malatesta was with him. Tricia tugged at my arm, and we joined them.

We were not only outnumbered but vastly outclassed. I wished I hadn't skipped my workout the last few days. It seemed to me that the chances were substantial that somebody was going to get physical, and what were a handful of tiny humans and an even tinier Mnimn going to do against a couple hundred fourteen-foot Ptrreek?

But they let us through. When we dragged him away, still shouting, they didn't follow. They just turned back to the skries.

"But really," Meretekabinnda gasped, "it is *incomprehensible!* Everything in the probe was *tested*. It's not possible that our engineering failed."

"Well, something did," I offered cheerfully.

He gazed sadly at me, the three-cornered mouth hanging limp. "Oh, my dear boy, what a *catastrophe*. I must go at once and communicate with the coordinators." He started away, then turned back to grasp my hand. "By the way," he added, "you were *splendid*."

And then he was gone, and the rest of us headed up to our rooms.

There wasn't any party that night.

We went to bed early. I didn't mind that, but, surprisingly, we went to sleep early, too.

When we came down the next morning there was no Binnda, no Barak, no "foreign" aliens visible at all, only Ptrreek. In spite of our recognized status as, well, as "sweethearts," Tricia turned down the idea of a quiet table for two at breakfast. She found a place to sit next to Norah, still grieving over her slowed-down Ephard Joyce, and I took the table with the sopranos and our recently speeded-up-again Spanish bass, Manuel de Negras.

It wasn't the happiest breakfast I ever had. I didn't blame Tricia for wanting to try to comfort Norah Platt, but I missed having her next to me. The sopranos were no help. They were having a lively conversation with de Negras, but unfortunately they were having it in French. It would have been interesting enough if my French had been up to following it, because he was telling them about his six hours (or fourteen years, depending on how you looked at it) in slow time, but they were going too fast for me. And by the time I got settled down even my scrambled eggs were cold.

I wondered what I was going to do with my day.

The night's opera was *Idomeneo* again, meaning both Tricia and I were off. It would have been a good time to do some sightseeing in the Ptrreek city, but when I leaned over to suggest it to Tricia she shook her head. Not while the blue sun was up, she said; she sunburned too easily. Not after it had set and only the red sun was in the sky, either, because then the opera would be on, and we owed it to Binnda to show up to watch it. I'd been complaining I hadn't been getting any exercise anyway, she pointed out, so why didn't I catch Conjur and find a place where the two of us could work out?

So I did.

We settled down in the place where we'd been having the cast parties; the room had been stripped bare after it had been cleaned up. It wasn't like Conjur's private gym, but he'd persuaded Binnda to include a basketball and a few other odds and ends with the theatrical baggage. We played a little racketball (no lines, no court, but plenty of room to swing in the high-ceilinged Ptrreek room) and went a couple of rounds with the big gloves to work up a sweat, with Ptrreek drifting in and out to stare at us. While we were jogging around to cool out Conjur panted, "Were you listening to Manuel at breakfast?"

"More or less," I said. "It sounded like a lot of nothing to do. I wonder how poor Joyce is making out."

"Screw poor Joyce," he said dispassionately. "Did you catch the part about the girl?"

I tried to remember and failed. "What girl?"

"Talk to him again," he advised. "But don't tell Tricia." Then he stopped, wiped sweat off his face, and said, "That's enough for today. Is that Tsooshirrisip coming in? I'm going to see if he can tell me where I can find a real shower."

But we didn't have any language in common with the Ptrreek. I went out to look for someone to translate, but by the time I found Purry and came back Conjur was gone. I asked Tsooshirrisip anyway, and he was amused at the notion. "In the kitchens," he advised me, through Purry, "there may be sprays to clean things. No doubt you can get under one of them if you wish." I started to thank him, but Purry interrupted. "Mr. Tsooshirrisip has more to say," he told me. "Mr. Tsooshirrisip wishes to tell you how much he enjoyed your Don Giovanni last night, and regrets that the terrible news about the probe so badly spoiled the evening for everyone."

"Oh, really?" I smiled up at the looming insect face. "Thank him for that, too." The Ptrreek might be an ugly alien monster that smelled like dead roaches, but he was the first person of any description to offer any consolation for my thwarted triumph. I didn't *need* to be soothed. But it had been a real downer, and I certainly would have appreciated it.

Tsooshirrisip was still going on, and Purry translated. "Mr. Tsooshirrisip thought the absolutely best part of the show was when you killed the old human and he returned from the dead. In the Ptrreek culture they have never evolved the human idea of 'ghosts,' and he thought it was quite amusing. Also the presentation of Ossps as what you call 'devils.'"

I kept the smile on my face, though he hadn't said a word about what the opera was really about, namely the singing.

I said politely, "Thank him again, but tell him, please, that I can't take any credit for the Ossps. That was entirely Meretekabinnda's idea."

But when Purry translated that, the Ptrreek spread his forearms angrily and sputtered what Purry rendered as, "Do not mention that Mnimn's name, Mr. Tsooshirrisip says. On this of all days, he says. It is entirely their fault that the good work of all the rest of the Fifteen Associated Peoples has gone for naught."

"Oh, but really," I began, but Purry stopped me.

"Please," he begged. "It is not a good time to disagree with him. Also there is more he is saying."

"What's that?"

"Mr. Tsooshirrisip points out that there is an old saying among his people, which he wishes they had borne in mind when they entered into the compact for the Andromeda probe. The saying is, 'When you have a Mnimn for an associate, you don't need an opponent.'"

We saw nothing of Binnda all that day, but when we got to the theater for the performance of *Idomeneo* he was waiting backstage, complete in his monkey suit, the green tongue working nervously in the hideous little mouth. "What a day!" he greeted us morosely. "Conferences, conferences— I shouldn't even be here now, but I have a duty to you all and to the audience. And at least," he finished, peering out at the auditorium, "it seems we will have a good house. I was afraid . . . But no, of course the people who appreciate opera will not hold the unfortunate destruction of the probe against us. Go take your places, everyone, please. I don't want to start late."

Until that moment it hadn't occurred to me to worry about what effects the probe accident might have on our performances, but as Tricia and I found our high-chair seats I began to.

Still, the performance went beautifully. Malatesta and Floyd Morcher outdid themselves, and so did everyone else in the cast. When it was over the Ptrreek applauded it wildly.

"I guess everything is going to be all right," I said to Tricia, climbing up on top of my chair to see better while the cast took their curtain calls. There were a lot of them. I was delighted to see it, even though they had almost as many as we'd had for *Don Giovanni* the night before. And then Binnda came trotting out from the wings in his white-tie outfit, modestly appearing for the final curtain call—

And the applause stopped cold. It shut off as though a switch had been turned. Every Ptrreek stopped clapping, and the only applause in that whole theater came from the hands of the humans of the opera company.

The Ptrreek were decent enough to show their admiration for the talents of us primitive Earth artists, but they were not now going to clap for a Mnimn.

I did not think an alien could weep, but Binnda's voice was choking as he called us all together after the performance. "My dear colleagues," he croaked, "you saw what happened tonight. For the good of the show, I don't think I should conduct again. I've asked our estimable Mrs. Norah Platt to fill in for me for tomorrow's performance of *I Pagliacci*. In any case, I must return for consultations about this terrible business. That is the bad news. The good news," he went on, "is that even the Ptrreek can't deny that you are all *superb*. The tour will go on. Tsooshirrisip"—I noticed that it wasn't "Mr. Tsooshirrisip" anymore—"will continue to make all the necessary arrangements, and I hope I can join you again at some later time. At least when we get to Hrunw."

It was a moving speech. Norah Platt and Maggie Murk were crying openly as he left.

There wasn't any cast party that night, either. When I suggested to Tricia that at least the actual human beings of the cast might get together she said, "Oh, I don't know if that's a good idea, Nolly. This is turning out to be kind of a jinxed tour, wouldn't you say?"

"Not for me," I told her, squeezing her hand to show her what I meant. "I think it's just great."

But in the long run I had to admit that she was right.

CHAPTER
36

From then on, the tour went all downhill. By the time we finished our remaining engagements on Ptrreek we were glad to leave. We were even gladder when we stepped out of the box at the next planet, which was called Hrunw, because the first thing we saw was Binnda's ugly, friendly face grinning worriedly up at us, with the bright green tongue licking out at us in welcome.

"Oh, Binnda *darling*," Norah Platt cried, flinging herself at him. Tiny as she was, Norah was about the only one of us who could do that without knocking him over. But all the rest of us gathered around, ignoring the natives and the Kekketies and the place we had come to. It hadn't been the same without little Meretekabinnda there.

"I can't stay," he said at once. "Really, I shouldn't have come at all, but how could I stay away?" And then he added, almost sobbing, "Oh, my dears, how *nasty* things are! Everyone at everyone else's throat. There hasn't been anything like this since that awful business with the Bach'het, and where it will end . . . But come, let's find a place where we can sit down and drink a little of this good The Earth whiskey"—he was waving a bottle in each three-fingered hand—"and you can tell me how things have been going."

A place wasn't hard to find. Binnda simply led us to what looked like a green lawn just a few yards away. It was unpleasantly squishy, as though it had recently been rained heavily on, although there was a warm, small sun in the sky. While the Kekketies struggled away with our baggage, Binnda listened to our stories.

There was plenty to tell him, because after he left we'd had one kind of trouble after another on the tour. Floyd Morcher flatly refused to kiss Sue-Mary Petticardi when it was his turn to play Don Ottavio to her Donna Anna—because that was an immoral act, he said, but more probably because he was upset. The reason he was upset was that Eamon McGuire had got away from him long enough to tie one on, so that he turned up for his fight scene with me roaring drunk. Bart Canduccio had had a terrible screaming fight with Ugolino Malatesta when he'd tapped on Norah Platt's door to console her over the difficulties Ephard Joyce was in and found Ugolino doing the job already. Worst of all, after our last *Pagliacci* there was something approaching a riot when a Ggressna—not Barak—tried to come to the performance and the Ptrreek had just about mobbed him.

"Yes, yes," Binnda said sadly, "there is so much hostility everywhere now. But, please, tell me about the *operas,* my dears! How have the performances gone?"

"Oh, very well," I assured him. "That part's been fine. I took three calls after *Don Giovanni* last night, and Tsoosh-irrisip gave us all medals."

"We all took curtain calls," Morcher added. "They didn't care about the kissing."

"Wonderful, wonderful," Binnda said, brightening as one of the Kekketies approached with a tray of glasses. "Will you pour, please, Norah? No, not for Eamon, if you don't mind; Eamon, you really must confine your drinking to when you aren't singing. And your Neptune? Was that well received?"

McGuire assured him that, really, the artistic affairs had gone very well. We all did. And when the drinks had been passed around we each lifted our glass—they weren't glass; they were made of something more like the inside of an oyster shell—and Binnda proposed a toast. "To your continuing success, my dears! And now"—he beckoned to one of the eight-foot natives, standing by—"let me introduce Mr. Nyoynya, who will be your impresario while you are here on Hrunw. I will return if I possibly can, but . . . well, things are really *quite* worrisome just now. Mr. Nyoynya will take excellent care of you, I'm sure. And I'll be with you in my thoughts always. And—oh," he said sorrowfully, "I do hate farewells! But I must go. Good-bye, all of you." And he turned and marched back to the box and was gone, leaving us in the care of an eight-foot creature that smelled of fish and resembled nothing as much as a shrimp made of Cellophane.

I'd read my book on the Hrunwians before we got there.

It told me that this new planet was named Hrunw. It didn't say how to say that word, and so it took me a lot of work before I could pronounce it well enough to satisfy even the opera company, much less the Hrunwians themselves. I came close by working my lips, the way my grandmother used to do when she was adjusting her dentures, and making a sound like a Hell's Angel jazzing up his engine at a stoplight.

Hrunw was even hotter and wetter than the Ptrreek place. The Hrunwians (which is not at all what they called themselves, but that I never did learn to say) did not live in skyscraper cities. They didn't live on the land surface of the planet at all. The kind of places the Hrunwians liked to live in were warm shallows without much tidal flow, and so their biggest communities floated in lagoons around volcanic islands in their oceans. They didn't use go-boxes to get around their low-rise, wickerwork cities. (Didn't *anybody* build with steel and stone on these planets?) They didn't use cars, either; transportation was walking, swimming, or riding in flat-bottomed airboats, with huge propellers at their sterns, along the canals of the cities. When we saw our "theater" we all groaned. It didn't have a roof. It was an outdoor arena, like a football stadium chopped in half. The Hrunwians were quite ugly to look at, with their transparent shells and tentacled eyes and nasty little clawed limbs, and when Eamon McGuire peered out at the audience before our first *Don Giovanni,* he muttered, "Bloody webfeet, they smell like fish."

Actually they did, a little. But after Eamon's third curtain call—the sounds of an enthusiastic Hrunwian audience were about like a few thousand people slapping clumps of wet seaweed together—he came offstage in a glow, declaring, "At least the bloody fish know good singing when they hear it. That calls for a drink!"

Eamon got almost as many curtain calls as I did. I thought he was milking them a little, stalking ponderously around the stage in his stone-statue makeup, but I didn't say anything. I did not begrudge the old man his success, and anyway I was still the one that was getting three and a half percent of the gross.

The Hrunwians had never heard of the institution of the cast party, and Binnda wasn't there to educate them. So McGuire didn't get his drink, at least not where I saw it.

Right after the *Don* performance, Tricia and I settled down in our room to wait for our dinner. It was officially "our" room now; we'd given up the his-and-hers, because the troupe knew all about us anyway and certainly the Hrunwians didn't care. The walls were wicker. I could hear Maggie and Sue-Mary murmuring to each other in the room next door. It was jungly humid and hot, but it was at least almost to a human scale, and there was a real bed.

That was a big plus. It almost made up for the food they had served us, which was a kind of a fishy stew, vaguely resembling bouillabaisse, followed by something like fish fritters and ending with a sweet chocolate-looking pudding that also tasted of fish.

"Well, we're only here for six performances," I said to Tricia when the Kekkety had taken away the dishes. "We won't starve in that time."

"Things are bound to get better," she told me, doggedly cheerful, but that was a very, very bad guess.

I suppose, really, we had all just been together too long.

Everybody was in a crabby mood. Morcher was on Eamon McGuire's case about sneaking drinks before breakfast. Tricia was hostile toward Floyd, because he had "church" services after breakfast (how could he know if it was Sunday?), and although Norah, the Italians, and three or four others attended he had kept her out. ("But I *always* go to church at home," she told me indignantly. "In Texas *everybody* does.") Sue-Mary and Maggie Murk had a low-voiced fight because the Spanish bass had made advances to Maggie, and when Sue-Mary dragged Maggie away he began hitting on plump little Eloise Gatt. Who was being true to the man she wrote letters to, back on Narabedla, and slapped de Negras to convince him of it.

We were getting on each other's nerves.

It wasn't just us humans. The larger affairs of the Fifteen Associated Peoples were a constant worry. Outside of the always-present Eyes of the Mother, scurrying around everywhere, there wasn't a single foreign alien anywhere in sight on Hrunw. "They've all gone home," Norah told us wisely. "It was the same when it was the Bach'het situation that got them all stirred up. Sometimes I think they're as bad as human beings."

"But the bedbugs are still here. I see them all the time," I pointed out.

"They're the Eyes of the *Mother*. They *have* to be allowed anywhere they want to go; it's the Tlotta-Mothers that run the peacekeeping program, don't you see?"

"So at least there's one race they all trust," I offered, and everybody laughed.

"Trust? Trust the *Mothers?*" Tricia giggled. "They're the last ones anybody would trust!"

"It's because they're so curious," Sue-Mary Petticardi explained. "They want to know everything. But they don't threaten anybody, because the Mothers don't move anywhere—they can't—and their neuter males just do what their Mother tells them. And their sexed males—well, I've never seen one of their sexed males, but as I understand it they're nothing but animated sexual organs. Like some other people I know," she said, giving de Negras a poisonous look.

"What you have to remember," Norah explained, looking around cautiously, "is that none of them trusts *anybody*. They'd all do anything they could get away with. And they're always squabbling among themselves."

"A lot like some other people I know," I agreed.

It was getting to be a pretty gritty existence. I could hardly remember that wonderful triumphant feeling of only a few days before. Depression was taking over. I hadn't even bothered to count the house for *Don Giovanni*. It was time for us all to go home . . . but we couldn't do that.

When we got to the theater the next morning Conjur Kowalski was stalking angrily around the stage, Purry trotting after him beseechingly. "Do you *know* what they have done to us?" he demanded of Tricia. "They have *canceled* us. They don't *want* us to do our thing for them."

Purry tried to placate him. "It's only your opening number they want to cancel, Mr. Kowalski," the little ocarina piped apologetically. "They do want the operas performed."

"But we are not *in* the operas," Conjur said savagely.

Since I was, I tried to be objective about the problem. "Maybe they have a short attention span here, you know? Even a short opera like *Pagliacci* is enough for one evening, maybe."

"Enough!" Conjur barked. "So if it's enough, how come they're putting in a bunch of creepy critters to replace us?"

"Mr. Kowalski is talking about the Drummers," Purry

explained. "They come from a protected planet, just like yours. They're really quite popular on some planets."

"I don't care *who* they are," rasped Conjur.

I tried peacemaking again. "After all," I pointed out, "you two are on straight salary anyway, so what difference does it make?" He looked at me in a way I didn't like, so I tried a different tack. "It's all Binnda's fault," I declared. "He's supposed to be with us just to handle situations like this."

"Damn freak," Conjur said bitterly.

Tricia said soberly, "Binnda can't really help it if he isn't here, can he? With all the troubles he's got over this Andromeda thing? Oh, heck! I have a bad feeling about the way things are going, you know?"

And Conjur reached out a great hand to clutch my shoulder. "Tomorrow," he said. "You and me and de Negras, Nolly. We're going to the zoo." And he stalked away without another word.

After I was made up as Tonio I sneaked out into the auditorium to watch the Drummers. In my opinion, the local Hrunwian impresarios were well within their rights in deciding that one batch of protected-planet primitives doing their rudimentary artistic endeavors was all they could ask their customers to sit still for. (Or, in the case of the Hrunwians, lie still for, as they watched the performances stretched out at full length on pallets.) We were on Hrunw, after all. On Hrunw we did what the Hrunwians wanted us to do, or we did nothing.

I didn't try to persuade either Tricia or Conjur of that.

The three of us watched the performance from pallets in the audience—the Hrunwians didn't bother to install seats for visiting dignitaries. Maybe they didn't consider us dignitaries. Tricia and Conjur were muttering resentfully to each other as the show began, and I didn't blame them. It wasn't any riveting spectacle to my taste, either. The Drummers were round-bodied, crustacean-looking little beasts, like fiddler crabs, and what they performed was a kind of musical mutual flagellation. They hopped and skipped around to their own music, which they produced by slapping each other's hard, horny shells with their hard, horny claws. As different parts of their shells gave out different sounds when struck, they did produce a kind of music.

I suppose I've seen more boring shows, but not often. Certainly not when I knew what I was getting into. Tricia settled down to a kind of bored attention. Conjur was not even looking at them; he was stretched out on his pallet, staring at the backs of his clasped hands.

Neither was very good company.

I twisted around curiously, trying to get an idea of how many were in the audience. It was hard to tell from our position, but there seemed to be at least five thousand. I did some quick accountancy. The Hrunwians did use money, which helped; but their currency had been falling on the Polyphase Index. As best I could figure, I was only going to get a little over half as much for this Tonio as I had been getting on the Ptrreek planet.

You win some, you lose some. It was just one more reason for wishing this tour over so we could get to a richer planet.

Conjur was still staring blackly at his hands. I leaned over to him and whispered, "What was that about a zoo?"

He didn't look up. "We're goin', my man," he said. "Tomorrow."

That was all I could get out of him. When I opened my mouth to ask why he was so hot for the zoo, Tricia poked me from the other side. "Leave him alone," she whispered. "He's in one of those moods. Anyway, the zoo's kind of fun. You'll see."

When the Drummers were finished they got a fair amount of applause (or the squishy Hrunwian sound that was their equivalent). I thought, listening carefully, that it was certainly not as much as Eamon had got in his curtain calls—not to mention me—but probably just a tad more than Tricia and Conjur had been given on the Ptrreek planet.

So maybe the Hrunwians had been right to make the substitution, but naturally I didn't say that. Anyway, I had to hustle backstage to get ready to sing.

Pagliacci was another triumph. But there wasn't any party. Most of the cast simply went to their rooms, and I began to count the days until the tour would be over and we would be back in friendly, human Narabedla.

The next day's opera was *Idomeneo*. Right after breakfast

Conjur rounded up all of us who weren't involved in the performance, like third-graders on a class trip, to go to the zoo.

Mr. Nyoynya had supplied us with transportation. We all piled into one of those flat-bottomed airboats, with the huge propeller thrusting us along the smelly canals of the basketwork city.

It was still hot and muggy, and the dead-fish smell was worse. Our Hrunw driver expertly slalomed past stopped boats and around the heads of swimming Hrunwians. They didn't even glance up as we passed. Neither did Conjur Kowalski. Considering that the whole thing was Conjur's idea, he didn't seem very interested in looking at the scenes we passed. He spent the trip poring over a map, scowling silently to himself.

When we got to the zoo our driver called something, and Purry translated it quickly as, "Hold on, everybody, please!" Luckily we all did. The boat didn't stop at the water's edge; it slid right up on the bank, bumping to a jolting stop. We got out and looked around.

The zoo was immense. It surrounded the dead-ended canal, which had terminated in a wide pool with dozens of other airboats drawn up on the bank or zipping along recklessly across the water. There must have been thousands of Hrunwians around, strolling, gaping, hurrying from one attraction to another; couples and groups and even families. (I explained to myself that I shouldn't be surprised that even alien monsters had families.) There didn't seem to be any cages, though that, I thought, might have been because of the clumps of feathery trees that almost encircled the pool, obscuring the view. But I didn't hear any roaring of giant jungle beasts, either. "So where are the elephants?" I asked Tricia, following her toward a gap between two clusters of shrubs.

"They don't have elephants," she told me. "How could they? Elephants are too big to get on the yacht. But don't worry. They have plenty of bigger things, and some of them have teeth and claws like tigers."

"Oh, really?" I said, smiling. "Where are those?"

She stopped and pointed. "Well, there's one now."

And indeed there was. It was bright green, scaly, and at least elephant size. It had teeth sharper and longer than Dr. Boddidukta's, and, like Dr. Boddidukta when I first saw him, it was sinking them into the throat of an orange-spotted creature with long antelope horns, the size of a horse.

All that I saw at first glance, but what I mostly saw was that it was not in a cage. It was no more than half a dozen yards away, and there was nothing between me and it . . . except two tiny, glassy Hrunwian young, so little that they wore nothing but a sort of transparent diaper around their transparent bodies, holding tight to each other's claws and feelers as they gazed up in fascination at the horrid spectacle.

I will say to my credit that my first impulse was to sweep Tricia out of the way and dash in to rescue the little Hrunwians. I didn't have to do that. I heard a bass bark of laughter from Eamon McGuire, and then Norah's silvery giggle. And then I began to understand.

"Oh," I said, over my shoulder, not quite sure enough of my ground to turn and face them. "They're in slow time, aren't they?"

"It gave you a real thrill right at first, though, didn't it?" Tricia grinned affectionately. "All the big things are slowed. That way they aren't going to hurt anybody, and if one of them starts out of the zoo, hey, the keepers just turn it around again when they close down for cleaning."

The two little Hrunwians had turned around at the sound of our human voices. Now they were staring at us, their little mouths gaping in astonishment. When I spoke to them they darted around behind the monster, peering out at me cautiously as I reached out to touch it. It felt slick and slightly warm—very much the way the "statue" of Dr. Boddadukti had felt while he was busy executing poor Jerry Harper. "All right," I said, taking my hand away. "Enough of this. We're scaring the kids. Let's go look at some other beasties."

There were plenty of other beasties to look at. The Hrunwians didn't bother having any of their own animals in their zoo, or if they did I didn't see them. Everything I saw was an exotic. Big ones with claws, big ones with wings and fangs, big ones that were hairy and muscular, like six-legged gorillas, big ones that I had never imagined even in a nightmare—all in slow time, moving millimeter by millimeter along the lanes or across the open spaces. And there were tiny ones in cages or pools or glass cubicles, hideouser than the big ones, and probably more dangerous because they weren't slowed at all. There seemed to be a section for each planet, though I had no idea which was which until Tricia tugged me around a corner and displayed the Earth quarter. An African lion was poised before me in soundless mid-roar. A zebu bull was frozen in the act of cropping grass. There was a cage of snakes (unfrozen), and a case of ants, and a mouse corral, with two or three hundred little rodents scurrying and playing around behind a transparent, hip-high fence. "Look," whispered Tricia, pointing to a family group of Hrunwians, the parents besieged by their three little ones. The parents (I *supposed* they were parents) conferred for a moment, and then indulgently put a few coins into a box, and all three of the little kids hopped over the fence.

Whistling and chirping in joy, they ran after the scurrying mice. Then each of them picked up one mouse by the tail and swallowed it. I could see the little animals writhing and struggling as they went sliding down those transparent digestive tracts.

"Let's get out of here," I said. "Now the kids are scaring *me*."

I had been talking to Tricia, but I got an answer from Conjur Kowalski, though I hadn't even seen him come up. "Good idea, Nolly. You come with me now, I got something that will interest you."

"Fine," I said, taking Tricia's arm, but he shook his head.

"You go keep the others company awhile, Trish," he ordered. "This is private between Nolly and me."

"Oh, really?" I said. He was looking quite tense about something. I glanced at Tricia, who shrugged good-naturedly and turned away. "Well, why not? Where is it?"

"Right down here," he said, marching ahead.

I followed, wondering what kind of freak was worth taking special notice of in this collection of freaks. A giant amoeba? A talking serpent? Maybe a captive human colony, trapped in slow time for the entertainment of Hrunw?

It was a human, all right. It was our bass, Manuel de Negras, chatting with Purry in front of a spiked, dinosaur-looking kind of creature in slow time. He turned to us without surprise; evidently he had been expecting this meeting.

Conjur didn't waste any time. "Ask him to tell us about the people he was in the slammer with," he ordered Purry. The little ocarina obediently translated it into Spanish, and the bass shrugged and began a long recital.

"There were more than forty people," Purry began. "Some had been there for nearly three days—that would be, Señor de Negras says, almost two hundred years. The oldest was an Englishman who—"

"No, not all that," Conjur interrupted. "Just the last one who came in right before Binnda sprang him. The girl. Tell him about the girl."

"Señor de Negras says that is correct," Purry reported. "There was a young woman. She arrived only a short time before he was released—far less than a minute. He didn't have any chance to speak to her."

I scowled at Conjur, beginning to be uneasy. "What's this all about?" I demanded.

He shook his head at me. "Ask him what she looked like," he ordered.

And Purry came back with the answer. "She had red hair and blue eyes. She was quite tall. Almost as tall as you, Nolly, Señor de Negras says. She was quite upset, but he only heard her say one thing."

"And what was that?"

Purry put the question and turned back to us. "Señor de Negras says, she said, 'Is Nolly Stennis here? Or Tricia Madigan?'"

I swallowed hard.

Conjur turned and looked at me for a moment. "All right," he said, nodding. "Thank the man for me, Purry. Nolly? Let's you and me take a little stroll."

I was having trouble with my breathing. "But that sounds like *Irene*," I told him.

"Well, my man," he said, pulling me after him, "you know, that's what I was kind of thinking myself. Shut up a minute."

One of the little Eyes of the Mother bedbugs was scurrying past. He waited until it was gone, looking around. There was no one but Hrunwians and zoo animals in earshot.

I was in shock. Irene Madigan! I hadn't exactly forgotten that she existed, but it had been a good long time since she had turned up anywhere in the conscious part of my memory. When Conjur opened his mouth again to speak, I cut him off. "Why didn't you *tell* me?" I demanded.

"And did I not?" he growled. "I been tellin' you, go talk to that Spanish cat. How many times do I got to say it? But no, not you; you been so fat and happy, countin' up your dough and playin' poker-poker with little ol' Trish, who could talk to you?''

"I thought Davidson-Jones had taken care of her," I complained.

"Well, he did, didn't he? His way. And what're you gonna do about it? Now here we get right to the point, Knollwood. You remember the dude I was tellin' you about, back in the waterfall pool?''

I hadn't taken him very seriously, but I hadn't forgotten, either. "You said there was somebody who might be able to get me back to Earth," I said. "But—''

"No 'but,' my man," he said savagely. "There is. He's here. Not half a mile away. You want to talk to him or you don't?''

"Well, I—I guess . . . Well, sure, I'd like to talk to him, only—''

"Then let's do it, all right?''

"All right," I echoed, not at all sure I meant it. "I'll go get Tricia—''

"No," he said, taking my arm. "We're leavin' old Trish out of this one. It's you and me that's got to see the Man, Knollwood. The lady can stay here. Better if she does. But us two got to get going.''

CHAPTER
37

Conjur was walking fast along the squishy duckwalks of the Hrunw city. He seemed to know where he was going, and he didn't want to talk.

I gave up trying. It took all my efforts to keep up with those long legs, and anyway I was concentrating on the idea of Irene Madigan, thrust into slow time. Of course, I told myself, I barely knew the woman. Anyway, I wasn't responsible for her problem—if anything, it was the other way around. Anyway, what could I do about it?

Conjur paused for a moment to look at his map, and I caught up. "Where are we going?" I demanded, panting.

"You'll see when we get there," he rasped, glancing around, as though trying to locate landmarks.

"Yes, but what does this have to do with Irene Madigan?" I persisted. He didn't answer. He just gave me a smoky, unfriendly look and started off again.

I followed. By then I didn't have much choice, because the zoo was far behind us and I was lost. Occasionally one of the locals would whistle and squeak at us, but Conjur ignored them and plowed right on.

We jumped over a couple of narrow canals, and hurried along the side of one larger one, filled with the airboat Hrunwian traffic. "Pedestrians"—by which I mean the locals—hurried vigorously along pathways of what looked like board overlaid with something more or less like straw matting. That was what we walked on. It got tiring, because the resilient surface gave a little at every step, like walking on piles of mattresses, but (Conjur growled at me when I complained) we didn't have far to go.

It wouldn't have been a bad walk if it hadn't been so sticky-hot, and if the place hadn't stunk so. It wasn't exactly a dead-fish smell, though that seemed to be in it. It was mostly a waterfrontish kind of mixture of salt sea, washed-up garbage, and sewer outlet. Pedestrians got fewer, except for one or two of the Tlotta bedbugs.

Then Conjur stopped, gazing across the wider canal at an unusually solid-looking building on the far side. It seemed to be made of something that resembled stone, unlike the Hrunwian reed igloos. Conjur looked at it, then at his map. Then he swore softly.

"That's it," he told me. "The Ossp embassy."

"The *what?*" I demanded, startled. I had heard of the Ossps. They were the ones everybody loathed, and what were we supposed to be doing with Ossps?

"It's the place we're going to," he said, looking up and down the canal. There was no bridge in sight. He swore again. Then he began untying his shoes and said, "Get 'em off, my man."

"Do what?"

"Take off the shoes and the pants," he explained. "There's where we got to be. You can keep 'em on if you want, but we got to wade."

We did.

The water was neither deep nor cold. Wading it was easy enough to do, though we had to wait for a lull in the boat traffic to splash across. The bottom was sticky mud with something sharp stuck in it, like shells—I *hoped* they were shells—but it didn't come much over our knees. On the other side we pulled our pants and shoes back on and marched up to the stone building.

A creature like a reptilian kind of bat appeared at the door. It looked us over silently for a moment. Conjur took a deep breath. "Wait for me here, Nolly," he ordered, and shoved past the Ossp. It squawked warningly at him, then hurried after him, slamming the door.

I did what I had been told to do. I waited.

I waited for quite a long time, and there wasn't a moment of that time that I enjoyed. First, what was I doing here? Nobody had ever forbidden me to speak to an Ossp, but then nobody had ever thought there was any likelihood I would. And certainly they had some kind of a bad reputation. Second, where was I? I had no hope of finding my way back even to the zoo, much less to the rest of the opera company. Third, what was Irene Madigan going through just then in her slow-time captivity? (Not to mention a stirring of the almost forgotten worries about Marlene Abramson back on Earth; was she going to show up there, too?)

And I was attracting attention. A pair of Hrunwian swimmers poked their heads out of the canal to whistle at me. I shrugged at them. I had no idea what they were trying to say, but it didn't sound friendly. One of the Mother's bedbugs scurried past, pausing to elevate itself on its hind legs and stare at me before proceeding on. I didn't like that. I supposed that the Hrunwians had some sort of equivalent of police, and that sooner or later a Hrunwian cop would stroll by and say the Hrunwian equivalent of, "What are you doing here, sir?"

I didn't think I had any good answer.

I didn't like the idea of going inside the Ossp embassy, either, but it was better than standing there in the watery Hrunw sunshine. So I was glad when the door opened again.

The Ossp was there, and next to him a Purry. I thought

for a moment the Purry was my own friend, but it wasn't. It was smaller and darker, and its English was oddly accented. "You are Knollwood Stennis," it stated. "You will come to the ambassador now."

The ambassador was waiting for me in a sort of a passage, too narrow to be called a room. It was hanging from a kind of clothes tree, and it wasn't alone. A pair of other Ossps were with it—these squatting on the floor instead of hanging from a rack—and so was Conjur Kowalski, leaning dourly against the wall. The place was dimly lit, with that all-over luminescence that didn't seem to come from any particular place, and, although it didn't have that Hrunwian smell of dead fish, it smelled far worse. It smelled like the bottom of a parrot cage.

"You're on," said Conjur. "The ambassador is willing to make a deal."

"What *kind* of a deal?" I demanded, but he just shook his head and pointed at the Purry, busily translating our conversation into a burst of clicks and musical-saw whines.

There was a quick exchange between the big bat on the clothes tree and one of those on the floor. Then the big bat clicked and whined back, glaring at me, and the Purry said, "The ambassador from Ossp speaks. You will give him some things that are of no value to you. Then he will see that you get transported back to your planet called 'Earth.'"

I turned and looked at Conjur. He didn't look back. He was standing there, holding the top of another of the coat trees, like a subway straphanger, staring vacantly at the ceiling. He didn't say anything.

I said to the Purry, "What are these things the ambassador wants?"

Clicks and metallic moans. Then the Purry said, "First you will be provided with suitable containers. You will ejaculate semen into these. Second, you will—"

I found my voice. "Hold it!" I yelled. "What was that first part again?"

Conjur crackled at me. "Don't argue with them, Nolly! Just listen to what the man says."

"But—"

"*Listen.*"

So I listened. The Purry went on imperturbably, "Second, you will procure an Earth-aboriginal female for the same purpose. When we have our specimens you will be conducted back to your planet."

I goggled at the Purry, then at the bat. "An Earth female—For the same p—Conjur!" I yelled. "What the hell are they talking about?"

"What they talking about," he said, "is, you beats your meat into a bottle for them, then you gets Trish to help out, then they sends you home."

"But—" I squeezed my eyes shut, shaking my head. It didn't get things clarified. "But that's not how it *works* with women!"

He said seriously, "Nolly, listen to me. They know that. They understand all about human reproduction, that's why they want the specimens. Do you want to go home or not?"

I gaped at him helplessly. He stood leaning against the coat rack, patiently waiting for an answer. The ambassador wasn't doing anything at all except to restlessly fold and unfold its wings, though the Purry was translating it all and I could feel the bat's bright little eyes watching me. I said, "Why me?"

" 'Cause they don't want no black jizzum," he said bitterly.

I said weakly, "Oh."

"Yeah," he said. "Oh. What they wants is good old WASPy come. You think I didn't try?"

"But . . . even if I did . . . I mean, they want a woman's ova, too? How could I handle that?"

"Trish," he said succinctly.

"But—" I began, but he was losing patience.

"You can stand there and talk all day, my man," he said, "only that gets *nothing*. Make up your mind. You want to go home or you don't want to go home? 'Cause here's your chance if you do."

"I couldn't ask Tricia to do that!" Conjur didn't answer, just waited me out. I tried a different tack. "What would they do with the stuff if they got it?"

Conjur jerked a thumb at the bat. "You want to ask him that question?"

"Uh, no," I said.

Because I didn't have to. There could only be one reason. The Ossps were the genetic wizards. They would know what to do with genetic materials. Human sperm and human ova could be converted into human babies even on Earth, with in-vitro fertilization and some kind of host mother. I had no doubt these creatures could do as well. As to what purpose they wanted human babies for . . .

I didn't want to ask that question even of myself.

I said stubbornly, "I need to think it over." The Purry translated. The bat was silent.

I said, "I'll let you know my decision." More translation. More silence.

I said, "I'm going to leave now. Come on, Conjur." And I turned and retraced my steps.

They didn't stop us, though my shoulder blades crawled as I retraced my steps. I blundered out the door into the warm, wet Hrunwian day, with Conjur right behind me.

We didn't talk on the way back. Conjur didn't offer any conversation; he just stalked along, face like carved ebony, not even looking at me. And I was busy trying to decide if I really wanted to go back to Earth—and to wonder if I were willing to help the Ossps in whatever nasty business they had in mind—and, most of all, to figure out just how to put the proposition to Tricia Madigan.

CHAPTER
38

I will positively *not*—you have got some terrific nerve just for asking—do *that*," said Tricia, eyes blazing, face twisted in repugnance.

I said, "But poor Irene—"

"No, not even for Irene! We'll get her out some other way. Don't even talk about it."

"But if we just got back home we could—"

"No! Do you know what the Ossps would *do* with that stuff? *No*," she said, and got up out of our bed and, clutching a dress in front of her but otherwise bare, stalked out of our room to hunt up some other place to spend that night.

And left me behind, tumescent and angry. She hadn't even given me a chance to argue.

If she had let me I would have explained to her that I had had plenty of time to think the matter over carefully. She didn't. I couldn't blame her for having some reservations about the Ossp's proposition. I had plenty of my own. I certainly was not keen about cooperating in whatever it was that the Ossps wanted to do with human semen and ova. I knew the Ossps' reputation. The first thing I did was check in the book Canduccio had given to me to make sure, and, yes, they were the galaxy's specialists in genetic manipulation.

It infuriated me that she could think I would participate in such a plan without careful study and, if possible, some sort of guarantee from the Ossps. I wasn't lighthearted about the prospect of permitting human babies—who would be my own children, after all!—to be generated in some alien laboratory, for purposes I did not want even to imagine.

So she had no right to go off in a huff that way, without even letting me explain. It was simply *unfair*.

I was steaming.

The funny thing was that the more I steamed the more I began to think that this particular offer, while not a very good one, was quite possibly the only offer of its kind I was ever going to get.

It had been easy enough for me to decide I didn't want to go back to Earth as long as it was impossible.

Now it wasn't impossible anymore. Only very, very—well—*risky*.

I asked myself: Did I really want to go back to Earth? Loud and strong the answer came back: *Yes*. Not just for my own sake. For the sake of all the captive humans on Narabedla—never mind that most of them didn't seem to object to their enforced captivity—and especially for the sake of bringing to justice Mr. Henry Davidson-Jones and all his crew.

Then, I asked myself, was I willing to do whatever had to be done to get there? There wouldn't be any easy choices, I told myself. Nobody was going to help me escape simply out of the kindness of his heart—even if he had a heart, about which, in a number of cases, I was doubtful. I would have to take risks. I would have to do things that were—well—I admitted it to myself, morally objectionable. Was I serious enough to accept that?

The answer was yes.

So then, I explained to myself, I should put qualms aside. The end would justify the means. You couldn't fight against the hordes of Attila the Hun by the rules of the Marquis of Queensberry.

At that time, in that mood, all those things made sense to me—not least, I think, because Tricia had left me not only angry but frustratedly horny.

It was a second puberty. True, I wasn't exactly a youth; but my glands were reborn, and they were flooding my bloodstream with all the itches of fresh testosterone. I was ready to join a street gang, fire-bomb a police station, charge a machine-gun nest; I was the typical rough, randy, riotous young male, looking for a turf to fight for.

In a calmer mood I would have been more rational. For starters, I would have forgotten all about the Ossp ambassador and started trying to enlist help from nicer sources. For starters, there was no doubt that everybody in the opera troupe would want to help get Irene Madigan out of the freeze. United, we could almost certainly cajole Sam Shipperton into finding her some kind of a job—she'd been at least an actress, or anyway almost an actress, hadn't she? Then we should be able to find even more potent allies. Among us we should be·able to persuade Binnda to help. Maybe Barak. Possibly Tsooshirrisip, or some other of the aliens—if they could get their minds off the crisis caused by the probe accident long enough to do something constructive. And then there was the consideration that, after all, I wasn't really doing so very badly in the Narabedla captivity. I was *singing*. I was getting *rich*. Before long there was every prospect I would be *famous*.

None of that deterred me. I wasn't thinking along constructive lines.

The funny thing was that I knew all this was happening. I knew who I was. I wasn't any comic-book superhero. I was L. Knollwood Stennis, CPA and opera star, a steady, mature (fairly mature) adult human being. That knowledge changed nothing. My glands had taken over. I sat there, with my legs dangling over the edge of that lumpy, empty bed, plotting ways to talk Tricia into donating a few ova for the cause—after all, what other use did she have for them? . . . or, failing that, trying my luck at recruiting Sue-Mary or Maggie Murk . . . or, failing that, wilder stratagems still, like getting my costume sword out of the *Don Giovanni* prop bin and putting it to the throat of that nasty little batty bit of business, the Ossp ambassador, and forcing him to get me into the go-box to Earth . . . and then, once I was back home, leading squads of cops and FBI agents on a raid of Henry Davidson-Jones's yacht, to do hand-to-hand battle with his troops and Kekkety servants and guards.

I think I would have been happy for a city to loot. But Narabedla would do until one came along.

I fell asleep in such musings of combat . . . and woke up to find they were real.

I wasn't alone in my bedroom anymore. It wasn't Tricia Madigan who was there. It wasn't ány human at all. The people dragging me furiously out of my bed, with their damp, chill, scratchy claws, were Hrunwians, whistling and chirping angrily. The one talking to me in English wasn't even a Hrunwian. It was one of the Mother's little bedbugs, rearing up on its hind legs to shrill at me, "Knollwood Stennis! You are under arrest! You have violated your terms of employment and must leave this planet at once!"

Ten minutes later I was being shoved into the big long-distance go-box. There wasn't any nonsense about being allowed to take my personal belongings. I was still in my pajamas. The Hrunwians giving me the bum's rush did not seem to be opera fans. They didn't let go of me, and they weren't gentle. When they released me from their wet, cold grip it was only to turn me over to a clutch of the Mother's bedbugs. "Get in," shrilled the English-speaking one, while a couple of others butted me inside and another scuttled up into the little overhead cubicle to gaze down at me.

The trip didn't take long, but it was long enough for me to realize that I was in the deep stuff. "Where am I going?" I asked. I didn't expect an answer, and didn't get one. But when the door opened there was Binnda, waving his ropy limbs in despair.

"Oh, *Nolly*," he cried. "How *could* you do this to me?

Have you no-loyalty to the company? Trafficking in germ plasm with the Ossp?—and you *know* what they will do if they get it! And—oh, my dear boy!—what about our *season?* We won't be able to do anything but *Idomeneo!*"

I didn't answer any of that. I hardly heard it, because I was staring around. The first thing that caught my eye was a batch of Kekketies at a silvery machine that looked ominously familiar. The second was even more familiar. It was Conjur Kowalski, seated in a chair.

He didn't look up to greet me.

He didn't move at all. His face showed anger, apprehension and disgust, and his eyes glared wearily at nothing. And would go on glaring in just that way for a good long time, because I didn't have to touch Conjur, and feel the slicky, oily *something* that surrounded him, to know that he was captured in slow time.

"Oh, God," I said.

Binnda hissed in despairing agreement. "There's a chair for you, my boy," he pointed out. "I suppose you might as well sit down."

I managed to ask, "How long?"

He twisted his upper body, as though shrugging. "Who can tell? Conjur admitted the whole thing—of course, once that Eye had been absorbed by its Mother, there wasn't any way to hush it up, anyway. And with everything in such a chaotic state . . . Ah, well," he finished, "we'd better get on with it." He leaned forward to give me a sad hug, then got quickly out of the way as the Kekketies began fussing with their machine.

"Anyway," he said consolingly, "everyone knows you are quite ignorant, even for an aboriginal from Earth. Perhaps that will be taken into consideration."

And that was the last I heard from him, because he, and everything around him, disappeared.

CHAPTER
39

What does being thrown into slow time feel like?

It feels like nothing much at all, except that everything around you goes crazy. There was a quick flash of orange-yellow light. Then something went wrong with my eyes. The Kekketies disappeared. Binnda was gone, leaving only a faint blur of motion to show where he had been. Something slammed against my shoulders, knocking me brutally against the back of my chair. I felt as though I were in a rocket lift-off as, chair and all, I was moved—moved again—set down. No, not *set* down, I was *dashed* down, chair and all.

And I stood up out of the chair and looked around, as Conjur did the same thing from the chair beside me.

I was in a place I had never seen before. It was a big room, maybe thirty feet square, furnished like the ambulatory patients' lounge in a rather nice hospital. It seemed really quite incongruously pleasant, considering what it was. Two elderly men were playing gin over in a corner, pausing to look up at the new arrivals, namely Conjur and me. Ephard Joyce was sitting on a couch, his head buried in his hands. There was a table along one wall with sandwich materials and a coffeepot, and a plump young man wearing a gold-braided uniform that looked as though it had come from World War I was lifting a cup to his lips. Corridors went off the room, and I could see, through an open door, a little bedroom with a tall, dark woman sitting on the edge of the bed and yawning.

I say I saw all this, but only in the way that you see a movie set on TV when you've just switched into the channel. I didn't make a careful examination of it. I was too busy looking at a young woman in shocked conversation with a short Oriental man. She (as best I remembered) looked very much like Irene Madigan.

It was she, all right. She turned toward me, eyes wide and wondering. She looked astonished, and shaken, and as though she were about to cry.

I had no doubt of what had happened. We were all in cold storage.

My big worry was how cold I was going to get—cold as in dead, maybe? Were they just holding me temporarily until Dr. Boddadukti or some even worse monster came to sink his fangs into my throat?

I couldn't believe that. I didn't want to believe it; but I reasoned that if they were going to make a Jerry Harper–type spectacle of me they'd do it in Execution Square.

All these things flashed through my mind and reached my senses at once. Very quickly.

"Nolly?" said Irene Madigan inquiringly, coming toward me.

"It's me, all right," I told her. "I'm sorry to see you here."

The little Oriental man was peering over her shoulder. "Who are you?" he asked politely.

I didn't get a chance to answer, because Irene was saying, "Is it true? What Gwan Lee has been telling me? We've all been captured by flying-saucer people?"

"She's quite upset," Gwan Lee said sympathetically. "I suppose you're feeling pretty shaken up, too. You'll want some clothes; but if you just put a note on the skry they'll bring them to you before you know it."

"And why *are* you in your pajamas?" Irene asked plaintively.

I held up my hands to slow her down. "It's a long story," I began. I started to tell it to her, but I didn't get very far. She made a soft, sobbing sound, and reached out for me. I put my arms around her. "It'll be all right," I whispered to her hair, holding her tight. She just sobbed again. I saw Ephard Joyce looking up at us from his couch, and Conjur standing by his chair, looking angrily amused.

"What's going to happen now?" I asked Conjur, still holding Irene Madigan.

He shrugged. "We stay here, is all. You got any better ideas?"

"Well," I began, patting Irene's back soothingly, "I guess—"

I didn't finish the sentence because something hammered

at my chest, where Irene was snuggled against it; I felt my
arms thrust away from around her. There was an instant,
almost subliminal orange-yellow flash—

My arms were still outstretched, but there was no one
inside them. Irene Madigan was gone.

I gaped at Conjur. "What the hell?" I shouted.

He opened his mouth to respond. . . .

Whatever it was he was saying, I didn't hear it. There was
another of those flashes, and two Kekketies were beside me,
holding me up, while another was turning off his silvery
machine.

An Eye of the Mother was peering up at me. "L. Knollwood Stennis," it piped, "the Mother wishes to see you."

I was out of slow time.

I stared about. Conjur was still opening his mouth to address the space where I had been, frozen still. All the others
were frozen, too.

I never got to finish any of those conversations. That's
not surprising. There's a limit to how much you can say in
something less than a minute . . . or (depending on how you
look at it) somewhere around a year and a half.

CHAPTER
40

The bedbug wouldn't say any-
thing else to me, but when it pushed the hanging bead curtain
aside to let me into the Mother's chamber Binnda was there,
pacing nervously back and forth. The bedbug quietly scurried to the edge of the Mother's pool and sat there, quietly
waiting, next to a Purry. No, not *a* Purry; it was my own
dear friend, because it whispered, "Hello, Nolly."

Binnda greeted me too, but sadly. "Oh, my dear boy,"

he said, "how good it is to see you again! So much has happened! But quickly, you mustn't keep the Mother waiting, off with those garments and in, please."

"But I want to know what—"

"Nolly! *In.* She's the *Mother*," he said sternly, and wouldn't answer any questions.

Things had been happening too fast for me. My resistance was low; I did as I was ordered, though not easily. Clothes are a kind of armor; when you don't have them on your defenses are weakened. I didn't like that, but I didn't see any choice.

A couple of those flying things buzzed me as I lowered myself into the Mother's shallow, smelly pool. I swatted them out of the way (one landed in range of the Mother's questing tentacles, and was immediately swept up into that obscene-looking orange mouth). I turned to Binnda for instructions.

"Closer," Binnda urged. "But not too close, of course."

I had no intention of disobeying that part. I waded slowly toward her. Little fishy things were nibbling at my knees and tenderer places, until I got within range of the Mother's tentacles. Then they stayed away.

The Mother took hold of me at shoulder, waist, and thigh and tugged me gently closer. The ring of tiny eyes regarded me silently as I tried my best not to move. Or even breathe.

Then the Mother began to moan in a gurgly sort of way—most of the time her speaking organ was under water. Her little bedbug translated from the edge of the pool.

"The Ossps are a race most foul," she said (through the bedbug). "They do not voluntarily abide by the agreed rules of association. They have in the past made war, viciously and harmfully, until they were defeated. Then they promised to refrain from antisocial acts. But even now they violate the accords."

"I know," I said.

There was a sudden flurry around my legs. One of the little marine animals had incautiously come close enough to nibble at my knee. It was a mistake. Instantly the Mother's tentacle slipped away from me and whipped around the thing, dragging it into her huge maw. The Mother went on imperturbably, and so did the bedbug. "I assure you, Knollwood Stennis, to deal with the Ossps is to risk very grave consequences to yourself and to the primitive planet you come from."

"I just wanted to go home!" I said bitterly.

The Mother's tentacles stiffened around me for a moment as the bedbug translated that. Then the tentacles relaxed again as the Mother moaned at me again.

"If that is so," the bedbug translated, "why did you not simply ask me?"

I gaped at those unblinking eyes. "But—" I managed. "But—but that was impossible! Henry Davidson-Jones wouldn't allow it!"

The tentacles whipped wildly about for a moment, and the Mother's huge, bright-colored barrel body shook with bubbly moans.

"The Mother is laughing," Binnda explained, his own voice sounding strained. "But really, my dear boy, what a foolish thing to say!" And he added a string of ho-ho-hos. Even Purry was chuckling softly.

Worse than being threatened is being laughed at. I suppose I was still on an adrenaline-testosterone high. "Cut this crap out," I stormed, turning to face them . . . and completely forgetting to move cautiously so near those long, striped tentacles of the Mother.

I had never felt the full strength in the Mother's tentacles before. They were like wire cables, lashing around me and jerking me toward that hideous, always-chomping mouth.

I yelled. I struggled. I squirmed as hard as I could; I battered against the many-colored, cold, clammy, solid flesh of the Mother, splashing up a Niagara of froth.

None of that stopped her for a moment, or even slowed her down.

It had been very foolish of me, I realized, to set off the feeding reflexes of the Mother. It was one more blunder, and probably the last one I would ever have a chance to make. There was nothing that could save me—

In that I was wrong.

There was a splash and a thud. Something heavy crunched against me, right between me and the Mother's remorseless mouth. The tentacles slipped away from me and caught it.

It was Purry, making noises out of all his mouths as the

tentacles deserted me to wrap around the plump, ocarina-shaped body of my friend.

"Nolly! Get out while you can!" Binnda yelled, running up and down agitatedly along the sides of the pool. "Are you *insane?*"

Getting out of that pool sounded like a great idea. I don't know if I could have done it by myself, but there were half a dozen of the Mother's drones suddenly in the pool with me, butting me away from the orange and blue and scarlet body, ramming me forcefully toward the edge. Binnda's clawed, sinuous arms darted down and hauled me out. I sprawled on the slick, warm floor, in pain. Dots of blood sprang up all along my shoulders and legs where the Mother's tentacles had rasped me raw, like metal potato-graters on my skin.

When I turned to look back I was shamed.

Purry had saved my life, but not cheaply.

He was actually being eaten, a mouthful at a time, held fast by the Mother's implacable tentacles. Little squeaky sounds were coming from those apertures in his skin. They weren't words. They weren't even cries of pain, although he was being devoured. They were just the sounds a bagpipe makes when you squeeze the last of the air out of the collapsing sack.

Then he managed words.

"Have you any orders for me, Meretekabinnda?" Purry gasped.

Binnda said sorrowfully. "Oh, no. It's too late now. Go ahead and get eaten." And there, right before my eyes, Purry did.

At least when I saw the Duntidon ripping out the throat of Jerry Harper it was only horrible. There was no sense of personal loss. I hadn't ever known Jerry Harper. But Purry—Purry was my *friend*. Purry was the one who had guided me around Narabedla, the one who had accompanied me when I wanted to raise my voice in song simply to celebrate the fact that I had a voice again . . . the one who had just saved my life.

And he was being eaten alive. Most of his body was gone now, pulled into that awful mouth. All that was left was his head, with one rabbity little eye looking sadly at me, then looking at nothing as it glazed over. And Binnda was not even watching. He was moving restlessly about the margin of the pool, pausing in front of me. He said, "As to the question of your returning to your The Earth—"

I didn't even hear him. I was staring transfixed as the last of Purry vanished into the Mother's mouth.

He was gone, and I was fighting the need to vomit.

Then what Binnda had said penetrated. I gaped at him. "What?" I demanded.

"That is possible," Binnda said.

I sat down, still naked, still bewildered, still with that lump of bile in my throat that wanted to come up. I rubbed the tiny blood spots on my arm. "What are you talking about?" I demanded.

He said, glancing at the silent, attentive bedbug, "The Tlotta-Mother wishes to see your The Earth. She has agreed to let you return, under certain conditions."

I shook my head. I said reasonably, "But you told me yourself that the Mother never goes anywhere. I know she said she wished she could go there and see it, but there's no way. She can't move; and if she could, my God, how could she disguise herself?"

Binnda preened himself. "It's true," he admitted, "that not everyone is fortunate enough to have nearly human anatomy, like me. Nevertheless, disguise is possible."

"Disguise *her* as a human being? But that's ridiculous!"

"Not necessarily the Mother herself," Binnda said, reaching out his arm to tap the bedbug by his side.

Which got up on its hind legs to address me. "And not necessarily like a human being, Mr. Stennis," it piped.

The Mother moaned a command, and one of the other bedbugs rushed out of the chamber. I said, dazed, "Are you really saying I can go back home?"

"Exactly, my boy," Binnda said sadly. "Oh, I'll miss you. The whole company will miss you—it's been terrible, trying to salvage the troupe, in these trying times, especially without our best baritone. But the Mother says you can go."

I shook my head. "But the rules—"

His bright green tongue sagged in misery. "Rules," he echoed. "Yes, there used to be rules. Much has happened while you were—away—my dear boy. The Eleven Asso-

ciated Peoples aren't the same anymore. Even I shouldn't
be here, but—''

"Wait a minute! *Eleven?*"

"There have been secessions," he said, licking the lips of
his three-cornered mouth.

"What about Davidson-Jones?" I asked, trying to take it
all in.

"Henry Davidson-Jones need know nothing about it,"
Binnda said forcefully. "He is not on his vessel. The crew
will obey the instructions of the Eye of the Mother. You will
simply—ah, here is the costume for the Eye. You see how
well it will work?"

I stared. The bedbug had scurried back, bearing what
looked like a small version of the kind of sheepskin you
throw over the corner of a couch to show you've been to
New Zealand. The English-speaking bedbug seized it and,
making faint mewing sounds of effort, slipped four of his legs
into the legs of the skin, pulled it over his body, and stood
there waiting for approval.

"A perfect copy," Binnda said proudly, "of one of your
The Earth dogs. You can take it anywhere."

I shook my head wonderingly. It didn't really look like a
very convincing dog, but it looked more like a dog than anything else. I began to believe that they were serious in all
this.

It was time for me to get serious, too. "All right," I said,
making up my mind. "I'll take that thing. But I won't
go alone. I'm not going unless Irene Madigan can go back
with me. She was kidnapped, just like me; she has every
right—''

I stopped, because the Mother was moaning at me. The
bedbug translated, its voice slightly muffled by the fur. "The
human aboriginal Irene Madigan may accompany us. It is
true to say that she was not validly here, and she has already
been released from the deceleration chamber."

"She's been staying with her cousin for nearly a month,
my dear boy," said Binnda, in confirmation. "It's been quite
a strain for both of them."

"All right," I said, pushing my streak. "Then Tricia
should have the choice of coming back, too, and Conjur Kowalski and Ephard Joyce—''

"*No,*" said the bedbug. "Only the two of you, each of
whom was brought here in violation of agreements."

"Even now," Binnda said sadly, "the Mother insists on respecting the regulations concerning aboriginals. What do you say, my boy? Do you want to go home to your The Earth?"

I had not forgotten Rule One of any negotiation: You push right up to the moment when the next thing would make them say no. Then you stop. That was the point we appeared to be at, so I made up my mind fast. "Let's go," I said, turning toward the beaded door.

"Very well," Binnda said, beaming in gratification. "But, my boy? Don't you think you should put your pajamas back on first?"

CHAPTER
41

The door that let us onto Henry Davidson-Jones's yacht hadn't changed. There was still the same mismatch in ceiling height, and we had to clamber up over the same high sill.

The bedbug, hampered by its poodle suit, had trouble making it. So did I, for a different reason. We were back on the good old surface of the good old Earth, and I found out that I was suddenly a good twenty-five pounds heavier than I had been for a long time.

I stood up to find myself looking into the eyes of a Kekkety, standing before us as motionless and unoccupied-looking as a suit of armor on a stand. I grabbed protectively at Irene's arm—pure reflex action; a little leftover testosterone, I suppose. But the Kekkety wasn't threatening. When our bedbug moaned something at it in, no doubt, the Mother's own language, the Kekkety jumped, touched its cap, and turned to lead us down that familiar metal-walled corridor.

"Where are we?" I demanded.

"We are at what you call your 'New York City.' Now please come with me," the bedbug said politely. We did.

I looked around warily. The last couple of times I had been aboard that yacht I hadn't known I was there, and wouldn't have been able to do anything about it if I had. This time it was different. This time we had the bedbug along, and it was in charge. When we got to the end of the corridor, the Kekkety opened a door for us and stood meekly beside it, waiting for orders.

We entered into Henry Davidson-Jones's personal cabin, the one that served him as an office on the yacht.

I had been there before, too. I had telephoned Marlene Abramson from that very desk, but now the desk was vacant. "Where's Davidson-Jones?" I asked.

"Mr. Davidson-Jones is not aboard this vessel. Only the ship's officers and crew are aboard. I will instruct them to say nothing. One moment, please, while I have this thing open this safe." The bedbug gave a quick command, and the Kekkety trotted over to the wall, spun a dial, and opened it. It was a big safe, and well stuffed. The bedbug clambered on a chair to peer inside, then pulled out a number of packets of papers and tossed them on the desk.

"Will this be enough?" it asked.

Irene glanced at what the bedbug had taken out of the safe. She looked up at me unbelievingly and whispered, "Oh, my God!"

What the safe had been stuffed with was sheaves of currency—all kinds of currency—francs and pesetas and pounds sterling, but most of all good U.S.A. dollars. Irene poked the nearest packet with a finger as though it might bite.

My attitude toward large sums of money had changed since going to Narabedla. I just shrugged. "Let's see what we've got," I said, and picked up a few handfuls of it to examine, stacking them crosswise to admire them.

"That's not ours," Irene said warningly.

"Excuse me," the bedbug interposed deferentially, "but the Mother informed me that you will need 'money' to carry out her instructions. Isn't that what this is?"

"It's money, all right," I confirmed. "Ms. Madigan just wonders if it belongs to us."

"Oh, yes, Mr. Stennis. Anything you want on this vessel 'belongs' to you," the bedbug told us.

Irene closed her eyes and sighed. Then she opened them and said resignedly, "Does that include clothing?"

"Of course," the bedbug confirmed.

"Then I think you ought to see if you can find some in Mr. Stennis's size," she said, looking at me. "Or were you going to go out in the street in your pajamas?"

When the bedbug was gone, Irene looked at me and sighed again. "Nolly," she said, "I'm not off my rocker, am I? This is all real, isn't it?"

"It's real. If it isn't, we're both off our rockers."

She nodded. "Just checking. There really are these flying-saucer people, then?"

"Fifteen different kinds of them, right. Each one weirder than the next."

"Uh-huh," she said. "And they're all fighting with each other because they had some big thing that blew up or something, and they've got all these captured human beings that can't go home—anyway, that's what Tricia told me."

"As to that," I said, "you know more than I do. I've been out of circulation for a while. But yes, that's the general idea."

She nodded, philosophically accepting that the world she knew had gone out of its tree. "Yes, I thought that was the way it was. Well, I see what looks like an empty dispatch case over there on the table. Don't you think we ought to fill it with some of this money?"

So that was what we did. A very practical woman, Irene Madigan.

If anyone should ever ask me how many ten- and twenty-dollar bills will fit in an ordinary dispatch case I can answer exactly. Enough to total $128,500. "What are we going to do with it all?" Irene asked.

"Use it."

"Yes, I understand that, but for what?"

I hesitated. Although the bedbug seemed to be on our side and in fairly complete charge of the situation, I didn't know who might, sooner or later, be listening. A plan was beginning to form in my mind, but all I said was, "We're going to get off this yacht with it as soon as we can. That's the first thing."

"And what's the second thing?"

"When we come to the second thing," I told her, "we'll figure it out then. All we can do is play it by ear."

When we walked down the yacht's gangplank there was snow on the ground and a mid-winter wind was coming up along the East River.

"Oh!" cried Irene Madigan, pulling up the collar of her light summer jacket. "I wasn't expecting this!"

Neither was I, but I felt a sudden rising of the heart, because I knew where we were. The yacht was moored at the Twenty-third Street boat basin. I had jogged along these very streets.

"We're only a few blocks from my apartment," I told Irene.

"Can we go there?" she said, shivering.

"Absolutely not! No. We're not going where anybody might look for us. Come on, if we go over to First Avenue there are always cabs going uptown."

And so we did, but by the time a taxi stopped for us, the bedbug was whimpering with cold, even with his fur coat on. "Gramercy Park," I told the driver, reaching for the handle of the door.

It didn't open. The driver had his hand resting on the door lock as he squinted out at us. "Is that a dog?" he asked.

"Yes, that's right," I said. "Open the door."

"I don't want no dog—excuse me, miss—crapping in my cab," he informed us.

I had almost forgotten what a New York taxi driver was like, but I hadn't forgotten how to deal with one. "If he does, I'll give you fifty dollars."

"Yeah?" The driver thought for a minute. "And you'll clean it all up, too? Because my doctor says I've got a real sensitive stomach, you know what I mean? Okay, let's go."

The hotel I'd picked was only ten minutes away. It wasn't a bad ride, apart from the bedbug scrambling up into my lap to peer outside at the buildings, the people on the streets in their winter parkas and boots, the cars competing with us for lanes through the jams at each corner. In spite of the traffic, the driver mellowed as we went along. By the time we got to the hotel he was at the friendly just-before-the-tip stage.

"That's a real nice, ah, pooch," he said admiringly. "Mind if I ask what breed he is?"

"He's a Lapsang-Oolang," Irene said smugly. "They're very rare in America. I think there are only half a dozen of them here, mostly in Beverly Hills."

And the bedbug obligingly said, "Woof."

When I registered us at the hotel I had a story all prepared. The damn airlines had lost all our damn baggage, even my credit cards—yes, it was certainly foolish of me to check my briefcase! But it wasn't necessary. The clerk wasn't interested. He didn't even ask how come I still had some kind of briefcase tucked securely under my arm. He simply took my two-thousand-dollar cash deposit, welcomed me to the hotel, and handed over the little plastic things they use instead of door keys.

The bellhop offered to relieve me of the dispatch case with the money, but I shook my head. "I'll carry it myself," I said, giving him a five-dollar bill. "Just show us to our rooms."

The rooms were actually adjacent suites, two of them, one for Irene Madigan and one for me to share with the bedbug. As soon as we all were in one of them the bedbug began to shed its woolly poodle suit. "It's very hot in here," it complained. "Why do you keep this place so hot? And it is very cold outside. You didn't tell me that water existed in the solid phase on this planet. Also I'm hungry."

It wasn't until it said that that I realized I was, too. It was not surprising. I hadn't eaten a thing since I was on the Hrunw planet—a year and a half ago! That was easy to remedy. After some discussion I picked up the phone and ordered from room service. The club sandwich, milk, and a piece of cherry cheesecake for me, the shrimp salad and a pot of tea for Irene Madigan, and, "How about that filet of sole? Can we get that without any breading or anything like that? Fine. We'll take two of them. And, oh, yes, we want them *raw.*"

I put the phone down and thought. The bedbug was already busy, exploring the suite, piling cushions on a chair to reach the thermostat, flushing the toilet, worrying up a corner of the carpeting so it could see what was underneath. I opened the hall door and peered outside. No one was in sight. "Come with me," I ordered the bedbug, and escorted it to the next-door suite, where I left it with the TV set (twenty-five channels to keep it amused; thank heaven for cable) and a "Do Not Disturb" sign on the door and returned to Irene Madigan.

Who was waiting with growing impatience. "Nolly?" she said. "What are we doing, exactly?"

It was an overdue question. "I think we can talk here," I said, looking around. "I doubt the bedbug can hear us through the wall."

"There isn't much to hear, because you haven't been saying much," she pointed out.

I said, "We're going to blow the whistle on Narabedla. There's nothing else to do, is there?"

She pursed her lips. "Well," she said, "I'm not exactly arguing with you, but couldn't we just go back to living our lives?"

I shook my head. "I don't think so. The Associated Peoples are all messed up right now, but what happens when they get back together again? Sooner or later they're bound to. And then there's Henry Davidson-Jones. The Mother let us come back, but he didn't. He's got a lot to protect, Irene. We're a permanent threat."

I paused to see what she would say. What she said was, "I'm listening."

"So we're going to lay low for a few days," I explained. "We're going to make affidavits. We'll write out everything we know about Davidson-Jones and Narabedla, and our own experience. Then we'll send copies to as many people we can trust as we can think of, with instructions that if they don't hear from us they'll send them to the police, the FBI, the CIA, their congressmen, *The New York Times*—everybody. And we'll include proof."

"What kind of proof is that?" she inquired.

"I've been thinking about that. First thing we need is a Polaroid camera, so we can take pictures of the bedbug with us; that should be a good start. Then we can tell them about all the people we know there. They can exhume some of the fake bodies and check fingerprints and dental records, like the one you buried thinking it was Tricia—"

She was shaking her head. "I had that body cremated," she pointed out.

"They can't all have been cremated. There's a whole list

that've come to Narabedla in the last twenty or thirty years; there's bound to be at least one they can check.''

She nodded thoughtfully. ''Say, that's true,'' she said. ''Maybe it is. Well, then, if all that works out, we go to Davidson-Jones and we tell him that if he doesn't leave us alone all that stuff comes out. So why do we have to blow the whistle on him now?''

''Why— Because— After all, Irene, they're *prisoners* up there! Even your own cousin.''

She said, ''But Tricia doesn't want to come back to the Earth. I asked her.''

''She doesn't?'' I blinked at her. ''At least Tricia should have the *right*, shouldn't she? And she's not the only one. Conjur Kowalski definitely wants to come back. So does Ephard Joyce. So do a batch of others—I bet nearly every one of the people we saw in slow time is there because they tried to escape.''

''Nolly,'' she said patiently, ''when I found myself in that slow-time place I thought I'd gone crazy. When Tricia got me out and took me to her place I was positive of it. I'm talking culture shock, you know? Even now, the only way I can handle it is by making believe it was some kind of a dream.''

''It's very disorienting, yes,'' I agreed.

''And what would happen to the whole world if they suddenly got exposed to it?''

I shrugged. ''I don't know. They'd just have to face up to the fact that we're not the only ones in the universe, or even the smartest.''

''And do you think they can? I mean, without going nuts?'' She got up and stood before me, peering down seriously at me. ''You're talking about two different things, Nolly. One is taking out insurance; that's fine. The other is pulling the trigger. Maybe that's right, maybe it isn't. All I'm saying is I think we should give that a lot of careful consideration before we do it. It scares me, Nolly.''

''But why? What do you think will happen?''

''Nolly, what scares me is I don't *know* what will happen. So, please, let's think it over before we do something we can't undo.''

By then the room-service waiter was knocking on the

door. I let him in, and tipped him, and escorted him out again, thinking hard.

It was possible Irene Madigan was right. By the time I had escorted the bedbug back to our dinner I had decided, at least, to hold off on anything irreversible for a while.

The bedbug ate its dinner sulkily. It not only wasn't very good, it wasn't anywhere near enough, it complained. Irene fished a few of the shrimp out of her salad, and it ate a few of them distastefully. Also it was fretfully anxious to carry out the Mother's orders. The TV set had kept it busy in the other room for a time, flicking the remote-controller from channel to channel, but that was not enough. "It is a very stupid system," it complained. "It is not even interactive. Can we go out now? I want to ride the subway."

I told it, "Pets aren't allowed in the public transportation systems unless they're in a pet carrier."

"What's a pet?" it wanted to know. And when I explained that that was its temporary status with us, as far as the rest of the planet Earth was to know, it seized on the idea of a carrier. "One with temperature control," it specified.

"But there aren't any of those, and you're too heavy to carry very much, anyway," Irene pointed out. "I'll tell you what we can do. We can get you a little doggy overcoat, and maybe even booties."

The bedbug demanded suspiciously, "What is an 'over-coat'? You mean there is something else I have to carry around? On only four legs? In this gravity?"

"It can't be helped," Irene offered, stroking its chitinous back.

The bedbug accepted the inevitable. "Then let us get this 'overcoat' for me," it said. "Although you may go on grooming me for a bit first."

Irene said obligingly, "All right. I suppose we ought to do some shopping anyway. I need a coat for myself, not to mention boots and maybe some other clothes, and I suppose you do too, Nolly."

I definitely did. The slacks and jacket I'd scrounged on Davidson-Jones's yacht were tight in the pants and loose in the jacket, and not really warm enough for a New York winter to begin with. "Also," I said, "we're going to need a Polaroid camera, and some film. And writing paper, and pens. And envelopes. And stamps."

"Hold it while I make a list," Irene said, searching the

drawers for hotel stationery. "Are you sure about wanting pens? To write these things out with? I'm sure the hotel could rent us a typewriter."

I thought for a minute. "No, it's better if they're in our own handwriting," I decided. "Put down a bottle or two of liquor, while you're at it, and some instant coffee. I wonder what time the stores close? What time is it, anyway?"

And when I called down to the desk to ask they told me it was a quarter after eleven. I didn't have to ask whether it was A.M. or P.M., because I could see out the window that it was night.

I hadn't thought of the time at all. "Well," I said, "maybe we ought to get some sleep first, anyway, and make a good start in the morning. Irene, would you like to keep this room? The bedbug and I will bunk in next door."

"I do not require to sleep," the bedbug piped up.

"All right," I said. "You can stay in the living room and watch television all night."

"But it is not my assignment to watch television! I must carry out the Mother's instructions!"

"Well, you *will*. Tomorrow. Probably. Meanwhile there are all-night news programs, movies—I think there's even a porno channel, if that interests you."

It chittered severely, "That is not the same thing at all. The Mother wants the firsthand experience from me. The sights, the smells, the tastes."

I tried to reason with him. "Yes, but you don't have to do it all yourself, do you? When you go back you'll just tell her all this. Why couldn't one of us just have told her?"

He reared up on his hind legs to gaze at me. "*Tell* her? What would be the use of *telling* her? No, Mr. Stennis, when I go back she will engorge me, and then all my memories will be hers."

I goggled at the thing. "You mean she's going to eat you?"

"It is the happiest thing I have to look forward to," he chittered with pride.

CHAPTER

42

It was a good thing we had a suite, because the bedbug was up all night with the television while I was trying to sleep in the bedroom next door.

I didn't sleep long enough. The bedbug woke me early, scratching at the covers over me and whimpering, "I have nothing here to eat, Mr. Stennis. My metabolism is not like yours. I must eat."

Room service wasn't open yet. If it had been, they probably wouldn't have had any raw fish on the breakfast menu; so there wasn't any help for it. I struggled into my clothes, cursing, and went out into the barely dawning morning outside.

If I had not been so cold and so sleepy, I would have been pretty happy. I was home! This was my own turf. My old apartment was only a few blocks away. There was my favorite sushi bar, next to it the neighborhood's best pie bakery. I had a quick cup of coffee in my regular coffee shop on Second Avenue, and found that the Korean open-all-night fish store was still there where I had last seen it, with the same busy, quick little Korean couple running it and the same display of Sun Myung Moon's ginseng elixir stacked on the counter next to the cash register. They didn't seem to recognize me. But then, they never had.

It was a homecoming. When I got back to the hotel room my shoes and socks were soaked from the melting snow, but I had a shopping bag full of seafood for the bedbug, a huge jar of instant coffee for myself, and about a hundred sheets of hotel stationery from the drowsing bell captain in the lobby.

I knocked on Irene's door to invite her to join us before letting myself into my own room. By the time I had finished laying out my purchases on the bathroom floor for the bedbug's examination, with its claws scratching excitedly on the

298

tiles, she came in, yawning and looking rumpled. "I *have* to have some clothes," she said drowsily.

The bedbug chittered in consternation over the fish. "It's all dead," it exclaimed.

"We don't usually eat our breakfasts here until they're dead," I informed it. Glumly it pawed over the slimy things. It nibbled at a filet of redfish, sniffed a cardboard dish of smelts, and finally, reluctantly, devoured three little squid and a dozen bay scallops, while I fixed Irene and myself some instant coffee out of the hot-water tap.

"That's a step in the right direction," she said, swallowing, "but I'm going to need more than that."

I nodded. I pulled the stolen dispatch case from under the bed, unsnapped it, and counted out a thousand dollars for her. "Get some breakfast for yourself," I instructed, "and then see if you can find any stores that open early on Twenty-third Street. Have you got that shopping list?"

She nodded, but protested, "I can't carry everything on the list! I don't know your sizes, anyway."

"Just get what you need. Then, when you come back, you can stay here with the bedbug and I'll go out."

"*No,*" said the bedbug forcefully, appearing between us with half a squid in its foreclaws. "You cannot leave me confined in this place when it is my duty to observe and experience. Take me with you!"

Irene scowled at him. "Later, okay? I'll take you anywhere you want—well, more or less—but I'm not really awake yet."

"Now," the bedbug said firmly. "Where is my costume? And, oh, yes, what is the excretory custom on this planet for 'pets'?"

"Maybe you'd better take a little more money," I offered, grinning. "You might have to buy a pooper-scooper."

She glared at me, then turned it onto the bedbug. "You," she commanded, "are to excrete into the toilet in the bathroom, and then flush it; that's a law, and do it before we go out. And close the door behind you," she called after the bedbug as it meekly turned to obey. Then she looked at me. "I'll take that extra money, though," she said. "It seems to me I'm going to deserve it."

They were gone for nearly four hours.

It wasn't really enough time for what I had to do. I was busy writing out my story on the hotel stationery. I started with the very first conversation with Woody Calderon, told of his "death," then of hearing from Irene, of having lunch with Vic Ordukowsky, bearding Davidson-Jones in his den, meeting Irene in southern France . . . I had filled twenty-five pages by the time Irene and the bedbug got back, and had only reached the point where I saw Norah Platt's dismembered body in Dr. Boddadukti's tub.

When they came in I quickly hid my notes under the desk blotter, because they weren't alone. Two bellboys followed them, laden with packages. Irene was not only carrying some bags of her own, she was wearing some of her purchases: red leather boots, calf high; a leather overcoat, with a fur Cossack hat on her head; and when she took the coat off I saw she was wearing a brand-new pants suit in a pale gray fabric. The bedbug, too, had a handsome new plaid wool overcoat buckled over his fleecy disguise.

"You both look very nice," I told Irene.

"Thank you, but will you tip the bellmen, please, Nolly? I don't think I have any money left," she said. While I was doing that she went into the bathroom and began running water into the tub. The bedbug scurried excitedly after her.

As soon as the bellmen were gone it began shedding overcoat and dog suit, chittering, "The fish! Please, put the fish in!"

"I'm doing it as fast as I can," Irene assured it, returning to the living room for a transparent plastic sack filled with water, in which three live ten-inch trout were agitatedly writhing and waving their fins. She untied it, dumped them into the filling tub, turned off the water, and left the bedbug in there. She closed the door, but we could hear the splashing and scratching noises anyway as it happily devoured its first decent meal on Earth.

"It's your turn to go out now if you want to," she told me.

"All right," I said. I showed her what I'd been doing. "You can start making your own report. We'll get them all Xeroxed and mailed out this afternoon. And remember, don't let anybody see the bedbug without his dog disguise. Above all, don't let him talk. When the maid comes to clean the room, tell her to do the other one first, then you and the bedbug can go in there while she cleans up here, and be sure you take the money with you.''

''Nolly,'' she said, sounding exasperated, ''I'm really a grown woman. I can take care of myself. Just *go.*''

And I went, feeling a little good-naturedly embarrassed at her reproof, but also feeling pretty good because things were going so well. It was even colder out than it had been earlier that morning, but I didn't head first for a men's clothing store to get a coat. I turned up my collar and walked briskly to the street telephone in front of the post office, because there was a call I had wanted to make all along and hadn't dared risk from the hotel room.

The street phone was still there. Remarkably, no one was using it; even more remarkably, it worked. I dialed the familiar telephone number for L. Knollwood Stennis & Associates, and waited for the ring, rehearsing the way in which I would disguise my voice in case of listeners and speak to Marlene in words she alone would be able to understand. . . .

The phone didn't ring.

Instead, there was a sort of clashing sound of ill-tuned chimes, and a mechanical voice told me, sounding like a more musical version of Barak's gaspy delivery, ''The number you have called . . . is no longer in service . . . please consult your directory.''

But I did, and the number wasn't there. The firm of L. Knollwood Stennis & Associates was no longer listed in the telephone book.

Almost anything could have happened in the best part of two years, I told myself.

But something certainly had, and none of the possible explanations I could think of were encouraging. I hesitated, then tried her home number.

That was a little better. I didn't get her, but I got her recorded voice, saying that although she couldn't come to the phone at that moment I should leave my name and telephone number, and the day and time I was calling.

I hung up. I was beginning to shiver violently in the open phone cubicle, anyway.

So I went down the block to a men's clothing store and bought a fleece-lined jacket and a hat; I needed more than that, but nothing as desperately. I stopped in the stationery store across from the post office for large envelopes. I picked up some more live fish for the bedbug, made sure the Xerox place was still there . . . and then dialed Marlene's home number again.

I got the same recorded announcement from her machine, but this time I was ready. "This," I said, "is Harrison Cham, Sylvia's husband." Sylvia Cham was an old client, which Marlene would remember, and she would not fail to remember that her husband, Harrison, had died five years earlier, because we'd gone together to the funeral. "It is important that I speak to you, but I must be in and out all day. Please call me at this number at three, six, or nine P.M." And I gave the number of the phone booth.

At three o'clock I was there. So was a small teenage girl, on tiptoes to reach the phone, having a long conversation in Spanish with, it sounded like, her mother. Three o'clock came and went and she was still on the phone. At five after she finally hung up, gave me a hostile glance, and departed. I took over, pretending I was talking with my finger on the hook.

But by twenty after there was still no ring. I took the statements Irene and I had written to the Xerox place and left them there as I went back to the hotel.

We spent the next hour or so taking Polaroid pictures of us with the bedbug. It didn't mind. It seemed to enjoy posing, and even climbed up in my lap so that Irene could snap us together a dozen times.

The photos looked pretty convincing to me. I suppose any Hollywood special-effects wizard could have created even better pictures with trick photography, but I couldn't think of any way of making them better.

At five-thirty I went out again. This time the bedbug insisted on coming along, and Irene decided she didn't particularly want to be left in the hotel by herself. All three of us picked up the Xerox copies, the bedbug obediently slinking under a table when I commanded, "Sit!" Irene and I stuffed the copies in the addressed envelopes, twelve copies going to twelve different people, and I left her waiting in line at the post office for stamps while the bedbug and I made the six o'clock check on the phone.

It didn't ring.

There was no particular reason for us to go right back to the hotel, and we were getting used to being out in the cold. Even the bedbug was contentedly doing his job for the Mother, sniffing at the tires of parked cars, rearing up to gaze into windows, pausing to investigate the aromas that came from pretzel vendors and hot-dog salesmen, and out of bars and restaurants. We strolled aimlessly down Third Avenue toward Union Square, and although people stared at the beast we had on a leash, and the hurrying crowds divided to let us through, no one offered any unwelcome questions.

"I guess I don't really *have* to talk to Marlene," I said, after a while.

"I suppose not," Irene agreed.

"But I wish I could! I'm worried about her. She wouldn't close down the office unless she absolutely had to."

"Well," she said practically, "what's our next step?"

Fortunately I didn't have to answer that just then. I frowned and shook my head, pointing down at the bedbug.

Which was whining up at us. I looked around. No one was very near. I bent down to listen, and it whimpered, "How does one manage with only four legs, Mr. Stennis? I'm getting tired, and this solid-phase water is very *cold*."

So we took it back to the hotel, and there I had plenty of time to answer Irene's question.

Or would have had. If I had had an answer. I was glad when it was time to go out again for a last check on the phone. There was no one in the cubicle this time, and not many people on the street at all, and I stood there wondering just what I was going to say to Irene when I got back to the hotel. I went over all the things we had done. We had distributed copies of our accounts in places where even the resources of Narabedla weren't going to find them. That was our insurance policy; Davidson-Jones would have to reckon with that before doing anything violent to us. The people we had chosen were good people. We could trust them . . .

But what should we do next?

I was so deep in concentration that the ringing of the phone was only an annoyance at first. Then I almost dropped it when I picked it up.

But then I heard Marlene's voice saying, "Nolly? It is you, isn't it? Oh, God, honey, I'm so glad you're *alive*."

* * *

On my way back to the hotel I almost ran, but when I passed the pet store on Lexington Avenue I stopped long enough to buy a few dozen tropical fish.

The bedbug was delighted. He promised to stay in the room while he enjoyed his meal at leisure, and I took Irene down to the hotel restaurant to celebrate. We found a quiet table in a corner, and over a drink I told her about my conversation with Marlene. "She sold the business," I told her, "to raise money to pay for private detectives. She didn't give up. She's been building up a whole dossier on Narabedla and Henry Davidson-Jones."

"Which will help support our story?" Irene put in.

"Which will damn *prove* our story," I corrected her. "She's going to get all the papers out of her safe-deposit box tomorrow morning. Then I'm going to go up to see her with a copy of our stuff, and we'll figure out what to do from there."

"Sounds good," Irene said, looking at me thoughtfully over her old-fashioned glass. "You know, Nolly," she commented, "you're really some kind of guy."

I shrugged modestly.

"I mean it," she said. "You're a regular Clark Kent. One day you're a mild-mannered accountant, and then all of a sudden you're taking on sixty-dozen wizard alien creatures with all sorts of high-tech jazz and rescuing the girl. I never expected it of you."

I said honestly, "I didn't really expect it of myself."

"It's a nice trait in a man. Is your drink empty, too?"

That was easily enough taken care of. When the waiter brought us the second round she frowned. "The funny thing is," she said, "I always thought I didn't really like jocks. You know? The kind of guy that figures he can take care of anything just by throwing some weight around? Do you suppose . . ."

She hesitated, fiddling with the orange slice in her new drink. Then she looked up at me with a peculiar expression, a little bit amused, a little bit embarrassed. "Tricia told me about your, uh, operation," she said. "Do you suppose that's why you're doing all this?"

Well, if I'd thought at all (I hadn't, actually) I would have been damn sure Tricia would not have missed the chance to gossip a little with her cousin. I didn't like that thought, but there wasn't anything I could do about it. I said shortly,

"How would I know if it was?" Then I said, more carefully, "I can tell you what lit my fuse this time. What got me going, Irene, was you. When I found out they had kidnapped you I wanted to—well, hell, I was willing to do anything I had to do to get you out."

"Thank you," she said, smiling at me.

"Don't mention it. Uh, what else did Tricia tell you?"

"Oh, well," she said vaguely. "Different things."

I was flustered. "I guess she told you that she and I—"

"Really, Nolly," she said, "what difference would that make? It's not important, is it?"

"Um," I said. "Uh. Well, Irene, you see, I didn't think there was any way that, for instance, you and I would ever see each other again—"

"Of course not."

"And we really didn't know each other very well, did we? You and I, I mean."

"Hardly at all."

"The only thing is," I said, "I felt kind of tacky about it, all the same."

"No reason you should have," she said firmly. "Don't you think we might order now? I'm starved."

And we ordered. And we ate. And we had a brandy with our coffee to finish it off. And when we were all done and the check was paid and we were lingering over the last brandy I said, "Well, we've got a busy day tomorrow. Do you want the room with the bedbug or the room by yourself tonight?"

And she said, "He's probably going to keep the TV going all night again, isn't he? So why don't we just let him have one of the suites all to himself?"

CHAPTER
43

When the city of New York decides to take a recess from winter it can change overnight. I came up out of the IRT at Seventy-second Street into bright sunshine. It was only a short walk to Marlene's block.

Marlene's apartment was one of those rent-controlled wonders that New Yorkers are willing to kill for, four big rooms in a well-kept building with an elevator for less than three hundred dollars a month.

It was a quiet block. There were still knee-high mounds of snow along the curbs where the plows had given up. Just behind one of them there was a parked ambulance. Its driver had the window rolled down to take advantage of the unexpected sun; he was wearing shades, a black man reading a copy of *Penthouse*. He looked vaguely familiar. An old woman was walking a dog—a real one; I saw it lift its leg to one of the city's always imperiled shade trees. An elderly man was peering out at the sunshine from the steps of Marlene's apartment house, trying to decide if it was warm enough to allow his old bones a walk to the 7-Eleven on the corner.

He looked familiar too. With good reason. As I climbed the steps he caught my arm. "Aren't you Stennis?"

As soon as he spoke I knew who he was. Marlene had brought him around to the office now and then. He wasn't a boyfriend, or even a date; he was just a guy she went to the movies with now and then. "Nice to see you, Mr. Keppler," I told him. "Is Marlene in now, do you know?"

"In?" He scowled at me. "Of course she isn't in," he went on in a disagreeable tone. "What do you think? Where've you been? She told me before she went to the hospital the first time you were someplace out of town. But didn't you know *anything?*"

I pulled my arm free, staring at him. "*What* hospital?"

"St. Luke's. Where she's dying from cancer," he said
bitterly. "So now it's too late you can finally take the time
to come see her, eh?"

I couldn't speak for a moment. I stood staring at him.

"I didn't know! Tell me!" I said finally, abjectly begging.
He did, with an old man's attention to the details of terminal
illness. According to Mr. Keppler, Marlene got sick the first
time over a year ago. She'd had to close down the office,
because she was facing at least six months of radiation and
chemotherapy. Then she'd been back in her apartment for
a while, but she'd regressed. He had gone to the hospital to
see her the day before.

She had, he said, no more than a month to live.

I cannot say how I felt then. I don't know the words to
describe it. It wasn't that I wanted to cry; it was a shock
too complete and unexpected for that.

"But," I said stupidly, "I just talked to her yesterday."

"You called her at the hospital? That's good," said Mr.
Keppler grudgingly. "You were lucky, because it's a real
miracle she could talk. When I went to see her last night she
was in a coma."

I let him go, my hand on the door to the building.

I watched him walk down the steps, leaning heavily on
his cane, making his way past the ambulance at the curb,
where the driver was looking sidewise at me from behind his
glasses.

It would have been a natural question to ask who it was
I had spoken to on the phone yesterday. I didn't have to ask
it. I already knew the answer. I remembered it from Henry
Davidson-Jones's office, when I had heard Marlene's voice
on a tape and it had not been Marlene speaking then, either.

The sun was still out, but the winter wind was chilling my
bones. Everything had suddenly become very different.

I turned around and walked quickly to the curb, not looking at anyone. When I got to the street I turned left, walking
along the parked cars. When I got to the ambulance I stopped
short.

I reached in the open window and grabbed the wrist of
the black man in the sunglasses.

"Nice to see you again since that time in Nice," I said
conversationally.

His reflexes were fast. He tried to pull his hand free, but I had it solidly. "Got a gun in your pocket?" I asked. "Or is it whoever's upstairs in Marlene's apartment that's got the gun?"

"Get your hands off me," he snarled, trying a sudden lunge. I put my elbow in his throat to stop that.

"You don't need a gun," I told him. "Just relax. If you want to take me to Henry Davidson-Jones you don't need anything at all, because that's where I want to go. Right now."

CHAPTER
44

It wasn't a man with a gun who was waiting for me in Marlene's apartment. It was Henry Davidson-Jones himself.

He was sitting at his ease at Marlene's dining-room table, and he wasn't alone. There was a Purry lying on Marlene's couch, regarding me with its little pop eyes—undoubtedly the one who had imitated Marlene's voice. There was a Kekkety in Marlene's kitchen, apparently doing dishes. And there was my friend from Nice and the ambulance, escorting me into the apartment, with his hand in his pocket.

"Hello, Nolly," said Henry Davidson-Jones. He looked tired, and he moved stiffly as he stood to reach out to shake my hand.

I didn't let him. He sighed and sat down again. "You can go, Arnold," he told my escort, and then as the black man reluctantly left, "I've just eaten something, Nolly. I'm sure the Kekkety can make something for you if you're hungry. No? Then," he called, raising his voice, "just bring us some coffee."

"I didn't come here for coffee," I said. "I want to make a deal."

"Well, do you mind if I drink some while we're making it? What deal do you have in mind?"

I said, "There are two people I want taken care of. One is Irene Madigan. I don't want her hurt, or confined in any way. I want her to be allowed to stay on the Earth. I'll ask her myself not to say anything to anybody, ever. I think she'll do it."

He clasped his hands and looked at his thumbnails. "Who's the other person?"

"Marlene Abramson."

He looked up. "Nolly," he said earnestly, "I give you my word I haven't done one thing to harm Marlene Abramson. I was very sorry to hear that she had become ill."

"I'm glad to hear it," I told him. "Are you sorry enough to take her to Narabedla to get fixed up?"

"Ah," he said, nodding in satisfaction. "I see what you're getting at. You think I'm a kidnapper, a profiteer, maybe a murderer—"

"That's right," I said.

"—and the Associated Peoples really ought to let the Earth in as a member, besides."

"I'm not quite as sure of that," I admitted. "But maybe so. At least we should have the choice."

"Yes. The freedom of choice. And in spite of all these wrongs, you're willing to let everything go on just as before, provided I arrange for Narabedlan medical treatment for one friend of yours."

"That's it exactly," I said.

The Kekkety padded silently over with the coffee. Davidson-Jones mused over what I had said while the Kekkety poured for him, then brought a cup over to me.

It would have been a proper gesture to refuse it, but actually it smelled pretty good. I took a sip. Then I got up, pulled the wad of papers out of my pocket, and dropped it on Marlene's dining-room table.

"We've sent out twelve copies of this," I told Davidson-Jones.

"Yes, so you told the Purry on the phone," he agreed. He riffled through the Xeroxes idly. "It seems quite complete," he said.

"They were only mailed yesterday," I told him. "There's

not much chance that any of them could be delivered today. The earliest would be tomorrow, just for the nearby ones. I don't know how you could intercept them, but I imagine you'd have a way.''

"Possibly," he agreed.

"I'll give you the names and addresses of all those people. Right now. If you give me your word about the two conditions.''

"What about yourself, Nolly? You haven't said anything about yourself.''

"I'll take my chances.''

"That's very commendable. And what makes you think I would keep a promise if I gave it?''

"I'll take that chance, too.''

"I'm flattered, Nolly," he told me, and he sounded very sincere.

He got up from the table and walked over to Marlene's window, gazing out at the bare trees in the snowy joint backyards of all the buildings on that block. "I hate winter," he said, rubbing his shoulder as though it pained him. "Nolly? There are pushing five billion human beings here on the Earth, and they all die sooner or later. Mostly sooner, and mostly in pain. Should I send them all off to Narabedla?''

"I don't suppose you could do that," I said reluctantly.

"So who do we save? Just the particular friends of Nolly Stennis?''

"I'm not asking for that. I'm only asking for Marlene Abramson.''

He turned and shook his head at me. "Oh, but Nolly," he said, chiding me, "you aren't making your best deal. You've got something to trade that, I admit, is valuable to me. It's worth a better price. Don't you want something thrown in for the human race? The secret of the go-box, for instance. Look at what that would mean. No more trains, planes, trucks, supertankers. No more sixteen-wheelers killing people on the highways—no more highways! No more jets from LaGuardia deafening the crowds at the Mets games. No more big tankers spilling their oil into the ocean. No more oil imports to bankrupt the high-energy countries. No more—''

I interrupted his catalogue. "All right," I agreed, "I'll take that, too.''

"Will you? It wouldn't be hard to do. The Associated

Peoples wouldn't object—they're too busy trying to patch up their own troubles. And it's just a matter of Einstein-Rosen separability. There are a lot of institutions right here that are close to finding it already. I've helped some of them, with money grants for research. Only—well, what about all those truckers and airline pilots and railroad workers? What are they going to do for jobs? How can you handle the unemployment that follows?''

"I don't know," I said, not liking the way the conversation was going.

"Neither do I," he said soberly. "I haven't known how to handle any of that, from penicillin to the silicon chip. I've helped them all, you know. For a long time."

I stared at him. "You mean with grants, and maybe little tips from time to time? But why do that when you could just hand all these things over?"

"Is that what you'd do, Nolly?"

"It's not my problem," I said shortly.

"But if it were?" he persisted. "Wouldn't you try to make all these changes gradually, so the human race would have time to adjust? And maybe even to give it a chance to keep its self-respect?"

"I might," I said, "but I wouldn't kidnap people."

He was silent for a moment, looking at me. He snapped his fingers, and the Kekkety glided up with more coffee. "I'm afraid I've made a lot of mistakes lately," he said. "I'm getting old."

"So go back to Narabedla yourself, and get fixed up."

"I have, Nolly, many times. I'm a good deal older than you think. It's time for me to retire."

I didn't like the way he was looking at me, because I didn't understand it. Then I began to understand it, and I liked it even less.

"Oh, *no!*" I cried.

"Oh, yes," said Henry Davidson-Jones.

CHAPTER

45

When Davidson-Jones's doctors got Marlene out of the hospital I was sitting in the ambulance, waiting for her. She looked terrible. She was tiny. A lot of her hair had fallen out. Her face was like death itself. She was in a coma, all right, and she didn't speak to me.

But when the Kekketies were gently lifting her into the box on the yacht I kissed her and whispered to her that everything was all right, and at least her eyelids flickered.

When the limo was taking us to the hotel Henry Davidson-Jones was silent. "Don't you have any instructions for me?" I demanded bitterly as we turned into Lexington Avenue.

"You give the instructions now, Nolly," he told me. "Just don't forget to make those telephone calls. Then, if you want to, come down to the office and you can get started. I'll be there. The car will come back and wait for you; it's your car now."

And I got out and stared after him as the limousine drove away.

It was early-evening dark. The streets were full. The hotel lobby was busy with well-dressed men and women intent on their own concerns.

They hardly glanced at me. They didn't know who I was—who I had suddenly become.

I had never been in charge of anything bigger than a six-person accountancy office, but I acknowledged that it was true, as Davidson-Jones had ordered, that money was money and if you knew how to handle a sum it didn't matter how many zeroes were at the end of it.

The second thing to do, I told myself, was to sit down with Irene Madigan and the telephones and call up each of the people we had sent those documents to to explain that they shouldn't open them, because they were a mistake, and someone would come around to collect them.

That wouldn't be too hard. The first thing would be harder.

In the elevator I found myself wondering whether I would ever have time to sing again, as I was trying to figure out how to explain to Irene Madigan that Narabedla was now ours—that the world was ours—to do with as we would and, most of all, to be responsible for.

About the Author

Frederik Pohl has been everything one man can be in the world of science fiction: fan (a founder of the fabled Futurians), book and magazine editor, agent, and, above all, writer. As editor of *Galaxy* in the 1950s, he helped set the tone for a decade of sf—including his own memorable stories such as *The Space Merchants* (in collaboration with Cyril Kornbluth). He has also written *The Way the Future Was*, a memoir of his first forty-five years in science fiction. Frederik Pohl was born in Brooklyn, New York, in 1919, and now lives in Palatine, Illinois.